Frank Jewett Mather

King Ponthus and the Fair Sidone

Frank Jewett Mather

King Ponthus and the Fair Sidone

ISBN/EAN: 9783743403512

Manufactured in Europe, USA, Canada, Australia, Japa

Cover: Foto ©Andreas Hilbeck / pixelio.de

Manufactured and distributed by brebook publishing software (www.brebook.com)

Frank Jewett Mather

King Ponthus and the Fair Sidone

BY

FRANK JEWETT MATHER, Jr., Ph.D.

FELLOW OF JOHNS HOPKINS UNIVERSITY, NOW INSTRUCTOR IN
WILLIAMS COLLEGE

BALTIMORE

THE MODERN LANGUAGE ASSOCIATION OF AMERICA

1897

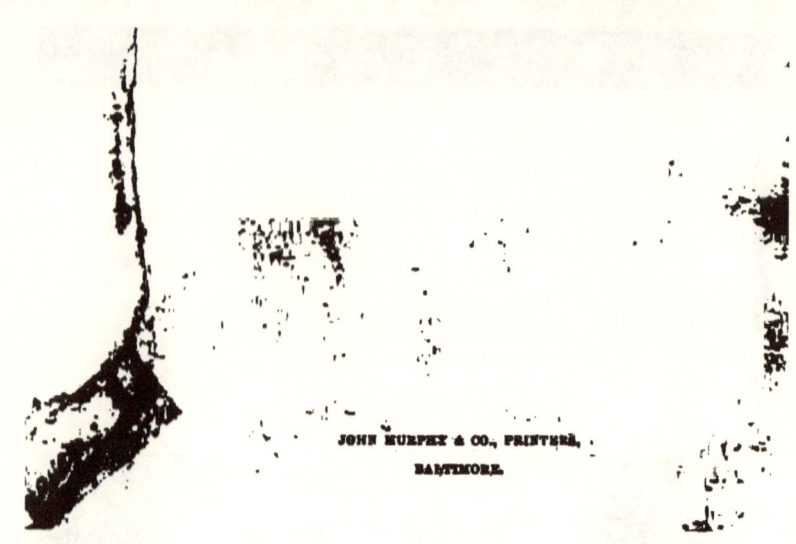

JOHN MURPHY & CO., PRINTERS,
BALTIMORE.

[Reprinted from the *Publications of the Modern Language Association of America*, Vol. XII, No. 1.]

PREFACE.

Apology will scarcely be necessary for printing an inedited English version of the story of King Horn, and, while the present chivalresque dilution of *Horn et Rimel* adds practically nothing to the general history of the legend, *Ponthus* has claims of its own to the attention of students of fifteenth century English. It was impossible for me to edit the French original; the reasonable limitations of publication in this Society's annual volume, forbade the reprinting of my transcript of Wynkyn de Worde's edition of 1511; my edition then assumes logically the modest proportions of an accurate reprint of the earliest and most interesting version of the English *Ponthus*, that of the Oxford MS. Digby 185. Where emendation appeared absolutely necessary, I have used my transcripts of the French original, MS. Royal 15, e. VI of the British Museum, and Wynkyn de Worde's print. I must crave indulgence for the inadequate study of this popular romance in its manifold versions offered in the introduction. Only the spare time of a summer in England, chiefly devoted to the mechanical work of transcription, was available for this purpoc The actual writing was of necessity done with only the scanty resources of my own books and those of a small library. Where practically nothing has been done, my notes may at least be of service to some more favored investigator. I could easily have trebled the amount of annotation by treating the portions of *Ponthus* which are derived directly

i

from *Horn et Rimel,* but this is, I believe, properly the work of the future editor of the Old French poem. I have gathered the important or difficult proper names into an alphabetical index. The few words that the professional student of English might wish to have explained, or the lexicographer, recorded, I have thrown into a glossary at the end of the introduction.

The pleasant duty remains of thanking those who have helped me in the preparation of this edition. The officers and attendants of the British Museum MS. room, of the Cambridge University Library, and of the Bodleian Library, extended to me all possible courteous assistance. Mr. George Parker, of the last-named library, did me a peculiar favor in early bringing to my attention the Digby MS., unrecorded in the scanty bibliography of *Ponthus.* Dr. J. W. Bright of Johns Hopkins University has helped me materially in seeing the text through the press; Dr. W. H. Schofield contributed the entire section on the Scandinavian rímur; and Dr. J. D. Bruce of Bryn Mawr sent me many suggestions, utilized in the introduction and notes, from the proof sheets. To all these, my most cordial thanks. May it some time fall my chance to show them, in Ponthus' words, that "ther be noo curtesie doon to a good hert bot that it is yolden agane."

F. J. M., Jr.

TABLE OF CONTENTS.

INTRODUCTION.

THE FRENCH PONTHUS.

ORIGIN, DATE, RELATION TO HORN ET RIMEL.

Just as the story of Melusine was written to glorify the family of Lusignan so the romance of Ponthus was written in honor of a member of the famous Tour Landry family of Anjou. Montaiglon, in the introduction to his edition of *Le Livre du Chevalier de La Tour Landry*[1] (Paris, 1854), has collected the little that is known of the Ponthus de La Tour, for whom our romance was named. The famous knight Geoffroy de La Tour Landry left a son, Geoffroy, who died, leaving his widow in possession of the family estates. Her second husband, Charles, assumed the name of La Tour and thus became head of the family. Their second son was our Ponthus.

Iu 1424, this Ponthus gave tithes of his estates at Cornouaille, to the convent of St. John the Evangelist at Angers. The 21 Mar., 1431, he was a sponsor (*ôtage*) at the wedding of the Count of Montfort and Yolande, daughter of the queen of Sicily. He appears to have been present at the battle of Formigrey in 1450. It concerns us immediately only to know that his activity covered the second quarter of the fifteenth century, and that in this quarter-century, in any case, some years before 1445, the probable date of the Royal MS., the French *Ponthus* was written.

Montaiglon (Intr., p. **xxiij** f.) continues :—Il est aussi bien a croire que c'est lui qui a fait écrire par quelque clerc le roman

[1] Wright, in his ed. of *The Book of the Knight of La Tour-Landry* (E. E. T. S., No. 33, Intr., pp. viii ff.), summarizes Montaiglon's study, but fails to make the genealogy of Ponthus of Tour-Landry sufficiently clear.

de chevalerie de Ponthus, fils du roi de Galice, et de la belle
Sidoine, fille du roi de Bretaigne, souvent réimprimé ; c'était
un moyen de populariser l'illustration de la famille et d'en
faire reculer très loin l'ancienneté,—Bourdigné, comme on l'a
vu, s'y est laissé prendre,—que de la mettre au milieu d'une
action à la fois romanesque et à demi historique. Les La
Tour Landry, ont voulu avoir leur roman, comme les Lusignan avoient Mélusine. Nous n'avoir pas à entrer dan le
détail de ce très pauvre roman, qui se passe en Galice, en
Bretagne et Angleterre, ni à suivre les péripéties des amours
de Ponthus et de Sidoine, traversées par les fourberies du
traître Guennelet et enfin couronnées par une mariage. Ce
qu'il nous importe de signaler c'est la certitude de l'origine de
ce roman. Le héros de l'histoire porte le nom fort particu-
lier[1] d'un des membres de la famille, et, parmi ses compagnons,
se voit toujours au premier rang Landry de La Tour. Tous
les noms propres sont de ce côté de la France ; ce sont :
Geoffroy de Lusignan, le sire de Laval, d'Oucelles et de
Sillié, Guillaume et Bernard de la Roche, le sire de Doé,
Girard de Chasteau Gaultier, Jean de Malevrier. Les quelques
noms de localités françoises concourent aussi à la même preuve :
c'est à Vannes que se fait le grand tournois, et, quand l'armée
se réunit, c'est à la tour d'Orbondelles, près de Tallemont ; or
Talmont est un bourg de Vendée (Poitou) situe à 13 kil. des
Sables. Un passage donneroit peut-être la date exacte de la
composition du Roman, c'est lorsque pour réunir une armée
contre les Sarrasins, on écrit à la comtesse d'Anjou : car, dit
le romancier, le comte étoit mort, et son fils n'avoit que dix
ans.[2] Mais c'est trop long-temps m'arrêter à ce dire, quil
étoit pourtant nécessaire de signaler.

Strangely enough, as M. Paul Meyer remarks (*Romania,*
xv, p. 275), those who have treated the King Horn story

---

[1] The name was I fancy not excessively rare, though I recall at present
only Pontus de Thiard, a somewhat obscure luminary of the Pléiade.

[2] Probably a mere pseudo-realistic touch of the romancer. The only
Duke of Anjou who at all fits the case, Louis I, claimant of the throne of
Naples, died 1384. His eldest son Louis II was ten years old in 1337. But
our romance could hardly have been written so early. Unfortunately we
are ignorant of the date of the historic Ponthus' birth. A theory that the
romance might have been written in 1387, when Ponthus was a child, for
his training,—within a few years too of the writing of the prose *Mélusine*
and perhaps in rivalry with it,—would be alluring rather than plausible.

have failed to note Montaiglon's very satisfactory theory of the origin of the romance of Ponthus. M. Montaiglon in his turn was apparently ignorant of the fact, known since the third ed. of Warton's *Hist.* that *Ponthus* is merely a *rifacimento* of the story of King Horn, more definitely of the Anglo-Norman *Horn et Rimel.*[1] That is, the romancer spared himself the responsibility and labor of invention by accepting as a whole the plot of the forgotten *roman d'aventure*, reshaping it on the lines of a book of courtesy, amplifying and adding details from his own invention and knowledge of the early prose romances, localizing most of the scenes in the provinces most familiar to his patron, Ponthus of La Tour Landry, and introducing incidentally many names of the local nobility.

I have endeavored to show concisely in the following pages the measure in which *Ponthus* (P) departs from its original *Horn et Rimel* (HR) by omission and by amplification. For practical reasons the references to P are made to this edition of the English *Ponthus*, which represents faithfully the story of the French version, rather than to my transcript of the French MS. of the British Museum (Royal 15, E. vi).

THE DEATH OF KING TIBER (THIBOR) AND THE ESCAPE OF PONTHUS (P, pp. 1–9, HR, ll. 1–114).

HR starts *in medias res* with the finding of Horn and his fifteen (13 in P) fellows in a garden by the African Malbroin. Master Thomas has already told

Cum li bers Aaluf est uenuz a sa fin.

It is possible that the early pages of P, the sultan of Babylon[2] and his three sons, the taking of Corunna[3] (Colloigne)

---

[1] Edited by Fr. Michel for the Bannantyne Club, Paris, 1845. I cite the convenient reprint of the MSS. by Brede and Stengel, Marburg, 1885 (Aus. u. Abhand, No. VIII).

[2] A prominent figure in the prose romances, as in the later Charlemagne romances, *Paris and Vienne* Roxb. Libr., p. 72, etc. There is a M. E. romance with this title (E. E. T. S., No. 38).

[3] For variant spellings see index of proper names. Wynkyn de Worde's print shows in the first chapter-heading and in the first chapter *Croyne* the usual English equivalent of Corunna.

by a strategem, etc., may preserve the outlines of this last poem of Thomas.[1] This could hardly be proved in any case, while it appears more likely that the romancer merely wished to give the three Saracen brothers a motive for their invasions, which in HR the five African brothers of the sultan of Persia, have nowhere expressed for them. The character of Sir Denis (p. 3, l. 25, Dampdenis), the priest, who hides the children and of Sir Patrick, the pretended Saracen, who saves them, are not in HR. In HR an *alchaie sur mer* advises the king Rodmund (the Brodas of P) to set the children adrift in a cranky ship, without sail or rudder: this is done in fact,—in P merely in appearance. The agreement of Sir Patrick and the Earl of Asturias (Destrue, pp. 6–8) to save the country by feiguing the Saracen religion, thereby becoming Brodas' lieutenants, is not in HR.

Minor differences are that in P Ponthus conceals his identity from the king, in HR Horn reveals it boldly, while the premonitory dream of the king that Ponthus in a lion's form[2] slew him (p. 6) is peculiar to P.

PONTHUS IN BRITTANY.—HIS MEETING WITH SIDONE (P, pp. 9–18; HR, ll. 115–1301).

The two versions show only insignificant differences. Herlant, the seneschal of king Hunlaf of Brittany (P. Huguell, R. Haguell?), is the single name common to the two. P mentions and describes briefly the princess Sidone when her father is first mentioned (p. 9), HR reserves the princess Rigmel till the love plot begins to open (l. 405 ff.). The insistence upon Ponthus' piety (p. 11) is as usual only in P. Horn chooses to have his fellow Haderof educated with him under Herlant

---

[1] Horn's statement, l. 278 f.:

> *Mis peres ifud pris par sa ruiste fierte*
> *Ki atendre ne uout ke uenist sa barne,*

points to a beginning like that of the English *King Horn*.

[2] See Mentz, E, *Die Träume in den Altfr, Karls- und Artus- epen*, Marburg, 1888; Ausg. u. Abhand, LXXIII, p. 53 ff., for a collection of similar lion dreams.

(l. 361 ff.). Pollides is educated separately by the Lord of Laval. In HR (ll. 588 ff.) Rigmel gives gift upon gift to Herlant, Sidone is content to give him a palfrey, reserving her gift of a cup (p. 17) till he has actually brought Ponthus; furthermore Rigmel (ll. 758 ff.) follows up the tardy Herlant with reminders from Herselote, her maid, that he is to bring Horn at once. The incident is absent from P. The action of Herland in substituting Pollides for Ponthus (p. 13) is left without expressed motive in P, in HR he explains (l. 693 f.).

> Qui merrai Haderof, par laparceiuement
> Quel semblant el li fra a cest assemblement.

Godswiþ, Rigmel's nurse, first recognizes Haderof in HR (l. 852 f.). Pollides in P declares himself promptly. Herselote, who has seen Horn at the feast, describes his beauty elaborately to Rigmel (ll. 950 ff.), Eloix (Ellious), Sidone's maid, uses a similar description as she sees from the window Ponthus coming. Sidone gives Ponthus a diamond ring at their first meeting (p. 17), Rigmel shows Horn this mark of favor only after his notable service in battle (l. 1790 ff.). These slight differences are only worth recording to show the freedom of the romancer's handling of his original. In a general way the descriptions of Ponthus' beauty, accomplishments and virtues are expanded in the manner of books of courtesy, while our author protests unnecessarily (p. 17) the innocence of the love of Ponthus and Sidone.

THE FIGHT WITH THE SARACEN MESSENGER AND THE DEFEAT OF THE INVADING SARACENS (P, pp. 18–32 ; HR, ll. 1302–1722).

Carodas, brother of the slayer of Ponthus father (in RH two kings, Eglof and Gudolf, brothers of Rodmund), sends a messenger[1] (in HR Marmorin) to defy king Huguell. Horn, having slain the challenger (l. 1541 ff.), presents the Saracen's head to Hunlaf as a trophy, Ponthus (p. 21) sends it back to

---

[1] The insolent Saracen messenger is a typical figure in the Charlemagne romances. Examples are hardly necessary.

Carodas by the two Saracen squires with a message of defiance. Immediately after the single combat Horn is appointed constable of Brittany (l. 1547 f.), Ponthus only after the general engagement (p. 37). Rigmel only hears of the duel after it is finished, then she gives Horn a pennon to bear in the battle (l. 1579 f.), Sidone gives Ponthus "a kerchef to beř on his spere" (p. 20) before the duel. Ponthus rescues the king of Brittany, who is unhorsed (p. 27 f.), but Horn, only Herland the seneschal (l. 1691 ff.).

The considerable elaboration of the course of the battle in P, as compared with HR where Horn and Haderof are the only prominent figures, was due to the romancer's desire to use prominently as many names of his French nobles as possible (see especially p. 24 and pp. 28–30).

PONTHUS CONSTABLE (pp. 32–34). THE FIRST TREASON OF GUENELETE (pp. 34–39). THE YEARS JOUSTING IN THE FOREST OF BROCELIANDE (pp. 40–59). THE GREAT TOURNAMENT AT VANNES (pp. 59–61).

Except the election as constable, which HR uses earlier, this entire chapter rests upon the romancer's invention and borrowings, in part easily identified, from other romances.

In HR Horn chastises the rebellious count of Anjou for king Hunlaf and makes all the king's subjects and neighbors fear him (ll. 1737–1749). Rigmel praises him and gives him a ring (l. 1790 ff.). None of this in P. Only Guenelete's motive for slandering Ponthus is borrowed from HR—that Ponthus refuses him the horse, Liard,[1] Sidone's present. In HR Wikel asks for Horn's *blanc cheval*, the gift of Herland, which Horn had already given to Haderof (l. 1850 f.). This scene in HR occurs just before Wikel slanders Horn to the king. The writer of P uses it to introduce this first treason of Guenelete, his own invention.

[1] The common name of a grey horse. Used of Herlant's horse (HR, l. 1696), in *Richard Cœr de Lion* (Weber), 2320, in *Ipomedon* A (Kölbing), 3892, 3911.

There are certain obvious borrowings in P. The *Fontaine des Merveilles* in the forest of Broceliande (Breselyn, p. 44) is the *Fontaine Perilleuse* of *Yvain* (Foerster, l. 380 ff.), but our author is more likely to have taken it from the prose Tristan (Löseth, *Le Roman en Prose de Tristan*, Paris, 1891; 82° fasc. de la bilb. de l'École de Hautes Études, p. 248). It is there Tristan, who, by pouring water of the well on the stone, arouses the knight of the tour. In P the incident is mere stage-setting.

The not uninteresting mummery for choosing the contestants by shooting at their shields (pp. 41–43) is probably borrowed, but I have been unable to trace the source. In the prose *Tristan* (Löseth, p. 321) the knight of the *Tour du pin rond* hangs his shield on a pine and jousts with all who will strike it, but this is scarcely parallel.

Again these detailed single combats and elaborate tournaments give the romancer the opportunity of bringing into prominence his chief minor characters, Landry de La Tour, Bernard de La Roche, Geoffrey de Lusignan,[1] etc.

GUENELETE'S SECOND TREASON. PONTHUS ACCUSED TO THE KING (P, pp. 63–69; HR, ll. 1818–2135).

Wikel's pretence of quarreling with Horn about the *blanc cheval* has been already used by P as the motive of Guenelete's first treason (p. 34). Envy is this time the motive.

Wikel in addition to charging Horn with Rigmel's dishonor,—the sole accusation in P,—makes him plot with her against the king (l. 1893 ff.).

The versions correspond very closely in Horn's words with the king and his refusal to swear (l. 1940 ff.), as in the entire section, but Horn sees the king once more after leaving Rigmel and reaffirms his innocence (l. 2071 ff.), and Rigmel exchanges rings with Horn (l. 2051 ff.), giving him a sapphire ring that will protect him from fire, water and

---

[1] This is the name of the famous hero of the Great Tooth, the sixth son of Mélusine. See the index of *Mélusine*, E. E. T. S., Ext. S. 68.

battle. In P Ponthus receives a ring, which has no talismanic properties, only at his first meeting with Sidone (P, 17).

PONTHUS IN ENGLAND (P, pp. 70–96; HR, ll. 2136–3681).

Horn assumes the name of Gudmod (l. 2160) on arriving in Ireland (Westir), Ponthus in England that of Le Surdit de Droite Voie,[1]—that is, *the accused one* who sought in vain the *straight path* of vindication by combat.[2]

The incident of the boar (P, p. 70) is not in HR. There Guffer and Egfer, sons of king Gudreche of Ireland have an agreement that the first two foreign knights arriving shall enter the service of Guffer, the elder, the third, that of Egfer (l. 2206 ff.). Riding together they meet Gudmod (Horn), who represents himself as the son of a vavasour; both desire his service, but it is Egfer's turn.

Gudreche, the king of Ireland, knew Allof, Horn's father, and Horn, when a child; he immediately marks Gudmod's likeness to Horn. Lenburc and Sudburc, daughters of the king, are immediately attracted to Gudmod. Lenburc, the elder, sends him a golden cup from which she has drunk, bidding him drink the rest and keep the cup (l. 2399 ff.). Horn reproves her and refuses the gift. Lenburc, still insistent, receives no encouragement. P omits all this except the general statement that the king's daughters loved Surdit (Ponthus) and goes on to the stone-casting (p. 72; HR, l. 2567 ff.).

Eglof, a vassal, outdid both the king's sons—in P, only Henry—in casting the stone. Implored by his master Egfer,

---

[1] Prince Philip of France, having relinquished his heirship to fight against the Great Turk, calls himself *Le Despurveu* (*Three Kings' Sons*, E E. T. Soc., Extra S., No. 67, p. 9). Iolanthe, feeling the name to be inappropriate, calls him *Le Surnome* (p. 36). Later the king of Sicily rechristens him *Le Nounpareil* (p. 55). *Noms de guerre* are common enough in all romances, but they seldom have any especial signification.

[2] As explained in the Royal MS. *Quant le roy ouyst quil* [Pontus] *se nommoit ainsi. Si pensa que cestoit pour ce quil lui auoit mis sur quil amoit sa fille* [Sidoine]. *Le seurnom, pour ce quil lui auoit refuse droicte voye, pour ce qui se voulloit combatre contre deux ou trois* (cf. p. 104, l. 18 of this text).

Gudmod without exertion equalled Eglof's boasted cast. Eglof casts a foot better. Again Gudmod equals his cast.
Eglof, with a supreme effort, casts half a foot farther. Gudmod, conjured by his love,—the allusion is turned to his
mother only in P,—outcasts him by seven feet (l. 2659 ff.).
In all this P follows HR with the slightest changes.

The two brothers go with Gudmod to disport themselves
(l. 2698 ff.) in Lenburc's chamber. A game of chess in which
Gudmod beats Lenburc—omitted in P—is elaborately described in HR (ll. 2726–2772).

Lenburc takes her harp and sings half the lay—all she
knows—which Baderof made to his sister Rigmel in Brittany.
Gudmod finishes the lay with marvellous sweetness, so that
Lenburc cries out:

Coe est Horn, cum ioe crei   (l. 2852),

and is with difficulty dissuaded. Wissman (*Anglia* IV, p. 394)
has already pointed out that this incident is probably imitated
from *Tristan*. In P, Surdit sings to Genever the lay which
he himself made to Sidone—the princess recognizes it immediately. They all make Surdit repeat it to the king.

The whole episode of the war with the king of Iceland,—
so in the Royal MS., in both English versions Ireland,—his
capture by Ponthus, his marriage to the king's younger daughter by Ponthus' advice, is apparently original with the writer
of P (pp. 76–82). P, on the other hand, entirely omits the
single combat with Rollac, slayer of Horn's father,—though
the long description in HR (ll. 3108–3210) may have yielded
certain details for the fight with Carodas' messenger earlier
(p. 20 f.),—and goes directly to the battle with Corbatan
(Corboran) the sultan of Babylon's third son. In HR Hildebrant and Herebrant, brothers of the African invaders of
England and Brittany, and of the *soudein de Perse, dan Gud-
brant*, l. 3000, are the invading kings.

The battle in P (pp. 82–86) is little dependent upon HR.
Hildebrant kills Guffer and is himself killed by Gudmod

(l. 3298 ff.); Herebrant (by mistake Hildebrant in þoth MSS. Harleian corrects to Herebrant on the margin) wounds mortally Egfer, Gudmod's master, but falls himself at Gudmod's hand (ll. 3359–3405). HR (l. 3497 ff.) dwells effectively upon the scene between Gudmod and his dying master.

In HR it is the king of Orkney (l. 3574 ff.) who tries to arrange the marriage between Gudmod and Lenburc, in P the king of Scots (p. 87). In HR Gudmond feigns to be betrothed to the daughter of a vavasour in Brittany (l. 3663 ff.), in P he offers only the general excuse of his low birth.

GUENELETE AND THE DUKE OF BURGUNDY.[1] OLIVER SEEKS PONTHUS IN ENGLAND (P, pp. 88–93; HR, ll. 3682–3917).

There is no change of scene to Brittany in HR. Only the barest details of Wikel's plot are told to Horn by Joceran, Herland's son, who appears as a palmer in the court and calls him by name. Modin (Modun), king of Fenenie, represents the Duke of Burgundy of P.

All the details of Guenelete's treachery, except the deposition of Herlant, such as Sidone's gaining time by pleading sickness[2] (p. 90), and Oliver's falling among thieves (p. 91), are original with P. HR offers only the slight differences that Joceran has wandered three years in search of Horn (l. 3702), and that Lenburc, hearing of Horn's betrothal, will become a nun and leave him heir to the kingdom of Westir (ll. 3875 ff.).

PONTHUS' RETURN TO BRITTANY. DEATH OF THE DUKE OF BURGUNDY. WEDDING OF SIDONE AND PONTHUS (P, pp. 93–106; HR, ll. 3918–4594).

[1] The son of the Duc of Bourgoyne is Paris' chief rival with Vienne (*Paris and Vienne.* Roxb. Libr., p. 57, 62, etc.); Vienne's father imprisons her because she will not marry the Duke (p. 62); is a character of *Three Kings' Sons* (see index); his brother Guy (mentioned P, p. 105, l. 33) bears the name of the hero of a *chanson de geste* (*Gui de Bourgogne*, ed. par Guessard et Michelant, Paris).

[2] Vienne, imprisoned, when her father attempts to force her into a marriage,—with her own lover disguised,—simulates a loathesome disease, by the unpleasant means specified on p. 85 of *Paris and Vienne*.

The chapter follows HR with few changes. In HR Horn first learns of the day and place of the wedding of king Modin from the palmer with whom he changes clothes (l. 3954 ff.). Horn's parable of the fisher to Modin and Wikel (l. 4046 ff.) is of course absent from P. The description of the custom of having thirteen poor men entertained at great feasts (p. 98) is not in HR. Horn merely pushes into the hall, having thrown the opposing porter under the bridge, with the press. He demands a drink of Rigmel (l. 4164 ff.) instead of waiting his turn. The pun on Horn (l. 4206 ff.) is necessarily absent from P. Rigmel knows Horn on the instant. Explanations then are made in the hall at the feast, not in the princess's chamber as in P (p. 99). She immediately offers to follow him in poverty, so the test questions of P (p. 99) are absent from the earlier version.

Horn tells Rigmel to persuade Modin to hold a tournament (l. 4323), in P it follows a wedding feast as a matter of course. Horn unhorses Modin in the tournament (l. 4479 ff.), then as Modin's people come to the rescue, blows his horn, summoning his concealed troops to capture Modin and take the town of Lions. In P the Duke of Burgundy, worsted by Ponthus, is precipitated into a pit by his unruly horse and killed (p. 102 f.). In HR Horn and Modin are reconciled (l. 4545 ff.), and Wikel pardoned for this treachery (l. 4565 ff.).

PONTHUS RECONQUERS GALICIA (P, pp. 106–119; HR, ll. 4595–4881).

There is a large loss of text in HR after l. 4594, so that the portion corresponding to the vow at the wedding feast (P, p. 108) and the invasion of Galicia, the finding of Sir Patrick and the Earl of Asturias at prayer in a chapel (p. 111), is missing. But at l. 4595, Hardre, formerly seneschal for king Allof, appears in the character of the Sir Patrick of P, deceiving the heathen king as to Horn's strength, and planning an ambush for the battle. Rodmund has dreamed that a wild boar gored his horse and wounded him mortally (HR, l. 4656 ff.), Brodas has dreamed that he became a wolf, and that a greyhound, accompanied by a "brachet,"[1] pulled him down (P, p. 113).

The strategem by which the town is taken (P, 115) is not in HR. Horn delivers his friend Haderof from desperate straits, in killing Rodmund (l. 4782 f.) otherwise the battle in P follows HR in a general way, with greater elaboration as usual and provision for a larger number of characters.

PONTHUS RECOGNIZES HIS MOTHER (P, pp. 119–122; HR, ll. 4882–4967).

The scene of recognition so sympathetically described in HR as to lead Michel to the rash appreciation, *Si j'étois forcé de choisir entre cet épisode et celui de la reconnoissance d' Ulysse par Pénélope, je ne sais auquel je donnerois la préférence* (Intr., LXII), is somewhat amplified in P, but presented with equal delicacy of feeling. Slight changes in P are, first, the queen enters the banquet hall as one of the thirteen poor people to be fed in honor of God and his apostles (p. 119, cf. p. 98); second, the Earl of Asturias, her brother, recognizes the queen,— a character missing in HR, where Hardre first recognizes her. The scene (l. 4928 ff.) where Horn returning from the chase meets his mother disguised at the door, is only in HR.

GUENELETE'S FINAL TREASON[2] AND DEATH (P, pp. 122–140; HR, ll. 4968–5215).

Horn dreams that Wikel attempts to drown Rigmel (l. 4968 ff.). Ponthus dreams that a bear devours Sidone[3] (p. 122). All the details of Guenelete's treason differ from the simple account in HR (ll. 5040–5146). The king and his daughter, warned by Wothere, Wikel's brother, that Wikel intends to imprison them in his new castle and marry Rigmel,

---

[1] See Mentz, *Die Träume*, u. s. w., p. 61, but there are no close parallels.

[2] In Caxton's *Blanchardyn and Eglantyne* (E. E. T. S., Ext. S., No. 68, p. 172 ff.; p. 197 ff.) Subyon plays a part very similar to Guenelete's. Left in charge of Eglantyne, he corrupts the commons, tries to force her to marry him, and besieges her.

[3] For bear dreams see Mentz, *Die Träume*, u. s. w., p. 56. Most like the present instance are those cited from *Berte aus grans piés*, l. 1678, and *Aye d'Avignon*, l. 2514.

defend the town, suffer hunger, and are forced to agree to a truce for fifteen days, and then to surrender, if Horn does not in the meantime return.

The elaborate description of Guenelete's forged letters, his corruption of the commons, Sidone's retreat to a tower, etc., is borrowed from Mordred's treachery in the *Morte d'Arthure*, usually appended to the prose *Lancelot*. The parallel is striking with the version represented by Füeterer's German Lancelot (Bibl. d. Litt. Vereins, No. 175, Tübingen, 1885, p. 348 f.). In this version Mordred, left in charge of the kingdom and the queen, wins over the people by great gifts, has a messenger bring a letter from Arthur, with word that he, lying at the point of death and all his people destroyed, makes Mordred king, and as a last request bids "Ginofer" marry Mordred. The queen doubts the letter, obtains four days' respite, in which time she shuts herself up in a tower, provisioned and garrisoned, to await rescue from Arthur and Lancelot. She upbraids Mordred for his ingratitude from a window as Sidone does Guenelete (p. 130 f.). Malory (Somner, p. 839) gives the same account with less detail.

Only in P (p. 133) Sidone dreams of her husband's coming.

The Earl of Richmond's journey to arrange the marriage of Genever and Pollides (P, p. 136 f.), and the details of the tournament (p. 138 ff.) are original with P.

PONTHUS' VISITS TO ENGLAND AND GALICIA (P, pp. 140–150; HR, ll. 5226–5250).

In the main P only amplifies tediously the score of lines in HR. Ponthus marries Genever to Pollides and reads him a homily (p. 145 ff.) on the duties of a prince, especially of one who has married above his station. Horn in Ireland has to provide for both princesses, Lenburc he marries to his former rival, Modin, Sudburc to Haderof, his companion, who, like Pollides, becomes heir to the kingdom. HR adds, Horn and Rigmel had a son Hadermod, who conquered Africa; Thomas could tell his story, but leaves it to his son Gilemot.

SUMMARY.

This tedious comparison shows:

(1) That P has used every essential element of the plot of HR, but has filled in the skeleton freely by invention, amplification, and occasional borrowings. I cannot find any clear instance where the French *Ponthus* has borrowed verbally from HR, but its general freedom of treatment makes a supposition that another version of the French *Horn* than HR was used gratuitous.

(2) P has definitely localized the story in Galicia,—instead of the Suddene (England) of HR, in Brittany,—in this agreeing with HR,—and in England, instead of Westir (Ireland). The Charlemagne romances may have caused the shifting of the early scenes of the romance to Spain, geographical proximity may have drawn the Irish episode of HR to England. All the geography of P is quite accurate, no more recondite reference than the index of Bædeker's *Northern France* is necessary to identify nine-tenths of the localities represented by the minor characters of the poem. All important proper names, those difficult of identification, or unidentified are collected in an alphabetical list at the end of the introduction. At times the scribe of the Digby MS. has bungled these proper names sadly; the necessary corrections have been made usually in the alphabetical list rather than in the notes.

(3) The only really important additions of the romancer to the plot of HR are: (1) Guenelete's first treason and the resulting year's jousting in the forest of Broceliande with its sequel, the great tournament at Vannes (pp. 40–61); and (2) the episode of the king of Iceland (Ireland) (pp. 76–82).

(4) The amplifications of the motives of HR, are either in the way of bringing out more definitely and elaborately the courtesy of the hero, or, in battles, etc., those imposed upon the romancer by the necessity of providing parts for a great number of minor characters.

ii

(5) There are demonstrable borrowings from the prose *Tristan*, and *Lancelot*. The names show that the romancer knew in a general way the legends of Arthur and of Charlemagne. Guenelete is clearly only a double diminutive of Guenes, the arch-traitor, Gener̃ (Genever) is as clearly the name of Arthur's queen, king Hoël of Brittany may have suggested, not given, Huguell (a mere diminutive of the familiar Hugues). These parallels Mr. Ward (*Cat. of Romances*, vol. I, p. 470) has already drawn. Beside these Carodas, son of the sultan of Babylon, gets his name from Carados of the Arthur legend (e. g. *The Prose Merlin*, E. E. T. S., vol. 36, p. 442, p. 594), while Fireague (Ferragu), a Saracen, who slays prince John of England, is apparently Ferragus, an insolent Saracen messenger familiar to the Charlemagne romances from the chronicle of Pseudo-Turpin to the English *Roland and Vernagu* (E. E. T. S., No. 39). It is probable that one more familiar than myself with the great mediaeval romances could supply many additional parallels, both in name and incident.

MSS. OF THE FRENCH PONTHUS.

I have examined only the three English MSS., of these the Cambridge MSS. only cursorily.

(1) Ms. Royal 15, E. VI, of the British Museum, which I cite constantly, from my transcript, as R, is a large folio in double columns, with many handsome miniatures. It was given to Margaret of Anjou, wife of Henry VI, presumably on the occasion of her marriage (1445), by the 1st Earl of Shrewsbury (died 1452). The description of this interesting volume of Romances in Ward's *Catalogue*, I, p. 130, is so accessible that I pass it here. The romance of *Ponthus* occupies ff. 207–226ᵇ. Mr. Ward (p. 470) counts 47 chapters with rubrics, but no numbers—I count 48. There is, as usual, no title.

The first rubric begins:

Cy commence ung noble liure du Roy Pontus filz du Roy thibor de galice le quel Pontus fut sauue des mains des Sarrazins. Et de puis fist de beaulx faiz darmes comme vous pourres oyr cy a pres.

The romance begins :

Compter vous vueil vue noble hystoire Dout len pourroit assez de bien et dexemplaire aprendre, etc.

Ends :

Le roy Pontus et la royne vesquirent asses longuement et regnerent au plaisir de leur pays. Et puis trespasserent Et moult furent moult [*sic*] regretes de tout le peuple Mais ainsi est de la vie mondaine. Car si beau sy bon sy riche, ne sy fort, nest que en la fin Ne conuienge laissier ce siecle
Explicit le liure du Roy Pontus.

The Royal MS. represents an earlier stage of the romance than either of the Cambridge MSS., with its absolute monotony of sentence structure,—endless *si's* and *et's* at the beginning of sentences, etc., but it shows also a version slightly condensed. All the long lists of names of knights are promptly cut off with an *et moult dautres*. In the closing chapters, corresponding to pp. 118–150 of the present text, R frequently condenses details more fully treated in all other versions, but never in a way to alter essentially the course of the story. This would render it inadvisable to make R the basis of an edition of the French *Ponthus*, in spite of its assured early date (between 1445 and 1452).

(2) MS. Hh, 3, 16 of the Cambridge University Library,— cited as H, fol. vellum, 82 leaves (originally 84),[1] written proba- bly about the middle of the 15th cent. The MS. contained originally 88 leaves as follows, a single fol. (2 leaves) contain- ing the rubrics of the chapters, ten gathers of four folios (8 leaves) each, a final gather of six leaves. Two leaves have been cut out, probably for miniatures they contained,—the second leaf of the third gather of eights, and the fifth leaf of

---

[1] At the end in an old hand (17th cent. ?),
Sum Jacobi Morranti & amicorum.

the sixth gather of eights. The leaves are not numbered.
The MS. in its present condition has 45 chapters with rubrics;
it probably had at least two more. The chapter divisions are
in the main those of R, but the chapter headings are quite
different in form, occasional differences from the text of R
appear to be revisions in the interest of varying the monoto-
nous style of the original. H has always the full reading
where R. condenses. It would undoubtedly, its two *lacunae*
filled from R, be the best of the English MSS. to print.

3) MS. Ff., 3, 31 of the Cambridge University Library,—
cited as F. Fol. paper, 15th cent. (probably late), ff. 33.
This MS. is only remarkable for its geometrical capitals, and
for a very dull prologue in octosyllabic couplets which M.
Paul Meyer has printed with a brief description of the volume
in *Romania*, xv, p. 275 ff. It is more minutely divided into
chapters than the other MSS.,[1] in place of the usual chapter
headings each capital at the head of the chapter contains a
motto or verse bearing upon the subject of the chapter
(Meyer, p. 276). The language is considerably revised and
modernized.[2]

I find two MSS. registered for the Bibliothèque Nationale at
Paris (see *Bibl. Imper. Man. Fran. Ancien Fonds*, Paris, 1868,
Tom. I).

No. 1486, vellum, 14th Cent. (The date is, of course, impossible, but it should, at least, be an early MS. to get such a
rating.) No. 1487, paper, dated 1462. I have no description
of these MSS.

A romance so popular as the French *Ponthus* was must
exist in many MS. copies. I have lacked the opportunity of
searching further the catalogues of the great libraries.

[1] E. g. there are 47 divisions in the portion of text corresponding to the
first 17 chapters of R.
[2] At the end of the MSS. are the following signatures of former owners,
John Dalton /1619/
William Townley of the parish of S.
Giles's in the Fields.

EARLY PRINTED EDITIONS.

Seven editions of the French romance within as many decades indicate the popularity of the book. Of these I have seen only the third, the others I cite summarily from Brunet, *Manuel du Libraire* (Paris, 1863), to which I refer the reader for exact bibliographical indications.

(1) Fol. 69 ff. without name, place or date, but published at Geneva, *circa* 1478.

(2) Fol.   Lyon Guillaume Le Roy, *circa* 1480.

· (3) Fol.   Lyon Caspar Ortuin, *circa* 1500.

This is No. 177 of the Douce Coll. in the Bodleian Library.

The first (a), fifth (e), and tenth (i) gathers are fours (8 leaves), all the others, including the eleventh and last (l), are threes. There are then 72 leaves in all (Brunet reports 71 because the final leaf is blank). Ai (front) contains only the brief title, PONTHUS ET LA BELLE SIDOYNE. Ai (back) contains the first text,

¶ Cy commence une excellent histoire le quelle fait moult a noter/du tres-uaillant roy ponthus filz du roy de galice et de la belle sidoyne/fille du roy de bretaigne.

A large woodcut of a mounted knight with a hawk, and a maiden offering a carnation fills the rest of the page, and the romance proper begins on Aii (front),

Conter vous vueil, etc.

There are in the text thirty-six rude but occasionally spirited woodcuts. The text ends on the back of the unlettered leaf of fol. l. ii (leaf 71, back),

Puis finerent leur vie a grant regrect de leurs pais.
Mais ainsi et [*sic*] il de la vie mondaine qui
nest si beau ne si riche ne si bon a qui au fort
ne conuienne laisser cest siecle et auoir fin.

Cy finist le tresexcellent romant du noble et
cheualeureux roy Ponthus et de la tresbelle Sidoyne fille du roy de bretaigne imprime par
maistre caspar ortuin a lyon :

The final leaf is blank.

This version agrees very exactly in all H's grosser variants from R. In its chapter divisions, and in the form of the chapter headings it represents closely the original of Wynkyn de Worde's edition. We shall return to this point in the discussion of that version.

4) Quarto, double cols. Paris, Jean Trepperel, after 1500.
5) Quarto, 58 ff.   Paris, Michel Le Noir, *circa* 1520.
5ᵃ)   "   "   "   Alain Lotrian, without date, reported from the Royal Library at Stuttgart. Possibly the same impression as 5.

6) Quarto.   Paris, Nic. Crestien, *circa* 1550.
7) Quarto.   Paris, Jean Bonfons.

These are all printed in the so-called Gothic character.

The remaining history of Ponthus in France may be told in a word. It is amusing, at least, to find that Jehan de Bourdigné, the Chronicler of Anjou and of Maine, accepted our romance as good history. In his *Chroniques d'Anjou et du Maine*, first printed in 1529,—I cite the edition printed at Angers, 1842,—Bourdigné gravely describes the descent of Karados upon the coast of Brittany (Cap. xvi, p. 74 ff.) and all the course of the battle precisely, in outline, as it is described in chapters ix to xi of our text. The names of the participants, even the list of slain, are the same. After the battle (p. 80) Ponthus jousting in the forest of "Brecilian" is rather mentioned than described. After the jousts Ponthus' expedition to reconquer Galicia is mentioned, with lists of the French champions and of the slain in the final battle quite as in the romance. Finally the chronicler states that these annals are, *extraictes de plusieurs cronicques, hystoires et livres anciens.* Pity that no bearer of the then extinct name of Tour Landry could see his family romance accepted as good history.

The condition of public taste in France in the 17th century did not, as in Germany, tolerate the survival of *Ponthus* as a *Volks-buch*, and the French history of "Ponthus" closes,[1] or

---

[1] I should confess that a reference in Büsching and Von der Hagen's *Buch der Liebe*, S., xlv, states that the French Ponthus is treated in T. ii, p. 180

possibly reopens, with the careful abstract presented in *Mélanges Tirées d'une grande Bibliothèque,* Tom. x, pp. 1–62. This abstract is based upon one of the editions in 4to, probably that of Jean Trepperel, about 1500. On p. 61 the author writes that Ponthus and Sidoine

eurent deux filz, don't l'aîné porta avec gloire la premiere de ces deux couronnes [Galice] & le second, nommé Conan Meriadec, est la tige des Rois & Ducs de Bretaigne.

I did not happen upon this bit of imaginary genealogy in " Bourdigné," and there is nothing of the sort in any version of *Ponthus* that I have examined.

THE ENGLISH PONTHUS.

General Description of the Digby ms. and Douce Fragment.

The earliest form of the English *Ponthus* is that of ms. Digby 185 of the Bodleian Library. The volume is a folio of 203 leaves handsomely written on thin vellum. The contents of the ms. are :—

1) Fol. 1–79. The prose chronicle usually called *The Brute of England,* with the prologue, ending with the capture of Rouen in the year 1418.

2) Fol. 80–144ᵇ. Thomas Hoccleve's poem, *De Regimine Principum.* At the place where the miniature portrait of Chaucer should stand there is an elaborate s-shaped flourish in the margin with the side note *Chaucer's Ymago* (I neglected to note the exact form of the second word). This shows that the poem was copied from a ms. that contained the miniature.

and 250, of the *Biblioth. des Romans.* Having searched everything that could possibly be cited as a T. II in that distracting collection, I came forth from its mazes empty handed. Some one who knows the way may yet find it. It probably signifies nothing that the index vol. does not contain the name of Ponthus.

3) Fol. 145–156. Hoccleve's story of the emperor Gere-
laus and his wife (published, E. E. T. S., Ext. S. 61, p. 140 ff.).
The prose exposition or moralization of the story follows on
fol. 156–157.

4) Fol. 157ᵇ–164. Hoccleve's story of Jonathas and his
paramour (E. E. T. S., Ext. S. 61, p. 215 ff.). The prologue
is lacking. The tale proper begins,

> Sum tyme an Emperour' prudent and wise
> Reigned in Rome.

The prose exposition follows on 164ᵇ and 165.

5) Fol. 166–203. *Ponthus.*

The facsimile (exact size) of Fol. 166ʳᵒ will give a sufficient
specimen of the fine and legible handwriting of the scribe,
while affording an excellent example of the heraldic illumina-
tion of initial capitals.

These heraldic illuminations make it possible to locate the
MS. and approximately to date it.

On page 1 of the MS. at the head of the *Brute* is this coat
of arms : Quarterly, 1 and 4, Argent, a chevron azure, with
a label of three points ermine ;[1] 2 and 3, gules, a griffin segreant or ;[2] crest, a friar's head, proper, hooded argent.[3] The
crest and arms quartered 1 and 4, indicating the family descent,
were borne by a Sir George Hopton of Swillington, who was
knighted by Henry VII at the battle of Stoke beside Newark,
June 9, 1487 (W. C. Metcalf, *A Book of Knights*, 1885, p. 14).
The Hoptons were descended from an illegitimate son of
Robert de Swillington, one Thomas Hopton who died in 1430
(Joseph Foster, *Yorkshire Pedigrees*, Vol. II), and they inher-
ited the manor of Swillington near Leeds, Yorkshire (*Loidis
and Elmete*, p. 232. T. D. Whitaker, Leeds, 1816). The

---

[1] These arms are attributed to the Swillington family in the Catalogue of
Digby MSS. erroneously,—Swillington arms in Burke's *General Armoury* are,
arg. a chevron az, and gules, a griffin segreant or (the Leicestershire family).

[2] Catalogue, [" Rivers or Swinlington ?"]

[3] Catalogue, "The head of a savage."

arms (gules, a griffin segreant or) quartered with the Hopton arms are given by Burke as those of the Swillingtons of Leicestershire, presumably related to the Yorkshire Swillingtons. The Digby MS. was then written for a head of the Hopton family of Swillington, not improbably for Sir William Hopton,[1] Treasurer for Edward IV (*circa* 1465).

The initial capital of Hoccleve's *De Regimine*, Fol. 80, contains the arms of Hopton described above, impaling quarterly, 1 and 4, Argent a bendlet sable, thereon three mullets argent; 2 and 3, gules fretty argent[2] (Beauchamp, *Cat. of Digby MSS.*). They are the arms of a daughter of the Hopton family impaled with those of her husband, probably a Beauchamp.

In an initial, Fol. 157[b], ten small coats of arms are introduced. The curious will find them described in the *Catalogue of Digby MSS.*

The initial letter of *Ponthus*, Fol. 166, see facsimile, contains the quartered arms of Hopton and Swillington, impaling those already described under Fol. 80. This indicates that the husband had assumed the arms of his wife, probably as heir to the titles of Hopton and Swillington. Thus the facsimile shows all the arms here described.

I have gone into this tedious matter of the arms, on the chance that some enthusiast in genealogy may be able to determine the marriage indicated by the second and third shields, and thus date the MS. My own cursory study of the matter was quite fruitless. It is of chief importance only for us to know that the MS. was written for a Yorkshire family residing near Leeds. This will prepare us for the language

---

[1] He would have been in his prime about the middle of the century, the probable time of writing of the MS., and of an age to have the married daughter whose arms are contained in the MS.

But this whole matter of the Hopton genealogy appears to be vague and is certainly incomplete.

[2] I could not identify these impaled arms. I fancy that Beauchamp is merely offered as a suggestion in the catalogue. Foster's *Pedigrees* and the county histories show no marriage in the Hopton family corresponding to this impalement. But all the genealogies are sadly incomplete.

of the text. It is also an admissible theory, and a pleasant, to feel that the book is a sort of a family book. A father, who must have played some small part in the history of his day, chose the prose chronicle of England; his daughter chose, perhaps for the education of her children, Hoccleve's *De Regimine Principum*; her husband, with a feeling for something less ponderous than Hoccleve, and yet sufficiently edifying, chose the new and fashionable romance of *Ponthus*. It wasn't a bad sort of book to have about a house.

DATE OF THE DIGBY MS.

On palaeographical grounds we are safe in dating the Digby MS. after the first quarter of the fifteenth century. It falls then within a period when palaeographical data are peculiarly uncertain. The Rev. W. D. Macray, of the Bodleian Library, who kindly gave me his opinion in the matter, regarded a date about the middle of the century as the latest possible for the writing of the MS. The difficulty of determining narrowly by the language the date of a text partly changed from its original dialect is considerable, but there is I think nothing in the language of Ponthus that is incompatible with a date of about 1450. A date much earlier I think improbable.

The MS. is written solidly, without paragraph divisions; chapter divisions are marked only by illuminated capitals; even punctuation, except for an occasional ¶ or ‖ is lacking. The short, downright stroke of the rubricator—see the facsimile—is used somewhat capriciously, usually in giving prominence to capitals, or initials, but often enough within the word (e. g., l. 18 of the facsimile *tHe cristen;* l. 19, *Doos anD moste*—the capitals represent small letters rubricated).

Catchwords occur at the end of every gather of 8 leaves, enclosed in rough pen-drawings.

Fol. 173ᵇ, lower margin. On an oakleaf folded back the catchwords, *haue a bett*re.

Fol. 181ᵇ, lower margin.   On the lower part of a knight's
    head and shoulders in armor, the catchword *Pon-
    thus.*
Fol. 189ᵇ, lower margin.   Across the side of a large fish, the
    catchwords, *And Pollides.*
Fol. 197ᵇ, lower margin.   In a scroll the catchwords, *you in
    this case.*

The matter of contractions and terminal flourishes is treated
in the section on the plan of my edition of the Digby MS.
Finally the Digby MS., though itself perfect, appears to have
been copied from a MS. of *Ponthus* that lacked a leaf (p.
57, note).

THE DOUCE FRAGMENT.

MS. Douce 384, of the Bodleian Library, is a miscellaneous
collection.   Its first two leaves are a folio (the leaves non-
consecutive) from a Fol. paper MS. of *Ponthus.* The text of
these two leaves is printed in full at the foot of the corresponding pages of text in this edition, pp. 33–35 and 42–45.
The gap between the two leaves corresponds in bulk to four
leaves of the same content.   The Douce fragment was probably then the second Fol. of a gather of four, possibly the first
of a gather of three.

The text is that of the Digby MS. with the usual unimportant variants.[1]   A chapter division (p. 34), corresponding
to Cap. XIII of D, shows that, like D, it lacked chapter headings.   The catalogue dates it merely 15th cent.   It must I
think be set towards the last quarter.

[1] The fly-leaf of the MS. contains the following note in Douce's handwriting: "This is a fragment of the Romance of " Ponthus of Galyce,"
printed by Wynkyn de Worde, 1511, 4ᵗᵒ. The language of this fragment
differs materially from that in the printed copy.   No perfect MS. of this
romance in English seems to be known."   Douce also entered on the margin of the fragment references to the corresponding signatures of W, and
occasionally variants from that text.

LANGUAGE OF THE DIGBY MS.

Though written at a period rather late for marked.dialect in Yorkshire, the Digby MS. shows every where the traces of its Northern scribe.

If we apply the time honored test of the inflection of the Pres. Indic. of the verb we shall find that beside the regular first persons singular, and plurals with no ending or only a final e, surely unpronounced, we have a fair number of specifically Northern forms.

First persons singular in -s only occur in verbs separated from a pronominal subject by another verb.

I loue and trustes, 68, 14. *I swer'* . . . *and has sworne,* 99, 28.

I haue commaunded and commaundes, 123, 23. *And here I leve of the kyng of Bretan and retournes,* etc., 124, 3.

Second person singular in -s: *havis,* 20, 30; *has,* 130, 32; 134, 28; *makes,* 130, 32; *says,* 97, 27; *thinkes,* 22, 18; *yeldes,* 130, 35.

Plurals in -s: *drives,* 68, 22; (people) *dwellys,* 26, 30; *has,* 87, 26; 94, 23; 95, 12; 117, 9; 134, 16; *laboures,* 26, 31; *losys,* 97, 15; *travells,* 26, 31; *was,* 129, 31; *ye loue God and dredys hym,* 62, 31.

Imperatives in -es: *calles,* 38, 13; *comes,* 25, 22; *meruelles,* 83, 16; *sendes,* 23, 22; 113, 2.

Participles in -nd: *dredand,* 5, 32.

The verbal noun *tythandes,* 63, 5.

Beside these northern forms are the midland plurals: *semen,* 4, 17; *ben,* 5, 14; 23, 19; *sayn,* 6, 31; *sayne,* 13, 18 and 21; *drawen,* 76, 15.

Singulars in -st and -th: 2nd person, *feylest,* 4, 21; 3rd person, *baketh, gryndyth,* 6, 32; *lieth,* 5, 15; 25, 22; *longeth,* 23, 4; *semeth,* 23, 9; 119, 12; and the imperative in -th: *goth,* 21, 32.

It is perilous to commit oneself to any statement of dialectal usage in the fifteenth century, while Prof. Wright's great dictionary is actually publishing. Certain words, however, in our text are clearly Northern: As, *bustus*, 73, 10; *boustously*, 49, 3; *gude*, 63, 26; *vngudely*, 128, 16; *gudelenes*, 143, 19; *gar'* (cause), 77, 33; *luke*, etc., 119, 13, 29, 31; *reiosed*, 98, 32; *reiose*, 132, 7; *trast*, 107, 18; *traysted*, 89, 9; *sall*, 87, 15; 134, 29; *suld*, 66, 29.

The use of *to* in the sense of till, 43, 19; 118, 33; 124, 2, and of *unto*, 38, 10; 39, 16, is Northern; likewise the great preponderance of *and* over *if* as the conditional conjunction. The invariable *awn* for the intensive pronoun must be regarded as a Northernism in a text of this date.

Stuffe in the sense of *provision*, frequent in this text, I believe to be a Northernism, though it occurs in W, and I have noted it in Malory (Somner, 839, 19). *Lugge*, 2, 24; *luges*, 27, 9, for *lodge*, is probably dialectal. It is barely possible that *there*, 15, 35 (note), is an isolated instance of the Northern demonstrative.

It may be well to note one or two phonetic matters, possibly dialectal.

An intervocalic *s*, but pretty certainly final in pronunciation, is frequently doubled, indicating the voiceless pronunciation, *pleasse*, 16, 27; 31, 33; 35, 5; 56, 5, etc. The single *s* is usual when the word is dissyllabic; e. g., *itt pleases me*, *if it pleasse my fadre*, 79, 32. Similarly, *rysse*, 139, 23, and *rosse*, 39, 19; 45, 25; 117, 22; 139, 21, etc.

Similar is the representation of a *v* sound by *f* in *gyf*, 2, 1; 11, 29; 103, 20; *gyfes*, 63, 1; *gafe*, 8, 8; these besides forms like *yevys* and *yeave;* so *relefe*, vb., 8, 20. The change of *b* to *p* in *warderop*, 14, 1; 67, 23, etc., was possibly more general. Precisely the reverse of this is the constant representation of life by *live*, *lyue*, etc.

Certain spellings appear to indicate that the *a* vowel was beginning to approximate its present front pronunciation: e. g., *sale*, 5, 26; *saled*, 5, 27 for *sail; prase*, 94, 7 and *prased*, 18, 2, beside *praysed*, 18, 5. *Wate*, 21, 15, and the verb, 65, 6. *Wale* (wail), 37, 15. *Captanes*, 111, 1. *Ordaned*, 111, 4; 112, 21; 123, 17, etc. *Agane*, 111, 7; 123, 16, etc., very frequent. This fronting of the *a* is usually set much later. There is evidence in the present text for such a pronunciation which should at least be considered. •

The dentals differ somewhat from standard English usage. *Hunderyth* regularly used for *hundred* is probably Northern. *Smoth*, 21, 11 for *smote* occurs but once. *Garthyn*, 3, 23 and *bothome*, 5, 26, 33 perhaps hardly call for mention.

In general apart from the singular of the verb the whole text has the look of London English of its time. The Douce fragment shows no Northern peculiarities. It would be difficult to disprove the thesis that the text might have been composed by a Northerner who knew standard English well and only occasionally lapsed into dialect, but it is far simpler to suppose that the translation was made in standard English of the time and slightly Northernized by the scribe, who prepared the present copy for the Hopton family of Yorkshire.

WYNKYN DE WORDE'S EDITION OF 1511.

The only known copy of this quarto is in the Bodleian Library.[1] Since the signatures misrepresent the make up of the book it may be well to give the matter a moment's attention. The book originally contained 100 leaves of which the

---

[1] In the Douce Coll. I transcribe one or two of Douce's notes from the fly leaf. Douce notes first, his MS. fragment and French edition (Ortuin's). Then continues,

"This romance is placed among the anonymous writers in Du Verdier's Bibliotheque Françoise."

"See it in Bibl. Reg. 15 E., vi, 6."

An instance of Douce's wide reading in obscure fields is the following:

"'From Pontus came Sidon, who by the exceeding sweetness of her voice first found out the hymns of odes, & praises and Posidon or Neptune.' See Cumberland's Sanchoniatho, p. 33. It is a whimsical coincidence of names at least."

"This romance is an enlarged version of King Horn, see Warton, Hist. of Eng. Poetry, I, 46, new edition."

"Concerning King Ponthus see Bourdigné, Chronique d'Anjou, xxxv, &c."

first two are missing. It is made up of alternate 8s and 4s (leaves) with the single exception that the last two signatures P and Q are both eights.

8s regularly numbered i–iiij + 4 unnumbered leaves, are,
a (i and ij lacking), c, e, g, j, l, n, p, q.
4s numbered i–iij + a single unnumbered leaf, are,
b, h, k, o.
4s numbered i–iiij, with no unnumbered leaf, are,
d, f, m.

Although a, i and ii are missing, the actual loss of text is but a single page,—exactly Cap. I of the present edition. We may safely assume then that the front of a, i contained only a brief title, that the back was blank, a large woodcut must have filled the front of b, i, leaving space, probably, only for the first rather long chapter heading (see the first rubric of R). The romance proper must have begun low on a, ij (front) or at the top of a, ij (back). Since a large portion of W is used to fill a gap in D (pp. 57–60), there printed line for line and letter for letter,[1] it will not be necessary to give specimens of the text here, beyond the beginning and ending. On a, iij (front) the text begins:

¶ **How Broadas sone to the Soudan toke Croyne and slewe the kynge Tyber.**

SO befell it as fortune it wolde one of the thre sones came as ꝯ wynde brought his navy by grete tourment that he passed besyde Croyne in galy ce and there he came up.

The romance ends q [iiij] front.

[1] Through my failure to give the printer sufficiently explicit directions the right hand margins are ragged and unsightly. Of course the "justification" was accurate in the original print. Otherwise the reprint represents as well as anything short of *facsimile* can, the typographical form of W.

But
thus it is of the worldly lyfe for there is none
so fayre nor so ryche so stronge nor soo goodly but at the laste
he must nedes leue this worlde.

Deo gratias.
q [iiij] back,

¶ Here endeth the noble hystory of the moost excellent
and myghty prynce & hygh renowmed knyght kynge
Ponthus of Galyce & of lytell Brytayne. Enprynted
at London in Fletestrete at the sygne of the sonne by
Wynkyn de Worde. In the yere of our lorde god.
M.CCCCC.XI.

Below this is the printer's mark,—a slight variation of No.
5 in E. Gordon Duff's *Handlist,* and a scroll bearing the name
of Wynkyn de Worde.

The book is divided (counting the missing leaves as the
first chapter) into sixty unnumbered chapters with headings.
There are fifty-four woodcuts of very crude and feeble execution.

Mr. Nicholson of the Bodleian Library kindly wrote to me
of a signature of four leaves (d, i and ij) of an unknown edition
by Wynkyn de Worde, in his custody, and had the fragment
copied for me. The transcript corresponds page for page with
signature d of the edition of 1511. Slight differences in the
justification of the lines, a variant spelling or two, the difference in designating the signatures (the fragment, d, i and ij +
2, unsigned; 1511, d, i–iiij, none unsigned), prove resetting.

In Lowndes' *Manual,* an edition of 1548 is noted. Repeated inquiries at the English libraries and at the great
London booksellers have brought me no information of this
volume or of its whereabouts. W. C. Hazlitt, *Notes and
Collections,* says characteristically, " I have not seen the book,
but is likely that for 1548 we should read 1648."

The printed edition shows nothing of unusual interest
linguistically. A few rare words are cited in my notes.
The discussion of the relation of W to its French source
and to R, falls to the next section.

THE RELATIONS OF THE TWO ENGLISH VERSIONS.

The problem of the relations of D and R offers unusual difficulties, which a statement of the general results of the comparison of the two texts will set before the reader. W is throughout a close and even slavish translation of its French original. Pp. 1–61 of D follow W so loosely that they might almost be regarded as an independent translation. D is in general shorter, condensing the narrative by cutting out superfluous descriptive details. Verbal correspondences of any length are rare in this portion. D, pp. 62–113, l. 6, agrees more closely with W. The versions are still fairly distinct, but frequent verbal agreement of long sentences makes it clear that one version is in some fashion a revision of the other. D, pp. 113, l. 7–150, is to all intents identical with the corresponding portion of W. The verbal agreement is unusually close for two prose documents of this period. Roughly speaking, then, the first two-fifths of D is a loose paraphrase of its French original, and only remotely connected with W; the second two-fifths is a close paraphrase, and closely connected with W; the final fifth is a close translation and virtually identical with W.

Before attempting an explanation of these phenomena it may be well to show by a representative example from the first part the relations of the two English versions to each other, and to the French text R. I have chosen Ponthus' fight with the Saracen messenger.

D (p. 21).	W (C. iij$^{ro.}$ ff.).
And Ponthus withdrewe hym a litle, and putt his sper' in the reste; and come with a goode will & smote hym betweyn his sheld and his hel-	& he afrayed hym a lytell & toke his spere & came to hym a grete pace and smote hym bytwene y^e shelde and the helme that he perced the

R (Fol. 210, Col. 1).

Il se eslogne ung pou et coucha sa lance et vient grant aleure contre lui et le fiert entre lescu et le heaul*me* tant qui lui perca sa manche et ses

iii

mett, that he brake his shuldre. And the

Saresyn smote Ponthus so myghtely that he brake his sper'. And when the kyng and the people sawe the iustyng, thei thonked Gode and said that Ponthus had wele iusted. Then Ponthus went forthre and drewe oute his swerd, and come to the Saresyn and gave hym suche a stroke aboue the vyser' of his helme that men myght se his vysage all open. Then hade the

Cristen ioye, and hope in Gode. The Saresyn drewe oute his swerd, whiche was a full grete blade of stele, and smoth Ponthus therwith so grete a stroke that he made his hede to shake and fire to smyte out of his eeyn: so he was sore astoned of that stroke, and sore was the feght betwen theym. Bot at all tymes Ponthus hade the bettre and lay in wate to smyte hym in the visage that

mayle and the doublet/& put the Iren & the tree bytwene yᵉ necke & the shoulders/& the tree brake well a two fote from the heed whiche greued hym moche/& the paynym smote Ponthus in the shelde & brake his spere in his breste. And whan the kynge & other sawe these Iustes/ they thanked god & sayd that Ponthus had lusted ryght fayre & prayed that god sholde helpe hym. Ponthus passed forth & made his cours & sette his hande on his swerde/& came towarde the paynym & gaue hym soo grete a stroke that he kytte a two halfe his ventayle & vnmaylled it so that yᵉ vyser bename hym the syght & the paynym rent it of so boystously yᵗ his vysage was all dyscouered/& than had the crysten men grete Ioy & grete hope/& the paynym drewe his swerde of stele & smote Ponthus so that he made all his heed to shake & his eyen to sparkle in his heed/so he felte hym astonyed of the grete stroke/& smote the hors wᵗ his spores & came agayne & smote him a grete stroke. So was yᵉ batayle bytwene them stronge & longe endurynge/& all wayes Ponthus wayted to smyte the paynym in

estoffes et lui mist le fer et le fust entre le col et les espaules, et fu rompue sa lance a deux piedz du fust, qui moult greua le payen. A pres le payen ferist pontus en lescu et brisa sa lance en pieces. Quant le roy et les autres virent ceste iouste, si mercierent dieu et disoient que bel auoit iouste pontus et que dieu lui aideroit. pontus passa oultre et parfait son poindre et met sa main a lespee et vient vers le payen et lui donne si grant coup qui lui abat et trenche la moitie de la bauaille tellement que sa visaigiere lui tollu la veue, tant que le payen la print et erracha tant quil eust tout la (?) visaige a descouuert, dont eurent grant Ioye le Cristiens et grant esperance en pontus quil gagneroit. A dont le payen trait le branc dacier et ferist pontus si grant coup qui lui fist la teste toute fremir tant que les yeulx lui estincesserent en la teste. Si se senti estourdy du grant coup quil eust. Si feri oultre et reuint et reffiert le payen si grant coup que merueille fu. Si fu forte la bataille dentre eulx et moult dure. Et touteffois estoit pontus tou-

was open; and so he mett with hym at a travers, that he smote of his nose and his chynne, so that it helde bot by the skynne: so he blede in suche wyse that his shelde and his nek wer' full of bloode, that vnneth he myght sitt on hors bake. Then Ponthus toke

the vysage/whiche was dyscouered /& soo moche that he wente to caste suche a trauers/that he smote the nose the mouth & the chyn/so y⁺ all helde not bot the skyn so bledde he strongely/& soo moche he bledde y⁺ all his shelde before was blody. The kynge & the people whiche sawe that stroke made ryght grete Ioye & thanked god. The paynym lost the blode & febled fast & so moche that unnethes he myght holde hym on his hors/& Ponthus ranne vpon hym sharpely tyll he caste hym doune as he that hadde loste his blode & myght holde hymselfe no more.

hym by the helme and pulled itt fro the hede, and aftre gave hym suche a stroke that he fell doune to the grounde. And when he had doon so, he smote of his hede and putt itt on his swerde poynte and broght itt to the squyers Saresyns and said to theym, "Fair Saresyns, I present you with the hede of *your* maistre."

Than Ponthus toke and rente of his helme from his heed/and afterwards smote hym suche a stroke that he made his heed for to flee too grounde. And he bowed downe and nyghed it with his swerde/and lyfte it vp and bare it vnto the two squyers sara-synes/and sayd vnto them in this wyse. Fayre lordes I present you with your maysters heed.

siours en a guet de le ferir par le visaige qui estoit descouuert. Et tant qui va getter trau*er*sse tellement qui lui couppa le nez la bouche et le men-*ton* tant que tout ne tenoit que a la peau. Si seigna si fort que tout son escu estoit senglant. Le roy et la peuple qui virent ce coup firent grant ioye et mercierent dieu. Le payen perdi le sang et affoybli tant que a paine se pouait tenir sur son cheual. Et pontus lui couroit sur asprement et tant quil reuersa *comme* cellui qui auoit perdu le sang et lui erracha le heau*lme* de la teste. Et puis le feri tel coup qui lui fist la teste voler a terre. Et puis senclina et la picqua & leua sus et la porta aux deux escuiers payens. Et leur dist. Beaulx seigneurs ie vous pre*sen*te la teste de vo*s*tre maistre.

Since in this specimen, as always, W is nearer the French original than D, it is clear that it cannot be derived directly from D. The obvious working hypothesis would then be the converse, that D is essentially a revision of W's original, a close translation of the French. The reviser setting out with the intention of rewriting and condensing W would then have carried out his plan for two-fifths of the way, flagged in the undertaking for the next two-fifths, from there out, sunk to the position of mere transcriber. But this theory that W represents a complete translation of which D is an early and partial revision is far too simple to account for the facts with which we have to deal, for there is a third term to be considered, namely, that in the revision of one version by the other there was reference to a copy of the French *Ponthus*. This is proved by the existence of variants which, while they could have come about by no process of scribal corruption in the English tradition, are readily accounted for as direct mistranslations from the French. Recognizing the possibilities of capricious revision in prose of this time I have limited myself to clear instances of independent use of a French text in D and W.

When Ponthus appoints the weekly jousting for a year in the Forest of Broceliande, being in disfavor with his lady, he appropriately calls himself *le chevalier noir aux larmes blanches*, to indicate his sorrow. W translates this properly "the black knight with the white tears" (see p. 58, l. 2 f.), but D always translates "white arms."[1] Now it will be perfectly clear that no miscopying of *teres* would result in *armes*, and that conversely *armes* could never suggest *teres* to the stupidest of scribes. Reference to the French sets the matter straight in a moment; the translator of D simply read in his original for the correct *aux larmes blanches, aux armes blanches*, this mistake, actually found in Ortuin's French print of about 1500, is one that any careless copyist of the French text would naturally make.

Another instance. Ponthus forced to leave Brittany and Sidone by Guenelete's slander naturally calls himself in W the "moost vnhappyest (R *le plus maleureux*) knyght that lyued;" in D (p. 67, l. 14) he holds himself "the mervellest knyght livyng" quite unaccountably, till we see that the writer

[1] *Armes whyte* 40, 10, 13, 28, 34; 42, 3; 43, 10, 13; 47, 17; 50, 32; 56, 4.

of D read *merveilleux* for *malheureux*. So (D, p. 49, l. 19),
Geoffroy strikes a stone with his "goode swerde" so that he
falls. W more naturally makes him strike it " w⁴ his fote,"
R "de son pie," out of the latter reading D, or a careless scribe,
managed to make *bon espee*.

Again in W the barons advise king Huguell to make haste
to offer his daughter to Ponthus because Ponthus is so rich
that he "setteth bot lytel by any *daunger*," that is, will bear
little haggling in the matter, and the king begins his speech of
consent "Fair lordes— ;" we have here a reading that a copyist
is little likely to have changed into, "he settes not by noo
daungerous lordes," while a careless translator might well have
so rendered the original R, [il] *en pris mains denger Seigneurs
dist le roy*—, construing *denger* with *Seigneurs* and supposing
the king's speech to begin only after *dist le roy*.¹   I would
not insist too much upon this, though it is the most probable
explanation.

Certain unimportant variant readings, which would appear
at first sight merely the work of a scribe's caprice, have MS.
authority. Thus in D (p. 2, l. 13) Brodas lands " he and xxi
men with hym," the detail supported, if not mathematically,
by F's *lui trente vngyesme* and H's *lui vintiesme*, is lacking
in W and equally absent from R. So D (p. 3, l. 3) sets the
number of Saracens disguised as merchants at forty, two
French MSS. at least give the decimal, F, xliiij; H, *Quarante
deux*, R gives no number; so W. Again D (p. 18, l. 13)
makes the Saracen host "twenty" thousand in number
following R's xx, W reads "thyrty" following O's xxx.

A final clear case of independent mistranslation by D is:—

D, p. 14, l. 25, "ye shuld vndirstonde wele not to bryng me another in
stede of hym."

R, "Anoy," dist elle, "si eussez encor attendu, non pas [mene] ung autre
pour lui."

¹ The full passages, parallel, will make the point clear.

R, "*il a tres grant tresor quil en pris mains nul denger.*" "*Seigneurs*" *dist le roy*,

D,   —*that he settes not by no daungerous lordes.*" *Sayd the king*—

W,   —*he setteth not by ony daunger.*" " *Fair lordes*" *said y⁴ kyng*—

W, "Do way," said she, "than shuld ye haue abyde as yet & not haue broughte a nother for hym."

That is, "you ought to have waited till you could get Ponthus." The mistranslation of D, especially the *vndirstonde*, is I think most easily explained on the supposition that the translator mis-read *entendu* for *attendu*, though it may be sheer mistranslation.

We come back then to the old problem with one term added. W and R cannot be independent translations, one must be a revision of the other with the use of a French text. The question then is, which is the antecedent translation?— which the revision? A general characterization of the two versions may throw some light on the question.

A glance at the notes on the lists of proper names in D (pp. 29, 30, 55) will show that the translator probably misunderstood these obscure French names and that successive scribes must have added to the confusion. W is singularly correct in this respect, so accurate that it is difficult to believe that it had ever been copied by one ignorant of the French original. In its chapter divisions[1] W practically agrees with Ortuin's print of about 1500, and the chapter headings are with rare exceptions exact translations of those of O. This may of course only mean that Ortuin's MS. was of the same class as the original of W. The coincidence is at least striking, when the three French MSS. in England differ so essentially in chapter divisions and headings. It is probably not fortuitous that D lacks chapter headings. The fact that it, the earliest German edition (1483) and the French MS. F, differing to be sure in chapter divisions, all appear without chapter headings, is at least an indication that the French *Ponthus* was originally composed without them, and that the

[1] The chapter division of W corresponding to xxv, p. 88 of D, is represented in O only by a break and a large capital, but W has apparently used what was originally a mere transition—"Now here I leue of Surdyte, etc.," as a chapter heading. Otherwise the chapter divisions are coincident.

varying rubrics are, as would be expected, the work of the scribes.

We are now in a position to test the theory that D is a revision of the version represented by W. First we must suppose that a scribe setting out before 1450 to condense, unsystematically, an English romance took the pains to use the French original in this revision, we must suppose further that a plan begun thus elaborately was gradually relinquished · till the reviser became mere copyist, finally we must suppose that a scribe careful enough to use a French MS. in revision, in at least two instances changed the obviously correct translation before him in favor of an error in his French original, which the correct translation would have made perfectly apparent. It is unnecessary to dwell upon the improbability of any or all of these suppositions.

Forced then to the theory that W is in some fashion a revision of D made with a French original, we shall find the motives for such a revision in the probable method of preparing W for de Worde's press. Suppose that Wynkyn de Worde planned to print the famous romance of *Ponthus* in English. He would pretty certainly have turned over one of the early printed editions of the French *Ponthus* to some hack with directions to translate it. This translator would naturally avail himself of the earlier English version, which Wynkyn de Worde, most conscientious of early printers, may have rejected as inaccurate,—keeping it open before him as he translated from the French. The early portion of D, being loose paraphrase, would have supplied him only with occasional phrases and sentences, the second portion, free translation, would have furnished him much material, the third portion, close translation, could have been transcribed for press with slight changes. The resulting version would then be W's rather slavish translation, which contains a large portion of the earlier D. The theory has more than *prima facie* probability to commend it. If W represents a translation made especially for Wynkyn de Worde's press, the unusual correctness of its proper names is immediately accounted for, and the coincidence of its chapter divisions and headings with those of Ortuin's edition ceases to be surprising.

There are only a few instances in which errors in W are more likely to be misunderstandings of D than of a French text. For instance, where Ponthus sings his song in the forest,—

D, p. 39, l. 28, "he made ther' a song of the whiche the refrete was this melodie:—"Of byrdes and of wordly ioy is to me no disporte," etc., following.
R. "Si fist une chancon et auoit ou reffrain, "Chant des oiseaulx, etc.
W reads, "[Ponthus] made a song where he was at the refraynynge of yᵉ byrdes, "No Joye shuld me reconforte." (Cf. note p. 39, l. 28.)

That is, W was misled by the form of D's translation into throwing most of the first liue of the song into the preceding description. D had already carried over the first word of the song (chant = melodie). W simply carried the process a point further. The mistake is not likely to have arisen directly from the French. Again W has just once the mistake "whyte armes" for "whyte teres" (the first occurrence of the phrase, D, p. 40, l. 10). This cannot be a genuine mistranslation, for the phrase is correctly translated three lines below. Only in the mechanical copying of D's reading when the attention had wandered a moment from the French text could the mistake have arisen. Only such a mistake of the eye would have escaped immediate correction.

Though the satisfactory demonstration of this solution of the problem would require the identification of the printed book from which W was translated,—a study which I have lacked opportunity to make,—I believe that the evidence is sufficient to establish, at least provisionally, this theory of the relation of the two English texts.

To recapitulate: D is a rough translation in its earlier parts, a fairly close translation in its central portion as the translator gained knowledge of French or warmed up to the work, finally, a literal translation. The only extant copy was made probably about 1450 by a Yorkshire scribe, from a standard English original. A copy of this early version, somewhat better than the Digby MS.,[1] lay before the man who prepared the version of W for the press in 1511. This reviser followed a French text, probably printed, closely. So he was obliged virtually to retranslate all the first two-fifths with only occasional assistance from the older translation, in the second two-fifths he revised the older work carefully from the French. The final fifth was so accurate that he merely transcribed it with minor corrections.

THE GERMAN PONTHUS.

Ponthus was early translated into German by no less a personage than the princess Eleanor, daughter of James I., of Scotland. Her motive is set forth in the first edition of 1483, where it is stated that the Archduchess of Austria [dise histori], *löblich von frantzosischer zungen in teutch getransferiert vn gemacht hat dem durchleüchtigen hochgeporenem fürsten vnd herren Sigmunden ertzhertzog zů österreich, &c. jrem eelichen gemahel tzů lieb und zů geuallen.* Eleanor married Sigismund of Austria in the year 1448. The earliest German MS. is dated 1465.[2] Between these dates then the translation was made, and from the middle of the fifteenth century to the present time the romance of Ponthus has been readily accessible in Germany. Only in Germany the romance passed the sixteenth century, there even in the eighteenth century it was published for popular reading. Probably the earliest allusion to *Ponthus* (the Fr. version?) in German, is in the colophon of the first German edition of *Mélusine*, printed 1484, but written in 1456. There the translator, Thüring von Rüggeltingen, mentions it in an interesting list: *Und ich hab*

---

[1] For W furnishes not a few emendations to D in the last part, pp. 113–150, where the versions are virtually identical. See the footnotes *passim*.

[2] So in Goedeke's *Grundriss*, I, p. 356. Büsching and Von der Hagen, *Buch der Liebe*, XLVI, give 1464 in their reprint of the exact form of the colophon of the Gotha MS.

*auch gesehen vnd gelesen vil schöner hystori vn bücher Es sey von
künig artus hof vn von vil seiner Ritter von der Tafelram Es
sey von her Ywan vn her Gawan/her Lantzelot/her Tristran/
her Parcefal/der ÿegliches sein besunder hystori vnd lesen hat
Dar zů von sant Wilhelm von Pontus von hertzog wilhelm von
Orliens vn von Malin* [? Merlin]. Büsching and von der
Hagen, *Buch der Liebe*, XL and XLV, cite passages from the
Adelspiegel of Spangenberg and the *Ehrenbrief* of Püterich
von Reicherzhausen which mention *Ponthus*. But the best
proof of the popularity of the story is the many editions of
Eleanor's rather dull version. The translation which I have
read in part in the edition of 1483 is a faithful rendering
of a very early form of the French text, showing all the
monotony of the French MS. R of the British Museum. The
second edition (1498) already shows revision and successive
printers worked it into the quite readable form of the 16th
cent. *Buch der Liebe*.

It could serve no useful purpose to repeat the matter in
Goedeke's *Grundriss*, Bd. I, b. 355 f., where all MSS. and
printed versions are described. I will simply enumerate the
editions with brief comment, marking with an asterisk those
which I have not seen.

(1) Fol. Hans Schönsberger, Augsburg, 1483. (2) the same,
1498. These like the early MS. described in Büsching and
von der Hagen, XLVI f., have no chapter numbers or headings. * (3) Fol. Martinus Flach, Strassburg, 1509. (4) Fol.
Sigmund Bun, Strassburg, 1539. This was the edition modernized by Büsching and von der Hagen in their "*Buch der
Liebe*," Berlin, 1809. It contains a long homiletic introduction
which tells "*wie und warumb si* [dise histori] *zulesen sei*," which
the interested will find at the end of Büsching and von der
Hagen's reprint. It is presumably only a publisher's flourish
to tell the reader that "*dise* [histori] *ausz Frantzösicher zungen
in das Latein und nachmals in unser Teütch sprach / bracht
worden sei*." The translation is still Eleanor's, but considerably revised and provided with chapter numbers and headings.

It enlarges the final paragraph exhorting the reader to recognize the shortness of life and follow the example of Ponthus. No other version has this modified ending. (5) Fol. 62 numbered leaves, no place or printer, 1548. Aside from its fine woodcuts[1] this edition has a certain interest as the source of the modified version of *Ponthus* found in the famous 16th cent. *Buch der Liebe.* The introduction of (4) is again used also the chapter divisions and headings of the immediately preceding edition, but there is one interesting change. Where all the earlier German versions following the French make Ponthus prepare for the tournament with a dwarf, this edition makes him consult with an "*edelmann*," and instead of the mummery of Ponthus disguised as a hermit, the masked old lady, shooting the shields, etc. (cf. p. 40 ff.), substitutes, in due form, a herald to direct the jousting. The change is evidently to make Ponthus' conduct conform more nearly to the actual code of the time.[2] * 6) 8⁰. Wygand Han, Frankfurt a. M., 1557. *(7) 8⁰. No date or printer. Frankfurt. *(8) 8⁰. Frankfurt, 1568. (9) *Buch der Liebe.* Fol. Feyerabend, Frankfurt, 1578 and 1587. Printed from a version showing the changes made in 5. (10[3]) "*Ritter Ponthus.*" 16⁰. Frankfurt [circa 1600], follows the *Buch der Liebe.* *(11) 8⁰. Nürnberg, 1656. *12) 8⁰. Nürnberg, 1657. *(13) 8⁰. Nürnberg, 1670. (14) 8⁰. Frankfurt, 1769. To these should be added *Ridder Pontus,* a Low German version, "Hamborch," 1601, the reprint in Büsching and von der Hagen's *Buch der Liebe,* 1809, and in Simrock's *Die Deutschen Volks-*

---

[1] Several of them bear the mark of Hans Schäufelin the younger, a monogram HS. and a small spade.

[2] Büsching and von der Hagen, p. l, had already noticed this difference between the version they printed (4), and that of the 16th. cent. *Buch der Liebe,* but they were ignorant of this ed. of 1548, in which the change first occurs.

[3] The edition is not cited in Goedeke, unless it is No. 7. It is not probable that he should have assigned so early a date to the book. I have seen 10 in the British Museum, it is if anything, later than the date assigned. My numbers 11–14 are Goedeke's 10–13.

bücher, vol. XI, Frankfurt, 1865, as usual without indication
of source. Since it has the additional didactic paragraph found
only in the ed. of 1539 and von der Hagen's reprint it is pretty
certain that Simrock merely reprinted von der Hagen's edition.
Since Simrock's series was popular rather than antiquarian in
intention, it closes a tradition of nearly four hundred years of
the popular survival of the romance of Ponthus in Germany.

THE PONTUS–RÍMUR.

It was a curious fate that the chivalresque *Ponthus*, which
had come through the stages of the heroic *Geste of King
Horn* and the French roman d'Aventure, should return
towards its origins by being done into a Northern rímur. I
learned first of the existence of this version through examining
a small paper MS., Bor. 106[1] of the Bodleian Library,—the
first page told me that it was the second part of a Pontus-rímur
and by Petür Einarsson. This is all I should have known
about it, if my friend, Dr. W. H. Schofield, had not come to
my aid. I print entire the notes he has kindly sent me
from Christiania.

"The Icelandic work usually called *Pontus-rímur* has not, so far as I know,
been published. It is, however, preserved more or less complete in at least
10 MSS. (outside of that one in the Bodleian to which you refer). Seven
of them are in the Arnamagnæan collection in Copenhagen, and may be
found described in the *Katalog over den Arnamaynœanske Håndskiftsamling*,
Copen., 1892–94, Vol. II, Parts 1-2, under the following numbers:

No. 1562 (AM. 611 g, 4ᵗᵒ—paper of 17th century).
"   1575 (AM. 613 e, 4ᵗᵒ— "   "   "   ).
"   1576 (AM. 613 f, 4ᵗᵒ— "   "   "   ).
"   1578 (AM. 613 h, 4ᵗᵒ— "   "   "   ).
"   1579 (AM. 613 i, 4ᵗᵒ—paper, ca. 1700).
"   1583 (AM. 614 d, 4ᵗᵒ— "   " 1656).
"   2611, 2, (Rask, 40—18th century).

[1] Ff. 163. The heading is, *Aflar Partur Pontus Rimna Orrturg: Petre
Einarssyne.* It is divided into 17 "fits." In Dr. Schofield's notes Einarsson is said to be the author of the last 16 songs of the *rímur*. The difference
may indicate only a scribe's subdivision of one of the original songs.

"Jón Þorkelsson in his Doctor's thesis entitled *Om Digtningen paa Island i det 15 og 16. Aarhúndrede*, Copen., 1888, p. 377, mentions three others: two fragmentary paper MSS. in Stockholm, and another fragment, I Bfél. Nr. 238, 8vo.

"From the last-named book, I extract the following information as to the *Pontus-rímur*, and its author:

"The work was begun by MAGNÚS JÓNSSON surnamed PRÚÐI, or GAMLI, who was born between 1520–25 and died in 1591. It seems to have been written in his 33rd year, for he speaks of his first wife as then dead. He, however, finished only the first 13 songs. His heirs decided that the poem should be continued by the priest ÓLAFÚR HALDÓRSSON (who died before 1639); but he got no farther than the 14th and 15th songs. Later in the 17th century, it was continued by Pétúr Einarsson of Ballará (still alive in 1665), who began where Magnús left off, and brought the work to a conclusion, writing songs XIV to XXIX. Thus we have two versions of songs XIV and XV.

"The corresponding saga is to be found in Thott's MS., No. 513, 8vo; but this seems to have been made up after the *rímur* by Magnús Jónsson digri (great-grandson of Magnús Jónsson prúði), died 1702. In (Uno von Troil), *Bref Rörande en Resa til Island*, 1772, Upsala, 1777, p. 164, we have a *Pontúsar saga* mentioned.

"Magnús was given the complimentary surname (*hinn*) *prúði, i. e.*, 'the elegant,' because of the distinction of his bearing, and the general esteem in which he was held. His other surname (*hinn*) *gamli, i. e.*, 'the old,' was doubtless not added until the last part of the 17th century, when his great-great-grandson was a grown man. His descendants raised a very costly monument to his memory, provided with a long Latin inscription.

"In *Historia Literaria Islandiæ*, auctore Halfdano Einari, Ed. nova, 1786, p. 85, we have the following insertion:

"*Magnus Johannis.* regionis Torskafiordensis Choronomus, illustri genere natus, fatis cessit 1596, Historiam Ponti, pulchro verborum delectu, carmineque numeroso gratiorum fecit. Tribuntur porro illi in quibusdam exemplaribus XII carmina, quæ historiam Ingrari, VIII, quæ Conradi Richardi Imperatoris filii, & nonnulla, quæ Amici & Æmilii complectuntur historias.

"Magnús Jónsson prúði was one of the most enlightened and cultivated men of his time. He was considered the best speaker then living, and one of the most learned of jurists. He was also an historian, and is said to have composed annals and other similar works. As a poet he was held in unusually high esteem by his contemporaries.

"Most of his shorter poems are lost, only separate verses being found here and there in chronicles and histories. Among other things of his, which are preserved, we have a *Amíkusrímur og Amilíus* (*i. e.*, rímur on Amis and Amiloun), on which see Kölbing in *Beit. zur Gesch. der deut. Sprache*, IV, 1877, pp. 271–314; also *Germania*, XIX, 184–189. This was edited by Kölbing in his *Alteng. Bibliothek*, II, Heilbronn, 1884, pp. 189–229. He, however, did not know the name of the author, and was wrong in dating it at ca. 1500, for it really should be dated ca. 1560–70, or about the same time as the Pontus-rímur (see þorkelsson, pp. 377–8).

"Magnús was very familiar with German. In his youth he spent several years in Germany, where he doubtless laid the foundation of his unusual and all-round culture. It looks as if it was, therefore, a German version of the Pontus story on which he based his *rímur*. Yet þorkelsson notes (p. 118) that there are certain verses on Pontus (preserved in other Icel. documents) which are not in Magnús's poem, and seem to point to an older poem on the subject. Séra þorsteinn Pétúrsson puts the *Pontus-rímur* in the 15th century. This is probably a blunder; but he may have known other older versions of the story than those preserved (p. 176).

"þorkelsson notes further (p. 117) that certain verses of the *Pontus-rímur* are still living in popular tradition in Iceland."

I need only add that the form of the proper names in the Bodleian MS. made it clear that Einarsson worked from a German, not a French version; in this it is probable that he only followed Magnus Jonsson. *Gendil*, f. 24ᵇ, 26, comes from the *Gendelot* of the German versions. *Geneve*, 40ᵇ, *Genefe*, 41ᵇ, is the German form of Guenever. Even more striking is *Produs*, 51ᵇ, for the French *Brodas*. *Tiburt*, 89ᵇ, is also the German, not the French form of the name of Ponthus' father. So *Henrich*, 39ᵇ, 59ᵇ.

LITERARY CONSIDERATIONS.

The late prose romances have found little favor with the critics, and with a certain justice, for most of them are clearly debasements, vulgarizations in the bad sense, of stories that had been better told. MM. Montaiglon and Mayer in their passing characterization of *Ponthus* as *pauvre livre* and *faible ouvrage*, evidently regard the book as at best an average example of its dull class. The indulgence of an editor for the foster-child of his fancy, if no more serious consideration, would make me bespeak for the book at least the mitigated condemnation of faint praise.

In its programme of " mervelles," jousts, battles and adven-
tures, the book, it seems to me, calls neither for praise nor
blame. Such descriptions have the inevitable monotony of
the *genre*, yet I believe the reader will find Ponthus' first
battle with the Saracen messenger convincingly sanguinary,
and Guenelete, at the last, a formidable villain of a melodra-
matic sort. The long lists of names, a sheer hindrance to the
enjoyment of the English version, constituted a very real and
legitimate attraction to the first readers of the romance. The
Angevin family of Tour Landry and their neighbors certainly
felt no less a thrill at recognizing their ancestors fighting for
the faith than did the high-born Athenian in reading familiar
names among the captains that sailed for Troy to avenge
Helen's rape. But as sheer romance, *Ponthus* is certainly far
inferior to Malory and in no way notable among stories of
adventure.

As a serious and consistent attempt to draw the portrait of
an ideal knight of the 15th century, in character as well as in
achievement, *Ponthus* has, I believe, a unique interest. No
great literary skill in the execution of this task was to be
expected ; and yet it must be said to the unknown author's
credit that he thoroughly believed in his own hero, and that
his ideal of the knightly character was high and manly. So
that in Ponthus we have a hero who has no vices and all the
virtues, and yet is distinctly not a prig,—no Grandison out of
due time. Besides the older duties of valor and generosity,
the author proposes for his hero above all things a certain
cleanness of life and a tactful kindliness that includes all
relations of life. In the attempt to express in incident some
of the finer emotions, I believe the romance rises well above
its class. Recognizing fully the incompleteness of perform-
ance in every case, it was no perfunctory hand that described
Sidone's sorrow at her lover's departure, Ponthus' farewell to
Brittany, his recognition of his mother, and many another less
notable scene of the book. The romancer then offers as the
chief virtues of his hero a certain sweetness and gaiety of

mind, purity and justness of life. Only in the instructions
to Pollides in the presence of his wife does Ponthus appear
to strike a jarring note. A modern reader would hope that
Genever's assurance, "Ser, he shall doo as a goode man owe
to doo," was spoken with a certain resentment. But we must
remember that the 15th century took its instruction, as well
as its transgression, sturdily. The whole scene and the long
homily that Ponthus reads his cousin must have been sufficiently in character when the book was written. Ponthus as
definitely represents the later ideal of knighthood,—the tone
of the book is often singularly like the life of the Chevalier
Bayard,—as Gawain represented the earlier ideal of knightly
courtesy. The later hero, obscurely represented in a single
romance, can never in any way rival the knight of Arthur's
court, celebrated by the great mediæval romancers, but I
believe that the character of Ponthus will hold a certain
representative value, permanent, if humble. It was no wholly
frivolous or contemptible motive that gave the book its con-
temporary popularity. It was the portrait of a knight that
men recognized and that men approved.

From the point of view of style, *faible ouvrage* the French
Ponthus certainly is. Better things may be said of the English translation. It will I believe be difficult to find any
English prose of the first half of the 15th century on the
whole so fluent and readable. Briskly and easily the story
chatters along, when most of the prose of the time lumbers
in hopeless monotony. Style, in the sense in which Malory,
Pecock, or a modern has style, the story has not. It is more
like good unaffected talk than anything else,—no slight merit
at the time, and a merit almost wholly the translator's. Just
as the homespun virtues and equally clear-cut vices of the
book cannot compete in interest with the subtle union of
sensuality and religious mysticism that in Malory exercises
a somewhat morbid fascination, so the clearness and bright-
ness of its English, excellent for its subject, may appear

insignificant, almost inaudible, when Malory resounds in full
volume; yet there is room for both, and none of the early
English prose romances is likely to suffer less by the contrast.
With all its defects of proportion, and they are many, it
remains a pleasantly told story "wherof a man may lerne
mony goode ensamples" of an ideal of character by no means
valueless to-day.   In the prose of the 15th century it should
gain and hold a modest place.

PLAN OF THE PRESENT EDITION.

The text printed is that of the Digby MS. with only the
following changes,—the representation of contractions by
the full form in Italic, the normalization of the use of capitals, the introduction of paragraphing and punctuation.   The
first change is now universal, the publishing of a fac-simile
page makes it unnecessary to follow the fashion of the MS.—
unsightly on the printed page,—in capitalization, the absence
of punctuation in the MS. except a rare ¶ and ||,—always
reproduced in the text,—makes the introduction of punctuation indispensable to the comfortable use of the text, finally
when it is once understood that the MS. is written solidly
with no breaks in the chapters, except the few marked by
¶¶, the division into paragraphs in the text, an obvious con-
venience, is in no way misleading.   Rare editorial changes
are clearly explained in the footnotes or, in the case of inser-
tions inclosed in brackets or parentheses, the former [] indicate matter supplied by the editor, the latter () emendations
from Wynkyn de Worde's edition of 1511.   To supply the
lack of any running analysis in the original I have written
the chapter headings inclosed in brackets.   That they should
be congruous with the text, I have followed the orthography,
and attempted to imitate the style of the Digby MS.   The
perils of this sort of composition have, I hope, been avoided
iv

by the use whenever practicable of material supplied in the
text itself, of the chapter headings of W, or the translation
and imitation of the chapter headings of the French MS. The
difficulty confronting every editor of texts of this period, the
treatment of terminal tags and flourishes, has been the less in
this case: first, because the fac-simile page gives all needful
information upon this point; second, because the Yorkshire
scribe of the MS. could have pronounced no final e's; third,
because most of these tags are clearly only flourishes. It
seemed advisable then to disregard all except the tailed r.
This is so much more clearly written than other tags and so
consistently used that it seemed desirable to represent it in
the text. An ꝛ was then cut to represent the tailed character
of the MS. Occasionally, usually after -rꝛ, I have printed
-rre, and -re, as more sightly.

It was at first my intention to insert all textual notes at
the foot of the page. All the readings of the MS., when
changed in the text, are so recorded. The impracticability of
holding the proof-sheets long, made it necessary to place the
longer textual notes, and a few that escaped my attention
among the general notes. The proper names are frequently
so thoroughly corrupted in the MS. that it seemed best in the
text to abide by the strictly palaeographical reading, and to
make the necessary corrections in the case of important names
in the alphabetical list of proper names, in the case of minor
names in the longer lists, in the general notes. Any formal
inconsistency in this matter will I trust be the more readily
pardoned, that the whole material is readily accessible. Finally
the reasonable certainty that W is a revision of D made it superfluous to swell this already bulky volume with its innumerable
variant readings. I have registered at the foot of the page or
among the general notes all readings of W which have any
intrinsic interest, besides the few that appear to represent
readings of the old translation better than those transmitted
in D.

NOTES.

CONTRACTIONS.

D. MS. Digby 185 of the Bodleian Library.
W. Wynkyn de Worde's Ed. of 1511.
R. MS. Royal 15, E. VI, Brit. Mus., of the French Text.
H. MS. Hh. 3, 16, Cambr., of the French Text.
F. MS. Ff. 3, 31, Cambr., of the French Text.
O. Ortuin's Ed., Lyon, *circa* 1500, of the French Text.

P. 2, l. 11, passed Spayne in Galice. The reading is justi-
fied by H, [il] *passa* par *en coste espaigne et en galice*, and F,
le vent le amena . . . . *passer toutte espaigne en galice*, but W's
reading *besyde Croyne* is the better. It follows R, [il] *passa
par jouste Coulloine en Galice*.

P. 9, l. 17, Armoric. W's reading *Morygne* appears to be
a corruption of R's *Montgrant*.

P. 9, l. 20, Mast. W, *sayle yerde;* R, *tref.*

P. 10, l. 5, Susteny. R, *susinio;* W, *suffone* (sic). Sucinio
is the name of a château, once the summer residence of the
Dukes of Brittany near Sarzeau.

P. 10, l. 17, Viceat. W, *verrac.*

P. 10, l. 30. W has only, *So made he theym to lepe upon
theyr horses & led theym to Vennes*, following R literally.
The easiest way out of the contradictory reading in D is to
read with W, *theym* for *hym* in both instances in l. 30 f., and
to suppose that the detail *behinde hym*, not in the French,
was copied in by mistake from the passage in l. 13. A later
scribe, wishing to emphasize Ponthus' dignity as a prince,
would have added the clause *and he . . . aloone.*

P. 11, l. 9, whete. W, *marchaundyse;* R, *fourmens.*

P. 11, l. 31. W names the game, *yf he played at the playe
of the tenys*, etc.; R. *a la pellotte;* O, *paume.*

P. 12, l. 5, breke his tayle. The expression is in the *Ro-
maunt of the Rose*, l. 6221 :

> Right thus whyl Fals-Semblaunt sermoneth
> Eftsones Love him aresoneth,
> And brak his tale in the speking.

P. 12, l. 8, live dayes. W interpolates with R, the following conventional description : *for he was grete and large in y⁰ brest & small in the waste/& y⁰ shuldres y⁰ armes y⁰ thyghes and y⁰ fete were made of ryght deuyse/y⁰ vysage was clere browne/the eyen so meke/the mouth rede/& the nose streyte/he semed lyke an aungell,* etc. In other respects also the versions differ slightly at this point.

P. 13, l. 11, palfrey. W adds with R, *and a meruayllous gentyll faucon.*

P. 13, l. 16, Norye. R, *nourriture;* W, *chylde.*

P. 14, l. 25, for . . . copp, which translates R, is not in W.

P. 15, l. 21 f. A mistranslation or arbitrary change. In W Sidone replies, "*I byleue the,*" *also as she whiche was caught w⁰ y⁰ loue of hym;* R, *comme celle qui ia estoit toute esprise de lamour de lui.*

P. 18, l. 29, fiꝑ-hows. W also uses the technical word *fyre hous;* R, *chascun feu.*

P. 19, l. 27, Susanne. Allusions to the apocryphal chapters of Daniel are, I believe, relatively rare, at least in English literature. In *Horn et Rimel,* l. 2082 ff., Horn tells the king that he will maintain his innocence by combat against five or six :

> Taunt me fi en cel deu. ki salua israel.
> Susanne deliuerad. par lenfant daniel.
> E lui meimes pus. des lions el putel.

In Shylock's taunting of Portia, "A Daniel come to judgment! yea, a Daniel," *Merch. of Venice,* IV, 1, 223, is the same allusion.

P. 19, *passim, the* and *thou.* As in all texts of this time *ye* is used in polite address, *thou* apparently only contemptuously. In the present instance Ponthus defies the Saracen with *the,* and the Saracen returns the contemptuous pronoun.

Similarly p. 20, l. 27, the Saracen in pitying scorn of Ponthus calls him *thou,* which Ponthus returns.

P. 22, l. 18, it is on the contrary used in prayer to Christ. W uses *ye* and *your* in this instance.

Ponthus, in giving the Saracen king, Corbatan, his death-blow, p. 85, l. 2, calls him at once *false Saresyn* and *thou*.

Ponthus chides his yeoman, p. 97, l. 15, *Hold thy peace*.

Guenelete, p. 97, l. 27, calls Ponthus, disguised as a beggar, *thou*, in anger.

The porter of the hall, rudely brushed aside, curses Ponthus with *thou*.

Sidone always calls Guenelete *thou* as she upbraids him for his treachery, p. 130, l. 30 ff. Ponthus similarly when on the point of killing Guenelete in the hall, p. 134, l. 28 f. With the single exception of the instance in prayer, it is always used in anger or in scorn in this text, never in intimacy.

P. 20, l. 2, kerchef. W, *pensell*.

P. 24, l. 4, Morteyne. W adds *paynel*.

P. 24, l. 5, Duches. W, *Countesse*.

P. 24, l. 6, deid. W adds with R, *and her sone was but x yere olde*.

P. 24, l. 6, Gouter. W, *payne de chateau Goutyer;* R, *payen;* O, *paon*.

P. 24, l. 29, Vale. W adds with R, the *lorde of dynaux* of ye brytons, *brytonauntes. And of Galos*, etc. The *Galyce* of D is then a corruption of *Galos*.

P. 24, l. 30, Edmund. W and R, *Guy.*—Dole. W, the later form *dueil.*—La Roche. W and R, *ronge*.

P. 24, l. 34, Mayne. W, *mans*.

P. 25, l. 14, Robt. de Sanguyn, Ranald de Sylle. The first name is hard to identify, probably a mere corruption. W, *Regnault de sully/and Aygret de poully;* R, *Robert de chenegue, regnault de sulli & aigret de prully*.

P. 28, l. 13, ryght. R, *senestre;* W renders *best*, apparently a printer's error for *left*.

P. 28, l. 14, Vicecounte Daniou. W, *Erle of Dongres* apparently the correct reading, but R has *le viconte de rohan* agreeing in the title with D.

P. 28, l. 15, Valoynes. W and R, *la Roche*.

P. 28, l. 28, Creton. W and R, *Craon*.

P. 28, l. 27–30. I give a characteristic variant of W, which agrees with R, *Kynge Karados helde with grete dystres the erle of Mans/and the lorde of Craon/and had ouerthrowen them and many of the manceaus and herupoys/as Hamelyn de sylle, Geruays de la porte, Thybault de matheselon, Peter de doncelles, Sauary de la hay, Gerarde de chateau goutyer, Guyllam de roches, Geoffrey de lesygnen/and Leoncel. But they defended them on fote/& were assembled whiche auayled them moche. Androwe de la toure/and Bertram de donne sette grete payne for to recouer theym/but there was too grete prees of saresynes/ and soo grete a folke that vnnethes myght they come to them/tyll that Guyllam de roches sawe Ponthus whiche that made the renges to shake with the helpe that sewed hym. " Syr it is nede se yonder a grete partye of our barons the whiche ben on fote."*

D certainly gains by dropping the list of names, but compresses so much that the incident is hardly clear.

P. 29, l. 6, Ralond de Avyon. Probably a corruption of R's *rol. de dynain;* W, *Guyllam de dygnan.*

P. 29, l. 24, Vaucay. W, *Bausaye mayle.*—Daniou. W, *daner.*

P. 30, l. 20, Peonny. W, *paynell.*—Wylron. W, *Villyers.*

P. 30, l. 21, Roger. W and O, *Hongres.*

P. 30, l. 22, Gaciane de Mounte Vyel. W, *Gassos de Mountreul;* probably for *Montreuil-Bellay.*—Tenull. W and O, *chenulle;* possibly an error for Chemillé in Maine.

P. 30, l. 23, Hundes de Prouere. W, *Endes de penaunces.*

P. 30, l. 24, Chastameny. W, *Gautyer de chateau neuf.*— Monte Agnant. W, *Androwe de Montagu.*

P. 30, l. 26, Mangon. W, *dauauger;* O, *dauaucheus.*

P. 30, l. 27, Deyner. W, *dygnan;* O, *dinant.*

P. 32, l. 10, lyve. W, *woman;* R, *femme.* We should probably emend by reading *love.*

P. 33, l. 3, for they had hym in theyr conceyte, *had* is subjunctive for *should have.* Cf. W, *to the ende that they sholde haue hym in the more fauour.* A semi-colon or period should follow grace.

P. 33, l. 8, that . . . taken, follows R, *El puis leur dist apres quilz auvient petitement aduise;* W mistranslates, *after that he had auysed hym a little.*

P. 33, l. 22, thre. W, *two;* R, *deux.*

Douce Fr., p. 34, l. 4, dyuers gyftis, dyuers is evidently a corruption of *dyners.* W and R concur in D's reading.

P. 34, l. 5, draghtes. W, *signes;* R, *signe.*

P. 36, l. 7. W, *y[t] is foly to sette her herre* [sic herte] *so on fledde folke,* an interesting translation of R's *gens de vollaiges.*

P. 36, l. 26, x. W, *a two;* R, *xv.*

P. 37, l. 13, putt fro. W, *benymme.*

P. 39, l. 29 ff. I give the text of the quatrain from R:

> Chant des oyseaulx ne nulle ioye.
> Ne me[1] puet[2] reconforter,
> Quant celle que[3] tant amoye[4]
> [5] Me veult delle[6] estranger.

P. 40, l. 9, wretyn in this wyse. R, *vnes lettres escrites en lettre de fourme;* W, *wryten in foure,* an absurd mistranslation.

P. 40, l. 33, swerd. W, *swerde with the gyrdell of golde & the crowne of golde.*

P. 41, l. 23, rede toune. W, *vyle ronge* by error for R's *ville rouge.*

P. 41, l. 34, Bellacion. W, *brylaunson;* R, *bellencon.*

P. 54, l. 1, Boloys. W, *bloys.*

P. 54, l. 2, Guyllem de Roches. W and R, *damp Martyne.*

P. 54, l. 4, Rosylyon. W, *Robert de resyllyon;* R, *tybault de roussilon.*

P. 55, l. 22, Averenses. W and R, *Osteryche.*

P. 55, l. 23, Barry. W and R, *bar.*

P. 55, l. 24, Mount Bernard. W, *Mountbelyart.*

P. 55, l. 26, Savye. W and R, *savoye.*

P. 56, l. 1, Bellacon. W, *Belenson;* R, *bellencon.*

---

[1] H, F, O; R omits.   [3] H, *que is.*   [5] H, *Si me.*
[2] O, *puēt.*   [4] O, *iamoie.*   [6] O, *du tout.*

P. 59, l. 18 ff. R, *Si commencerent menestrelz a sonner de toute manieres et heraulx a crier que len eust pas ouy dieu tonner, que tout le bois retentissoit.*
I have not happened upou this conceit outside of Chrêtien. Cf. Yvain (Foerster, l. 2348 ff.) :

> Li sain, li cor et les buisines
> Font le chastel si resoner
> Qu' an n'i oïst Deu toner.

P. 60, l. 14, Ponthus. W adds with R, *& his hors al whyte with a grete rede rose that betokened his lady.*

P. 61, l. 11 f. As W explains, because Ponthus thought that Bernard should have had the prize Monday.

P. 65, l. 14, messe-booke. W, *holy gospels;* R, *saincte euangiles.*

P. 65, l. 27, thre or fouȓ. W and R, *two or thre*; so p. 66, l. 13.

P. 70, l. 26, Henry. W, always *Harry.*

P. 72, l. 4, Droyte Voy. W reads always, perhaps, by a printer's error, *driot voyce*; so p. 91, l. 20 and 104, l. 17.

P. 74, l. 27, demaunded hym. W, *resoned hym;* R, *la* (sic) *raisonna,* read *l'araisonna.*

P. 76, l. 1, grete rumour. W, *rygour,* omits *grete;* R, *grant guerre.*

P. 80, l. 20, is not myche worthe—misses the point. W, *is onely but selfewyllfulnes of hertes of grete lordes;* R, *le debat nest pas chose fors de grans seigneurs.* This is the necessary introduction to Ponthus' words on the duty of princes.

P. 81, l. 31, stedes. W adds with R, *& syxe coursers.*

P. 82, l. 11, Corbatan. W and R, always *Corboran.*

P. 84, l. 8, Fireague. So O, *Feragu;* but W, *Feragne,* and R, *Ferragny.*

P. 84, l. 22, voyde place. W, *grete way.*

P. 86, l. 1. R, *La nef fu a merueilles grande et painte et ystoriee;* W, *yᵉ shyppe was passynge grete and wele poynted.* Both English versions appear to have misunderstood the description of the decorated ship, uɴless *poynted* is an error for *paynted*.

P. 86, l. 9, Coffyrs and trunkes. W, *hutches and these grete cofers;* R, *huches.*

P. 89, l. 5, Mounte Belyard. R, *Montbliart.*

P. 90, l. 21, fonde of Guenelete. W, *affonned on G.* I do not know the word, are the *n's* misprints for *u's?* R, *affole.*

P. 90, l. 30. It is perhaps worth while to have this certainly comprehensive description in all the versions. W, *for men saye y' he hath many euyll condycyons/& also he is aged and corsyous and lame and dronklew;* R, [il] *est si gras si viel des monnyacle et yurongue.*

P. 97, l. 30, make his berd. I do not know this expression in the sense of give one a beating. It usually means to outwit, as in the *Reves Tale*, l. 176,

> Yet can a miller make a clerkes berd,

also, *Wife of Bath's Prol.*, l. 361,

> Yet could I make his berd, so mote I thee.

P. 98, l. 22, gallerye. So R; W, *tresaunce.* Bradley-Stratmann has only one instance of the word, *Pr., P.* 502.

P. 100, l. 31, by x and x. W with R, *by .xx. by .xxx.*

P. 102, l. 12, Doule. W, *Dueyl;* R, *dueil.*

· P. 103, l. 26, As Gode live, etc. I should have emended *Gode* to *goode*, cf. W, *Ponthus sayd y' good lyfe gyue hym god as to his lorde*, following R.

[P], *lui dist que bonne vie lui donnast dieu comment a son souuerain sires.*

P. 106, l. 28, conne you thonke. W continues, *for that ye haue done so well for his soule/for all his frendes shall thanke you & gyue you grete pryce. Ponthus sayd thynges that ought to be shall fall/ye ought not for to be full gladde ye shall haue none dower by cause ye set neuer fote in his bed with him/& thus he bourded with her & talked of many dyuers thynges. And than he wente to the kynge*, etc. All this in R.

P. 108, l. 2. W adds that they should assemble *at the toure of derbendell fast by the thalamount;* R, *talemont,* and further expands the passage, following R.

P. 110, l. 23, gyftes. W substitutes for the following sentence, *And then came Guyllam de roches a good knyghte Paraunt de rochefort/the lorde de douay, Pyers de donne, Gerarde de chateau goutyer, Johñ melcurier with the herupoys. Of the manceaus/beaunmount la vale, Sygles de doncelles and other of the countre of mayne. Of Tourayne baussay mayle hay and of other tourangeaus. Of poytw/the vycount of toures/the erles brother of marche/maulyon chastemur/la garnache & dyuers other.* The list is not in R.

P. 111, l. 12, any pouere man. W omits *pouere;* R, *Sil trouast aucuns pour scauoir lestre du pays.* D has apparently doubly translated *pour,* or it may have been repeated in D's original, once as *poure,* "poor," and again as the preposition.

P. 112, l. 5, and caste—othre. W, *wepte bothe two;* R, *pleurent tous deux lun sur lautre.*

P. 112, l. 28–30. This speech is Sir Patrick's in W. The Earl first sees Pollides and gives the command with l. 31 ff.

P. 115, l. 14, to-stowpe?

P. 115, l. 17, ay to. W, *a two,* probably the original reading.

P. 116, l. 13, Herupoys. W, *Herupoys, Hubert de craon, Pyers de chenulle/& of knyghtes Thybault de bryse, (H. de M.* as in D), *Eustace de la poyssoner.*

P. 116, l. 18, Hardenyr. W and O, *Ardenne.*

P. 116, l. 20, William. W and O, *Rycharde.*—Pamell. W, *Paynell;* O, *panel.*

P. 119, l. 16, vowes to the pope. The detail is neither in W nor R. I do not know of any other instance of vowing to the pope at a feast. It appears that we should read *po* and regard the ceremony as a peacock vow.

P. 135, l. 8, our author need not have known Chrêtien's

Les iauz li beise et puis le vis   *Yvain,* 6694.

P. 136, l. 20, a twenty. W and R, *a twelve.*

P. 140, l. 7, Chateawbreaunce. W, *chateau bryaunt.*

P. 146, l. 6, so shuld ye wors reioys. W, *wherof ye sholde reioyse;* R, *Et lamour donc vous deueries iouyr.* D mistranslates the clause.

P. 146, l. 9, withdrawe it. I. e., you would not be able to recall her fancy (*plesaunce*) from her lover, when you would do so.

P. 149, l. 17, Malle. W, *Mailles.*

NAMES OF PERSONS AND PLACES.

The names of minor characters in the story are omitted; also such common names as *Spayne, Fraunce, Englond,* when the modern, geographical equivalent is obvious. An interrogation point indicates that I have not been able to identify the name. The variants from W, given in the notes, should always be consulted for the longer lists of names in the text.

Amroy, *error for* Auray *near Vannes*, 96, 30.

Andrewe, *see* Landry.

Aniou, Duches of, 24, 5.

Aragon, 1, 6; *Arragonne, Kyng of,* 121, 32.

Armoric, *for* Armorica, Brittany, 9, 17.

Auncenys, Geffray d', Ancenis, 116, 12.

Aurences, Vicecounte d', Avranches *in Normandy,* 24, 3; *error for Fr.* Auteriche, 55, 22 (*see note*).

Avyon, Ralond de, *error for* Dinan,? 29, 6 (*see note*).

Babilon, Sultan of, 1, 10; *Babilone,* 117, 31.

Baniers, Ser William de,? 55, 25.

Bausy, Hondes de,? 149, 17; *Vaucay, Lorde,* 29, 24.

Bellacion, *another name for the* "Welle of Mervells," 41, 34; *Bellacon,* 56, 1.

Boloys, Tybould de, Blois, 54, 1.

Breales, a Saracen, 29, 3; *Fr.* Broalis.

Breselyn, *forest of,* Broceliande, 39, 16; *Breselyne,* 40, 12.

Breste, 24, 21.

Dorbendelle, *toure of,* Derbendelle *near Talmont* (*Vendée*), 110, 19 (*see p.* 5).

Doune, Piers de, ? 149, 14.

Douncelles, Lorde, 30, 21 ; *Oliver' de,* 116, 18.

Ellious, *Sidone's maid,* 14, 2 ; 68, 9 ; *Elious,* 14, 7 ; *Ellyous,* 15, 7 ; 127, 23. *Fr. Eloix.*

Fireague, *a Saracen,* 84, 8 (*see note and p.* 18).

Galice, Galicia, 2, 11.

Galyce, *error for* Galos (*Gaulish Britons*), 24, 29 (*note*).

Gener, *elder of the English king,* 73, 8 ; *Gener',* 74, 11 ; 136, 22 ; *Geneuer',* 137, 18 ; *Geneuer,* 143, 16 ; 144, 8.

Gloucestre, Earl of, 95, 36 ; 140, 15 ; *Duke of,* 138, 16 ; 139, 1.

Gloucestre, Rolande, 72, 30.

Guenelete, *Treacherous companion of Ponthus,* 34, 19 ; 63, 11 ; 88, 31 ; 97, 21 ; 124, 11 (*see p.* 18).

Hampton, *English port,* 70, 22.

Henry, *younger son of the king of England,* 70, 26 ; 84, 12.

Herland, *seneschal of Brittany, Ponthus' guardian,* 10, 19 ; 38, 29 ; 90, 19 ; *Herlande,* 10, 3 ; 13, 10.

Hungary, 57, 8.

Huguell, *king of Brittany, Sidone's father,* 9, 25.

Irland, king of, 76, 22 ; 77, 21 ; *Irelond,* 76, 4, 21 ; *Irlond,* 76, 2.

John, *elder son of the king of England,* 83, 2 ; 84, 9.

Karodas, *son of the sultan of Babylon, invader of England,* 27, 16, 25 ; 28, 27 ; *Carodas,* 18, 22 ; *Karados,* 27, 10. W and R always *Karados.*

Lay Forest, Amaulry de, ? 116, 17 ; *Hulland de La Foryste,* 30, 25.

Lay Garnache, John de, ? 116, 16.

La Hay, *Fresell de,* ? 30, 23.

Lay Poys, Eustace de, *for* La Possonnière *Maine,* 116, 15 (*note*).

La Roche, Bernard de, *Brittany,* 29, 32 ; 43, 4, 19 ; *Barnard,* 31, 17 ; *Guyllyam de,* 28, 29 ; *G. de Roches,* 24, 7 ; 29, 5 ; 110, 23 ; *Roger' de,* 24, 30.

GLOSSARY.

Abowed, p. ptc. *bent, bowed,* 45, 9.

Alblasters, *Arbalasters,* 83, 6.

Ale, *ail,* p. ptc. alyd, 36, 25.

Aloigne, Fr. *aloigner,* 63, 16.

Alowed, p. ptc. *praised,* 30, 33. W, *praysed;* R, *eust grant loz.*

Arased, p. ptc. *sprinkled,* 68, 10.

Attempe, *tempt,* 64, 19.

Availed, *lowered* p. ptc., 10, 12.

Avenaunt, *suitable,* 53, 21.

Balengere, *a large row boat, etymologically, a whale-boat,* 2, 13 ; ballengers, 133, 23, etc.

Batell, *a battalion,* 24, 28, etc., in b., in battle array, 27, 13.

Bente, p. ptc. of bend, *bent, pitched* (of a tent), 41, 34.

Ber̃, *a bier, or litter;* hors-ber̃, 50, 21.

Boude, probably an error, *bow,* 42, 29.

Celed, p. ptc. *hidden, concealed,* 93, 34.

Chalanged, p. ptc. *opposed, refused,* 89, 29.

Chaces, *coursing hounds,?* Fr. *chasses,* 4, 13.

Cherty, *affection,* 136, 30.

Comon, vb. *associate,* 147, 11.

Comoners, probably *participants* in a tournament from the vb. *comon,* but the notes suggest deliberate coinage from the vb. *come on,* 139, 4, 33.

Cosen, *for chosen* p. ptc., 53, 24.

Cowardyue, *cowardly,* 27, 20.

Cronocles, *coronets,* 108, 10.

Dawyng, n. *Dawn,* 3, 7.

Demaundes, *questions,* 10, 21 ; 16, 11; 16, 22.

Devise, *spy out,* 24, 25. R, *espier.*

Discesed, *died,* 150, 9.

Discolored, *blanched,* 67, 6.

Dismated, *dismayed* p. ptc., 29, 17.

Draght, *allurement, encouragement,* 75, 15; draghtes of loue, 34, 5.

Drogman, *dragoman, interpreter,* 18, 24.

Dunyon, *citadel, donjon* (fig. *protection*), 25, 21.

Dystrakked, *distracted,* 129, 16.

Enhauntes, *exercises, follows,* 1, 20.

Erst, *before,* W, 135, 16 (note), miswritten *herfte,* 67, 2.

Farrome, a, *at a distance,* the weak dat. plu. of the adj. *feor,* 48, 31; farrom, 141, 15.

Fiꝥ-hows, *building where there is a fire, dwelling house,* 18, 29; also in W.

Forfeted, p. ptc. *done amiss,* 65, 4.

Fouuysch, *foolish,* 64, 1.

Fylloy, *follow,* 39, 13.

Gaꝥ, *make,* 77, 33.

Garnysche, *provide, garrison,* 23, 23.

Gaynstondyng, n. *opposition,* 3, 15.

Gogle, *joggle, stagger,* 51, 11; gogyllyng, 52, 18.

Gоweꝥ, *a brooch,* ? 61, 12 (note).

Grifyns, *falcons,* 4, 14.

Gyrtelles, *for Kyrtelles,* 121, 27.

H, initial, inorganic: harme, 28, 8; 29, 16; 68, 9; vn-h, 46, 16; helboys, 6, 5; herely, 5, 23; holde, 24, 27.

Haviꝥ, *Fr. avoir, possessions,* 144, 34.

Labre, v. *labor,* 7, 1, etc.

Langoure, *languish,* 68, 6.

Laseꝥ, *leisure,* 127, 34. Frequent in Barbour with this spelling.

Lay, for Fr. *la* in proper names, 46, 8; 116, 15, 16 and 17.

Lesse, *shorter,* 137, 22.

Livelode, *patrimony,* 108, 30.

Lovyng, *laudation,* 50, 7.

Luges, *huts or tents,* 27, 9.

Lugge, v. *lodge* Inf., 2, 24; p. ptc. *lugged,* 3, 2.

Manhened, pret. *maimed,* 114, 29.

May, for Fr. *ma, May dame,* 36, 32.

v

Mokkyng, *mocking*, 12, 3.

More, in the sense of *taller*, 48, 1.

Neghtboures, *neighbors*, 23, 19; 81, 14.

Nobylley, *nobility*, *splendor*, 53, 13.

Norye, *foster-child or ward*, 13, 16.

Pensy, *pensive*, 39, 27, etc.

Pensynes, *pensiveness*, 37, 4.

Perchen, *to pierce*, p. ptc. perched, 44, 13; 84, 15, etc.

Peyns, *garments*? or *plumes, tufts,* ? 82, 1 (note).

Pris, n. *praise*, 31, 16.

Proloyne, *absent itself*, 66, 30.

Protestacion, *protestation, solemn assurance*, 63, 23.

Refrete, *refrain*, 39, 29.

Refuse, *avoid*, R, refuser, 7, 33; cf. Barbour (glossary).

Reiose, in the sense of *enjoy*, 132, 7.

Repenyd, p. ptc. *repined*, 46, 28.

Rokkette, *a small crag*, 95, 4; W and R, *roche.*

Serve, *deserve*, 17, 3.

Skale, *to scale* (a wall, etc.), inf., 2, 27; *scaled*, p. ptc., 10, 23; 94, 26.

Somers, *sumpter beasts*, 97, 19.

Strenghtes, *strong places*, 26, 30.

Stuffe, v. *provision;* pt. stuffyd, 5, 23; 124, 24; 128, 8, etc.; frequent in Barbour.

Subarbes, *suburbs*, 134, 10.

Suyd, p. ptc. *issued*, 43, 11.

Symphonys, *musical instrument*, 44, 1.

Tempe, *tempt, try*, 35, 2; *pret.*, 124, 19.

The, *for they*, 2, 26; 69, 14; 86, 23; 100, 17; 119, 11; 129, 9; 130, 15; 135, 5.

Titter, *sooner*, 130, 12.

Topp, *top* (*nautical term*), 6, 19.

Trast, *trust*, 107, 18; pret. traysted, 89, 9.

Vndretaken, p. ptc. *surprised;* R, seurpris, 27, 14.

Unnes, *with difficulty*, 67, 8; 103, 3.

Ure, *probably fortune, lot,* as frequently in Barbour, 131, 26 (note). The meaning *man,* A.S. *wer* suggested by the note is hardly possible.

Voward, *van-guard,* 25, 9.

Vyser, *visour,* 21, 8, etc.; vyssour, 41, 29, etc., *a musk.*

Ware, for *vair, fur,* 141, 8.

Wate, lay in, 21, 15, *lay in wait.*

Warne, *direct, govern,* 96, 4.

Wordle, *for world,* 38, 31.

Wordly, 9, 30; 39, 30; 46, 29; 67, 16.

FRANK JEWETT MATHER, JR.

[KING PONTHUS AND THE FAIR SIDONE,

NOW FIRST PRINTED FROM THE UNIQUE MS. DIGBY 185 IN
THE BODLEIAN LIBRARY.]

[Cap. I. Of kyng Tiber of Spayne and his sonne Ponthus;
and how the Sawdeyn of Babilon sent his thre sonnes to
werre vpon the Cristen.]

[Fol. 166.] N¹Ow I wolle you tell a noble storye, wherof a man may
lerne mony goode ensamples, and yonge men may here
the goode dedes of aunciente people that dide muche goode and
worschip in their days—how itt happenyd to the kyng Tiber
5 of Spayne. That kyng had to his wyf the kynges doghtre of
Aragon, a full holy womman. So thei had betwen theym a
sonne that was called Ponthus, the moste famose childe & the
moste gracious that euer was seyn in that tyme. The kyng
his fadre was a full worthy man and debonere.

10 In that tyme itt happened in the Est that the sawdeyn of
Babilon was of gret power of havyng men of armes. So
he had four sonnes; wherthurgh he ordayned that the eldest
schuld haue his empire, and sayd to the othre thre, "Fair
sonnes, take ye noon hede to haue any of myn heritage, for I
15 wolle ordeyn that eueryche of you shall haue thirty M¹ men
of armes, for the whiche I schal paye their sawde for thre yer,
and schall yeve you schippyng and all that you nedes to haue.
And eueryche of you thre schall goo in his aventure to conquer contrees and realmes vpon the Cristen ; and which of you
20 thre that best doos and moste conquerys and moste enhauntes²
the lawe of Mahown schal be the best cheresyd with me, and

---

¹A handsome illuminated initial N, extending through twelve lines of
text. See the description of the MS. and the facsimile page.
    ²*Enhauntes*, to exercise or follow, corresponds closely in meaning to
szaucera of the French original. See Bradley-Stratmann for instances of
this rare word.

1

I schal gyf to hym the moste of my goodes." So the sowdeyn ordayned his thre sonnes and yeave theym that thei nedyd for to weṛ vpon the Cristen. And thei went to the sce all thre to gedre.

5 [**Cap. II.** How Brodas sonne to the Sawdeyn toke Couleigne and slewe the kyng Tiber; and how a Cristen knyght named Patrices saved Ponthus and the xiij children in a schip.]

S¹O it happenyd as fortune wold, that oon of the childre of 10 the sowdeyn come, as the wynde drove hym and his navye by gret tourment, that he passed Spayne in Galice, and toke londe nygh to a gret citee that was called Couleigne, and went to londe in a balangere, he and xxi men with hy*m*, and toke of the people theṛ aboute the londyng. And when he 15 asked who was lorde of that londe, the[i] answeryd and seyd that itt was the realme of Spayne and that kyng Tibeṛ was kyng of that londe. Then askcd the sowdeyn's sonne what lawe he held, and thei answeryd and seyd, the lawe of Ih*e*su Criste.
Then made he to withdrawe his (navy),² as thogh he wold 20 withdrawe hym fro the contree, and toke two and twenty schippys and sent theym to the porte of Couleign and charged theyme to make theyme as marchaundes of cloth of gold, of silke, & of spices; and that thei schuld in the evynnyng goo into the town and lugge theyme with fovrty men of armes, 25 with habyrdions undre theiṛ govnes; and in the morow erly that the[i] schuld come vpon the walles at the wateṛ gate, & that thei schuld gete the gate, and thei schuld assey to skale the wall and to come vp into the tovne. And as they deuysid,³ itt was so doon.

---

¹ This capital S extends through three lines of text; so, unless there is a note to the contrary, all initials marking chapter divisions.
² The scribe has apparently omitted *navy*, here added from W. The French has *Lors fist retraire son nauire.*
³ MS. *deuydid*, a sheer blunder due to the ambiguous French verb. R, *Et ainsi comme il deuisa il fu fait.* W, *and so as he had deuysed it*, etc.

So come the xxij vesells and made theym marchaundes of
Ciprice and sold theiꝛ marchaundys goode chepe. And aftre
that, the fourty men that weꝛ lugged in the toune as marchaundes, nygh to the wateꝛ gate—thei made theiꝛ hostys to
5 ete and drynk with theym, that noon ingyne schuld be thoght.
And when thei had disported theym, thei went and had take
theiꝛ avice to be vp on the gate on the dawyng, to goo aboute
and deuice theiꝛ dooyng. And when itt come to the houre,
thei went vpon the wall; and att the same houre, the sonne of
10 the sawdeyn, that was called Brodas, come to the foote of the
[*Fol. 166ᵇ.] wall with a grete * navye¹ of ladders. And sume went on
theym on hygh & thei that wer above pullyd up theym that
weꝛ benethe, so that within a while ther was a thosand or moo
vpon the walles, and wanne the wateꝛ gate, and so enteryd into
15 the toune withouten ony gaynstondyng. And thei made gret
martirdome of the people, and forwith thei assailed the castell
in the which the kyng Tyber was, and thei toke hym by
strenght, not withstondyng the kyng defendid hym and wold
not be taken, and so he was slayn.
20   And the quene went oute prively into the wodes. And
the kynges sonne Ponthus, and xiij childre whiche was
lordes sonnes, and a goode preste that toke theym,² went out
prively and hidde theym in a roche in a garthyn; and theꝛ
thei weꝛ twoo days withoute mete or drynke. And the goode
25 preste which was called Dampdenis had so grete drede, when
the childeryn wold goon oute of the cave, he wenyd to haue
died for theym; and seyd, "Goo ye not oute bot if ye wolle
dye." So he kepyd theym twoo days therin. Bot on the third
day Ponthus sayd to his maistre, "Itt is bettre to dye on the
30 swerd then forto dye with hungre, for then we schal be cause
of ouꝛ own dethe; and if we goo oute, we may by the grace of

---

¹ Some word representing the *nombre* of W and R, or the *foueson* of H &
F would be more natural. I have let *navye* stand in the text in the sense
of a ship, because I have no emendation probable on palaeographical
grounds.

² MS. *theym and.* See note.

Gode happely fynde sume remedye." And the goode preste
sayd he hade leuer̃ dye for hungre then goo into their̃ handes,
and tremelyd grettly for fere.

 Bot fers[1] Ponthus and his cosyn german Pollides and all the
5 othre lepe oute of the roche, and anoon thei wer̃ aspyed and all
taken, and ledde to the toune to the kyng Brodas, that made
hym selve kyng of the londe. And when the kyng sawe the
thirten childre, thei semed to hym ryght fair̃. So he asked
whoes childre thei wer̃. And Ponthus answerd and seyd thei
10 wer̃ childre whiche the kyng norisched for the loue of Gode
and for theyr service when thei schuld be men. "And of
what seruice?" said the kyng Brodas. "Ser," said the childre,
"some to kepe his grehoundes and his chaces, and sume to kepe
havkes of the toure, and sume to kepe grifyns, and othre to
15 doo seruice in hall and in chaumbre." "What!" seyd the
kyng Brodas, "Clothed he his seruauntes so worthely as ye
bee?—for by your̃ clothes that ye were, ye semen to be grete
lordes sonnes." "Ser," seid Ponthus, "we be the childre bot
of small gentylmen." "By hym that I serue," said the kyng,
20 "I can not see what ye be, bot of beaute and of fair̃ speche
thou feylest non; bot ye muste lef your lawe that is noght
worth and take the lawe that we leve on, and I schal doo you
muche goode; and if ye wolle not, I schal make you for to
dye: and so chese you whethre that ye wolle." "Truly," said
25 Ponthus, "of the dethe ye may wele ordayn to your̃ plesir, bot
for to leve oure lawe and to take youres—we wolle not for to
dye therfore." "No!" seid the kyng, "Then shall ye dye an
evyll dethe."

 And then come a knyght Cristen, that had taken their̃ lawe
30 for drede of dethe, the whiche all way had his hertt and thoght
vnto Ihesu Criste, the whiche the kyng loved myche, and sayd
vnto the kyng, "Deliuer̃ theym to me, for if they wolle not
beleue vpon our̃ lawe, I schal ordayn in suche wyse that thei

---

[1]Adverbial for *fersly*. R, *Et au fort Pontus sailli.* . . . H, *Mais en la fin.*
W, shows a similar mistranslation: *and by strengthe Ponthus sterte out of
the caue.*

schal neue*r* doo harme vnto youʔ lawe." "I pray you," sayd
the kyng, "and I yeve theym vnto youʔ goue*rnaunce."* Then
trowed Ponthus and his fellawes to be deid. The knyght led
theym to his hous and manasshed theym sore before the Sara-
5 zyns; and when the Sarasyns weʔ withdrawn, he said to assey
[*Fol. 167.] theym, "Ye muste beleve on Mahounde, * or elles ye muste
dye." And thei answeryd thei wold not, bot ratheʔ to dye.
And when he sawe theym so stedfaste, he had gret ioy in his
hert and he asked theym if thei had oght etyn of late tyme.
10 And thei sayd, "Not thes thre days haue we nawtheʔ ete ne
dronke." Then he made theym to ete and drynke. And as
thei ete oon of theym sayd to his fellawes, "Wherfor ete we,
when we schal dye anoon?" "Say ye not so," q[uo]d Ponthus,
"in the grace of ouʔ Lorde ben mony remedyes. If itt like
15 hym, we schal leve; if it like hym, we schal dye; for all lieth
in hym. So lete vs have good hope in hym, and he wolle save
vs." And so thei ete and prayd to Gode to have me*r*cy on
theym.

The knyght herd what Ponthus sayd and prased hym muche
20 in his hertt, and seyd, "Itt weʔ to gret pitee to lete so fayʔ
childre dye." And so he went fro theym and soght a schipp,
and by nyght stuffyd itt with vitell for a monethe, and herely
in the morowe he ledd the childre to schipp, and putt therin a
schipman with theym that was a *Crist*in man, and putt theym
25 in the bothome of the schipp; and when the childre weʔ in
the bothome of the schipp, thei pulled vp the sale, and the
schipp saled into the hygh see. Then the schippman come
vp fro benethe and toke the goue*r*naill of the schipp and asked
theym whedir thei wold goo. Then Ponthus said, "Syth Gode
30 has sent you vnto vs, faiʔ frende, lede vs to the coste of
Fraunce." And he said he wold, and bad theym not be ferd
ne dredand, for thei had vitell enogh for a monethe; and told
theym how the knyght had putt theym[1] in the bothome

---

[1] W and R have *hym* and *lui*, a far better reading. But the repeated,
therefore consistent, blunder may be the translator's. See l. 24 f. and p. 6, l. 1.

of the schipp and the vitell with theym by nyght. Then
sayd Ponthus, " Faiῤ Seris, knele we all down and thanke we
Gode of the grete goodnes that he hath sent to vs, and pray
we all to be to his plesaunce." So did the children nyght
5 and day vpon theiῤ knees and helboys, praying to Gode full
devoutly, aud (had) alonely theiῤ truste and stedfaste beleve
in almyghty Gode.

[Cap. III. How the kyng Brodas dremed that Ponthus become a lion and devouryd hym; how Patrices councelled
10   hym to lete the Cristen people yeld tribute; and how
Patrices delyuered from prison the Erle of Destrue.]

SO lete we lefe of the fovrten childre and retourne to the
knyght that putt theym into the schipp. The knyght
was called Patrices, and he went and told the kyng how he
15 had venged hym vpon the xiiij childre that wold not beleve
on Mahounde. "How have ye doon?" sayd the kyng. "Ser,"
said the knyght, " ye schal neuer see theym, for I haue putt
theym in a faiῤ schipp full of holles, withouten vitell, and lete
drawe vp the sale to the topp, that broght theym into the hygh
20 see. Have no drede, for ye schal neuer see theym."
" I wolle wele," said the kyng, "for I haue dremed this nyght
that I sawe the xiiij children in a wodde, and that the faiῤ
childe that speke to me become a lion and devouryd me and
hurte me in suche wyse that I dyed. So I haue be sore affrayd
25 in my slepe." "Ser," sayd the knyght, "itt is bot a dreme
and malyncoly. Of theym ye be quytt." " I wolle wele," said
the kyng.
Then said the knyght, " By Mahounde Ser, me aght to councell you truly to my poweῤ, if itt like you, that no man be
30 putt to dethe, bot if he stonde at defence; for ye have a faiῤ
conquest. For men sayn in scorn, that as mytch is a mylne
worthe that gryndyth not as an oven that baketh not. Now
lete euery man beleve on that lawe that he wolle; and that
all the strenghtes & contres come to youῤ obesaunce and to

[*Fol. 167ᵇ.] yeld you tribute; * and lette theym leve and labre, and ye schal be as ryche as ye wold be." Then said the kyng, " By Mahounde ye counsell vs truly. Goo ye and so serche prisoners; and thei that wolle beleve vpon ouꝛ lawe—thei schall 5 be worschipped with vs, and we schall yeve theym of oures; and thei that wolle not, shal beꝛ tribute to vs aftre theiꝛ poweꝛ; and we putt all the gouernaunce of ouꝛ law in you." So was the knyght charged with the gouernaunce of the prisoners and of the contre.

10 And the knyght, whiche was a worthye man and that took noon hede bot forto save the Cristen people at his poweꝛ, went aboute to take oute prisoners and to putt theym to a lyght ravnson. Among all othre prisoners he founde the kynges brothre of Spayne, that was Erle of Destrue, that was sore 15 wounded with two woundes; and when that the knyght knew that he was the kynges brothre of Spayne, he toke hym by the honde and led hym aloone into a chaumbre and said to hym, "Ser, I wote ye be the kynges brothre. Ye haue gret desiꝛ to save the countree and the people that ben fallen to 20 gret myschief into the tyme that Ihesu Criste putt remedye therin. I sey to you in goode feith secretly that I schal putt the best remedye thurgh youꝛ goode councell that I can putt therin." Then the Erle had gret ioye to heꝛ hym speke of Ihesu Criste, and said that he knew wele that he wold the 25 welfaiꝛ of the Cristen people and said full sore syghyng,

[Cap. IIII. How by the councell of the knyght Patrices the Erle of Destrue feynyd hym a Saresyn vnto the tyme that Ponthus schuld relefe the contree; and how thei made all the contree tributorie to the kyng Brodas.]

30 "Ryght swete Ser, I wote not whethiꝛ ye say thus to assey me, bot wold Gode that youꝛ hertt weꝛ as youꝛ movthe says." Then said Patrices and told how he was take in the batell, and forto refuse the dethe and for the welefaiꝛ of the prisoners of the batell and of all Cristen, he become

Saresyn, bot his hertt was all wey to Gode. And told hym
how he savyd the xiiij children, and how he made that
the kyng putt noon of theym to dethe, and that euery man
schuld hold his own lawe and beꝛ to hym tribute and seruage,
5 and how he hade doon this vnto the tyme that Gode wolde
putt sume remedye therin, and how he was charged to raunson the prisoners. And then the Erle fell down vpon his
kneys and gafe thonkyng vnto Gode, wepyng. Then the
knyght toke hym vp and thei kyssed to gedre and thonked
10 Gode.

And when thei had wepyd envgh for pite, thei said that
Gode had semelyd theym to doo sume goode to the people
that weꝛ in poynte to be distroed. Then said Patrices, "Faiꝛ
Ser, yitt I hope to Gode that he wole haue mercy vpon the
15 contree and his people, & I pray you to feyne you a Saresyn
as I doo, and the kyng wolle haue of you gret ioye, and so by
the grace of Gode we schall putt suche ordinaunce that schal
be profittable for to abyde the grace of Gode. And I say to
you as myn hertt says to me, that the childre that I haue
20 savyd schal relefe the contree—and in maner the kyng hath
tolde me in a dreme, how that he dremed of the xiiij children,
and how that the grettest become a lion and devoured the
kyng." Then said the Erle, "I reioyse in myn hertt, for he is
my nevew and my Gode son—Gode gyde hym." Then thei
25 sweꝛ to hold companye to gedre—in goode and in evyll to
enduꝛ. And so thei toke theiꝛ avice to gedre.

Then Patrices went to the kyng and said, "Ser, ye ought
to thonke Mahounde, for I haue conuerted the kynges brothiꝛ
of this contree, that is the Erle of Destrue; and so by litle
30 and litle he schal helpe to encrese the lawe of Mahounde and
he schal make you to haue grete tributes and grete wynnyng
of the contree; and he and I schal ride into the contree to
[*Fol. 168.] cites and townes; and thei that wolle * obey schal be cheresed,
and thei that wolle not sall be punyshed."
35 The kyng hade gret ioye and made the kynges brothre to
come before hym; and so thei accorded that thei schuld ride

with the kyng into the contree. And so the kyng roode from
toune to toune with thirtee thovsand men of armys; and so
thei made all the contree tributorie to the kyng.

So itt happened aftre mony mervelles and pestilence[s] in
5 the contree. So forto passe ouer the matier, the kyng reignyd
xv¹ yer as by a vengeaunce of Gode, and aftre the londe was
relevyd agan.

Now lete we retorne to the children that wer in the see full
sorye and full dredfull of their live.

10 [Cap. V. How Ponthus and the xiij children arived in Litle
Bretayn and Herland the senyschall broght theym to the
kyng Huguell that lete norysh and teche theym. How
Herland governed Ponthus. Of the grete speche of the
goodlyhede of Ponthus. And how Sydon the kynges
15   doghtre desired in hir hert to se hym.]

Bot fortune that was mervellous led theym to the contre
of Armoric, which be called now Litle Bretayn. So
was the wynde strong and the tourment of the see that made
theym to arive vpon a roche ayeinst a forest. And as Gode
20 wold, the mast fell betwen twoo roches; and so thei lepe vp and
savyd theym selve vpon the roches eueryche of theym. And
when thei wer vpon the roche, thei held vp their hondes and
thonked Gode of his grace and said that Gode forgetteth not
his seruauntz, bot he sendes theym socour.

25   N²[ow] that tyme reigned in Litle Bretayne kyng Huguell,
a worthie man and a true, bot he was olde and he had bot oon
doghtre a live of all the children that he hade by hys wyfe, the
whiche was sustre to the kyng of Normandie. This doghtre
was the fairest, most curtes, and devoute that myght be founde
30 in anye contre. Sche was the most wordly³ ioye that hir fadre

---

¹ MS. xv as. As cancelled by the rubricator.

² The N in this text is very like a large & in form, but neither W nor R
has an &, while such a reading would be awkward.

³ A characteristic spelling for worldly which I have retained here and elsewhere, see glossary.

hade, and comforth and chere. Was no feste bot hiꝛ beautie
and hiꝛ wommanhode was spoken of.

So it happed that Herlande that was senyschall of Bretayn, a full goode knyght and a trew,[1] was gouernouꝛ of
5 Bretayn, and he hunted that day in the forest of Susteny.
And, as (of) aventuꝛ, an hertt went to the water nygh to the
roche theꝛ the children weꝛ. So Herlande loked vp and
beheld the children vpon the roche. Then he come toward
theym and asked theym what thei weꝛ. Thei answerd and
10 said thei weꝛ aventured in the see. Then the seneschall smot
his hors with his spurris and come to theym, for the see was
availed and withdrawn—then the hors went vp to the belly
in the see—and made theym to lepe vp be hynd hym and his
knyghtes and his esquiers, and broght theym to the londe.
15   Then he asked theym of what lande thei weꝛ. And thei
said thei weꝛ of the kyngdome of Spayne. Then said oon
called Viceat, "Ser, Loo her Ponthus! that is the kynges son,
and theꝛ Pollides his cosyn german, and thes othre ben barouns
sonnes of Spayne." And when that Herland herd that Pon-
20 thus was the kynges son, he made hym goode cheꝛ and did hym
grete honour, and asked of hym demaundes. And the childe
that was full wyse answeryd hym full wysely and told hym
how that Brodas the Sowdeyn son hade scaled Coleigne and
sloy his fadre and toke the contre; and how thei weꝛ taken
25 and putt into a schipp, and all the maneꝛ as ye haue herd afore.
And when the Senyschall herde the sorow of the roalme of
Spayne, he hade grete pitee of the kyng and of the realme
of Spayne that any suche (folke) schuld haue dominacion of
the Cristen.

30   So then he made hym lepe vp behinde hym—and he toke
Ponthus and his cosyn horsse to ride aloone[2]—and led hym to
[*Fol. 168ᵇ.] Vennys theꝛ as the kyng was. * And when the kyng sawe and
hade herd of the kynges dethe of Spayne, he was full sory

---

[1] MS. *trew that was*, etc. I amend by omitting *that*, following R. *Si aduint
que herlant . . . . estoit tout gouuerneur de bretaigne et chassoit celle iournee, etc.*
[2] See the note on this apparently contradictory passage.

and hade grete pitee on the contree and wepyd, for he loved
myche the kyng of Spayne, and said that he had doon myche
goode and goten grete worschip vpon the partes of Spayne
wheᵽ as he had ben in werre ayenst the Saresyns, in the com-
5 pany of the kyng of Fraunce. "And I say," q[uo]d the kyng,
"itt is grete hyrt to all Cristendome of the dethe of the
kyng, for he was a full goode knyght and a worthie; and as
to vs Bretaynes, we haue more harme than any othiᵽ nacion,
for we sent thediᵽ to chaunge ouᵽ whete with theiᵽ goode
10 wynes, and so we haue lost mytch more than othiᵽ men. Bot
Gode of his grace deliueᵽ the contre of that fals lawe, and I
thouke Godde that he has sent me the kynges sone and the
children of the barounes, for I schal lete norysh theym and
teche theym as I wold myn awn. Then he called to hym the
15 senyschall and betoke Ponthus to hym, and to diuerse of his contre he betoke the remeynaunt. And so he departed theyme¹
into the ende of iij yers and charged theyme to teche theyme
wele in havkyng and huntyng—in all maneᵽ of disportes.
So were the xiiij children departed, as ye haue herd, to the
20 barounes of the contre. And Herland gouerned Ponthus and he
lered hym all maneᵽ of disportes—hawkyng, huntyng, playng
at the chesse, daunsyng, and synghyng. Myche was the worschip thurgh oute all Bretayn that sprong of the grete beautie,
governaunce, and curtesie of Ponthus; and thei spake of hym
25 both farre and neᵽ. And aboue all thing he loued God and the
chirche, and his first ocupacion in the morowe was to wesch his
hondes, to say his prayers, and to heᵽ his messe full devoutely,
and wold neuer ete ne drynke vnto the tyme that he had his
prayers all said. And of suche as he hade, he wold gyf to the
30 poeᵽ men prively parte. And he wold neuer sweᵽ grete othe
bot "Truly" and "As God me helpe." And he wold be as
glade when he loste and when he wan; if any man dide hym
wrong, he wold sey att few wordes in faire maneᵽ that he had

¹ MS. thenne. Clearly a scribal blunder for theym. A form theime, on the
analogy of thei, would be better palaeographically, but is found nowhere in
the MS. N, And so departed he theym. R, Et ainsi les departi.

wrong, and he wold yeve upp his gamme in faire maneř rather
or he wold strive; and no man couth make hym wroth in his
playng. And he lovyd neuer mokkyng ne scornyng. And if
any man speke of any vices or harme by man or womman, he
5 wold breke his tayle. And he wold neuer play at gamme that
was hurt or angre to any man, for he was the best taght that
any man sen in any place, and the best and the fairest schapen
in his live dayes. He semed like an aungell. The more that
a man beheld hym the bettre hym schuld like hym.
10 Theř was no speche bot of hym, in so myche that the reporte
of his goodelyhede and of his semelenes was myche spoken of in
the kynges courte. Sydon the kynges doghtre herd so myche
worschip spoken by Ponthus that she had grete desiř in hiř
hertt to se hym; and sche was hold the fairest, the comeliest,
15 the most womanly in all Fraunce or Bretayn, and best couthe
behaue hiř in presence of all maneř of people, both of high
degre and of lowe degre.

[Cap. VI. Of the grete feste at Vennys; and how Sydon bad
        Herland bryng hir Ponthus, that was his norye, and he
20   broght hir first Pollides for drede of evyll speche; and
        when Ponthus was broght, Sydon began for to loue hym,
        withouten any poynt of velanye, and chose hym as for hir
        knyght. How tithynges come that the Saresyns wer
        landed in the Ile of Breste.]

25 A ftre itt happed that the terme of iij yeres was comen
     vp, and that the kyng helde a grete feste in the Whis-
son tyde at Vennys; and he sent govnes of oon suyte to the
xiij children; and sent to theym that thei schuld come to
the feste; and eueryche baron schuld bryng his childe. And
30 Herland broght Ponthus, and the Lorde de La Vale broght
his cosyn german Pollides that was most faiř, most goodely,
[*Fol. 169.] and best in behavyng * of theym all except Ponthus.
When Ponthus was comen euery man beheld hym. And
when the kyng sawe hym, he had gret ioye and praid to Gode

to save hym and to send hym myche worschipp, and said that
he schuld serve hym of his copp at the feste.

The kyng made his fest with his barones and his knyghtes
in oon parte¹ and his doghtre in an othiꝛ parte. Grete was
5 the feste and the ioye and the grete sportes. Sydon, that herd
the grete speche of the beautie that was in Ponthus and of his
demeynyng, sche was day and nyght in grete thoght how sche
myght fynd an way, with hiꝛ worschipp, to speke with hym—
for drede myche of spechc of menn. And when sche had
10 thoght envgh, sche sent for Herlande the senyschall; and
when he was comen, sche gave hym a right faiꝛ palfrey,
and sche made hym ryght grete cheꝛ. Herland mervellyd
of the grete cheꝛ, bethynkyng hym what sche mente, and
doubted; and aftre werd sche said all, "Ay, fair Senysshall,
15 faiꝛ and swete frende, we pray you that we myght see your
norye Ponthus, that is wele taght and right wyse, as men
sayne; I pray you bryng vs hym this nyght that we may see
hym, for men sayne that he can daunce and syng." "Ma
dame," said the senysshall, "I schal bryng hym to you, sith
20 that itt like you that I doo soo." "Then goo," seid sche,
"and I schall see if he [be] suche oon as men sayne, or not."

The senysshall toke his leve and wente on his wey. He
was a full goode knyght, wyse and redie, and wente thynkyng
that the goode cheꝛ that he hade was for the love of Ponthus.
25 And so he was troubeled in his thoght and said to hym selfe,
"Ay Sainte Marie, if I schuld bryng Ponthus, he is so faiꝛ, if
this woman sawe hym, sche myght be so take with love that
sche wold haue noon otheꝛ bot hym; and sche myght schew
to hym suche love as sche myght (be) perceyved; wherthurgh
30 she myght haue blamc, and the child loste, by envy. I wot
not what to doo." So he then thoght that he wold bryng his
cosyn german in stede of hym, for mony causes, and for he
doubted myche the kyng, and for drede that any harme schuld
fall therby. He come agayne and broght Pollides with hym.

¹ The word is entered over the line.

Sidon went into hiꝛ warderop and sche made [come] a
damesell named Ellious, the whiche sche loved myche and
trusted vnto more than to any othiꝛ, and she said to hiꝛ that
she hade grete desiꝛ to se the faiꝛ childe Ponthus, of whome
5 all men spake. So sche had a litle wyndowe wheratt sche
loked oute ofte tymes, if any thyng come that wey; and so
she called Elious to se that all hiꝛ aray weꝛ wele dressed
vpon. So att the laste, as thei loked, thei sawe comyng the
senysshall and Pollides that was ryght faiꝛ and goodely. And
10 so she come doune into the chaumbre and made grete cheꝛ and
ioy, and toke Pollides by the honde and wold haue made hym
to sytt doune by hiꝛ. And Pollides said, "Ma dame, I wolle
not sitt doune by you, for itt is no reason." "Truly," she
said, "itt is reason. Ye be a kynges son." "Ma dame," said
15 he, "that be I not, bot I am his cosyn german." "Ay," said
she, "I went that ye hade ben he." So she made hym as
faiꝛ cheꝛ as she myght. Not withstandyng, she was wrothe
and said to the senysshall, "Iape ye with me?" "How
Madame?" said he. "Ye schuld haue broght the kynges
20 sone of Spayne," said she, "and ye haue broght his cosyn
german. Wherfore dide ye so? Hold ye me such a foell."
Then the knyght kneled doune and said, "Ma dame, I crie
[*Fol. 169ᵇ.] you mercy, and be * ye not displeased, for in goode faithe I
thoght bot wele; for I myght not at that tyme bryng hym,
25 for he served the kyng of his copp." "Yitt," said she, "ye
schuld vndirstonde wele not to bryng me oon othre in stede
of hym. Ye doute of me. I am not now so yong bot that I
wold kepe my worshipp." "Itt is no doute Ma dame," said
the senysshall. "I thynk bot wele; bot I doute my lorde youꝛ
30 fadre that loves you so myche—for if ye make hym a litle
more chere than any othre, men wold haue envy of hym—
and leste any evyll myght come therof, for the worlde is full
evyll; for where that ye thinke bot goode and worshipp, yitt
thei thynke othre wyse." "Ay," said she, "Ser, thinke ye no
35 doute, for I hade leveꝛ be deid than any myght reproche me
or my worshipp for any thyng—be right sure." "Ma dame,

Gode wold that euery man wold as wele as I, for I wold youꝛ
worshipp and welefaiꝛ as wele as any man on live; and sith
ye wolle, I schall bring hym." "I pray you," said sche, "and
tary not long."
5 The senysshall went his way to fetche hym. Sydon went
into hiꝛ warderopp to loke att the wyndowe, if she myght se
hym come. So she said to Ellyous here best beloved damesell,
"Yeve me my myrrour and se that I be wele." "Sothely Ma
dame," she said, "ye be ryght wele." Then said she, "Loke
10 ye if that he come." And so thei loked ofte, if thei myght se
hym comyng. So att the laste Ellyous went rynnyng to hiꝛ
ladie and said, "Ma dame, se ye wheꝛ he cometh, the fairest
of the worlde."
And Sidone lepe vpp and come rynnyng, and sawe hym
15 come, and the senysshall with hym. So she sawe hym faiꝛ,
sanguyn, broune, and high—of faiꝛ stature, so that she hade
of hym grete mervell. Then she said to Ellyous, "Damesell,
me semys he is mervellous faiꝛ." "Ma dame," said Ellious,
"he is no man—he is an aungell. I sawe neuer so faiꝛ an
20 erthely creatuꝛ. Gode made hym with his aun hondes." "By
my faith," said Sidon, "ye say verray trauth. I trowe she
that be take with his love be fortunate." And so she went
doune into hiꝛ chaumbre to hiꝛ ladies and gentylwomen. And
anoon aftre, Ponthus and the senysshall come vpp into the
25 chaumbre; and so Ponthus went forth toward Sidon with full
lowe curtesie, saluyng hiꝛ and hiꝛ ladies. So Sidone toke hym
by the honde and welcomed hym goodely and praid hym to
sytt doune by hiꝛ. And he said, "Ma dame itt is not for me
to doo so." So thei made grete curtesye. Then said she,
30 "Wherfore make ye all this curtesie? Be not ye the kynges
son of Spayne?" "Yis, Ma dame," said Ponthus, "bot yitt
I be not like you, for ye be doghtre to a grete kyng and a
myghty, and I be a kynges son disheret; and so I haue noght
bot by the goodeness of my lorde your fadre, that so myche
35 goode has doon to me." "Ay, Ponthus," said she, "leve these[1]

[1] MS. there.

wordes, for Gode has not made you suche as nature schewys
you, bot forto doo for you ;[1] for ye be made and fouremed to
haue as myche worschipp and goode, and more, then euer you?
fadre had—the which Gode sende you." "Ma dame, I am
5 not in that way, bot in the mercy of Gode is all."

"Now sytt ye," said she, "I you pray and commaunde."
So he satt a litle benethe hi?. Then said she to the ladys,
"I pray you of sume dissportes to the senysshall aud to the
knyght, and that we may he? Ponthus syng and se hym
10 daunce." And Sidone, that myche desired to talke with Ponthus, putt hym in demaundes of mony thinges. So she thoght
hym passyng wyse of his age. Among all othre thinges she
said, "Ponthus ye haue bene long tyme in Bretayn withoute
seying of vs." "Ma dame, I be in gouernaunce and so me
15 oght to obey." "Itt is reason," said she, "bot I demaunde
[*Fol. 170.] you, haue ye envy to see vs and ou? ladies * that be here?"
"Ma dame, nay for sothe, for here is a full fei? company to
see." "I you demaunde," said she, "haue ye any wyll to any
ladie or gentylwoman, to be hi? knyght?" "For sothe Ma
dame, nay; for the seruice of me is bot litle worthe." "Pon-
20 thus," said she, "save your grace, ye be of the place to be of
worschipp to serue the grettest ladye and the fairest of all
Bretayne." So thei hade enugh of diuers demaundes betwen
theym, in so myche that she said, "I wolle that ye take the
state of knighthod, and that ye be hold as for my knyght.
25 And when I here that ye doo you? selve worshipp, I wolle
haue ioy of you." "Ma dame," said he, "Gode thonke you
and Gode send me grace to doo that may pleasse you and all
your ladys, for the dedes of a poue? man be litle worthe."
"Yitt," said sche, "I wolle wele that ye wytt how that I
30 holde you as for my knyght, and when that ye doo bettre
then any of my knyghtes, I shall loue you for the beste, and
ye schal wante no thing that I haue; and I wolde that ye
made surement to serue me aboue all othre, in worschipp;

---

[1] "To aid you"—R, *Dieu ne vous a pas fait . . . . pour vous deffaire.* W, *for
to vnmake you.*

and thinke ye not bot that I thinke worschip." "Ay, Ma
dame, I thonke you of the grete worshipp that ye offre to me
as myche as I may. Gode yeve me grace to serve itt vnto
youꝛ worthynes." "I shall say you," said she, "that I wolle
5 loue you as my knyght, and that ye be of suche maueꝛ that I
may perceyve that ye thinke noon othre wyse bot forto kepe the
state and the worshipp of me; and if ye thinke any velanye,
I shall neuer loue you." "Ma dame, I hade leueꝛ be dede
than to thinke any thyng that shuld turne to youꝛ diswor-
10 shipp or to my lorde your fadiꝛ[1] dishonuꝛ." "Then wolle ye
promys me, so as ye be a kynges son?" "Yea Ma[2] dame, by
my feyth," seid he. Then she yeave hym a ryng with a dia-
mounde and she said that he schuld bere that for the loue of
hiꝛ. "Ma dame," said he, "Gode thonke you." So he toke
15 itt and putt itt vpon his fingre.

And aftre that, she lede hym to daunce, and aftre sche praid
hym to syng. And so he dide hiꝛ commaundement, as he that
felyd hym self take with loue. So he song so goode and so
swete a song that it was mervellous to heꝛ. Then he was loked
20 vpon with ladies and gentylwomen and gretely praysed. And
then eueryche of theym disired in theiꝛ hert the felischipp of
hym and said omong theym, she was full happy that hym list
forto loue and cherys. And aftre that thei hade daunsed, theꝛ
come furth spices and wyn; and so Sidon yeave to the senys-
25 shall a copp of golde full of wyn, and the senysshall thonked
hiꝛ myche. And when thei hade wele disported theym, the
senysshall said, "Ma dame, we beseche you of leve, for itt is
tyme that we goo to the kyng." So she yeave theym leve, and
she prayd the senysshall that he shuld come ofte and se hiꝛ,
30 and he said that he schuld. So she and Ponthus loked full
amcrously at theiꝛ departyng, bot she keped hiꝛ as coverte as
she myght.

[1] The flourish of the r is bolder than usual. It possibly represents an es.
I have preferred to regard *fadir* as the old Gen.
[2] MS. *my dame.*

2

And when thei weꝛ goon, she asked of the ladies, "How say ye of Ponthus?" Theꝛ was noon bot thei prased hym gretly; and theꝛ was sume said that she was right happy that myght haue suche oon to hiꝛ loue. She myght wele say she had the 5 fairest and the flouꝛ of the worlde. So the ladys praysed gretly Ponthus and that was grete ioy and comforth vnto Sidone to here, if she durste say bot litle, bot that sche said he was faiꝛ enugh, and prayd to Gode to kepe hym from all evyll tunges.

10 The feste dured thre days with grete ioy and welfaiꝛ and all maner of dissportes. So itt happened theꝛ come mervellous tithynges, that said that the Saresyns weꝛ londed in the Ile of Breste and were mo then twenty thovsand. So the courte was gretly trovbelyd, so that thei couth make noo cheꝛ.

15 [Cap. VIƮ. How tithynges come to the kyng of Bretayn that the Saresyns were come in to his lond; how Ponthus answered the Saresyn that said that his lawe was better then the Cristen; and how the kyng made Ponthus knyght.]

20 Aboute the myddes of the day theꝛ come furth a knyght
[*Fol. 170ᵇ.] and twoo * squyers Saresyns in message fro the kyng Carodas that was sonne to the sawdeyn, oon of the iij sonnes that ye herde of before. The knyght was huge and grete, stronge and horrible to se. A drogman he made to say, and 25 said on highe, that the son of the sawdeyn was comen into the contree to do a wey the Cristen lawe and to puplisch the lawe of Mahounde; and badd the kyng of Bretayn to forsake the Cristen lawe and take hym vnto the lawe of Mahounde; and to haue tribute of hym and of euery fiꝛ-hows in his realme; 30 and if he wold not, he wold distroy all Bretayn and putt all to the swerde.

The kyng herde the manashyng and grete pride of theym. He wyste not what to sayn and said no worde.

Then loked vpp Ponthus and saw that noo man spake noo worde. He lepe furth and said, "I am a simple child, I wolle not soffre hym to dispyse ouᵽ holy lawe afore me." And so he knelyd doune before the kyng and asked leve to answeᵽ the
5 Saresyn. The kyng graunted hym, when he sawe noon otheᵽ wold speke. Then said he to the knyght Saresyn, "I shall answeᵽ the, and say, that youᵽ lawe is bot temptacion and dampnacion, and live of the fire *cuer* lastyng, and ouᵽ lawe is helthe and saluacion and ioy that shal endure; and as to yeld tribute
10 to you, we be free, and suche *seruege* shall we neu*er* doo to you, by the grace of Almyghty Gode."
Then said the Saresyn knyght, " Be theᵽ any too men that wolle fyght ayeinst me, that Mahounde is not grett*re* then youᵽ lorde Ihe*su* Criste?" Then answeryd Ponthus, "If it pleasse
15 Gode, we wolle not putt too ayeinst the. I am yonge and feble, I caste myn hodde to a wedde for to defende thes wordes befor the kyng." And the Saresyn stode vpp and said, "Undirstonde that I wolle fyght with the and oon otheᵽ." " I aske bot my self," said Ponthus. The kyng and the Barounes weᵽ
20 wrothe that Ponthus had waged batell with the Saresyn and that he had caste doune his wedde; bot it wolde not be amended.
Then said the kyng, "Ay Ponthus, ye haue putt vs in grete disease of hert, that ye haue ben so hasty to cast doune youᵽ wedde—ye that be so yong—ayeinst yonde knyght, that be so
25 stronge and myghty." " S*er*," said Ponthus, " knowe not ye that at the request of Daniel, that was bot a child, thurgh whome[1] Gode savyd Susanne? Mervell ye not of the *mer*velles of Gode. Whome Gode wolle haue keped, shal be keped. I hold me sure and hardy ayeinst hym. Doute ye not of me."
30 When the kyng herd hym thus speke, he weped, when he consideryd the goodnes and the hardenes of hym; and for the

---

[1] The omission of *thurgh whome* would set the sentence straight, but there is no reason to suspect scribal corruption in this case. Inconsequent constructions are so common in this text that I shall never indicate them, except where a probability of scribal error justifies emendation.

pitee that he hade of the childe, he besoght Gode full humblely
with all his herte to helpe hym att the iorney.

"Ser," said Ponthus, "make ye me knyght and yeve me
armore, and I shal goo and doo my devir." The kyng maked
5 hym knyght, and girde hym with a sworde, and kyssed hym &
he weped sore, that he myght not speke oon worde; and then
he lete arme hym with the beste armour that he hade, and
yeave hym the best stede that he hade; and when he was
armed and on hors bakk, he was so faiꝛ to se, and satt so
10 streght and so wele vpon his hors, that it was grete ioy to see
hym. And his xiij fellawes weped for pite and for fere of
hym; and Herland the senysshall was full sory; and so was
all maner of people sory and wrothe, that he that was so
yonge shuld fyght with oou that was so strong; for men
15 said that he was the myghtehyst and the hardeyst among
all the Saresyns.

Grete was the speche of Ponthus that he wolde fyght: in so
myche that worde come to Sidone. It is not to be demaunded
*Fol. 171.] whethre that she made any sorow or hevynes for * hiꝛ knyght.
20 She sent hym a kerchef to beꝛ on his speꝛ; and when he sawe
itt, he reioysed hym in his hertt and thonked hiꝛ; and she
went prively into hiꝛ warderopp and said hiꝛ prayers for him
devoutley.

[Cap. VIII. How Ponthus slewe the Saresyn and sent his
25   hed to the Sawdeyn.]

And when he was on hors bak, the Saresyn said to hym:
"Goo fetche an othre to helpe the, for thou be to yonge;
and I haue grete pitee of the, for thou be so faiꝛ a child. Itt
weꝛ grete harme that I schuld sloo the, by Mahounde. Ther-
30 fore it is goode that thou gaynsay all that thou havis said and
pray Mahounde to foryeve the thy evell wordes that thou hast
said of hym." "Knyght," said Ponthus, "leve thes wordes.
Thov shall see anoon the vertue of Ihesu Criste. Defende the,
if thou wolle."

And Ponthus withdrewe hym a litle and putt his sper̃ in the reste; and come with a goode will & smote hym betweyn his sheld and his helmett, that he brake his shuldre. And the Saresyn smote Ponthus so myghtely that he brake his sper̃.
5 And when the kyng and the people sawe the iustyng, thei thonked Gode and said that Ponthus had wele iusted. Then Ponthus went forthre and drewe oute his swerd, and come to the Saresyn and gave hym suche a stroke aboue the vyser̃ of his helme that men myght se his vysage all open. Then hade
10 the Cristen ioye, and hope in Gode. The Saresyn drewe oute his swerd, whiche was a full grete blade of stele, and smoth Ponthus therwith so grete a stroke that he made his hede to shake and fire to smyte out of his eeyn: so he was sore astoned of that stroke, and sore was the feght betwen theym. Bot at
15 all tymes Ponthus hade the bettre and lay in wate to smyte hym in the visage that was open; and so he mett with hym at a travers, that he smote of his nose and his chynne, so that it helde bot by the skynne: so he blede in suche wyse that his sheld and his nek wer̃ full of bloode, that vnneth he myght
20 sitt on hors bake. Then Ponthus toke hym by the helme and pulled itt fro the hede, and aftre gave hym suche a stroke that he fell doune to the grounde. And when he had doon so, he smote of his hede and putt itt on his swerde poynte and broght itt to the squyers Saresyns and said to theym, "Fair̃ Saresyns,
25 I present you with the hede of your maistre. Goo and ber̃ it to the sawdeyn sonue your̃ kyng. And (tell hym)[1] it was at his requeste—this batell for the prevyng of our̃ feyth and his, and that God shewed by a childe that he is verray Gode, and thus by hys poer̃[2] he schall shewe that ye hold on a fals lawe;
30 and say to hym in shorte wordes that itt shall be hastely knowen and shewed, whethir̃ that my God or his be more myghty. So goth oon your wey, for ye shall goo save and sure—for a messynger̃ shall haue noon harme, bot if he require dedes of armes."

[1] R, *Et lui dictes que. . . .*   [2] R, *puissance.*

The squiers toke the hede and the body and broght[1] itt to
theiꝛ kyng and all his lordes Saresyns, and told hym and
theym all the maneꝛ of the request of the batell, and how the
Cristen was of the age bot of xviij yeres at the moste. So
5 the kyng and all his lordes Saresyns was full wroth and sorofull of theiꝛ knyght, and thei had mervell of that aventuꝛ, for
he was holde (the best knyght) and the strongest on theiꝛ
party. So thei buried hym aftre theiꝛ maneꝛ. So lefe we of
hym and retourne we vnto Ponthus.

10 [Cap. IX. How Ponthus gave thonkynges to Gode for the
victorie, and how he auised the kyng to assemble
the princes and barounes ayeinst the Saresyns. How the
Cristen ordeyned their batells.]

POnthus smote his hors with the spores and rode streght
15   to the hygh chirche, yeldyng thonkynges vnto Gode
full devoutly, and said, "Ay, swete Ihesu Criste, thi dedes be
mervellous, for by thy grace I haue the victorie of myn enemys,
[*Fol. 171ᵇ.] and I knowe that thou thinkes * on thi poueꝛ seruauntz; and
goode Lorde haue mercy of me that am thy povere seruaunt,
20 and on this contree that is in thyn honde." Then he made his
offeryng and lepe vnto his hors and so went vnto the kyng.
It is no demaunde whethiꝛ the kyng & his barounes weꝛ
glade and made of hym grete ioy and grete chere. The kyng
toke hym aboute the neke and kyssed hym, sayng thes wordes,
25 " My faiꝛ swete frende, we truste in you that ye schall delyuer
vs and ouꝛ countre frome ouꝛ aduersaries that wold ouergoo vs."
Aftre this itt is no question if Sidon and hiꝛ ladies made
ioy ; and thei said, that beautie, bounte, and manhode weꝛ
assemelyd in his person—"this was mervellously doon of hym.
30 We pray to Gode to save hym from all evyll."
Aftre this the (kyng) sent for all his barounes and knyghtes
to here howe the Saresyns weꝛ comen to his countre, and the

---

[1] MS. broght a. The a is cancelled by the rubricator.

kyng asked of eueryche of theym his avice. So thei weř all
abasshed and astoned for the grete multitude that thei weř,
that thei couth gyve noon answeř. So the kyng asked of
Ponthus his avice. "Ser," said Ponthus, "to me itt longeth
5 not to speke, that ben so young,—of litle reson, befor so mony
knyghtes." The kyng commaunded hym to say his opinion.
"Ser," said he, "for youř worschipp and to fulfyll your commaundement I shal speke as a clerke of armes and as a childe
among wysmen, bot all'wey foryeve my folye. Ser, it semeth
10 me that this people, how many so euer that thei be, [be]¹ not
gretely to be dovbted, for we be, and shall be,² (in Gode
Almyghty) that may save or distroy with fewe people mony
of theym; for in this case sett oon agayn oon hunderyth in
kepyng of his feith, for this tovcheth all Cristentie, that be
15 seruauntz of Gode,³ and all Cristen people wolle come to helpe
you at that tyme; for if thei wynn ouř contree, all othre contres wolle not be sure ne sikeř. Wherfore I wolle counsell
you, by the goode avice of your knyghtes that be here present,
to send to princes and barounes that ben your neghtboures,
20 that thei be here within xv days; and by the help of Gode
and of ouř goode diligence men schal doo theym suche harme
and angres that theiř gode schal neuer amende itt. Also sendes
to garnysche your fortresses of men and vitell, & make strong
youř tovnes and castells—and in especiall, theym that be next
25 the countree that thei be in—and withdrawe and distroye vitell
frome theym."

¹ The obvious emendation of the passage is the insertion of a second *be*
following the French. *Il me semble, combien que ceste gent soient grant nombre,
ne douient pas estre tant doubtez, car nous seruons et sommes a dieu tout puissant,
qui puet sauuer*, etc. The passage might stand without emendation if *how
many so euer* might be regarded as a clause in opposition to *people*. This
seems to me incongruous with the style of the text.
² MS. *be of gonde myght enoghe*. The context shows clearly that *goode*, as is
the case a few lines beyond, must be a corrupt reading for *Gode* and necessi-
tates the emendation of the clause. I have adopted the reading of W *for
we shall be and ben in gode almyghty;* which follows the French, *vid. supra.*
Both English versions appear to have had an original reading *serons* instead
of the *seruons* of R.   ³ MS. *goode*.

This counsell was holden goode aboue all othiꝛ and was
fulfylled. And messyngers was sent throgh oute the contre
that was next: as in Normandie to the Vicecounte d'Aurences,
to the Erle of Morteyne, to the Erle of Mayne, to the Lorde
5 de La Vale, and of Sylle; and to the Duches of Aniou, for the
Duke was deid; also he sent to the Lorde of Chasteaue Gouteꝛ,
and to Guyllen de Roches, to Bortane de Doune, and to Landry
de La Toure; into Petewe thei sent to the Erle of· Peyters, bot
he was goon to Rome, and thei sent vnto Geffrey de Lazenyen,
10 to Lernell de La Mauelyon, and to Henri de La Marche : so
thes knyghtes weꝛ chosen for the best that was in thos dayes
in thoos contrees aboute theym. And all thos that weꝛ sent
vnto, they sent to the contre aboute theym, that thei schuld
in all the haste come in theiꝛ best aray, that thei myght come
15 to gedre to helpe the kyng of Bretane ayeinst the Saresyns
that wold distroye the Cristen people.

It is noo question bot all *maner* of people weꝛ comyng
toward the iourney in theiꝛ beste array; and so by the xv
days' ende thei weꝛ comen to gedre—a grete mayne of all
20 *maner* of people, of the which the kyng made grete ioy. And
so they toke theiꝛ wey togedre toward Breste and to Seynct
Malewe, wheꝛ was the oste of the Saresyns, that pylled and
distroyed the Cristen aboute theym.

[*Fol. 172.] Bot the Cristen ordeynyd fouꝛ thosand * horsemen to ride
25 aboute theym and to devise the oste. So the Sarcsyns doubted
of batell, thei weꝛ so neꝛ aproched. Then the kyng and Ponthus ordenyd theiꝛ batells; and by cause the kyng was holde,
he hade to helpe to governe his batell the Vicounte de Leon
and the Lorde de La Vale and othiꝛ barounes; and of Galyce,
30 Edmund de Vitry and Rauland de Dole, Rogeꝛ de La Roche.
In the secund batell was Ponthus and Herland the senysshall.
With hym weꝛ Normandes, the Erle of Morteyn, the Vicounte
of Averences. The third batell was taken to gouerne to the
Erle of Mayne and barounes and knyghtes of Aniou,[1] Guyllen
35 de Roches, Andrewe[2] de La Toure. And of the fourte batell

---

[1] MS. *Avyen* read with R and W *Aniou*.   [2] MS. *landrewe.*

hade the gou*ernaunce Geffray de Lazynyen[1] and Leonell
de la Maleon, in the which we? Normannes, Manseons, and
Petievynnes.[2] The Normannes we? by estimacion ix^c men of
armes; Angevynnes and Petevynnys we? fou? thovsand wele
5 fyghtyng men, as by estimacion.

[Cap. X. How the four batells of the Cristen rodc toward
the pauellons of the Saresyns aboute the poynt of day.]

A nd so the? we? fou? grete batells, in the whiche Ponthus
and Herland had the voward; so thei rode toward
10 thei? enemys, and the kyng and othre that we? with hym in
the rerewarde, and luged theym vpon the feldc; and thei
ordayned the halfe to wake, whiche watched, whils the othi?
halfe dide slepe. So the? happed a grete affray aboute mydnyght; for Robt. de Sauguyn, Ranald de Sylle and a grete
15 company de la Breste[3] come rydyng with iij$^{M l.}$ men of armes
toward the batcll and thei we? aspyed and knowne; and thei
made grete ioye of thei? commyng; and of thei? desi? thei putt
theym in among the Angevynnes.

Then said the kyng to Bertam de Doke[4] and to Landry de
20 La Tou?, "Fair Seris, thonke we Gode ye be worthie men and
of grete worship; ye be ou? strenght and oure dunyon; in
youre hondes lieth myche of oure hesynes. Comes not to the
besynes vnto the tyme that it be nede."

Ponthus and Herland ordaned the Bretaynes in array.
25 Then said Ponthus to the kyng and to the lordes, "Seris I
councell that we sett vpon theym before day, or aboute the
poynte of day, before that thei be armed or thei? horses
sadylled and or thei be putt in ordinaunce. Thus thei schal

---

[1] MS. *De la Zynyen.*   [2] MS. *petie tynnes.*

[3] I do not understand this *de la Breste.* R reads: . . . *venoient a la besogne
a bien trois cens escus,* which W translates literally. Our translator's original may have made the reinforcements come from Brest.

[4] Apparently a mistake for Bertam de *Doune* mentioned above. So in W
and R.

be more easly discomfytt." "Truly," said the kyng and the
lordes, "this counsell is goode. Let vs goo to hors, for itt is
tyme." Then euery man armed theym and lepe to hors.

The wediȝ was faiȝ and bryght and the mone shone full
5 bryght. So thei rode toward the Saresyns, that was ayeinst
Breste in theiȝ pavellouns, and toke theiȝ counsell thus : bot
if thei shuld be foghten with, thei wold ouerride all Brotan.
And thei broght with theym engynes and laddirs forto con-
queȝ the contre and thei dovbted not, for thei trowed to haue
10 no batell, and thei made bot litle dowtes by cause of the grete
multitude that thei weȝ of.

[**Cap. XI.** How the Cristen and the Saresyns ordaned their
batells. How Ponthus rescoued the kyng of Bretayne
and slewe the kyng Karodas, and aftre that the Saresyns
15   wore putt to flyght, wanne the grete tresour. And how
Sydon made grete ioy of the worschip, that he receyved
in this batell.]

A ¹ftre itt happed that the batells approched so nygh that
thei sawe the Saresyns, the whiche had mony pavyl-
20 louns of dyuers colours. Then said Ponthus, that gyded
theym that weȝ in the firste batell, to his people, "Se here the
Saresyns that wold disheryte vs of oure faithe. We ben in
the seruice of Almyghty Gode, wherfore noman haue noo
doute bot that oon of vs is worth mony of theym; and I pray
25 you of too thynges: oon is, aboue all thyng to truste in Gode,
for by hys poweȝ we shal come aboue oure enemys; the secunde
is, that ye take no thyng to pyllage ne to noo covetyse, bot
oonly to discomfytt oure enemys and to putt theym oute of
oure contrey, in the worshipp of oure faithe and for pitee of the
30 pouere people that dwellys oute of strenghtes in the feldys—
that laboures and travells, in whome we lyve. Therfore be
[*Fol. 172ᵇ.] we strong and stable to * defende the chirche and theym."

¹A extends through two ll. in the MS.; so also the initial A of Chapter VII.

And when he had said to theym thus, he said, "Nowe goo
we forth my frendes, and eue*ry* man thinke to doo wele."

Then eue*ry* man toke hert to theym, and smote thei͛
horses toward the tentys and began to bete doune tentys
5 and pavyllouns, and to sley sume as thei we͛ armyng theym
and sume naked ; and so thei made in that syde mony to
dye. Grete was the noyse and the crye among theym. So
cleryd the day. Then thei began to loke vpp, and the Bre-
tayns laid on and putt fire in they͛ luges—and in so myche
10 that the kyng Karados was on hors bak in a playne with a
grete batell, and said to his people on hyghe, "Eue*ry* man
drawe to his captayne and putt theym in ordinaunce, for itt is
nede." Then ye myght see the Saresyns putt theym in batell,
notwithstondyng thei we͛ vndertaken, for there were sleyne
15 of theyme vij^{ML.} and that was the fourte[1] pa*r*te of thei͛ people;
bot the kyng Karodas was a me*r*vellous goode knyght and of
grete corage, and when he was on his hors, he toke his bane͛
in his honde to releve his people. And when thei herde his
voice and his horne, itt conforted thei͛ hertes and recoueryd
20 the hertes of the cowardyue.

And aboute the sonne rysyng was grete crie and grete noyse,
for aboute that tyme thre batells of oure people were comyn
to gedre in the syde of the Saresyns, the͛ myche was to doo,
to feght—and ou͛ people to putt fyre in thei͛ lugyng. Then
25 the Saresyns drewe theym to gedre aboute the kyng Karodas.
Grete were thei͛ strokes on both sydes and grete was the crye
of theym that we͛ slayn and hurtt.

In that othre side faght the kyng of Bretayn, the whiche
was fallen of his hors in the grete prese. And Ponthus by
30 aventure loked vp and saw that the kyng was fallen doune to
the grounde. He was full sory and wrothe, for he was like
to haue be deid, ne had Ponthus and the Lorde de La Vale
ben besyd hym to helpe hym. And Ponthus, that toke litle
hede of hym selfe, that sawe his lorde in distresse, he laid

[1] The *e* of *fourte* is written over an unfinished *h*.

aboute hym with his sworde on euery syde, so that he slowe
both hors and man; so that euery man mervelled of his
myght and thei fled fro hym for ferde of his strokes: so that
by the helpe of Herland the senysshall and his cosyn germayn
5 Pollides—for thes thre keped theym euer to gediȓ, and they[1]
dide so mony grete dedys of armys that they rescoued the
kyng and lyght adoune forto helpe hym vp, for he had his
harme broken, the whiche grevyd hym sore, for he was nyghe
oon hunderyth yeres olde. A goode knyght he was and of
10 grete corage. So he was on his hors bak in disspite of his
enemys, and he was ledd oute of the batell.

Grete was the batell egrove[2] on that oon parte and on that
othre. So Ponthus behelde the batell on his ryght honde,
that hade myche to doo, and therin was the Vicounte Daniou,
15 Gautier de Rays, Bernard de Valoynes, Geffrey Dancen, Breut
de Quyntyn-Monford, and mony othre barounes of Breytayn
that weȓ bett doune and in grete aventure of theyȓ lives, for
theȓ weȓ x Saresyns ayeinst oon Bretayn. Then said Ponthus
to his fellawes, "Loo heȓ oure people that has myche to doo,
20 and nede of helpe! Goo we to socouȓ theym." Then they
smote theiȓ horses with theiȓ spurrys so fersly that thei threw
doune theym that was before theym. And Ponthus went all
afore and dide sloo the hardiest that wold abide. Thei dide
so myche, within a whyle they rescoved theyr men and putt
25 the Saresyns to flyght and made theym to resorte into the
grete batell the which was grete and hyddous.

[*Fol. 173.]   Bot the kyng Karodas helde full shorte[3] the Erle of *
Mayns and the Lorde Creton and the othre Maunceouns.
Guyllyam de La Roche sawe Ponthus and cried to hym and
30 said, "Loo here of youre people on fote!" Then come Pon-

---

[1] The French and the context suggest the reading *he* (Ponthus) here and
below, but the departure from the construction is characteristic.

[2] *egrove* can only be the p. ptc. of growe, the *e* representing the original
ge prefix. *v* with the value of *u* or *w* is not infrequent in this text, but I
have no other instance of its intervocalic use. R, *Moult fu la bataille cruelle
dune part et dautre,* which W translates literally.

[3] R. . . . *tenoit moult a destroit.*

thus and brake the presse and rescoued the Erle and othre
that hade nede. And when thei were remo[n]tcd,[1] the batell
was full cruell. The kyng Karodas and Breales and Corbadan,
his vncle, dide mervellously dedys of armes and most harme
5 to the Cristen. They had bett doune Guyllyam de Roches
and hade slayn Ralond de Avyon and mony othre. Then
said Ponthus to Herland and to Landry de La Toure, "Take
hede of the kyng and of too knyghtes. If they endure any
while, they wolle doo myche harme; and if we myght putt
10 theym to dethe, we shuld haue the victorye of all othir."
"Ser," said Landry de La Toure, "goo we to theym." Then
said Ponthus, "I wolle goo vnto the kyng." And so he went
to hym and smote hym so grete a stroke that he fellyd hym to
the grounde—that he brake his nek; and Landry de La Toure
15 bett doune Corbadan; and Herland smote doune Breales and
kytt of hys harme. And when thes thre wer bett doune, the
Saresyns weȝ gretly dismated and gretly dyscomforted, and
stode as shepe withoute an herdman. Then thei begayn to
flee, and oure men ran aftre with grete crye and toke of
20 theym; and they wyst not wethiȝ to flee bot toward theyr
shyppes. And the Saresyns turned agayn and faght strongly,
for mony faghte for the kynges dethe, and mony of theym
knewe not of his dethe. And they hade bett doune the Lorde
Vaucay, Geruast Daniou, the Lorde de Mounte John, and
25 Lewpeyne[2] de Rocheford, and distroyed and slew mony of
oure men.

So at the last oure men toke herte, with comforte of Ponthus,
so that thei bett theym doune. Ponthus dide mervellously,
for he stroke doune hors and men and all that wold abide
30 hym. So they bere hym companye—Geffray de Lazynyen,
Landry de La Toure, Leonell, Guyllen de Roches, and Bernard de La Roche, and Herland; and as they went they made
way—and so that noon durst abyde theym. Ther Ponthus
cried and said, "On theym! On theym! They flee as shepe."

[1] R. *remontez.* The scribe has omitted the nasal mark.
[2] Probably *Le Payne.* W, *payne de R.*

And ther they slewe so many of theym within a whyle that
all the felde ran of bloode and lay full of deyd bodyes, that
it was mervell to see.

And they that myght ascape fledd to their shippes, and
5 Ponthus aftre and toke a bote and slew xxxᵗʸ and toke foure
scoore and asked theym wher the ship was that the kynges
tresour was in. And they schewed itt to hym, whiche was a
fair, grete shipp. So they led hym and Pollides into itt. And
they caste ouer the borde all the men that they fonde in itt.
10 And so they saw an other fayr shipp that his golde and syluer
was in. Then said Ponthus to six of hys men, " Kepe ye
thys, and I wolle goo see if there be any that wolle lyfte upp
his hede ayeinst vs in that vessell." So he went into itt and
toke itt.

15   Ther ye myght see Bretanes, Maunceouns, Petevynes, and
Normanes—sume goo to shippes and sume to tentes, and so
ther was not the powrest, bot that he wanne grete riches. Then
aftre they serched the felde for the Cristen men, euery man for
his frende. So ther was fonde deid on the felde the Vicounte
20 d'Auerenses, John Peonny, Turnebeufe, the Lorde Wylron;
and of Maunceouns, Roger de Biamount, the Lorde Douncelles,
and the Lorde Sylle; of the Hyrpos, Gaciane de Mounte Vyel,
Roland de Tenull, Hundres de Prouere, aud Fresell de La
Hay; off Petoy, Gauter de Chastameny, Andres de Mounte
25 Agnant, Hulland de La Fo[r]yste;[1] and of Bretanes, Pier de
[*Fol. 173ᵇ.] Doule, Ryoud de Rey,* Iohn de Mangon, Herdy de Lyon,
Hubberd de Deyner, Gaudyffry de Rouen, Aubry d[e] Rays,[2]
and mony goode knyghtes. Eueryche caryed home his frende
and buryed theym that wer deid and healed theym that wer
30 hurte.

Ponthus made the grete tresour come to Vennys to hys hous
and departed therof full largely and yeave to hys knyghtes
and to his men, so that he was gretly alowed of all men.

---

[1] R abridges the list of slain earlier. W, *Hubault de la forest.* O, *Urbain
de la forest.*
[2] MS. *aubryd Rays.* O, *Aubri de Rais.*

The kyng drew hym to Quynpartorentyn and ther he dide assemble all the grete lordes, and made to theym all a grete feste and yeave to theym grete gyftes to eueryche aftre his estate, and said to theym, "Fair Lordes, ye be comen, Gode
5 thonke you, to the seruice of Gode and of the chirche and of the pouere people, and by the helpe of the Grete Lorde and of your grete worthynes and hardynes, ye haue delyueryd this contree of Saresyns that wold haue distroyed our lawe and our laudes. Thonke we God of his grace, that has
10 yeaven vs suche victorye, for agayns oon of vs ther was six of theym."

So itt was gretly spoken of theym that faght the beste and gave the grettest strokes and did the moste dedes of armes. Bot withoute comparacion Ponthus hade the name and the
15 laude afor theym all, and they said that he had all wonne and gete. Also they gave grete pris to Geffray de Lazynyen, to Landry de La Toure and to Barnard de La Roche, for they wer thre of the best aftre Ponthus. The kyng held his feste thre days; and aftre they toke theyr leve of the kyng;
20 and Ponthus convehed theym furthe; So euery man went home into his awn contree; and the kyng repared to Vennys.

It is not to aske if Sydon made grete ioy; and she said to Ponthus, "My swete frende, blessed be Gode of the grete wor-schipp that ye haue receyved in this batell; for as Gode me
25 helpe, I haue so grete ioy of the worschipp that I her spoken of you that it puttes myn herte in full grete gladnes, and there [is] no thyng that dos me so myche goode, as the goode name that euery man yevys to you." "Ma dame," said Ponthus, "it is not as euery man reportes, bot I thonke you
30 of the worschip that ye wold doo me; and Ma dame wytt ye wele, that if God sende me grace to doo any goode, itt comys of you; and I wold fayne doo so, that I myght fall in his goode grace, and to doo to you suche seruice that myght pleasse you." "Ponthus, your seruice I take wele a worthe,[1] whyls

---

[1] Paraphrasing R, *vostre seruice prens ie bien en gre de tout mon* . ♥ . *Tant comme ie vous trouuery loyay* (sic) etc., which W translates literally.

that ye be trewe and withoute thinkyng of vylanye to me,
for I wold that youꝛ love be clene and sure; and wytt ye wele,
that if I perceyve any othre wyse that ye thynke, then to
youre worschipp and myn and to my frendes, as myche as I
5 love you, I wolle hate you." "Ma dame," said Ponthus,
"ne trowe ye not ne thynke ye not that I wolle ymagyn ne
thynke bot to youꝛ worschipp, for I haue fonde you so goode,
clene, and trew, that I loue and prayse you a thowsand tymes
the more—fore theꝛ is no fayreꝛ thyng in thys wordle then is
10 a goode, clene lyve."

So they loued mytch to gedre and of trewe, clene love. Bot
envye that may not dye comes aftre vpon theym, as ye shal
here more playnly heꝛ aftre. So lete vs leve to speke of theym,
and turne to the kyng.

15 [Cap. XII. How by the voice of all the barounes Ponthus
    was chosen constable for the kyng. How he kepyd the
    ryght of Bretayn, and how he was loued of all men, and
    in especiall of fair ladies and gentylwomen.]

The kyng come afore all his barounes and said to theym,
    "Faiꝛ Seris, I shal say you that I am full olde and I
20 may not travell as I was wont to doo; and fro now forward
me must take myn ease. Wherfor by your councell I wolle
chese a constable that shal haue the besynes of the londe of
Bretayn, and suche oon as the barounes and the comons of the
londe wolle beste obey vnto. So like ye, who be the moste
25 profitable?—for I wold fayne that he weꝛ chosen by youre
avice."

"Ser," said the barounes all with oon voice, "we wot not
[*Fol. 174.] wheꝛ to * haue a bettre, if itt lyke hym, then Ponthus, for he
is moste worthie to gouerne ane empyre, as for bountie, beautie,
30 of wytt & gouernaunce and gentylnes—as a kynges sone, and
with the beste begynnyng of his knyghthode that thys day is
lyvyng."

When the kyng herd this, he hade grete ioy, for itt was all
that he soght and desired, bot he wold not withoute theiͬ
desire and speche, for they had hym in theyr conceyte and
grace, and so theͬ was noo gaynsayng.

5   So was Ponthus called furth and theͬ itt was said to hym
before all, that the kyng and the barounes hade chosen hym
constable of Bretayne,[1] as for the moste sufficient. So he
thonked the kyng and all his barounes and said to theym
that they had a small avice taken, and that he had nawtheͬ
wytt ne valure to gouerne itt, and that he was to yonge. Bot
10 to blame hym selfe it avaled not, for he was charged therwith, all excusacions laid aparte.

So he was in office welbeloued and dred; for if theͬ weͬ
any dyscension betweu the barounes and the knyghtes, he
wold sett theym in peace, and acorde theym. He kepyd the
15 ryght of Bretayn withoute dooyng wrong to any man. He
was loued of all men. He iustyd and made festes and revellys.
He was ryght plesaunt to grete and small, and in especiall
among ladies and gentilwommen. He was curtes: if any did
of his hoode to hym, he wold doo of his as sone to hym. He
20 wold here the pouere and doo theym ryght. He wold not
that the pouere weͬ grevyd. And he loued Gode and the
chirche. He herd euery day thre messes at the leste. He
loued woddes and ryvers and all honest dissportes.

[Fol. 1.]   ¹ Douce Fragment A begins here: I normalize partially the capitalization but retain the punctuation of the MS.

Bretayn. as the most sufficient. So he thankyd yͤ kyng and the barouns
and sayd to theym that they had take a small [avice] and that he had not
5 wytt ne gouernaunce ne valour to gouerne it and that he was to yong But
to blame hym self yt avayleth not for he was then chargyd wold be nold he.
So he was in his office well belouyd and dred for yf there were eny dissen-
cion by twene the barons and the knyghtis he wold set theym in peas and
concord. He kepte the right of Bretayn without doyng wrong of eny man
10 he was louyd of all men he iustyd and made festys and reuelles. He was
plesaunte with gret and small and in esspeciall amonge ladyes and ientil-
women he was so curtes yf eny man dyd of his hode to hym he wolde do of
his as sone. He herd the pore and he dyd theym ryght. He wold not that
pore people were grevyd. And he lovyd God and holy churche he hard

3

If he come into a toune, he wolde send for ladyes and gentylwomen and make theym to daunce and syng. All dissportes
and ioy come ther̃ as he was; for he wold make to theym
dynnars and sopers. He was beloued of mony fair̃ ladies and
5 gentylwomen, that shewed to hym mony fair̃ draghtes of loue,
bot he neuer disired loue of ladies ne of gentylwomen othre
wys then to their̃ worship, for any cher̃ that they made hym.
So they wold say among theym oon to oon othir, "She was
full happy that was belouyd of Ponthus;" and dyuers said
10 to theym self, "Wold Gode, he wold loue me as myche as I
wold loue hym." //

Myche he was beloued of grete and of small. Bot envy
that neuer lakked was putt in oon of his xiij fellawes of his
contrey, that was a grete speker̃ and a flater̃ef̃¹ and couth
15 mony fals engynes.

[**Cap. XIII.** How Guenelete had envye of his maistre Ponthus; and how by his evyll spekyng he put dyscencyon
betwen Ponthus and Sydone.]

20 SO he hade to his name Guenelete, that sawe of Sidon the
loue, and of his maister̃ Ponthus. He had thcrat envye,
and forto assey hym, he asked of Ponthus oon hors that Sydon

euer two masses and after he louyd to go to the woodys and to the revers
and to all disportis Yf he come to a town he wold sent (sic) for ladyes and
ientyll women and made theym to daunce and syng and all dyssporte come
there he was and ioye also for he wold geue theym dyuers gyftis He was
5 louyd of many a feyre lady and gentyll woman. that shewed to hym meny a
feyr draught of loue but he never desired loue of lady no ientylwomen.
none other wyse than to theyr worshippe. for eny chere that they made to
hym. So they wold sey one to another. She was full happy that was
[*Fol. 1ᵇ.] belouyd of Ponthus. Another said wold God that he * louyd me as moche
10 as I wold do hym Moche he was belouyd of gret and small but envy that
lackyd not [was] put in one of his xiij felowes that was a gret speker and
a flaterer and couth meny fals wrenchis.   *   *   *   *

He was namyd Evenylet (sic) that saw the loue of Sydony and his
mayster Ponthus He had gret envye and for to asay [hym] he askyd
15 Ponthus an hors that Sydonye gaue hym. So he thought well that he mygt

¹ MS. flaterer.

hade yeven hym. So he wyst wele that he myght not haue
hym, bot for to assey hym and forto tempe hym ‖ he said,
"Maistre, yeue me Liard that Sydon yeave to you." "Truly,"
said Ponthus, "that wolle I not yeave you, bot goo to my stable
5 and (take) oon othre—suche oon as wolle pleasse you, for ther
be more fairer then he." "For sothe," said Guenlete, "I wolle
noon hors haue, bot if I may haue Liard." "Ye may not haue
hym," said Ponthus. "How so?" said Guenelete, "Thinke ye
myche of oon hors to me? I owe to truste full litle in you."
10 "How so?" said Ponthus, "Is it not sufficiaunt to you to chese
of all myn horses oon of the best? And if ye be not pleased
with oon, take you twoo of the beste."

Guenlete passed ouer and made hym ryght wrothe and said
in his hert, "I wote wele I shal fayle of hym, bot he shal be
15 dere boght, if I live long." He thoght full evyll, as he that
was full of envye and of flaterye, and thoght to goo and hyndre
him first vnto Sidone.

So he spake with a damesell that was the privyest with
[*Fol. 174ᵇ.] Sydone and * glossed hir with wordes and said that he loued
20 hir myche and that he muste tell hir a grete councell; and
made hir to swer by Gode and by all his saintes, that she
schuld not discure hym. Then said he, "I loue so myche the
kyng and my lady his doghtre, as theym that norysched me,

not haue hym and to tempte hym. Mayster. he sayd geue me Lyard that
Sydony gaue you. Trewly said Ponthus that wyll I not geue you. But go
to my stable & take such another as wyll please you for there be more
feyrer. For soth sayd Guynelot I wyll none hors haue but Lyard Ye may
5 not haue hym sayd Ponthus What sayd Guynelet let ye to geue an hors to
me I aught full litull to tryste to you. How so seyd Ponthus suffichith
not to you to chewse of all my hors. And yf ye be not pleasyd with one
takyth two of þᵉ beste Guynelot passyd ouer and made him right wrothe
and seyd in his hert I wot I shall fayll of hym & he shall be dere bought
10 yf that I lyve longe. He thought full evyll as he that was full of envye and
of flatery. And thought to hyndre hym to Sydonye. And that in haste.
So he spake to a damysell that was privye of councell with Sydonye. And
glosyd her with wordis and said that he louyd her moche and that he muste
tell her a gret councell where fore she swerith by God and by all seyntis
15 that she wold not discouer hym. I loue so moche—

therfore I wolle hide no thyng that schuld be agayne theym.
Know ye[1] not," he said, "that Ponthus my maistre makes
my lady and youres to beleve that he loves hiꝛ more than any
othre in the worlde? Wytt ye wele, he bot iapes with [hiꝛ],
5 for I haue perceyved that he loves an othre bettre by the
halfe: so it is folie for hiꝛ to sett hiꝛ hert on any man that
be so chaungeable, for suche wold stond in grace of mony,
and they be full disceyveable. Therfore it is goode that my
ladye take goode hede to hiꝛ self."

10   Then said the damesell, "In good faithe, I trowed that he
had ben more trewe then he is, bot at all tymes I wote wele
for certayn that he desired neuer thyng of my lady bot goode;
bot nowe I se wele he is not suche on as hym semyd."

Then the damesell trowed that he said trewe and come vnto
15 hiꝛ lady and said to hiꝛ, "Ma dame, ye must promys me that
ye wolle not discure me of that thyng that I wolle tell vnto
you." And aftre that, she told hiꝛ of all that she had herd—
howe that Ponthus loued an otheꝛ bettre then hiꝛ.

When Sydon herd that, she was full sory and full heuy in
20 hiꝛ hert, what cheꝛ so euer she made. So at the laste Ponthus
come to se hiꝛ as he weꝛ wonte to doo, makyng glade cheꝛ.
And Sidon made mornyng cheꝛ and was thoghtfull and she
mad[e] to hym bot sadd cheꝛ. And Ponthus was abasshed
and come to hiꝛ damesell Ellyous and asked hiꝛ what
25 Sydon alyd. "Truly," said Ellyous, "I wote not, bot
it is nowe x dayes and more sithe she made goode chere[2]
as she was wonte."

Then Ponthus went vnto hiꝛ and said, "Ma dame, what
cheꝛ is with you? Haue ye any greuaunce? Is theꝛ any
30 thyng that I may doo for you? Commaunde me as youꝛ
awn." And she said, "Noon may wytt to whome to trust;
this worlde is so mervellous to know." "Ay, May[3] dame,
mercy," said he, "say ye me wherfore ye say thes wordes. Is

---

[1] ye entered above the line.
[2] chere entered above the line.
[3] may for ma and lay for la are not infrequent. See glossary.

theꝛ any thyng that I haue doon, or any othre, that has
displeased you?" "Nay," said she, "bot so myche I say
to you." So he departed and went into his chaumbre, full
of sorowe and of pensynes. Ponthus myght no more come
5 forto haue goode cheꝛ as he was wonte, so he perceyved wele
that he was hyndered to hiꝛ by sume fals flatereꝛ. And so he
went agayn, trowyng to wytt the cause, bot it was for noght,
for he couth wytt nomore at that tyme.

That nyght he was full sorowful and lay thinkyng with-
10 oute slepe, sayng, "Allas, sorowfull catyve! What haue I
doo? Who has hindred me to my lady? Alas! What is he
or she that wolle slo me, distroye me, murthre me so vntruly
with oute any deseruyng? Who be they that wolle putt fro
me my most ioy worldly and make me nyght and day languꝛ
15 and wale?"

So hertly and petuosly complenyd Ponthus; and if he had
hevynes, Sydone hade myche more. She said, "Allas! Who
shall haue truste in any man? I am deceyved, for I trowed
that he hade bene true aboue all othre knyghtes. Howe has
20 natuꝛ thus fayled to make oon the most faire, the most
gracius, the most best hold of worship, most curtes, most
large, of all goode maners, withoute any thyng wantyng—
howe has thou forgete to putt in hym truthe and stable-
nes? Allas! it is grete pitee and reuthe." Thus sorowed
25 she, the faiꝛ Sydone.

[Cap. XIV. How Ponthus, that got no chere of Sydone, departed from the courte secretly.]

[*Fol. 175.] *And by this meane theꝛ was myche trowble betwen theym,
so vntruly was thes too treue louers put in to greuaunce
30 and sorow by this flatereꝛ.

Ponthus, that had litle reste and slepe, rose vp in the mornyng
and went to here messe; and aftre he sent for Ellyous to speke
with hiꝛ, the whiche he loued wele, by cause that Sydon loued

hiꝛ the best and was the most secrete aboute hiꝛ; and he said
to Ellyous, "My swete frende, I mervell mych of that that
my lady says to me, in so myche that I trowe that I moue
neuer haue ioy in myn hert." "Ay," said she, "ye may not
5 doo so, for I supposse my lady doos itt bot to assey you, or
ellys it is by sume reporte that shal be founde a lesyng, and
therfor I wote not wherfor ye shuld be so discomforted."
"Ay," said he, "my loue, I wot not what ye thinke, bot I
wole a while oute of the contree and I wolle not come agane
10 vnto my comyng a gane may please hiꝛ."

He said no mor at that tyme, bot withdrewe hym into his
chaumbre and called to hym oon auncient squyeꝛ, his name
was Gyrard, and said to hym, "calles iiij yomen and lete
trusse myn harnes prively, for I wolle goo awhile hens, bot
15 not full farre, nygh to the ende of oon yeꝛ; and I wolle
Herland be for me leutenaunt, for he is a goode knyght and
a worthie."

Then he went to the kyng and said that he wold goo a
whyle from thens. The kyng said to hym, "My dere frende,
20 goo ye not farre bot that I may se you ofte tymes, for in you
is all my ioy and the sustenaunce of my life and the gouernaunce of my reaume." "My Lorde," said he, "I thynke not
to goo into noo place, bot and I here that ye haue any thyng
to doo that touches your worshipp, bot that I wolle come to
25 you in shorte tyme." Nevyꝛ the les he had myche to doo or
he gate leve to goo.

So he toke leve of the kyng late in the evynnyng full
prively, that noo man perceyved hym; and so he wente into
his chaumbre and sent for Herland the senysshall and said to
30 hym lyggyng on his bedde, "Herland my swete frende, I
wolle goo a while forto se more of the wordle, and to aquante
me with goode knyghtes; so I haue spoken to the kyng that
I wolle leve you as for lyeutenaunt. Also I pray you as ye
loue me to be goode frende to my cosyn german Pollides and
35 to myn othre felowes." "Ay," said Herland, "whethre woll[e]

ye goo my faiꝛ frende?" Said he, "I goo bot a litle way hens.
I wolle not tarry long. I wolle also that nooman knowe therof,
for a cause." Then Herland wold nomore enqueꝛ hym and
dovbted not that he wold tarry long.

5   And when Herland was departed from hym, he then sent
for[1] his clerke and made hym to make twoo lettres. Oon was
to yeve his poweꝛ to Herland the sensshall and that othre
was to recommaunde hym to his fellawes, prayng theym to
doo goode seruice to the kyng and to obey Herland, and that
10 he son wold come agane. And so he sealed theym and betoke
theym to his clerke and bad that he shuld not delyuere theym
vnto that othre morowe at nyght. He dide so for doute that
his fellowes wold fylloy hym.

When it come to the houre of myd nyght, he rosse and
15 arrayed hym and went furth as prively as he myght and rode
all that tyme vnto he come to the forest of Breselyn.[2] And then
he wente into the pryore that was nyghe besyd—and nyghe to
itt theꝛ was an hermytage that stode all solitarye in the depenes
of the foreste. Theꝛ he was vj days. And euery day he rosse
20 erly vpp to goo to the hermytage to heꝛ messe, and did myche
[*Fol. 175ᵇ.] abstynence, for he fasted thre days in the woke and * euery
friday he wered the hare.

So he thoght myche vpon the kyng, that he was olde, and
that the reaume was intendaunt to hym. So he thoght that
25 he myght not goo farre, lest any disease or trouble weꝛ in the
contree; and so he was all pensy and heuy in his thoghtes.

He herd the byrdes syng swetly and merrely—and [it] was
in the myrre moneth of Apryle—and so he made theꝛ a song
of the whiche the refrete was this melodie:—"Of byrdes and
30 wordly ioy is to me noo disporte, sythe that she that I loue
the beste has me enstraunged and of hiꝛ loue dyscomforthed."[3]
And he made therof a wele goode note.

[1] MS. *fro.*
[2] MS. *Bres ỹn lyn, yn* cancelled by the rubricator and *e* inserted above it.
[3] A quatrain in the French original. See note.

[Cap. XV. How Ponthus sent a dwarfe thurgh all the contrey of Fraunce to anounce and shewe of dedes of armes
that shuld be made in the forest of Breselyn euery tuysday of the yere.]

5 A nd aftre, he thoght to make entirpryse, wheꝛ as he wold
   doo fetys of armys. And so he made his ordenaunce,
and made to fetche a dwarfe and arrayd hym wele in a goone
of sylke and betoke hym a yoman and a hors and a lettre
wretyn in this wyse:—

10 "The blake knyght wyth armes whyte gyves knoleche
to the best knyghtes of euery contre, that they shall fynde
by the Welle of Aventures in the forest of Breselyne a
paveloune blake with armes whyte all the tuysdays of the
yeꝛ, and at the houre of prime; and theꝛ they shall fynde
15 (a tree) whervpon his shelde shal be honge; and theꝛ shal
be an horne that a dwarfe schall bloo; and when the horne
blooys, theꝛ shall come oute ane old damesell and bryng a
cercle of golde; and an hermyte with hiꝛ, the which shall say
to theym what they shall doo and shall bryng theym into a
20 medow, wheꝛ they shall fynde the blak knyght armyd at all
pecys, the whiche wolle iuste a course with a speꝛ and aftre
that smyte with a swerd trenchand withoute any poynte[1] to
the vtterance. And he that he conquerys shall aske of all the
knyghtys in verray certayne, who be the most faiꝛ beholde in
25 the roialme of Litle Bretayn among all the ladies and gentylwomen, and to hiꝛ he shal yelde hym prisoneꝛ; and she to
doo hiꝛ wyll with hym, in the name of the blake knyght
soroyng beryng armes white. And it is to wytt that all thos
that has iusted with [hym][2] shall graunte to come the Whys-
30 sontyde nexte aftre into the forest to a fest that shall be holden
theꝛ. And he that has the best iustyd, shall haue the speꝛ and
gofanoun and a cercle of golde full of margarites; and he that
has[3] smyten the moste hardy with a swerd, shall haue a swerd
harnyshed, with gold frenged. And if it happen that any
35 conqueꝛ the blak knyght, he may send hym to prison to what
lady or gentylwoman that hym lykes."

  [1] MS. poynte wantyng. R, le quel [cheualier] . . . . se combatra de lespee
trenchant sans pointe iusques a oultrance.
  [2] R, qui auront iouste a lui.   [3] MS. has the.

When Ponthus had taken thes lettres to the dwarfe, he commaunded hym to goo thorowe all the contres of Fraunce wheᵲ as festes and iustys weᵲ holden and to yeve theym knolege of the dooyng.

5 [Cap. XVI. How there come of euery londe knyghtes to do
        dedes of armes with the Blak Knyght; and how they
        were chosen by the smytyng of theyr sheldes. How
        Ponthus iustyd with Barnard de La Roche the first
        tuysday of the yere, and sent him prisonner to the faire
10   Sydone.]

The dwarfe, that was wele spoken, wente thorow oute all
    the contre and gave to all men knolege of the assembely. So they mervelled myche of what contre the knyght
was that wold doo thes entrepryses, and that he did chese the
15 beste knyghtes of euery contrey. Mony arrayd theym to goo
thedre and said that grete worship shuld be vnto hym that
myght haue the swerd and the speᵲ, and myche more vnto
hym that myght conqueᵲ the knyght. It was not long bot of
Bretane and of othre contres theᵲ come en[o]we.
20   Ponthus had his menne sworne to hym, both the prioure
and the covent and the hermyte, that they shuld not dyscouer
hym to noo body. And so he did sende to Reyns, that befor
[*Fol. 176.] was called the rede toune, to feche * that hym neded. He
sent to seke an olde damesell that shuld be his secrete,
25 and she suld haue hiᵲ (cote) and mantyll of sylke and a
circle of golde vpon hire gray hede and a kerchyf befor
hiᵲ vysage, be cause that noman suld know hiᵲ. And Ponthus was in the array of an hermyte with hede and berde
white with a vyssouᵲ befor his face, and held in his honde
30 the ordinaunce.
    It happenyd that the same thuysday in the morow theᵲ
come mony knyghtes for to doo fetys of armys with the blak
knyght. So they weᵲ at the Well of Mervells—sum called it
the welle of Bellacion. So they sawe a faiᵲ tente bente and a

grete pavellon. It tarryed not long bot a dwarfe come oute
of the pavellon, a full lothly on to se, and come to a grete
tree, wheꝛ as hynged an horne and the blak sheld with whyte
armys; and the dwarf toke the horne and blew it on hight;
5 and when he had doon so, then come the damesell oute of the
pavylloune and the hermyte, that held hiꝛ by the gylten reyne,
and they come streght to the sheld & made the dwarfe to crye
that euery knyght that wold doo fetys of armes with the blake
knyght shuld hyng his sheld vpon the grete tre, the whiche
10 was sett a boute with sperys and smetyn full of crochetys,
that euery man myght hyng his sheld vppon; and so euery
man that was theꝛ did hyng vpp theiꝛ sheld. And when the
sheldes weꝛ hynged vpp, the dwarfe said to the damesell, " I
muste say to you that the ordenaunce is, that ye shall doo
15 chese among all the sheldes iiij sheldys by the advice of the
hermyte, to the whiche ye shall shote, to eueryche ane arowe
fethered with golde; and hym that ye smyte the furste shal
goo arme hym for the furst tuysday; and that sheld that she
smytes with the secunde arowe shall be redy ayenyst the
20 secunde tuysday; and that she smytes with the thirde arowe
shall be redy the thyrd tuysday; and that she smytys with
the fovrt arowe shall be redy the fovrt tuysday." And so
was it doon euery moneth of the yeꝛ, so theꝛ shuld be · lij ·
knyghtes delyuered in the yeꝛ, of the best and of the worthiest
25 that she couth chese by his advyce; and this dured all the
yeꝛ vnto[1] the tyme that he myght fynde oon that by fetys of
armys myght ouercome hym.

And when the dwarfe had thus said, he entred into the
pavellon on hors bak and broght a feiꝛ Turquys boude[2] and
30 fouꝛ arowes fethered with gold; and the damesell and the

---

[1] Douce Fragment B.—the tyme that he couth fynde hym that by fete
of armes ouer come hym. And whan the dwarffe had þus sayd he enteryd
in to the pavelyon on hors bak and he brought forth a feyr Turkes bowe.
And four aroos feddaryd with gold. And the damysell and þͤ hermyte
[2] *Bowe* is the obvious emendation following R & W, but the spelling is
likely enough to be the scribe's.

hermyte went aboute the tree to se the sheldys; and the hermite councelled the damesell and tolde hiꝛ the whiche that
she shuld smyte. So sche schote the fouꝛ arowes and smote
fouꝛ sheldes: the furst was Bernardes de La Roche, that was
5 holde the best knyght in Bretane; the secunde was Geffray
de Lazynyen, for the beste of Peytou; the thyrd was Landry
de La Toure, for the best of Angevynnes; the fourte was the
Erle of Morteyn, for the best of Normannes.

And when she hade shote, the hermite led hiꝛ into the gret
10 tente that was blake with armys white; and anoon he lyght
doune and armyd him at all pecys and suyd oute of the tente,
the shelde on his nek,[1] the speꝛ in his honde, vpon a gret blak
hors trapped in blake with armes white, and richely arrayed.
The knyght was grete and large, and was sore drede and
15 myche loked on—mervellyng myche what he schuld be—for
the comon voice was that Ponthus was goon to the roialme of
Poleyne and of Hungarye, forto enqueꝛ what was to doo theꝛ
beyonde; wherfor noman thoght that it was he.

It was not long to Bernard de La Roche, the whiche hade
20 the furst arowe in his shelde, come ryght noblely arrayd with

went about the tre to se the shyldes. And than the hermyte councellyd
the damysell and told her which sheldys that she shuld smyte. And so she
shot.the four aroos and smote the iiij sheldys. þe first was Bernard de La
Roche. that was holdyn the beste knyght of Bretayn The second was þan
5 Geffrey de Lazinyne for the best of Paytaye. The third was Landry de La
Tour. for the best of Angeowns The iiij[th] was the Erle of Mortayn for the
beste of Normandye And whan she had shott the hermyte led her in to the
gret tent that was blak with white armes. And he alightyd down and armed
hym at all pecys And anon he com forth of þᵉ tent with a sheld on his bak
10 and a spere in his hond with a gret blak hors trappyd with blak and white
armes and richely arayed. The knyᵹt was gret and large and was sore drad
and gretly lokyd on. And the people mervelyng moche what that he shuld
[be]. for the comon voyse was that Ponthus was gone into the realme of
Polayn and of Hongrye for to enquere what was to do there by yond. where
15 fore that no man thought that it was he. Hyt was not long that Barnard de
La Roche which had the first aroo in his sheld come right nobely armed
with gret foyson of * harnesse and with trumpettys. symphonyes and oþer
    [1] R, *Lescu au col.* The reading of the Douce Fragment, *bak*, is clearly
wrong.

grete foyson of hornys,[1] trumppys, symphonys, and othre myn-
[*Fol. 176ᵇ.] strelces,[2] whiche made grete noys.*

The blak knyght toke a copp of gold and putt itt into the
well and wett the ston that stode beside the well; and the wateȓ
5 spred aboute vpon the ston; and then it began to thonneȓ and
hale[3] and made strong wedre[4]—savyng itt lasted bot awhyle.
So the straungers mervelled myche of the mervells of the well;
and euery day the ston was wett befor that they faght.

Aftre that, he lepe vpon hors, with his helmete, and toke his
10 speȓ in honde and smot his hors with his spurrys and come
toward Barnard, and Barnard toward hym agayne ward. And
so they gave grete strokes with theiȓ sperys in suche wyse that
they perched[5] both theyr scheldes, and come agane and smote
to gedre in suche wyse that Barnard and his hors fell. Bot
15 Barnard keped[6] hym vpon his foote and lyghtly lepe oute of
the sadle. And when the blak knyght sawe him vpon his fote,
he lyght doune and come rynnyng vpon hym with his bryght
swerd and gave hym grete strokes wheȓ as he myght areche

instrumentys which made gret noyse The blak knyɟt toke a cupp of gold and
put yt in the well and wet the stone and the watre spred aboute. And than
yt be gan to thundre and to hayre (sic) and made straunge weder save yt
lastyd but awhile. So the straungers mervelyd of the mervelles of the well.
5 And euery day the stone was wet be fore they faught. After he lepe vppon
his hors with his helmet and his spere. And stroke his hors with his
spurres toward Bernard [and Bernard] to hym. So they gave gret strokys
with her sperys vnder suche a wyse that they partyd theyr sheldys in sondre
that Barnard and hys hors fell down. But Bernard lepyd vpon his fete. And
10 when that Ponthus saw hym on fote he alight on fote. and come rennyng
vppon hym with his sword and gaue hym gret strokys afore that they brake

[1] R, a grant foison de cors. Harnesse in the Douce Fragment is obviously
a corruption.
[2] Not in R. or W.
[3] R, gresler. I do not understand the hayre of the Douce Fragment.
[4] R, fort temps.
[5] R, percerent les escus. The partyd . . . . in sondre of Douce is apparently
due to mistaking a c for a t. The word in the scribe's original was probably
contracted as in our text.
[6] R, sailli sur piez would make the lepyd of the Douce Fragment appear
the original reading. The clause and lyghtly lepe oute of the sadle is neither
in W, R, nor Douce; therefore a scribal amplification.

hym. And Barnard defended hym with all his myght; and
Ponthus smote so grete strokes and sore that he brake all that
he raght, and gave hym suche a stroke that he smote doune
the vyssoure of his helmete and all the cyrcle, and hurtt hym
5 a litle in the vysage. And Barnard left vp his swerd and smote
Ponthus, bot Ponthus putt itt sumwhat by, and the stroke lyght
vpon the sheld so sore that he hade gret payne to pluk itt oute.
And Ponthus drew to hym his swerd with so grete myght that
the swerd abowed in sundre;[1] and as son as Barnard sawe
10 that he was with oute swerd, he made grete sorowe. And then
Ponthus said to hym, "Knyght itt is tyme that ye be goo
to oon of the fayrest of this roialme—damecell and madyn."
And Barnard spake noo worde to hym, as he that was angre
and wrothe. And Ponthus said to hym, "Gode defende that
15 I shuld stryke you when ye[2] haue not wherwith to defende
you." Then Barnard come and wenyd to haue taken hym
with his hondes. And Ponthus that was grete and strong
avaunced hym and smote hym on the helme and drewe hym
to hym so myghtely that he made hym fall to the grounde,
20 whethiꝛ he wold or not; and putt hym vndre hym and said,
"Knyght I wolle lete you goo to hiꝛ prison, that be ryght
fayꝛ; and grete hiꝛ wele in the blak knyght name." And so
he withdrewe hym.

And Barnard sawe the benygnyte of the knyght, and prased
25 hym myche, and rosse vp and come to the knyghtes that beheld

all that they raught and gaue hym suche a stroke that he brake down his
visare of his helmet and the sercle and hurt hym a litull in the vesage. And
Bernard lyfte vp his sword and smote Ponthus and Ponthus put up his
sheld afore hym that the sword stake in the sheld with so gret myght that
5 the sword abode. And whan Bernard saw that he was with out a sword he
made gret sorow And than Ponthus sayd to hym Knyght yt is tyme that
ye go to the mercy of þᵉ feyrest damysell and mayden of the realme and
Barnard spake no word to hym ageyne as . . .

[1] R, *Pontus* . . . *tire a soy lescu de grant force. tant que le branc sen vint avec
lescu.* Douce has apparently omitted *and Ponthus drewe to hym his swerd*
after *sheld.* But the reading *abowed in sundre*, "broke," is a corruption of
the *abode* of Douce.

[2] *y* written over an *h*.

the batell and said, "Fayꝛ Lordes, I haue fonde my maystre. Sith I was borne, fonde I neuer so myghty knyght ne so cur- tesse. Now theꝛ is no more bot I wold witt of you, in goode feith, whiche be called the fayrest madyn of this reaume."

5 So they sayd itt was the kynges doghtre Sydone, and she had the voce of theym all. So he departed and went vnto Vennys.

So leve we a litle of Barnard de Lay Roche and retourne to Ponthus.

[Cap. XVII. How aftre the batell Ponthus rode his way
10   prively into the forest.]

POnthus lepe on hors bak and entred into the forest, ryd-
   yng by ways certan that he knewe wele, in suche wyse that noo man wyst wheꝛ he become. And so he come at resonable houre to the same place wheꝛ he was before and 15 entred in and shytte the doeꝛ vpon hym and lyght doune and did vnharme hym; and the damesell, the dwarfe, and othre [*Fol. 177.] with vyssers abode in the tentys * vnto the nyght; and then went theyꝛ way, when all men was withdrawn.

So leve we to speke of theym and retourne to Bernard de 20 La Roche and to Sydone &c.

[Cap. XVIII. How Barnard de La Roche yeldcd hym
   prisonner to the fair Sydone, and of the grete chere that she made hym.]

SYdon was day and nyght in sorowe and mysease, when 25   that Ellyous hiꝛ damesell had told hiꝛ that Ponthus wold goo awhyle oute of (that) contre. She thoght that it was for the evyll chere that she made hym; so she mervellously repenyd hiꝛ and cryed oftyn tymes, "Allas wreche! Now haue I lost by my gret folye all my wordly ioy. Blame haue 30 they that first broght me that worde, for I knowe wele and se wele, that and it weꝛ not for the grete fere that he has by cause I was wrothe with hym, he had not lefte the contre;

and sothely that was grete foly of me, for I doute not bot that
he is of a¹ trewe hertt as any lyvyng. "Then she wept and
sorowed in heꝛ hertt, for she dred to haue loste hym. And
so she sorowed day and nyght.

5 Grete languege was theꝛ of Ponthus in the contrey. The
kyng myght not be in peace in no wyse, which gretly wey-
mented; and so did his cosyn german and his fellawes;
and all maner of people, grete and small, of the courte
weꝛ sory.

10 And son Barnard come to the courte and asked aftre fayꝛ
Sydon and said that he was hiꝛ prisonneꝛ. The kyng sent
for hiꝛ; and she come with a grete felysshipp of ladyes and
gentylwommen; and theꝛ assemelyd all maner of people to
here Barnard de La Roche. And when he was comyn into
15 the hall, he kncled doune and said vnto Sydon on hyghe, that
euery persone myght here, "Ma dame," said he, " vnto you
sendes me the blak knyght with armes white, whiche has me
conqueryd by his worthenes in dedys of armes, and said to me
that I shuld yelde me prisonneꝛ to the fairest madyn of this
20 reaume so I haue enquered of all knyghtes and squyers that
theꝛ weꝛ, whiche was the fairest madyn; and they said all
with oon voice that it was ye; and thus I yelde me vnto youꝛ
prisoune as your knyght, and doo with me as ye wolle. And
yitt he badde me that I shuld recommaund hym vnto you in
25 hys name."

Sydon waxed rede and was sumwhat asshamed by cause
that they helde hiꝛ for the fairest. "For sothe," said she,
" God thonke theym, for they bot simpley avysed theym to
chese me; bot I thonke the knyght that sent you hidre, and
30 I beseche you to tell me what he is." "For soth," said he,
"I knowe hym not." "How so?" said Sydon. "Ma dame,"
said he, " he wolle not be knowen—what he is, bot sothely he
is the fairest knyght that euer I se and the best cann stryke
with a speꝛ and with a sworde, and me semys he is a little

¹ The emendation a[s] is tempting, but *as any lyvyng* probably means "as
much as, etc."

more[1] than Ponthus, and myche lyke hym; bot it is not he, for it is a comon sawe that he is goone into the reaume of Polleyne and of Hungary to a werre that ther is."

Enughe was itt spoken of the blak knyght, and how that
5 the next tuysday he shuld feght with Geffray de Lazynyen, and the next aftre folloying with Landry de La Toure, and the next tuysday aftre with (the) Erle of Morteyne.

The kyng and the ladys made grete cheȝ to Barnard, and they ete all with the kyng in the hall. Sydone iapyd with
10 Barnard de La Roche and said, "Ser, I haue grete ioy to haue suche a prisonner, and so ye shuld haue grete drede what
[*Fol. 177ᵇ.] prisoun ye shall endure." And Barnard began to laghe * and said, "Ma dame, and ye doo me noo soreȝ prisonment than this, I shall endure itt more easly; and knowe ye wele that
15 or the yeȝ be passed, ye shall haue more largely of prisonners, for I shall not be alloone."

Aftre dynneȝ begane the dauncers[2] and the carralles. Bot Sydone daunsed bot a litle, and yitt she[3] wold haue daunsed lesse bot for drede that any shuld perceyve hiȝ sorowe.
20 So leve we of theym and of the courte and retourne agayne to the secund tuysday.

[Cap. XIX. How on the secund tuysday Ponthus conquered Geffray de Lazynyen.]

The day was faiȝ and clere, and the knyght de Lazynyen,
25 the which was a mervellous goode knyght, was armed at all peces and come before the well. And the blak knygth come oute of the pavyllone, the shelde on the nek and the speȝ in the honde. And sone they lete theyȝ horses renne, and smote to gedre, and gave grete strokes, so that theyȝ
30 horses fell vpon theym, and in so myche that almuste they ouerthrewe theym self. Theȝ they withdrewe theym a farrome and toke awthre of theym a grete, sharpe speȝ and come to

---

[1] R, ung pou plus grant. W, he is somewhat more than was Ponthus.
[2] R, dauncers, though strange, is apparently right. Commencerent le dames a dancer mais Sidoine ne danca gueres. W, began the daunces and the karolles / bot, etc.
[3] MS. ye.

gedre as hastely as they myght, hors and man, and gave so
mony grete strokes vpon their sheldes, that both the knyghtes
fell and theyr horses—so boustously that Geffray hors fell
vpon his body, the hors hede vndre, so that the hors ne the
5 man myght remeve; for he hade his thye and his legge vndre
the hors and was grctly bressed.   Bot Ponthus helped vp the
hors and the knyght both, and hade had grete shame to haue
ben so drawn doune; and so he beheld the knyght, that myght
not drawe hym oute frome vndre his hors, for his foote was
10 oute of ioynte, that he myght not stonde bot on oon foote—bot
allway he putt his honde toward his sword, as he that was of
grete corage and hardenes.   Bot when that he sawe that he
myght not stonde bot on oon foet, so Ponthus thoght then
that he wold not smyte hym; and said to hym, "Knyght, I
15 see you in the feblear partie, wherfore it wer shame to assayle
you."   And Geffray said vnto hym, " I holde me not yit dis-
comefeted, in so myche that I may holde my sworde."   And
so he payned hym to smyte Ponthus, and Ponthus leped by,
and so he smote a stone with his goode swerd so fersly that he
20 fell doune to the grounde.
      Bot Ponthus helped to releve hym and said to hym, "Ser,
and ye wer hole, I wold rynne vpon you, for I se wele by
your worthenes ye wold not yelde you to me; bot ye shall
yelde you to the fairest lady of Bretan, that wolle take you to
25 hir mercy, and shall grete hir wele for the blak knyght.   So, I
pray yow, lete vs doo noo more, for we haue donne enughe;
for I wote wele, and ye wer hole, ye wold not soffre me to be
so hole as I am ; for I knowe your worthynes long agoo."
And when Geffray knewe the goodnes of hym, he praysed
30 hym in his hertt, and said to hym, "Ser, I wolle go thedre as
ye commaunde me, and if I wyst that I shuld not dysplease
you, I wold wytt your name."   And Ponthus answeryd, "Ye
ne noon othre shall knowe itt yitt."
      Then Geffray wold aske ne enquer noo more of hym, and so
35 toke leve of hym.   Then the blak knyght went into the forest
by his pathe ways, as he was wonte to doo.
      4

And so the knyghtes and the people mervelled myche vpon
the knyght when they sawe the batell, and said, ryght curtese
was the blak knyght and gentle; and said iche of theym to
othre, "Sawe ye not the grete benignite—howe that he wold
5 not tovche the knyght, by cause he sawe hym hurte, and how
he had two tymes releved hym?" Wherfore they made grete
[*Fol. 178.] talkyng therof and * gave hym a grete lovyng.[1]

And Geffray de Lazynyen, that myght not wele meve hym
ne styrre hym, said to Landry de La Touꝛ, "Fair frende, I
10 wolle abyde vnto the nexte tuysday, for to bere you companye
to se the faiꝛ Sydon, bot if ye putt bettre remedy than I
haue doon." Said Landry de La Touꝛ, "Of aventure of armys
theꝛ may nooman iuge, they be so mervellous; and ye be noo
thyng wars for this aventure, for this was by the fall of your
15 hors, for the whiche may nooman kepe hym; and (I) thinke
to haue noo shame, if I be suche a knyght as ye be founde
in dedes of armys." And also they spake of Barnard de La
Roche and of mony thinges.

And then they toke Geffray de Lazynyen in the softest wyse
20 that they myght and led hym to Mountford; and theꝛ he was
arrayd in suche wyse that he myght ryde vpon an hors-beꝛ
the tuysday next followyng, whiche was a faiꝛ day and a clere.

[Cap. XX. How the third Tuysday Ponthus conquered
Landry de La Toure and sent hym prisonner to the
25   faire Sydone, and aftre, the Erle of Morteyn; and so
euery Tuysday of the yere he sent a knyght of the best
that was in the reaume. And of the grete feste that he
made the Whissontyde at the yeres ende at the Welle
of Mervelles.

30 A nd itt happed the same tuysday theꝛ come of all contrees
to se the batell. Then the blak knyght with armes
white yssued oute of the pavyllone—he and his olde damesell

---

[1] R, *grant compte et grant loz.* W, *greete loos.* See Bradley-Stratmann for
lovyng, "laudation."

and his dwarfe, and on that otheꝑ side come Landry de La
Touꝑ. So they laid theyr sperys vndre theiꝑ sides, with theyꝑ
gonfaunons hyngyng, and with grete myght they stroke to
gedre, withoute any faile; and passed ouer, and come agayne
5 so myght[e]ly that they perched[1] theiꝑ sheldes, and brake
theiꝑ speres, and ranne to gedre with theiꝑ swerdes, and gave
grete strokes, wheꝑ they myght, ofte and thyke. So they weꝑ
long tyme on hors bak. And then Ponthus dressed hym wele
in his styrropes and smote Landry de La Toure with all his
10 strenght, that he was astoned; and when Ponthus hade yeven
hym that stroke, then he sawe hym gogle, and toke hym by
the helmete and drewe with all his myght, and all astouned
drewe hym doune to the grounde. Not withstondyng, he rosse
vp as sone as he myght.

15   And when Ponthus sawe hym at the grounde, then said he
to hym selfe that he wold not assayle hym on hors bak, lesse
it myght turne hym to shame and repreve; bot then he lyght
doune on foote and putt his shelde afore hym and toke his
swerd in his honde and assayled hym. And Landry made
20 hym redy to defende hym in the best wyse that he myght,
for he knewe wele that he hade not to doo with noo childe.
Then Ponthus come and smote hym a grete stroke so that the
stroke fell vpon the scheld and stroke doune and quarteꝑ;[2] and
Landry smote hym with grete strokes, wheꝑ he myght areche
25 hym, and mervelled myche howe Ponthus myght endure agane
hym so longe, for he was a mervellous goode knyght. Bot
Ponthus gave hym ofte so grete strokes that with grete payne
he myght vnneth drawe his brethe, ne Ponthus navtheꝑ. And
they rested theym a litle while on theyꝑ swerdes.

30   Then spake Landry and said, "Gentle Knyght, I wote not
what ye be, bot so myche may I say, that I wenyd not in the

---

[1] R, percerent.

[2] R, Pontus fiert moult grant coup et le branc descend en lescu si que il en abat
ung quartier. W translates literally. Our translator appears to understand
a quartering blow, possibly from another reading, or perhaps we should
read a for and.

mornyng to haue founde so myche strenght and valuꝛ in you
as I haue prevyd; bot or ye ouercome me, ye muste doo moo
dedes of armes then ye haue doon." "Yea," said Ponthus,
"avtheꝛ shal ye yelde you to the fairest made of Bretane, or
5 elles ye must ouercome me with dedes of armys."

And then he lyfte vp his sworde and smote Landry, as he
that had grete shame that he endured hym so longe, and he
stroke hym in suche wyse that the bloode ranne doune to his
fete. And when Landry felyd that he was so smyten, he
10 gave Ponthus so grete a stroke vpon the temple of the hede
[*Fol. 178ᵇ.] that the helmete * was gretly enpared. Then turned Ponthus
the sheld and toke the swerd in bothe his hondes and smote
so grete a stroke that Landry was all astoned. Bot that was
no mervell, for to long hade that batell endured betwen theym.
15 And so he smote sore, stroke vpon stroke, that he was almost
dysmated with the grete plente of strokes that he hade taken
and gyven; and he hasted more and more when he sawe a
litle gogyllyng,¹ and then he come and smote hym with all
his myght in suche wyse that he bett hym to the grounde—
20 and fell bothe two. Bot Ponthus fell aboue, and Landry
myght not ryse ne helpe hym selfe.

And Ponthus said to hym, "Knyght, yelde you." And
Landry spake noo worde and endured with grete payne, and
as he that was lothe forto yelde hym. And he that was full
25 of curtesey said, "Knyght, yelde you to the faiꝛ damesell, I
pray you,—and that theꝛ be no more debate betwen vs, for
we haue assayd authre othre enughe." Then knewe Landry
the curtesy of the knyght that he faght with and said to hym,
"To hiꝛ wolle I yelde me, sithe itt lykes you." "Itt is suffi-
30 ciaunt to me," said Ponthus.

Then he rose full sore and full wery of the strokes and
travell that he hade gyven and taken of the grete batell that
so long hade endured. So come Ponthus to his hors with grete
payne, and lepe vp, and rode faste into the forest, so that he
35 was fro the syght of theym all anoon.

¹ R, et quant il vit ung pou chanceler si le boute. W, sawe hym staker.

And Geffray de Lazynyen and mony othre knyghtes come
to Landry de Lay Touȓ and asked hym howe he dyde; and
he said, well—aftre the evyll that he hade founden his maistre.
Then said Geffray to Landry, "I shall bere you companye,
5 for ye and (I),[1] we wolle goo to gedre to the faiȓ Sydone."
"I wolle wele," said Landry, "for itt is no reason that ye goo
thedre withoute me." Thus they bourded oon to an otheȓ.
And then he was vnarmed and had mony woundes, bot he
had noon bot that he myght ryde.

10   And so they went and yelded theym to Sydon. And the
kyng made theym gret cheȓ and did theym grete worschipp,
as for the best knyghtes that myght be founde in any contrey,
of nobylley of knyghthode. And sone aftre they went to
Sydone and putt theym in hiȓ mercy. And she, that was full
15 of curtesey and of wysdome, receyved theym with grete ioy
and fested theym and worschipped theym and gave theym
grete gyftes. So they thonked hiȓ, and said that they were
wele prisoned, for itt was noo grete payne for to endure itt.
"Serys," said she, "I wot not what the knyght is that has
20 sent you hidre—for ye and he doos me grete honour withoute
cause; for ther be more fayrer and more avenaunt in this
reaume than I be, who so wolle seke theyme." "Wele Ma
dame," said they, "we owe to beleve the comon voice, for all
has cosen you for the fayrest." And thus they bourded of
25 mony thynges. Theȓ they weȓ twoo days with the kyng, and
all the othre days wyth Sydon.

And aftre she gave theym leve to goo, and then they went
furth to se the batell of the Erle Morteyn, that was a full
goode knyght.

30   Son aftre issued oute the damesell and the dwarfe, and had
his Turquis bowe in his honde and the arowes. And the
heremyte with the vysouȓ, that lede the damesell aboute by
the gylten reyne, made signe whiche schelde sche schuld smyte,
[*Fol.179.] as * for the next moneth folowyng. The damesell shote fyrste

---

[1] R, *nous yrons vous et moy ensemble.* W, *we shall go you & I togyder.*

the sheld of S*er* Tybould de Boloys that was named a wele goode knyght; and that othre was the shelde of Guyllen de Roches; the third was the shelde of Henry de Mounte Morency; and the fourthe shelde was the sheld of Rosylyon.[1]
5 Thes was iiij knyghtes of grete name of knyghthod, whoes scheldes weꝛ hongen vp for the next iourney. And when she hade shote hiꝛ fouꝛ arowes, she withdrewc hiꝛ into the pavyllon.

And son aftre the blak knyght issued oute of the pavyllone
10 armed att all peces, the shelde in the nek, the speꝛ in his honde. ·In that othiꝛ side come the Erle of Morteyne full rychely arrayd, with a grete multitude of mynstrells. And as son as they sawe aythre othre, they ranne to gedre with theyꝛ sperys, and gave authre othre grete strokes. Bot Pon-
15 thus reu*er*sed the Erle, that he lakked bot a litle that he was doune. Then they putt theiꝛ hondes to theyꝛ swerdes and ranne to gedre full fersly. Bot Ponthus smote so grete a stroke that his sworde cutted that he smote; and the Erle defended hy*m* at his poweꝛ. So the batell dured longe. Bot
20 Ponthus that was *m*ervellous[2] toke hym by the helme, and drewe to hy*m* so myghtely that he pulled hym doune to the grounde, and yeave hym a grete stroke with his sworde, and said to hym that he suld yelde hym—for he smote hym bot with the flatt of the sworde. And the Erle endured myche,
25 bot at the last he must nedes yeld hym, whedre he wold or noo.

And thus he co*m*maunded hym to yelde hym vnto the fairest ladye and madyn in Bretan; and so he de*p*arted and went into the forest as he was accostomed to doo.
30 And the Erle went and yelded hym vnto Sydone as the othre knyghtes had doone. And theꝛ she dide hym grete worschip; and so did the kyng hiꝛ fadre.

---

[1] MS. *Rosy lyon.*

[2] R, *qui grant et fort estoit a merueilles.* W, *which was grete and strong toke.* It is a temptation to throw in the *grete and strong* of W, after *mervellous*, but *mervellous* is often used independently in our text.

The nexte tuysday they faght agane ; and so they did the
next folowyng, to the monethe come to an ende. Bot itt weꝑ
to long to tell the batells and the iourneys that he dide—and
that otheꝑ parties also ; for theꝑ were mony grete batells
5 and mony sharpe stowres of armes whiche weꝑ to longe to
tell, who wold all devyse. Bot all weꝑ ouercomen by his
dedes of armes and weꝑ sent to prisoune to the faiꝑ lady
Sydone.

So was theꝑ founde in the yeeꝑ .lij. knyghtes prisonners, of
10 the best that they knewe or myght fynde in any londe, to
wynn or conqueꝑ worschipp ; for euery of the beste knyghtes
that herd therof went to assay hym ; and then he chase of
the beste knyghtes to doo dedys of armes with hym, and
eueryche hade desiꝑ to be of the nombre to assay theym with
15 hym, in so myche that the high renowne ranne thorowe oute
Fraunce and by mony othre reaumes and contreys. And
Ponthus chase euer by reportyng the best, and faght neuer
bot with oon of a contrey, whiche was holden for the beste ;—
forto make hym to be known, that if theꝑ weꝑ any man that
20 wold requiꝑ hym to doo any thyng for his lady sake, that he
wold be redy alwey to delyuer hym. And theꝑ was of the .lij.
knyghtes propre names—that is to say : the Duke of Averenses, the Duke of Loreyne ; the Duke of Barry ; the Erle
of Mount Bernard,[1] the Erle of Mountford, and mony othre
25 erles and dukes ; and Ser William de Baniers, Ser Arnold de
Hennolte, the Erle of Savye, and mony othre knyghtes ; and
of theyꝑ names I passe ouer at this tyme and goo to my mateꝑ
agayne.

[*Fol.179ᵇ.]   When * itt befell that Wyttsonday was comen at the yeres
30 ende—that[2] all prisonners come to yelde theym, theꝑ as itt
was ordayned, Ponthus lete make a grete hall couered with
grene boghes, by the Welle of Mervelles, otheꝑ wyse called

---

[1] MS. Mountbernard.
[2] The same ellipsis is in W and R. R, tant quil aduint que la penthecoste
vint . . . . que tous les prisonniers vindrent.

Bellacon, and sent for all maner of vitelles and dyuers wynes, and wrote to the kyng a lettre, sayng thus :—

"To the goode kyng of Bretane the Blak Knyght with armys white recommaundes hym with all his seruice and
5 honour. And prays hym mekely, that itt may pleasse hym to be at this feste of Wytsontyde in the forest of Breselyne at the Welle of Mervelles, with the companye of the fairest ladys and damoselles of Bretane, to knowe to whome the pris shall be yeven and to enquiꝛ who has best iusted and who that has
10 the beste and the myghtest foghten of thes .lij. knyghtes of euery tuysday in the yeꝛ."

And when the kyng had red the lettre, he had grete ioy therat; and said that grete worshipp did hym the blak knyght and that he wold be theꝛ.

15 And then he sent for his doghtre and tolde hiꝛ thes tyth-ynges and charged hiꝛ to enquiꝛ of the fairest ladies and gentylwommen of his reaume to come with hiꝛ at the feste of Wytsontyd;—"and faiꝛ doghtre," said the kyng, "ye aghte forto doo itt, for he has doon you myche worship; for by his
20 swerd he has sent to youꝛ prisoune so mony goode knyghtes and lordes, wherof grete worschip is comen to you and to youres and to all ouꝛ reaume; wherfore I am myche beholden to the blak knyght." Faiꝛ Sydonc kneled doune and said, sith it liked hym, so sche wold doo his commaundement.

25 And then she lete write to the grete ladyes of Bretayne, that they schuld be redy on the Wytsontyd even, and that they shuld bryng with theym the fayrest ladys and gentyl-women that they myght fynde in theyꝛ contrey. The ladys at hiꝛ commaundement hade grete ioy and arrayd theym and
30 come at the day. Theꝛ was ryght grete assembley that come at the Wytsontyd to the Welle of Mervelles. So they broght with theym tentes and pavyllones, and dide hyng theym and pyght theym aboute, in suche wyse that it semed a grete oste.

Ponthus furth before the kyng come ryght sone—and had
35 sent xiij govnes of a suyte to his xiij fellawes, and oon to Herland the senysshall, and had sent to fetche theym the day before. It is noo demaunde to aske if that his cosyn

germane and his fellawes had grete ioy of the worschipp that
God had yeven to hym.   They went aganes the kyng.   And
when the kyng sawe and knewe that it was Ponthus that so
mony fetys of armes hade done, it is noo questyon bot he made
5 grete ioy.   And at the feste and worshipp that he dyde hym,
he myght not forbeꝛ bot that he called hym, & kyssed hym,
and said, "Wheꝛ haue ye ben so louge hyd frome vs.   It was
said that ye weꝛ in Poleyne and Hungary in the werre; bot
in travthe myn hertt said euer that itt was ye that so mony
10 mervelles did."   Ponthus waxed rede and said noo worde, for
he was sory that the kyng prased hym so myche.

Therfore he went his way aganes Sydone—grete was the
company with hiꝛ of ladys and of gentyllwommen[1]—

And

15 salewed her mekely | & she yelded him agayne his salu
tacyon | as she that had all Ioye ẏ herte myght thyn-
ke | & than she sayd vnto hẏ smylynge O Ponthus
ye haue hyd you lōge tyme frō vs in this forest I doute me ẏ ye be become an ermyte & wylde. A madame
20   Pon.   G. iiij.

[*] sayd he saue your grace I am easy to tame. And than
he departed frome her as he that was all taken in the
loue of his lady that of lōge tyme he had not sene her
And than he wente too se the ladyes the whiche were
25 all dysguysed with grene bowes & garlondes | and he
sayd vnto them. My ladyes I praye god that eche of
you haue that ẏ your hertes desyre | for in good fayth
it is a good syght to se soo fayre a company. The lady

---

[1] The Digby MS. has an omission corresponding to about a page and a
third (MS.) of text at this point, though the MS. shows no break of any
sort between *gentyllwommen* and *And furth* (p. 60, l. 14). It is highly improbable that we have to do with deliberate condensation—far more likely
that the scribe copied from a smaller MS. that had lost a leaf. F has two
chapter divisions in this space which might have been marked by miniatures
in a MS. of its class, thus suggesting a motive for the mutilation of the MS.
before the scribe of Digby. I have filled the gap with the corresponding
portion of W, printed diplomatically. The French MSS. R, H, and F contain all this matter.

es yelded hym his salutacyon | the whiche were full of
Ioye for to se hym for they loued hym meruayllously
well aboue all knyghtes. And the one sayd to another
It is Ponthus the good and fayre knyghte thanked
5 be god of the grete worshyp that he hathe sente hym
and I praye god that he wyll kepe hym vs as the best
knight of the worlde | and this was there speche ferre
and nere. So they arryued at the fountayne bothe ẙ
kynge and the ladyes | with grete Ioye. And on that
10 other syde came the knyghtes straungers. The kynge and the ladyes made them grete Ioye. And there
was grete sowne and noyse of dyuers maners of mẙ-
stralsy so that all the wode ronge of it. And the kynge
and ponthus dyd grete worshyp to the dukes and lor-
15 des | as to the duke of Ostrytche of Lorayne & of ba-
ar | & to the erle of dampmartyn of Sauoye of moũt-
belyart & to other dyuers grete lordes. So they wente
and herde masse that the bysshop of Rennz sange | af-
ter that they came to the halle. And the kynge | the du-
20 kes and Sydoyne were sette at the hygh dese | and af
ter euery man after as he was. Greate was the feest
and grete was the hall | and on the syde were hanged
the .lii. sheldes of the knyghtes conquered. Ryght stra
unge and fayre thynges were made bytwene the cour-
25 [*] ses as armed chyldren that fought togyder | & dyuers
other thynges | and syxe olde knyghtes | and syxe olde
squyers | some bare the spere & the gouffanon blacke
with the whyte teeres of grete margaretes & oryente
perles | & a ryche cercle of golde meruayllously wrou-
30 ght of ryche perles and of good stones. The other ba-
re the ryche swerde with the pomel of golde | And the
gyrdell of sylke wrought with golde & grete margare-
tes and perles | & with precyous stones that it was a
fayre syght to se. And this rychesse had ponthus won
35 in the shyp of the Soudans sone. So he sayd hymself
that he myght no better beset them than afore so ma-

ny notable prynces and grete lordes | for he shewed all
his dedes ryght honourably.   The knyghtes and ẙ ladyes wente aboute the halle syngynge as though they
wyste not to whome they sholde presente them.   And
5 than they came before the lorde de Lesygnen and presented hym the spere and the ffouffanon (sic) and the ryche
cercle of golde ẙ whiche they set vpon his hede | for ẙ
beste Iuster.   And after they came to Androwe de la
toure and presented hym the ryche swerde and the ry-
10 che crowne set vpon his heed | whyther he wolde or no
for he excused hymselfe moche & wende to haue refused it saynge that they dyde hym worshyp that he had
not deserued and that there were dyuerse other that
had better wonne it than he had and he wexed rede &
15 was ashamed | but Ponthus hadde so ordeynèd it for
he sayd iu good fayth that he had yeuen hym moost a
do as fore one daye.   Also Geffrey hadde ryght wel Ius
ted.   Than beganne mynstrelles for to playe of all ma
ner of mynstrelsy and also the herauldes began to cry
20 that men sholde not haue herde thoudrynge | for al rō-
[*] ge bothe wood and forest of the noyse.   There was gy
uen many dyuerse meases and good wynes and also
grete yeftes vnto heraudes and mynstrelles.   Ponth’
came behynde the kynge and sayd to hym in his ere.
25 Syr & it please you we shall do crye the Iustes ayenst
to morowe | and on tewesdaye at Vennes bycause ẙ
ye sholde knowe these prynces | and these dukes | for it
shall be your worshyppe.   A sayd ẙ kẙge in good fayth
it is a good and a trewe counseyll and I praye you
30 that it be done.   Than Ponthus called an heraude and
made hym to crye that the whyte knyght with the rede rode (sic, rose) shall be this mondaye and tewesdaye in ẙ cy-
te of Vennes with fyue felowes and hymselfe shall
make the syxte for to withstande all maner of knygh-
35 tes with speres.   And he that shall haue the pryce on ẙ
mondaye without forth (sic) shall haue the gyrdell and the

gypsere of ẙ fayrest of the feest. And he that dooth best
on the tewesdaye shall haue the sparohawke mewed
with the loynes of perles and margarytes | and a cha
pelet that the fayrest of the feest shall gyve hym. And
5 he of the ynner partye that shall Iuste best shall haue
a rynge of the fayrest.

¶ How Ponthus made a Iustes to be cryed in the cy-
te of Vennes and how he smote downe the strongest
that he recountred.

10 ON y morowe after they departed by tymes | &
wente and herde masse at saynt peters of Ven-
nes | and than they wente and dyned | and after dyner
the kynge & the ladyes wente to the schalfoldes.

¹And furth with come Ponthus and his v fellawes whiche was
15 named, Barnard de La Roche, the Vicount of Lyon, the
Vicount of Daunges, Pollides,² and Herland. And Ponthus
was all in whyte bothe [he] and his hors, with a grete rede
rose whiche signified his lady. The iustys weᵽ grete aud the
dedes of armes, bot aboue all othre Ponthus iusted beste, for
20 he threwe doune hors and man and did so mervellously that
euery man doubted to countre hym. Also he putt his hertt
and his wyll to gedre for his lady sake that was before hym.
[*Fol. 180.]	* Grete and litle prased hym myche. And then spake the
ladys and said, "See ye hym theᵽ that berys all doune before
25 hym? He is not wyse that comes aganes hym. His speᵽ
spares noon, bot itt hurtes and makes theym to fall." Sydone,
that herde the ladys prays hym, said noo worde, and she loked
that noo man perceved the gladnes of hiᵽ ne the ioy that she
hade in hiᵽ hertt.
30 Right wele iusted the Duke of Averences, and the Duke of
Loreyne, and the Erle of Savye, the Erle of Mount Belliart,
and mony othre. It weᵽ to long to tell of the goode iusters

---

¹ MS. Digby resumes.　　² MS. *Polleyne.* R, *polides.* W, *Polydes.*

that iusted the moneday and the tuysday. And they weꝑ wele
fested the tuysday at mete and at sopeꝑ. The pris of monday
was yeven to the Erle of Mounte Belliart. He hade the gyrdle
and the gypseꝑ of Sydone—for she was chosen for the fairest.
5 The price of the tuysday was yeven to the Duke of Averences.
And he hade the sparhawke with the ryche loynes and the
chaplete, of Sydone. Bot not withstondyng, Ponthus iusted
the best; and wold take noon of the prices, in so myche
that he ordaned theym. Bot the ladys sent to hym a
10 ryng with a rubye, for the most worschipfull knyght that
was of theym all; also they sent to Barnard de La Roche
a riche goweꝑ.[1]

Then heroudes and mynstrelles made grete ioy and grete
noyse. And aftre sopeꝑ they hade carralles, daunces, and
15 songys to mydnyght. And aftre they dranke and ete spyces.
And aftre the straungers toke theyꝑ leve of the kyng and of
Sydone and of [the] othre ladys, and departed.

The wedynsday erely aftre messe Ponthus convehed theym[2]
to Castellyon,[3] wheꝑ he hade lete ordayne theyꝑ dynneꝑ; and
20 aftre dynneꝑ wold haue convehed theym—bot the lordes wold
not soffre hym. So he offred hym myche to theym, and toke
leve eueryche of othre. Gretely prased bothe the grete and
the small the goode cheꝑ and fellyschipp of Ponthus—and
that[4] they trowed that he was the beste, the fairest, the most
25 curtes, and the most gracius knyght of the worlde, to theyꝑ
intente, and that he hade noo fellawe. And also they prased
gretly Sydone of hiꝑ beautie and of hiꝑ curtesy—and that[5] he
were ryght fortunate that myght haue hiꝑ.

[1] The word is doubtful, but has clearly something to do with M. E. *gorgere.*
O. F. *gorgiere.* R, *fermail.* W, *ouche.*
[2] MS. *hym.* W, *them.*
[3] R, *a chasteau guyon.* W, *to ye castell of gyron.*
[4] An elliptical construction like that in W, *prasyed . . Ponthus . . . . and
that trewly he was*—but cf. R, *Et disoient vrayement cest le meilleur . . . . cheualier.*
[5] Both W & R show the ellipsis: *praysed . . . . Sydone . . . . and that he that
sholde haue her sholde be well eurous,   louaient S. . . . et que bien seroit eureux qui.*

[**Cap. XXI.** How Sydone made grete ioy that she sawe agane
Ponthus.   And how Guenelete, that had grete envy at
his maistre, accused Ponthus to the kyng, that he loved
Sydone to hiͬ dishonur.]

5 POnthus turned agane to the kyng and to the ladys.   And
the knyghtes of Bretane toke leve of the kyng and of
his doghtre.   So the kyng and his doghtre come huntyng[1]
and playng by the way.   So on a tyme spake Sydon and
Ponthus to gedre.   Then said Sydon, "Long tyme haue ye
10 keped you frome vs full secrete, and we gretly mervelled that
we herde no thyng frome you."   "Ma dame," said he, "I
sent you euery woke a knyght in stede of a messynger."   "Ye
say sothe, my swete loue.   Ye sent the moste noble messyngers that myght be founden.   Notwithstondyng, it wold haue
15 doone me more goode to haue knowen who hade sent theym
to me, for euery body said that ye weͬ goon into Hungarye;
so I was gretly amervelled that ye gave noon othre knowleche
of youͬ gooyng.   Wherfore myn hertt was full hevy."   "Ay,
Madame," said he, "I was full nyghe you and so was myn
20 hertt and thoght.   And all that I did, I thoght to doo itt for
youͬ honouͬ and to encresse youͬ goode renoune, for I wyst
wele that ye shuld be chosen for the fairest in Bretane.   So I
haue doone so myche, that the best knyghtes that myght be
founden or knawen come forto see you and to putt theym in
25 youͬ mercy.   Bot in goode faithe Madame, it was not I, that
dide the aventures of armes, bot it was ye; wherof I thonke
youͬ goode ladyshipp—for the myght and the hardenes that
I haue, I haue itt of you, for of my selfe I couthe not vndre-
[*Fol. 180ᵇ.] take itt."   "Ponthus," said she, "I knowe wele that this
30 goodnes and worshipp comes to you * frome Gode and frome
noon otheͬ.   The cause is that ye loue God and dredys hym,

---

[1] *Huntyng* is strange, but I have no reasonable emendation. R, *Et le roy
sen vint esbatant, lui et sa fille vers susinio.* W, *came syngynge & sportynge theym
towarde syclynere.* Digby omits the name of their place of destination.

and therfor he gyfes you that grace and hardenes; and so[1] ye
shuld [thynke] how[1] to thonke Gode." "Ma dame," said
he, "so I doo; bot I trowe that the entrepris comes of you."
"Now Ponthus," said she, "leve we thes wordes, for in goode
5 faithe the gladdest tythandes that myn hert myght haue, was
to her goode tydynges of you—as longe as I fynde you trewe
to kepe my worshipp and my lordes my faders." "Ma dame,"
said he, "therof truste ye verrely; for I hade levyr be deid
then to have thoght othre wyse, by my faithe."

10   And vpon thes wordes come oon of his xiij fellawes, called
Guenelete, whiche was named full envious and a fair speker
and a grete flaterer, and hade grete envye at his maistre Ponthus. And at that tyme ther was noo grettre maistre in the
contre then he. So he see the kyng olde, and thoght by fair
15 speche and flattery that he wold be maistre: and so he thoght
to aloigne his maystre Ponthus, whiche was full secrete with
the kyng; and he thoght, if that he myght a litle enstraunge
hym fro that courte, that he shuld then be maistre and most
privey with the kyng.

20   Thus he couthe not refreyne hym selfe fro dooyng of treson.
And so he sawe the kyng allone in a wode, wher as hunted he;[2]
and so he said vnto hym, "Ser, I wolle telle you a grete counsell, so that ye wold ensure me and make protestacon trewly,
by a kynges worde, that ye shall not dyscouere me." Said the
25 kyng, "I swer and promys you faithfully that I shall not dis-
couere you." Then Guenelete said, "My ryght gude Lorde,
ye haue noryshed me, and all the goode that I haue, comes of
youre goode grace; so I haue cause to loue you more then my
fadre, or modre, or all the worlde. Wherfore myn hert may
30 not soffre your harme ne dyshonour; and not withstondyng
I loue Ponthus more than any thyng bot you, for sothe itt is
this,—that Ponthus loues my lady your doghtre. Wherof I
make you wyse, for he is a full fair knyght; so I doute lest

---

[1] MS. *so she shuld and how.* I emend by changing *she* to *ye*, inserting *thynke*
to complete *shuld*, and dropping *and.* W, *so ye ought for to thanke hym hyghly.*
R, *si len deues moult mercier.*   [2] MS. *he was.* Om. *was.*

any fouuysch love be betwen theym, wherof ye myght haue
shame or dyshonour." "Ay," said the kyng, whiche thoght
noo thyng bot goode, "Guenelete I see wele that ye loue me
and that ye wold not my dyshonour. I am beholden to you
5 at all tymes and thonkes you gretly herof." And thus the
kyng thonked hym, as he that wenyd that he had said him
trauthe. And Guenelete said, "My Lorde, ye shuld not thonke
me, for I be so myche beholden vnto you that theꝶ is noo thyng
that a mortall man (myght do) for youꝶ Lordeship bot that I
10 wold doo itt, if I shuld dye therfore, forto lenght youꝶ live, if
nede weꝶ; and Ser, I wold tell you howe ye myght best preve
hym, and he say that he loues hiꝶ not,—bid hym make an othe
thervpon, and peraventure ye shall see that he wolle not sweꝶ."

And so Guenelete herde Ponthus say that in the parties of
15 Spayne noo kynges sone shuld make noon othe to credaunce,
whylst that he myght fyght—and if he dide, he weꝶ dys-
honored; and therfore he said the same to the kyng, for he
wyst wele that he wold not sweꝶ; and therfore by that maner
he wold attempe hym, and by thoos meanes to enstraunge hym.[1]

20 [Cap. XXII. How the kyng required an othe of Ponthus;
and he, that myght not swore, offred hym to fyght with
thre or with four. And how Ponthus wold not abyde
in the courte in mystruste and in susspeccion, bot toke
leve of Sydone for vij yeres.]

25 The kyng was thoghtfull of the tythyng, as he that mervellously lovyd his doghtre and he that had grete drede
of his dyshonour; and when he was comen fro the wodd and
lyghted doune fro his palfrey, so furth with come Ponthus,
[*Fol. 181.] wenyng to haue taken his swerd and his gloves as he was
30 accustomed. Then the kyng turned hym an othre * way and

---

[1] R and W have an additional sentence. *Et par ce il . . . . lestrangeroit de
la court, car nul enuieulx ne peut riens souffrir. for to estraunge hym from the
countree for to haue the more rule gadered in to his owne hande | for an envyous
man may no thyng suffre.*

nawthre made to hym countenaunce ne spake. And when
Ponthus perceyved that he was wrothe to hym, he said, "Ser,
be ye wrothe with me? Say to me, if it like you, for Goddes
loue, what I haue forfeted." And the kyng, which was right
5 wrothe of suche fals informacion, said, "Ponthus I haue
made a simple nurture in you, when ye wate to dyshonour
me." "Howe Ser?" said Ponthus, "By what way?" Then
said the kyng, "For ye loue my doghtre to dyshonour me.
And I haue noomoo children bot hiꝛ, whiche is all my ioy
10 and the lenghthyng of my life." "Ser," said he, "Who said
you this? And theꝛ be any man that dare say itt, or mayn-
tene itt, I am redy to shew my body that he lyes falsly—save
youꝛ worshipp." "Nay," said the kyng, "bot and ye wolle
sweꝛ vpon a messe-booke that ye loue hiꝛ not as I haue said,
15 peraventure I wolle leve you." "Ser, for to say that I loue
hiꝛ not as the doghtre of my ryght goode lorde—aftre my
dutye, I owe not to say; bot if theꝛ be any man that wolle
say that I loue hiꝛ to dyshonour you or hiꝛ, in wylle, dede,
or in thoght, I shall answeꝛ as a true knyght shuld doo. And
20 Ser ye knowe wele, othre thing ye shuld not disiꝛ of me, youꝛ
worshipp saved, for ye wote wele that noo kynges sonne shuld
make noon othe of fals vndirstondyng, whils that he may
defende hym with his hondes. And suche is the custome of
the contre whiche I am of." "I wote not howe itt is,"
25 said the kyng, that was ryght wrothe of the wordes that he
held.[1] "Ser," said Ponthus, which was right sory, "I offre
me to feght with thre or fouꝛ; for I fele myn hert so sure
and so true that I am certan that God wolle helpe, as he is
true Iuge of this dede and of all othre." "Ay," said the
30 kyng, "ye hold you so strong and so knyghtly, that ye wote
wele that theꝛ (dare)[2] no man feght with you." "Ay Ser,"
said Ponthus, "offre me to doo that thyng that I may doo to

---

[1] The emendation *herd* is probable, but *held* makes good sense, regarding
Ponthus as the subject of the clause—*le roy, qui moult fel estoit des paroles,
quil auoit ouyes.* W, *had herde* keeping the construction of R.

[2] R, *nul noseroit combatre.*

5

saue my worschipp." The kyng passed ouer and said theꝛ
shuld no batell be doon for that dede.

And when Ponthus herd this, he was ryght sory and wrothe.
By cause that he was a kynges sonne, he had shame to make
5 the othe that turnyd hym to shame; and that othiꝛ side, he
was sory be cause that the kyng wold doo hym noo ryght.
And then he come to the kyng and toke his leue and said
that he wold byde no lenger in his courte in mystruste ne in
susspeccion.

10   So he departed and come to Sydone and told hiꝛ how the
kyng had said to¹ hym, and howe the kyng wold not doo
hym ryght, and howe that he had offred hym to feght with
thre or fouꝛ, and how that he wold putt hym to his othe, to
his grete shame and dishonuꝛ. And when Sydone herd this
15 and vndirstode itt, it nedes not to aske if that she had any
sorowe in hiꝛ hertt; for she was so sorofull that she was
almuste loste. And when she myght speke, she said, "Ay
Lorde Godde, who be [thes]² traitours and flatterers that so
myche fals lyhyng has founde?—for in goode faithe, I wolle
20 swere on the sacrament, that theꝛ is noo vyllanye thoght in
ouꝛ loue. Bot sothely it is,³ that envy may not dye."

"Ma dame," said Ponthus, "ye say sothe. Bot I wolle take
leve of you with suche regrete and sorowe as euer knyght did,
and toke, of his lady." "Ay," sayd she, " my swete loue, me
25 semes it weꝛ bettre for to sweꝛ, for ye may doo itt surely, and
excuse vs." "Ay Ma dame," sayd he, "I dare not be seen in
my contrey, if I dide soo ; and God graunte I be not the first
kynges sonne that makes the furste othe, for at all tymes itt
suld be reproche to me and to myn heyers. Bot Ma dame, not
30 withstondyng thoghe the body proloyne for a while, the hertt⁴
[*Fol. 181ᵇ.] shall day and nyght * dwell with you. And if it pleasse God,

¹ MS. after to, hir' cancelled by the rubricator.
² W, these. R, ces.
³ R, Mais ainsi est. W, But thus it is.
⁴ The scribe has run down a flourish from this word into the lower margin
of the Fol. inclosing in it a heart.

at the ende of vij yeȝ I shall see you agane, and I live, bot if
I come herfte;[1] and if itt like you to kepe you vnmaried vnto
that tyme—if ye may—I wold pray you." "Ay," said she,
"the terme is long and farre. And how many sorofull days
5 and nyghtes shall be betwen you and me in the meane tyme!"
And with thes wordes she fell in swone and was all discolored.
Thus was the hertes of theym bothe so sore knytt[2] to gedre
that with grete payne they myght vnnes any thyng say, bot
[th]at[3] they cleped aythre othre and the terys fell doune from
10 theiȝ eeyn.

Then Ponthus putt his hoode afore his eyne, and departed
and went frome hiȝ vnto his chaumbre, and shitte the doore
vpon hym. And then his hertt beganne to swell and said to
hym selfe that he was the mervellest knyght livyng; that for
15 hym that lady myght receyve blame or shame with oute cause;
and on that side,[4] he losys all wordly ioy, when he losys the
contrey and the syght of hiȝ, of the whiche he has bot litle
recoueryng. And thus he complenys hym and wementys hym
ryght sorofully. And when he hade ben a while in that
20 sorowe, then he comforted hym selfe to make goode cheȝ and
refrenyd hym selfe ryght myche.

And if he hade sorowe in his hertt, Sidone had as myche;
for she entred into hiȝ warderop and called Ellious vnto hiȝ,
and when she sawe that theȝ was noon bot they twoo and that
25 they weȝ alloone, then beganne hiȝ sorowe, so grete and so
mervellous, that it was pitee to see. "Ay," said she, "my
swete love goos a way—the faiȝ, the goode, the floure of
knyghthode and of curtesy, and the beste that levys and the
best manerd and enteched aboute[5] all maner of estates and

---

[1] I read clearly *herfte*, which I fail to understand, in the MS. Some
word meaning earlier is required. R, *se plus tost ne reuien*. W, *yf soner I
come not.* | Is it possibly *herste* (illogical *h* and long *s*) for *erste*.

[2] MS. after *knytt*, W, cancelled by the rubricator.

[3] The conj. *at* may be a genuine colloquial form, that has slipped into
the text. W, *saue onely that.*

[4] R, *Et dautre part.* W, *And also he leseth.*   [5] R, *En tous estas.* W, *among.*

among all mane*r* of people—and that is goode reson that he
be so, for he loues God, dredes hym, and worshippes hym;
and has the olde and the wyse in reu*e*rence. He is humble to
the moste and to the leste; he is myrroure of all noblenes and
5 largenes; his swete hertt is gentle, humble, and debonere.
What shall myn hertt doo aftre his depa*r*tyng, bot langoure,
and weymente day and nyght, wi*th*oute any ioy or reste?—
for I knowe wele his swete hertt wolle haue no lesse."

Then she toke Ellious by the harme hastely and furth with
10 fell to the grounde in swone. And Ellious weped, and arased[1]
hi*r* lady with a litle wat*er*, and conforted hi*r* in the best wyse
that she myght; bot it avayled hi*r* not, she was so sory. And
then she said to Ellious, "I may not in noo wyse kepe my
hertt ne counsell close frome you, so myche I loue and trustes
15 you. Bot love, this sorowe comys on me when I thinke[2] the
grete vntrauthe that has ben putt vpon vs, and that we neu*er*
thoght vyllany, for mor true*r* loue was neu*er* betwen two per-
sounes; and aftre, I thinke the wordes[3] that be said of grete
wrong, and that for me he loses the contrey whe*r* he was so
20 wele beloued of grete and small, and all the evyll that he shal
soffre and haue shall be for my sake; and thus I shall be
cause of his myschief. All thes thinges drives sorowe to myn
hertt." Gretly she wemented and aftre dryed hi*r* eyn. And
itt was long or she come to the chaumbre of astate among hi*r*
25 ladys and gentylwommen; and made no semelance, bot as it
greved hi*r* bot a litle. She was right wyse and wele couthe
kepe hi*r* conten*a*unce. The ladys and the gentylwommen
weped and wemented of the depa*r*tyng of Ponthus an*d* said
that cursed was he that suche falsed fonde and contreved.
30 Bot Sydon reconforted theym full gentylly and womanly.

And thus I turne agane to Ponthus.

[1] R, *et Eloix pleure et arouse sa dame. Arased* then means "sprinkled,"
Fr. *arroser.* W shows a combination of a curious blunder and a correct
translation: *toke rose water and bespryncled her lady.*

[2] R, *ie pense la grant desloyaulte* translated slavishly. W, *thynke on.*

[3] R, *ie pense les paroles.* W, *thynke on.*

[Cap. XXIII. How Ponthus departed from the courte and
   saled to England; and how the kynges sonne of England, that was called Henry, welcomed hym and toke
   hym to the courte wher as he was ryght wele cherysed.
5   And how the kyng of Irlond made werre vpon theym,
   and Ponthus toke hym prisonner; and aftre councelled
   theym to make peace betwen the reaumes, and the kyng
   of Irlond to wed the kynges doghtre of Englond.]

POnthus called his chaumberlayne, a squye̅r, and com-
10 maunded hym to trusse and to putt in males all that
was nede, and toke leve of euery persone of the courte.   So
was the̅r noon bot they made sorowe for his departyng and
weped; and euery man and womman had as myche sorowe
and doyll in thei̅r hertt as the[i] wold haue hade, iff all they̅r
15 frendes had ben deid—so myche they loued hym.

Then he departed from the courte; and the barounes, the
knyghtes, and who so euer myght lepe on hors bak conveyd
hym wepyng, and wenyd varely to have withholden hym with
fai̅r language, sayng, that the kyng was olde and not wyse,
20 and that he shuld not take to hert that that he said.   Bot he
wold not abyde for all they̅r langage.

And when they had conveyd hym twoo myles, he aboode
and prayd theym to turne agane; and so he made theym to
turne a gane, whedre they wold or not.   In takyng leve was
25 wepyng enughe.

So they retourned and made grete sorowe for his departyng,
sayng, "Ay Bretan, thou oughte to be dysmated and wepyd:[1]
when the fai̅r, the goode, the most worshipfull knyght takes
his leve, the whiche keped theym in peace and ioy; for he
30 keped theym, as the hen did hi̅r byrdes vndre hi̅r weng, from
all evyll neghboures and aduersaries.   The barounes and the
people also wepyd and regreted, in cursyng theym that the fals
wordes had founde and contrevyd.

---

[1] Adj. in the sense of sorowful, for *biwepyd.*   R, *bretaigne tu dois bien
plourer.*   W, *thou oughtest wele to wepe.*

Ponthus rode to Sainte Malo de l'Ysele,[1] and thedre made come a shipp, and on the morowe herd messe, and aftre went to take the see. And so Herland the senysshall and his fellawes wenyd to haue goone with hym; bot he wold not soffre

5 theym, and said, that the kyng had norysshed theym and made theym,[2] and that he myght doo theym, myche goode; and therfore he counselled theym for to abyde styll with the kyng. And thus with grete payne they departed frome hym full sorofully and toke leve of hym wepyng. And when the shipp

10 was oute of theyr sight, then begau theyŕ doyll and theiŕ grete sorow—bot if itt weŕ Guenelete, which made semelante as he had wepyd, and was no dele sory, bot hade grete ioy in his hert inwarde, what cheŕ so euer that he shewyd outewarde.

And Ponthus went his way, and thus he losys the syght of

15 Bretan. Then the teres fell doune frome his eyne, and softely said, "Blessed be Bretane and the faiŕ, the goode, the [most] trusty, that lyues[3]—Sydone, and all othre ladys and gentylwommen for loue of hiŕ and goode knyghthode, for I neuer sawe ne hard of noon[4] bettre."[4] Grete sorowe then his hertt

20 had for Sydone. Not withstondyng, he keped his sorowe in the most covert wyse that he couthe or myght.

And within a whyle he arryved at Hampton and come rydyng toward London. And theŕ passed by the way a grete bore; and a grehounde toke the bore; and then Ponthus with

25 his sworde clove hym in the myddys in twoo peces. And Ser Henry the kynges sonne sawe the stroke and had grete mervell therof; and prayd hym to dwell with hym. And Ponthus graunted hym.

[1] MS. lysele. R, saint malo. W, saynt Solo (sic).

[2] W, And yᵗ he was of power to make them & doo them good. R, le roy les auoit nourris et fais et leur feroit des biens asses.

[3] MS. loues. I emend the passage following R, benoist soit bretaigne. Et la belle et la plus loyale qui viue et la meilleur.

[4] MS. more bittre. Cf. W, for better nor sweter was there neuer. Both English versions depart from R's, Car onques plus doulz pays [Bretaigne] ne feust. The emendation may appear somewhat heroic, but clearly there is confusion in the passage as it stands.

And the kynges sonne enquired of his estate. And he told hym not as yete, bot tolde hym that he was comen to the courte of Englonde to see itt, by cause of the grete renoune that he herd of the kyng, and of his twoo sonnes; and that
5 he come also to see the estate and noblenes of the same contre and reaume. "Ser," said Henry, "ye be ryght welcome. And I be oon of the kynges sonnes, and I pray you to be with me." "Ser, in Godes name, savyng that it pleasse yow."

[* Fol. 182.] Thus they wente to gedre toward the courte, spekyng of
10 mony thynges.[1] * And when they come to the courte, the kyng was even[2] sett to mete. Henry commaunded his men that they shuld delyuere chaumbre and stable to his newe knyght. And itt was so doon. The kynges sone entred into the hall and his knyghtes with hym. The kyng asked hym
15 howe he had hunted and the quene bothe. And he tolde theym. Then the kyng asked hym prively what was the faiȝ knyght. And he tolde hym howe he had hym founde, and of the grete stroke that he gave the bore. And Ponthus was gretly loked vpon, for on euery syde they come to beholde
20 hym, and hade grete mervell of hym.

The courte was anoon full of the tithynges that theȝ was comen with the kynges sonne the fairest knyght that euer any man loked vpon. The ladys and gentylwomen beheld hym, and in especiall the kynges twoo doghters. Eueryche of theym
25 said, "Se heȝ, a mervellous faiȝ knyght!" "Yea," said sume, "if he be feyȝ, he is more amyable and plesaunt." They made hym sitt among the ladis, and aftre dynneȝ they went furth of the hall; and then was broght furth the bore, whiche was the bore that they had sen before, whiche was cutt in twoo peces.
30 "Loo!" said Henry to the kyng and to the quene, "what my newe knyght has doone with oon stroke of a swerde." And Ponthus turned hym an othre way and shamed that they prased hym so myche.

---

[1] The -es is nearly erased.
[2] R, le roy estoit ia assis a dîmer. W, yᵉ kynge was set at dyner.

The kyng and the quene asked hym of whens that he was.
And he said, of the reaume of Fraunce. "And what call they
you?" said the kyng. "Ser, they call me Le Surdite de Droyte
Voy." And so they asked hym of the tydynges of Fraunce,
5 and of mony thynges. And the kyng herde hym so wysely
spoken and answeryng, that he gretly mervelled. Then he
said to the quene, that he had not herd a bettre avysed ne
bettre attempred in language then he was—"and for sothe
myn hertt yeves me that he is grettre of byrthe, and more
10 noble, then he makes hym." And thus they tarryed a grete
whyle; and the more that they sawe hym, the more they
loued hym and prased hym.

Grete doylle made the kynges eldest sonne that he had not
the furst mett with hym, before his brodre Henry; for Pon-
15 thus knewe notablely of all maner games—of huntyng, of
hawkyng, and othre disportes; and euer he made as thoghe
he knewe no thyng, ne he prased neuer hym self in nothyng
that he dide. Gretly was prased his connyng and his maners
among all the people. He loued God and the chirche, and
20 euery day he herd messe; and gave his almus secretly to the
pouere people. And he wold neuer swer̃ by God ne by noon
of his saintes.

Uppon a day itt befell that the Erle of Gloucestre sonne,
which was a ryght fair̃ knyght and a strong, and was right
25 presumptuous, cast the stoone with the kynges sonne Henry,
and mony othre noble knyghtes that was ther̃. And he hade
passed Ser Henry nygh four̃ fyngers, and he avaunted hym
selfe therof before the ladys. And of his boste Ser Henry was
evyll plesyd, and called Ponthus to hym and said, "Surdyte
30 my frende, I pray you to revenge me, for Rolande Gloucestre
makes his boste afore the ladys that he has passed me to
myche."[1] "Ser," said Surdyte, "sith it please you, I wolle,
bot I am vnlykly." Then he toke the stone of his maistre
and caste itt easly frome hym, and passed hym negh by twoo

[1] R, se vente .... quil ma passe de trop.

fyngers. Then the thothre² toke the stone and reforced hym
and did so myche that he caste as farre. "Ay," said Ser
Henry, "by the faithe that ye owe to the lady that ye beste

[*Fol. 183.] loue in the worlde, caste itt as farre as ye may."

5   And when he herd hym thus require * hym, he remembred
hym of his lady, and toke the stone, and said, "Ser, ye haue
sore required me, for I owe grete feithe to my lady, my modre."
"Ay," said Gener the kynges eldist doghtre, "be ye so myche
waxen, and be to seche with ladys vnto nowe?"¹ "Ma dame,"
10 said he, "I am so fonde and bustus that noon deynes to loue
me." "God knowes that itt is trewe," said Gener. And then
she said in hiȝ hertt, "Now wolde Gode that he wold loue me
as wele as I loue hym."

And then Surdyte toke the stonne and cast it vij fote ferthre.
15 And when the kyng and the ladys sawe the cast, they mervelled
therof gretly. The Erle sonne of Gloucestre was abasshed and
said that he was ouercomen. Then said Henry to Surdyte,
"Why haue ye so longe abyden to cast that grete caste?"
"Ser," said he, "and ye hade not so sore desired me, I wold
20 not haue melled therwith, for I haue doone the Erle sonne of
Gloucestre dyspleseȝ—and that dyspleses me, if it weȝ not to
fullfyll youȝ commaundment; for it longes not to me to dys-
plese any man." So his maistre sawe wele the curtesy of the
knyght.

25   So come Gener to hiȝ brothre Henry, and said, "Faiȝ
brothre come and sporte you in my chaumbre, ye and youȝ
knyght, I pray you." "Sustre," said he, "I wolle." And so
they went to dysporte theym in hiȝ chaumbre. There they
had wyne and spices and aftre they begane to ·daunce and
30 syng. Bot with grete payne they myght vnnethe make Sur-

¹Apparently a case of "tother," dentals are irregular in this MS., so I
have let it stand.
² W, *Surdyt Surdyt* | *it may not be that ye be now* | *vnpurchased and be so moche
& so goodly.* R, *Sourdit, Sourdit a peine estes si grant creu que vous en soies a
pourchaser dun autre.* Our translator apparently had an original differing
from R.

dyte de Droyte Voy to daunce, for he said he couthe noo
thyng doo; bot when he was in daunce,[1] he daunced so that
noo man daunced like hym. And also vnneth they couthe
make hym to syng. Bot at the kynges doght*re* praye͞r, he
5 song a songe whiche was passyng swete.

And aftre when they had so*n*gen, the kynges sonne and his
sustre beganne to harpe. And when they had harped a whyle,
they prayd Surdyte to harpe. Bot they had grete payne to
make hym to doo any thyng as towchyng to harpyng, syng-
10 yng, or daunsyng; bot at the last he harped a newe lay that
was me*r*vellous. "Goode faithe!" said Gene͞r, "I haue grete
ioy that ye can this, for we haue had grete desi͞r to knowe
itt—for it is the lay that the goode knyght Ponthus made for his
love, as it is told vs." "Madame, I wote not who made itt,"
15 said he. Bot yitt he was a litle aschamed, and waxed rede,
when he thoght on hi͞r that he made itt for. Then Gene*r* and
hi͞r sust*re* lerned itt, and had itt wretyn.

And anon went the kynges sonne and his twoo susters to
the kyng they͞r fadre and to the quene, and told theym that
20 Surdyte couth the lay that Ponthus made in Litle Bretan.
And the[2] kyng co*m*maunded hym to harpe itt be-for hym
and the quene; and they thoght itt me*r*vellously goode, and
said to thei͞r twoo doght*er*s, "Truly, fai͞r doght*er*s, we wold
that ye lernyd itt, for itt is ryght goode, and the knyght doos̓
25 itt wondrely wele—and of all dyssportes and ˙plays he canne
enowe."

And on a tyme Gene*r* dema*u*nded hym and sayd, "Surdyte
se ye any lady in this londe, whe͞r ye lyst putt you͞r hertt and
plesaunce vnto? I pray you, tell ye me; and in goode faithe,
30 I am she that wolle you͞r worshipp." "Ma dame," said he,
"God thonke you at all tymes, for I haue grete nede of you͞r
goode helpe; bot in this case, I loue all as goode ladys."
"Ay," said she, "Be they all comon to you, or be the͞r any
that has avauntege before any othre?" "Ma dame," said he,

¹ R, *fu a la dance*.   ² MS. *ther̓*.

"all be so good that noon may honour and worshipp theym
so myche as they be worthie; and as tovching me, the honuȝ[1]
of so pouere a knyght is litle worthe." "Ay," said she, "he
[*Fol.183ᵇ.] is not pouere that has the beautie, the hountie, the * goode
5 maneres, and the feyȝ countenaunce, that ye haue; for in
goode feith, I knowe not so grete a lady in this lande bot that
she myght hold hiȝ worshipp, if that she were love vnto suche
a knyght as I trowe that ye be." "Ma dame," said he, "I be
farre frome suche worthynes as ye say that I be of." "Ay,"
10 said she, "I say noo thyng bot that me thynkis[2] sothe." "Yea
Ma dame," said he, "Itt likes you forto dysporte with me, that
be so pouere a knyght." And thus he held hym all vpon iapes,
and made noo semeland to be in any throwes of love[3]—wherof
itt dyspleased hiȝ gretly; for and she had founde any cause or
15 draght of love in hym, she wold haue dyscouered her more
largely. And that perceyved Surdyte ryght wele ofte tymes,
by hiȝ and by mony othre ladys and gentylwommen, which
cast to hym mony coverte wordes and contenaunce—whiche
with goode wyll wold haue loued hym, and he hade wold.
20 Bot he shewed to eueryche elyke goode chere withoute any
contenaunce of love; wherfor the[re][4] were many sorofull,
and in especiall the kynges twoo doghters.

Ryght wysely he aquanted hym with, and did plesaunce to,
euery body. Mony nyghtes he thoght on his lady and made
25 dyuers lays, wherof the wordes of oon lay ended in contenyng
of sorowe[5]—that he wold loue hiȝ withoute any eschaunge;[6]
and in thes thinges at sume tyme he toke myche of his com-
forthe, and lyghtnes of his straunge thoghtes.[7]

---

[1] R, lamour. W, loue. The translator probably read lamour as lonour in
his French original. [2] MS. thynk is.
[3] R, effray damer. W, wyll for to loue. [4] R, dont il y en eust.
[5] R, Et faisoit lays et virelays et tous les noms cheoient en regart de doulceur
(sic). W, the whiche fell in complaynyng of sorowe.
[6] R, sans changer.
[7] R, prenoit moult de confort a la guet de ses estroites penses. W, blunders
in this passage: & in these thoughtes he toke ofte tymes grete dyscomforte (sic) &
sometyme allegyaunce of his heuy thoghtes.

Then itt befell that there was grete rumo*ur* of werr*e* betwen
the kyng of Englond and the kyng of Irlond; for there
was taken truse, which was broken vpon a Myghelmes, the[1]
[whiche] was twoo days passed. And the kyng of Ireland
5 had at that tyme ryden wi*th* a grete armye. And anoon the*r*
come tydynges to the courte therof. And the kyng sent oute
p*r*ivey seales, and le*tt*res of comm*au*ndement, thorow oute his
reaume; and ordaned to send furth his twoo sonnes.

Surdy̆te asked his maistre, "S*er*, what title has the kyng
10 to werr*e*?" And S*er* Henry toke hym that he had goode
title, and toke itt vpon per*e*ll of his saule. Then said Surdyte, "S*er*, I wolle goo with you; for in no evyll title of
Cristen werres I wold not goo, for noo thyng. For we oughte
mo[2] to loue ou*r* saules then ou*r* bodyes that be mortall, and
15 from day to day drawen to an ende—and the saule may not
dye, and it behoves to haue it[3] rewarde of Almyghty Gode,
authi*r* goode or evyll." His maist*re* herkened hym wele, and
prased hym myche in his hertt, notwithstondyng he wenyd
that his fadre hade goode ryght.

20   The armye made,[4] they beganne to goo aganes the kyng of
Irelond, which had taken a castell and held itt—the which
he had wonne with a sawte. And when the kyng of Irland
herd by his spyes that the kynges twoo sonnes come to the
batell, anon he come against theym; for he was an hardy
25 man and a worthie. And he had six batells and had mony
comons with hym.

---

[1] R, *La quelle estoit passee de trois iours.* W, *and was passed a thre days.*

[2] MS. *me.* R, *mieulx.* W, *better.*

[3] Reading *his* for *it*, or dropping *it* from the text would amend the passage.
It, in any form, as a genitive is of course impossible at this date. R, *son
guerredon.* W, *her rewarde.*

[4] R, *Mais touteffois cuidoit il que son pere eust droit en larmee. Ce fait ils
partirent et allerent contre le roy dislande.* Apparently the translator has
rendered *ce fait, the armye made* (*i. e.*, put in order) deceived by the proximity of *larmee* in his original. The blunder is a surprising one, but it
appears better to tally with the texts than the obvious but unsatisfactory
emendation *beginne* for *beganne.* W, *The armes were assembled & wente.*

And the kyng of Englond*es* twoo sonnes had bot fouꝛ
batells with theym : wherof the Erle of Northampton, that
was marshall, hade the furste batell; the secund batell had
the Lorde Henry; and the third had the kyng[1] eldyst sonne,
5 in the which weꝛ mony Barounes; the fourte batell had the
kyng of Cornewale, which was a full good knyght and nevewe
vnto the kyng, and with hym weꝛ the Walshmen.

The kyng of Irland had the moste parte of his men on fote.
Bot the Euglyschmen weꝛ the most parte on hors bak. At
10 the sembly weꝛ grete showtes and cries, and mony knyghtes
beten doune so that they had no poweꝛ to relief theym self.
So had the Erle soffred twoo batelles to come vpon hym. And
[*Fol. 184.] when Surdyte, that was in the * secunde batell, sawe theiꝛ
men withdrawe theym, he said to his maist*re*, "S*er*, itt is
15 tyme that we meve vs. Youre men losys grounde." "Ye
say sothe," said the Lorde Henry.

Then they went furthe and entred into the batell and felled
doune mony knyghtes in theyr entryng. And aftre they toke
theym to theyꝛ swordes; and then began the feghtyng strong
20 and fersly. And anoon the Ireschmen drewe bȧk, so that the
othiꝛ batell come in, in the whiche was the kyng of Irland
and the best knyghtes that he had. Theꝛ was grete noys of
trumpys. Itt was not long afteꝛ bot all the batells assemelyd
with mony grete iustys, bot itt weꝛ to long to tell all, how
25 they weꝛ doon.

Surdyte, that had grete desiꝛ to doo fetes of armes, bett
doune mony *with* the tronchon of his speꝛ; and aftre toke
hym vnto his sworde and began fersly, and smote on aythre
syde hym//and made rowme before hym, so that he was knawn
30 of theym that neu*er* saw hym befor. He did so manfully that
mony left theiꝛ feghtyng to behold hym.

Then said the kyng of Irlond, that if yonde knyght shuld
live long, he wold gaꝛ his men lose grounde. And so he
smote the hors *with* his spurrys; and *with* a gret short speꝛ

[1] The *g* has a large tag much like the usual flourish, unlike the -*es* con-
traction.

he smote Surdyte at a travers, that he had nyghe ouerthrawen hym. Notwithstondyng, he fell not. And when he was re-dressed vp agayn, he said in his hertt that he was bot litle worthe, bot if he weꝑ revenged. He knewe wele that it was
5 the kyng of Irland for othre mervelles of armes that he sawe hym doo, and he sawe (hym) rychely arrayd in pereles and precious stones.

Then Surdyte avaunced hym and smote hym vpon his helme so grete a stroke that he was astoned and bowed bak
10 vpon the arson of his sadle; and then he wold smyte hym noo more, for fere lesse he shuld sley hym; and thoght in his hertt that itt was not Godes wyll, that he shuld sley so goode a knyght. Then he toke hym by the shulders and drewe hym to hym, furth of his sadle, and cast hym before hym
15 and bare hym as the wolfe beres his pray. The Iresche men trowed to have rescoued hym; but Surdyte smote so sore aboute hym that they durst ꝺot tovche hym and he bare oute of the batell, and putt, hym in save garde.

When the Ireschmen sawe that theyꝑ kyng was taken, they
20 loste theyꝑ córage and hardenes; and toke theym to flyght, thos that myght—sume to the woddes and sume to the hylles. And mony weꝑ beten doune deid. And at nyght euery man toke that they myght, and drewe theym to theyꝑ banneꝑ and to theyꝑ stondard, and luged theym in the felde in signe of
25 victorye. Bot the Lorde Henry had gret ioy of his knyght, that had taken the kyng. Myche was the speche of Surdyte, that all the felde was wonne by hym. And on the morowe they went before the castell that the kyng of Irelond had taken; and within a whyle it was yelden vp, and mony othre
30 tounes and castells that they had taken.

Grete was the ioy (of the tydynges) that come to the courte[1]
—howe by Surdyte the kyng of Irlond was taken and all his men dyscomfetyd; and at theyꝑ comyng home the kyng and the quene went aganes hym with grete ioy, and said, "This

---

[1] MS. *courte and.* R, *Moult fu grant la Ioye et la feste des nouuelles . . ., comme le Sourdit auoit este vainquer.*

knyght is welcome, whiche is the floure of knyghthod." Surdyte was ashamed of the grete worshipp that they did hym ;
and said to the kyng and to the quene, that they did hym
shame to putt hym to so grete worshipp, that had not diserued
5 itt. "Ay," said the kyng, " I trowed that I had doon wele,
bot syth it displeasses you, I wolle doo noo more so."

Menne asked the kyng what he wold doo with the kyng of
Irlonde, and he answeryd and said, " Like as Surdyte wolle ;
[*Fol. 184ᵇ.] and that he * be not sett in prisoune, bot if he commaunde
10 itt." And Surdyte answerd therto and said, "As the kyng
wolle, so be itt doon ; and if itt like hym, by myn advice, it were
wele doon to doo hym worshipp, and that he myght ete and
drynk in the hall." And the kyng said the counsell was goode,
and commaunded his yongeᵉ sonne to bryng hym into the hall.
15 And the kyng of Irland was full semely and a full faiᵉ
knyght, of thirtee yeres of age, and was richely arrayd in a
coote of purple and a mantyll of sabyllyn doune to the foote.
He was gretely beheld of all the people. The kyng and the
quene made hym cheᵉ. for the loue of Surdyte ; and he was
20 sett betwen the kynges twoo doghters. Bot he made bot
symple chere. And Surdyte come to hym, and said, " Ser, be
ye of goode cheᵉ, for ye haue goode and easy prisoune betwen
twoo faiᵉ ladyes." " Truly," said the kyng, "sithe Gode hath
sent me suche prison, me oght not gretly to be dysmated."
25 Aftre dynner Surdite made hym to talke with the kynges
yongeᵉ doghtre, and said to hiᵉ, " Madame, howe likes you the
kyng of Irloud ? If I knewe that it liked you, I wold speke
of a mariage betweu you and hym, althogh it long¹ not to
me—for pouere men has bot litle voice among grete men
30 and lordes." "Ay," seid she, " Surdite haue ye said as ye
thoght?" " Yea Madame," said he, "if I wyst that it weᵉ to
youᵉ pleasure." " For sothe," said she, " itt pleases me, if it
pleasse my fadre and my brethre,² sith that I may not haue

¹A large *g* tag may represent an -*es*, but is probably merely a flourish.
²The first *e* looks like an *o*, in which the pen has slipped downward in
making the left stroke, but there is no doubt that the reading is *brethre*, not
brothre.

an othre, that be navthre kyng ne duke—bot he is the fairest
knyght of the world, and the best." "Madame," said he, "it
is a straunge thyng to knowe the beste, for theŕ be mony
goode." And he thoght that she said it by hym. And so
5 she did. Bot he wold not comforth hiŕ therin. And aftre
they went furth for to dysporte theym in the gardyns, and
playd att the chesse and att the tables, and at mony othre
dysportes.

On the morowe the kyng of Englond held a grete fest
10 and a counsell,—and theŕ was the kyng of Scottes, that had
weddyd his sustre, and the kyng of Cornewale, and princes,
dukes and barounes,—to wytt what shuld be doon with the
kyng of Irlonde. And thus they spake of dyuers ways.
And at the last the kyng asked Surdyte and badd hym say
15 his advyce,—"for itt is reason that we take ouŕ advice att
you that has hym vndre subieccon." He excused hym to
sey, bot the kyng commaunded hym to sey, "Ser, sith me
must nedes speke, foryeve me my rude and my simple speche.
It semes me that the quarell and the debate that I haue herde
20 is not myche worthe, for itt is not the lawe ne the commaundement of Gode to be all wey in aduersite—for he sais, ' Loue
thy neghbouŕ as thy selfe ; ' and also, when Gode was borne,
the aungell come to the shepherdes, and shewed to theym the
message of Gode, and aftre went vp into hevyn synghyng,
25 Gloria in excelsis Deo et in terra pax hominibus, &c., that is
to say, ' Glorye and worshipp be vnto Gode in high places,
and in erthe, peace to all people.' [1] Also God said to his
apostylls dyvers tymes, ' Peace be among you.' So if God
haue sent you grete realmes, kyngdomes, and lordeshipps, itt
30 is not for to werre, the stronng ayeinst the feble; for ye werre
also ayeinst the pouere people, whiche ye oughte to kepe in
reste and peace, and they ben sleyn and distroyed. That is

[1] W and R have nothing corresponding to *in high places;* they substitute
for *all people.* W, *men of good wyll.* R, *hommes de bonne voulente.* The verse
from the Vulgate is completed in W by the addition of *bone voluntatis;* in
R it stops at *Deo.*

grete pitee for the Cristen to here of. And I shall say you
what wolle make goode peace betwen you, by myn advice,—
ye shall yeve to hym youꝛ doghtre in mariage, and all this
[*Fol. 185.] debate to be cessed." All lordes said, "Blessyd be * he for
5 his counsell." Soo itt was hold and keped.

Then seid the kyng of Scottes, "Faiꝛ frende, sith that youꝛ
faiꝛ speche be so plesaunt to all people, goo ye now to the
kyng youꝛ prisonneꝛ and bryng to vs the reporte of his wyll ;
for we charge you with that occupacion." And Surdyte said
10 he wold with a goode wyll, sith that itt liked theym. And
anoon he went and spake with the kyng of Irlond, and told
hym the subieccon that he was in, and the perell that myght
fall to his reaume ; and aftre told hym howe that God loues
hym that loues his neghtboures, and how mony has ben lost
15 by theyꝛ corage and excesse of covetyse. "Nowe what say
ye, and I laboure so that ye may haue[1] the kynges yongre
doghtre and that your raunson and debate be foryeven in the
mariage ; and so euer aftre to be frendes." "Ser," said the
kyng, "and ye may bryng itt aboute, I am myche beholden
20 to you, aftre God, most of any man." "Wolle ye,"[2] said
Surdyte, "that I doo itt and bryng itt to a conclusion?"
"Yea," said the kyng, "with all myn hertt, for I desire it
most of any thyng."

Then departed Surdyte from hym, and come to the coun-
25 sell, and reported to theym that the kyng was ryght glad of
the aliaunce, and forto haue peace.

Thus was itt concluded and fulfylled. And the kyng
and she ensured[3] befor the Archebyschop of Canterbury ; and
within a moneth aftre they weꝛ wedded with grete fest and
30 ioy, for the kyng of Irlond had theꝛ a hundreth knyghtes of
a suyte, and gave to Surdite iiij stedes couresoures, and x
thowsand besantes of gold, and grete plente of clothes of golde,

---

[1] The MS. repeats *may haue.*   [2] MS. *yeu.*
[3] W, *The kyng . . . made yᵉ archebysshop . . . for to handfest theym.* R, *fist . . .
fiancer.*

6

of purpyll, and of sylke, and also grete peyns[1] of armyn and
of sables. And within a while the kyng sent [the] quene
into Irlonde, wheꝛ as she was coroned, loued and worshipped.

[Cap. XXIV. How Corbatan the third sonne of the Saw-
5   deyn londed in Englond, and how Ponthus slewe hym
       and toke his tresouꝛ. And the kynges two sonnes were
       sleyn in the batell. How the kyng offered to Ponthus
       to wed Genere his doghtre and to be kyng aftre hym.]

SO itt happened in the vij[te] yeꝛ aftre that Surdyte come
10   into Englond, that the thirde son of the sawdeyn, which
was called Corbatan, had pylled mony iles and reaumes, and
doon grete harme vnto the Cristen people, and made mony
londes tributary to hym, and londed in Englond as his twoo
brethre had—that oon in Spayne, and that othre in Pety
15 Bretan. Anon theꝛ was a grete noys that he was londed with
ix C vesselles, grete [and small],[2] and defyed the kyng and
bad hym voyde the londe, or to forsake theyꝛ beleve and pay
tribute.

All the contre for grete fere tremelyd,[3] when they harde of
20 the grete noumbre that the hethyn weꝛ of. The kyng had
counsell forto send hastely aboute, and so he sent hastely for
the kyng of Scottes his brothre, and for the kyng of Irlond
his son, and for the kyng of Cornewale his nevew, and for
the Erle of Wales, and for all othre erles and barounes of his
25 reaume. And when they weꝛ assemylyd, theꝛ was a grete
armye. Also he sent his twoo sonnes and Surdyte; and they
come in ordynaunce bot iiij[4] Englysch myles fro the Saresyns,
and ordaned theyꝛ batelles: wherof the kyng of Scottes and
the kyng of Irlonde hade the furst; the secunde hade the

---

[1] R, de bonnes pennes (on an erasure) de gris dermines et de sebelines. W,
goode furres of veer and of sables. See pane, a garment, in Stratmann-Bradley.
[2] R, que grans que petis. W, what grete what small.
[3] MS. tremelyd mony.
[4] R, a trois lieues. O adds anglesses. W, well a foure myle.

kyng of Cornewale; the thirde, the Erle of Wales; the iiij[te]
the Lorde Iohn, the kyng eldyst son; the v[te] the Lorde Ser
Henry, the kynges yongre son; and Surdyte had the vj[te].
Ther[1] vj batelles wer, grete, and noumbred to moo than xxx[te]
5 thovsand horsmen, beside theym that wer on fote, as archers
and alblasters.[2] And Corbatan the kyng, which knewe of
theyr commyng made xij batelles and had moo then fourtee[3]
[*Fol. 185b.]thovsand, besyde theym * on fote, and they were ryght fers,
as they that had not ben dyscomfeted in xii yere, sith they
10 departed from the sawdeyn of Babilone.

And our people rode wele enbatelled and on a rowe; and
when they sawe the Saresyns oste,[4] that held so grete a countre,[4] they gretly amervelled.   They had all herde messé,[5] that
the Bishop of Canterbury had songen,[5] and wer shreven and
15 howselyd, and then they held theym myche more sure.   Surdyte come by the batelles, and said, "Feir Lordes, mervelles
not of the grete noumbre, for we be vndreneth the banner of
our Lorde Ihesu Criste, which fulfylled v[M] people with v
barley lovys and twoo fysches; for so he may (gyue) victorye
20 to oon aganes C.   Therof haue we goode hertt, and smyte
we sharply aganes theym; for he that wolle,[6]—nedes the
defendaunt comonly voydes and makes way.   So goo we in
Goddes name vppon theym withoute any delay, for they haue
no Gode to defende theym, ne helpe them; and lete vs be
25 hardy withouten any fere, and they shall be anoon dyscomfeted, with the grace of God."

[1]A tempting emendation is thes for ther', but ther' . . . wer translates R, si
furent.
[2]W, arbalasties. R, arbalestriers.
[3]R, quinze. O, l. mille. W, xl.
[4]W, the same, translating R, qui tint si grant pais. "Who occupied so much
space ?"
[5]The clause is neither in W or R.
[6]I. e., smyte sharply. I render, "Who sharply attacks—of necessity the
defensive party yields," following R, Car qui bien assault et se deffent len lui
vuide lentree et se fait ou voye. W, condenses, for he that well assaylleth or
defendeth rpon theym that haue no fayth God helpeth hym.

Then they smote their horses with their spurrys and come
to gedre oon aganes an othre. There was grete cry and noys
of trumpes, and anon wer ryght mony ouerthrawen and dede.,
And the batell endured iiij houres[1] and more. Ther myght
5 men here and see swordes breke and clatre on the helmetes
of stele.

Surdyte made way wher so euer he went, for as mony as
he ouerraghte wer deid or distroyd. Fireague, oon of the
Saresyns, had slayne Ser John, the kynges eldest son, of
10 whiche was grete harme. The batell was ryght cruell.

Corbatan the kyng did ryght mervellously dedes of armes
and sawe Ser Henry rychely arrayd, and how that he did
mony fair dedes of armes. He toke in his honde a grete
shorte sworde[2] and stroke hym at a travers, in suche wyse
15 that he perched his goode harnes, and stroke hym into the
body alfe a fote. Surdyte then dressed hym and made the
Saresyns to flee befor hym with the grete strokes that he gave
theym, and beheld his maistre fall to the grounde, and hurte
in the body. It nedes not to aske whethre that he was ryght
20 sory or not. And then he stroke on the ryght hond and on
the lefte honde, so far furth that he, with the helpe of the
kyng of Irlond, made a grete voyde place; and anoon he
lyght doune and helped his maystre vpp, and asked hym
howe he dyd. And he said, " Wele "—so that he wer revenged
25 vppon hym that had gyven hym that. "And what is he?"
said Surdyte. " It was Corbatan the kyng of the oste."
"Ser, doute ye not," said Surdyte. " I wolle dye, bot.if I
son revenge you." Then was the kynges son sett vpon hors
bak and putt furth of (the) prese.

30   And then Surdyte associate hym with C men or moo, and
behelde the gonfanoune of the kyng Corbatan and went that
way, and stroke on euery side thwarton and endway, and
brake the prese and sawe the kyng, which did mervellously
with his hondes and was rychely armyd and had a ryche

---

[1] R, dura la b. tant qui heure de tierce. W omits.
[2] W, a spere grete & sparte (?). R, une espee grosse et court.

croune of golde vpon his hede. Surdyte said vnto hym, "Ay,
false Saresyn, thou shall goo no ferther, which has hurtt my
maistre." Then he come vnto hym and smote hym with all
*his myght, that he astouned hym and made hym to fall vpon
5 the arson of his sadle; and then Surdyte smote hym agane
vndre the lasys of his helmete so strongly that he smote of
his helmete and his hede with all.

And then he toke the hede and bar itt to his maistre oute
of the prese. And as sone as he sawe itt, he said, "Blessed
10 be God, and I dye, I shal dye more ioyfully; and graunte
[*Fol. 186.] marcy,"[1] said he, "to Surdyte." "Ser," * sayd he, "thinke
not to dye, for ye shall see within a while thes Saresyns dyscomfeted, seyng that theyr kyng is deid."

And he said sothe; for as sone as they wyst that theyr
15 kyng was deyd noon of theym stode at defence, bot were sory
and abasched, and began to dyscomforth theym self. And
Surdyte entred into the presse and began to doo fayr fetes of
armes, and to reioyse his felleschipp, and to thrawe doune
Saresyns; and faght so mervellously that all men knewe hym
20 by the grete strokes that he gave. So they fled all afor hym, as
doos the hayres afor the grehoundes,[2] and toke theym all to
gedre as they that were oute of array, and fled by the contre
as bestes.

And then ye myght see Englisch, Scottysch, and Iresch, men
25 showte and crye strongly vpon theym, and sloo theym vpon
euery side, so that the feld lay full of deyd bodys. The
Saresyns wyst not whethir to flee, ne wher to hyde theym.
Ther wer mony that fled to theyr shippes; bot Surdyte and
the Englisch pursued theym son, that they myght flee noo
30 ferther; and then they wer cast into the see. There was grete
slaghtre.

And Surdyte come to a shipp and entred into itt, and spake
Latyn, and asked where the shipp was that the kyng was in
and his tresour. Then a Saresyn shewed hym the shipp and

---

[1] R, *grant merci.* W, *grammercy.*
[2] R, *comme le lieure fait deuant les chiens.* W, *as shepe before the wolfe.*

went oute with hym into itt, which was grete, faiř, and large,
and wele stuffed, that it was mervell to see. And theř weř
sume in the shipp that wold a[1] defended theym; and Surdyte
leid hond on his sworde and sloo all theym that was therin,
5 save thre Saresyns that come in with hym—the whiche said
they wold be cristened, by cause that Mahounde soffred so
mony to dye. And they wer cristened; and Surdyte yeave
theym myche goode. Then said oon of the Saresyns, "Ser,
see ye on of yonde coffyrs and trunkes, that be full of gold
10 and syluer—the which the kyng Corbatan had wonne of
mony of the Cristen people in mony realmes, iles, and contrees—so myche that itt is mervell to see?" And the Cristen
lordes toke vesselles and shippes, for theř weř the noumbre
of ix C sales. They had mony grete wynnyngges, wherof they
15 weř all ryche.

And Surdyte delyuerd his shipp to suche as he trusted best,
and badd theym bryng itt to London; for he thoght theř to
yeve to sawdeoures, to men of armes, and archers, for to goo
into his contrey of Spayne, that the Saresyns keped in seruage.
20 Notwithstondyng, he gave so grete gyftes that euery man mervelled for the grete largenes.

The nyght passed—it was on a tuysday—and on the wedynsday the[i] serched the feld to fynde the Crysten that were
slayn. And theř they fonde the kynges twoo sonnes, the Erle
25 of Wales,[2] the Erle of Gloucestre, twoo barounes,[3] and aboute
xl[4] knyghtes, and ij[MI] comons. Sum weř led into theyř contrey and the remenaunt weř buryed in a white[5] abbey.

The kyng, the quene, and all the contrey had grete ioy of
the victorye that they had. And they said all that the good
30 knyght Surdyte was the chief cause of all; for had not God
and he ben, they had loste the feld. So he had the lavde and
the prise.

[1] Undoubtedly a colloquialism for *wold haue.*
[2] W adds, *the baron of staunford.* R, *staffort.*
[3] R, *trois autres barons.* R, *thre other barons.*
[4] R, *bien cinquante.* W, *.XII.*
[5] W omits. R, *en une abbaye blanche.*

Bot sorowe and wepyng was theᵽ myche for the kynges
twoo sonnes that weᵽ deyd. The kyng, the quene, the ladys
and lordes made grete chere and thonkyng to Surdyte, and
Śeyd, by hym they had ouercomen theiᵽ enemes. Surdyte
5 weped when he sawe the kyng wepe for his maistre; bot the
kyng toke hym to comforth and said, that in more mery ne
in bettre seruice myght he not dye, then in the seruice of God
and in defendyng of his contrey agancs the Saresyns.

Itt taryed not long bot that he assemelyd his councell.
10 And theᵽ was the kyng of Scottes, his brothre, the kyng of
Cornewale, his nevewe, and all his lordes. And the kyng
[*Fol. 186ᵇ.] said, " Faiᵽ * Seris, ye see the mervelles that be comen to this
londe, and howe I haue lost my two sonnes. I be olde, and
the quene is not yonge; so we must devyse who may haue
15 this roialme aftre, and who sall gouerne itt in myn age."
The kyng of Scottes stode vp, and said, " I haue wedded youᵽ
sustre and ye haue wedded myn; so ye owe to holde me as
youᵽ brothre. I wold councell you to yeve youᵽ dignite to
Surdyte; for then ye shall be dovbted and dred, and youᵽ
20 roialme worshipped and wele gouernyd."   And then they
answerd all with oon voice, that the consell was goode; and
the kyng accorded therunto.

And the kyng of Scottes, desyryng to wytt the wyll of
Surdyte, said vnto hym, " Surdyte, ye ought to thonke God,
25 for ye be faiᵽ and welebeloued of all people; for the kyng
and his lordes has chosen you to haue his doghtre, and to be
kyng aftre hym—and in his live to gouerne his roialme."
" Ser," said Surdyte, " God thonke the kyng and all theym
that wolle me goode and suche worshipp. It is bot febly
30 counselled, for it longes not to a kynges doghtre, and suche
an heirytoure, to haue suche oon as I am, and of so lowe lyn-
nage; and Gode forbede, that as by me shuld be lowed the
bloode riall."   " What is itt that ye say?" said the kyng.
" We be all comen of oon fadre and modre. And mor ouer,
35 theᵽ be so myche goode and worshipp in you that ye be
worthie to haue a grettre."   So they spake myche to gedre of

this mateẜ. Bot the kyng of Scottes myght neueɼ fynde in hym any wyll that he wold assent, for he made so faiẜ excusacions that it was meruell to heẜ.

And when he sawe that he myght not bryng itt aboute, 5 he retourned to the kyng and to the counsell, and said to theym the answeẜ that he had, and how that he thonked the kyng and his counsell, and wysely and worshipfully excused hym. "Truly," said the kyng, " he is maried, or has betravthed sume lady, for ye may heẜ that is hertt is sett on 10 sume womman." "Truly," said they all, "we trowe he be maryed or travthe-plyght."

The kynges doghtɼe was ryght sory that she myght not haue [hym]. "Truly," said she, "I see wele that his hertt is sett in sume othre place, or elles he is wedded." She com- 15 plenyd myche in hiẜ hertt and sorowed, for aboue all men lyvyng she loued hym the best.

Nowe leve we of Surdyte and of the courte, and retourne we to Sydone and to the kyng of Bretan.

[Cap. XXV. How Guenelete, that made hym maistre aboute 20   the kyng of Bretayn, wold lete marye Sydone vnto the kyng of Burgone. And how Sydone toke terme vnto the Whissontyde at the seuen yeres ende. How Herland sent his sonne Oliver to serche all contrees for Ponthus, and he found hym in the courte of Englond.

25 When Ponthus had taken his leve of Sydone and taken his shipp to passe oueɼ the see, itt is noo question bot Sydone had grete sorowe day and nyght; bot she keped itt so secrete that noo man wyst therof bot Ellyous, the whiche comforthed hiẜ gretly. Sydone said in hiẜ lamentacion : "Allas! 30 for my sake is goon the best and the fayrest of the world."

So itt happened that Guenelete had all his desire and was all maistre aboute the kyng. He was so flateryng and so faiẜ spoken that he putt Herland oute of his office, and made (the) kyng his heuy lorde;[1] and he laboured so that he had the kyng and all the courte in gouernaunce.

Sydon was desyred of mony kynges and dukes. And among all othre, the kyng of Burgone hard say, and was reported to 5 hym by the Erle of Mounte Belyard his cosyn, that Sydon was the fairest and the wysest that any man knewe. Then was the kyng of Burgon so amerous that he myght not endure, bot if he myght haue hiꝛ loue. He desyred to knowe by whome the kyng was gouernyd and in whome he traysted moste; and 10 men told hym it was a knyght called Guenelete. And anoon he sent to hym grete gyftes, that he shuld labre to the kyng [*Fol. 187.] of Bretane for hym. And Guenelete was * covetous and spake to the kyng and said, "Ser, lete marye youꝛ doghtre, while ye be in hele—and ye shall alie you with sume goode 15 kyng, and then doo ye wysley. Loo heꝛ the kyng of Bur- gone desires to haue hiꝛ! He is a worthie, and a ryche, kyng. Itt weꝛ folye to refuse hym."

Guenelete said and did so myche, that the kyng spake to his doghtre, and sayd, "Faiꝛ doghtre, I be olde and feble and 20 I haue noo child bot you, and ye be desyred of mony kynges and grete lordes. And I haue herd say 'He that reson refuses, reson wolle goo fro hym; and so he myschevys wyllfully;'— wherof God defende that in this case itt be so doon. Faiꝛ doghtre, the kyng of Burgone desires you, whiche is nevyewe 25 to the kyng of Fraunce, and he is a myghtey, ryche kyng. Me semes he oghte not to be refused; and as for me, if it please you, I accorde therto." "My Lorde," said she, "as yitt is noo nede forto be maried." "Truly," said the kyng, "ye haue so ofte tymes chalanged,[2] and I wot not wherfor; bot I 30 shall (neuer) love[3] you, bot if ye agree you to hym."

---

[1] R, *le* [Herlant] *fist mal du roy.* W, *heuylorde.* What is a *heuylorde?* Per- haps "a displeased, unresponsive, master." This would tally roughly with R.

[2] R, *vous mauez tant calenge.* W, *ye haue so longe forborne.*

[3] MS. *leve.* R, *ameray.* W, *I shall neuer loue you.* The context shows clearly that the reading of W is the original.

She was gretly abasshed of hiꝛ fadre wordes, that weꝛ so
harde to here. Then said she, " My Lorde, ye wot wele that
theꝛ is noo thyng that ye commaunde me bot that I wolle
doo itt. My swete Lorde, I wolle say to you in counsell that
5 I haue a grevaunce and a dysease in me that I dare not tell
you, bot itt wolle be Whyssonday or I be hole, and then I
shall fullfyll your commaundement." " Wele," said the kyng,
" itt suffices me and that terme I wolle yeve you."

And the same Wytsontyd was the ende of the vij yeres
10 comen oute, that was promysed betwen Sydone and Ponthus.

The kyng held hym pleased, and told Guenelete the terme
that she had taken. Guenelete said that itt was wele, and sent
to the kyng of Burgone, and did so myche, that the day of
the mariage was sett the tuysday aftre Whyssontyde.

15   Sydone was passyng sory and sent mony tymes to herkyn
of Ponthus and myght here noo glad tithynges of hym, by
cause that he had chaunged his name. She was in grete
sorow day and nyght. And when the tyme approchied, she
was gretly abasshed, and sent for Herland, and sayd, " My
20 true frende, I mervell mych of my lorde my fadre, that he is
so fonde of Guenelete—and in suche wyse that he has made
hym doo mervellous dedes, as to putt you oute of youꝛ office ;
and also by his fals wyles he caused the best and the manliest
knyght of Cristeantie to departe oute of the contrey,—that is
25 Ponthus, whiche ye noryshed and taghte thre yeres, whiche
ye louc so wele ;—and mony vyolente[1] dedes he has caused
my fadre to doo, as he that is so grete a flatereꝛ, and as
deccyvcable as euer was man ; and in like wyse he caused me
to be gyven to the kyng of Burgone ; agane my wyll—for itt
30 is tolde me that he is evyll condicioumed, fatt, olde, scabbyd,
and frentyke. Bot I may not refuse the commaundement of
my fadre ; and so I haue taken terme vnto the tuysday aftre

---

[1] MS. *vyolence*. R, *villains fais*. W, *shamefull thynges*. *Vyolence* myght be a
corruption of R's reading, but probably the original was that of O, *vaillans
fais*, which myght well have confused the translator, and have led to the
rendering in our text.

Whissontyde. And I wote wele, and Ponthus knewe itt, he
wold putt a remedy therin; and in trouthe theꝛ be noo man
in this worlde that I wolde haue dysclosed my counsell to bot
to you."

5 " Ma dame," said Herland, "God defend that he cause you
to haue any husbond ayeinst youꝛ wolle, or any that has so
evyll taches and manᴇrs. I shall tell you Ma dame,—Oliveꝛ,
my sonne, be oon of the kynghtes that Ponthus most louys;
and he shall goo into Englond, Scottlond, and Irlonde, and
10 all aboute, and if he live, he shall make hym to come to
you." "Ay," said she, " In goode faithe, ye say wele." And
anoon Herland spake to his son of this mateꝛ, whiche went
with full goode wyll.

ᵒl. 187ᵇ.] And Sydone and Herland charged Oliveꝛ with the message
15 and gave hym money enughe for his dyspenses. Aud * he
passed the see and come to Hampton. And he enquered and
fonde wele, that vij yere afor that tyme theꝛ come a knyght
into Englond—the fairest and the best named in worshipp,
and he chaunged¹ his name and called hym Snrdyte de Droyte
20 Voye. Then Sᴇr Oliveꝛ thoght that itt was Ponthus by the
signes that he harde, and said to hym self that he chaunged
his name for sume cause.

And he and his yomen went furthe, and as they come by a
wodde, they mett with thevys; and by cause they knewe not
25 his langueege and sawe hym rychely arrayd, they ran vpon
hym and toke frome hym all that he hade and hurted hym;
and he escaped and went fro theym into the wodde to save
his live. And theꝛ he soffred hungre and pouᴇrtie, dysease—
and almost naked. So he wayled and sorowed, for he founde
30 noo comforth of his dysease; bot his tarryng and lettyng
greved hym more then dide all his losse and disease. Bot as
sone as he myght, he passed the forest and went sekyng his
bred for the loue of Gode fro dore to dore, vnto the tyme

¹ This lapse into the writer's point of view is only in D. R, *Et se nommoit.*
W, *but he named hym.* But probably the scribe's eye caught *chaunged* from the
passage below.

that he come vnto the kynges courte, that same [day], at the
aftre noon, that the kyng of Scottes spake vnto Surdyte for
the mariage of Geneꝛ.

And then Surdyte was at the courte wheꝛ as he beheld the
5 dysportes of yong gentylmen that dyssported theym in dyuers
maners. Ser Oliveꝛ, the son of Herland, come into the courte
almust naked and dysspoled, and as he loked aboute, he sawe
Ponthus and knewe hym. Anoon then he come befor hym,
knelyng doune, and said, "My Lord Ponthus, God yeve you
10 good grace and long live and encrese you in the worshipp
that ye be in." Ponthus, a litle abashed and alf asshamed,
said to hym; "My frende to whome speke ye?" "Ser, said
he, "I speke vnto you, for I knowe wele ye be the kynges
son of Spayne, that has forgetyn the contree of Bretane. And
15 if I be pouere and naked, I be the son of Herland—Oliveꝛ,
which ye sum tyme loved wele; and I be comen to seke you."

And when Ponthus hard that he knewe hym wele, he did
from hym his mantell and cast itt vpon hym and toke hym
in his armes and kyssed hym, wepyng, and myght speke no
20 worde to hym. And then he led hym into the chaumbre and
lenyd bothe vpon a beddes syde. And when he myght speke,
he said, "Ay, swete trusty frende and brothre, how doo they
in that contrey, and who dysspoyled you thus?" And he
said that he had mett with thevys. Grete wepyng was betwen
25 theym twoo. And Ponthus did array hym newe with the
beste arayment that he had; and when he was fully arrayd,
he semed a full faiꝛ knyght to see. And then he told hym
what p[er]elle he was in, among thevys, and howe he escaped
and begged his brede fro dore to dore; and told also that
30 Guenelete had all the covrte in revoll, and that þe[1] kyng
loued hym most of any man, and howe he had putt oute his
fadre fro his office; and aftre told hym howe Sydone wold
not assent to noo mariage, and of the grete dysease that she
had soffred,—and att the farthrest, she myght not lengeꝛ
35 abide vnmaried, bot to the tuysday aftre Whitsontyd, and

---

[1] Entered in a different hand above the line.

that then she shuld be maryed to the kyng of Burgon, the
which be full evyll condiciouned,—"bot Guenelete causes
itt, for he has taken myche gold of hym. Sydone sendes to
you prayng you to sett a remedye therin, for all the loue that
5 be betweyn you twoo." And when Ponthus herd the grete
loue and travthe of his lady, the teres fell doune from his
eyne; and said, and God wold vouchesaue, that he wold
[*Fol. 188.] (sett) a remedy therin. So they spake enughe * to gedre of
mony thynges.

10 [Cap. **XXVI.** How Ponthus retorned to Litle Bretayn; and
there he chaunged gounes with a pouere pylgreme, and
went to the feste of the kyng of Burgone and of Sydone.
How Sydone gaue drynk to hym, as to a pouere man,
and she knewe hym by the ryng that he lete fall into
15 the cupp. How Ponthus come dysgysed to the iustyng
wheᵽ as of aventure he slewe the kyng of Burgone.]

The tithynges come thorow oute the courte that theᵽ was
comen a man fro Litle Bretan that knewe Ponthus,
which named hym self Surdyte. When the kyng and the
20 courte herd this, they had mych mervell, and the kyng said
to the quene and to the kyng of Scottes, "Me thoght euer
that he was of hygheᵽ degre then he said he was, for the
noble dedes that he dyd and for the goodnes of hym." "Ay,"
said the quene, "I mervell not thogh he wolle not take ouᵽ
25 doghtre in maryege, for I haue herd say that he loues ouᵽ
cosyn Sydon of Bretan withouten any vyllanye." "Truly,"
said the kyng, "it may wele be, when he wolle not marye
hym self in this contrey."

When they went to soppeᵽ, Ponthus come into the hall
30 and his knyght with hym, which was ryght wele arrayd with
riche clothes of sylk furryd with sables, and he was ryght
faiᵽ to see. The kyng of Englond and the kyng of Scottes
went ayeinst hym. And then he said to Ponthus, "Wherfor
haue ye so long celed you frome vs, and said that ye weᵽ a

pou*ere* knyght sonne, and ye be a kynges son ? Thus we be
dysceyved and has not doon to you the worshipp that we
ought to doo to you ; bot ye be worthie to haue the blame,
for in good faith, we haue not doon itt bot of ignorance."
5 And when Ponthus sawe the gentyllnes of the kyng, he said,
"All thogh it be so, that I be a kynges son, it is bot litle
worth ; for a man dysheryte ought full litle to p*rase*[1] hym
selfe." "Ay," said the kyng, "save you*r* bettre advice, (he)
that has the noblenes, wytt, beautie, and bountie—with the
10 goode maners and the worthenes that is in you, is more worth
than a reaume ; for ye be aquanted with goode frendes, that,
by the grace of Godde, ye may conque*r* you*r* awn agane, and
mony othre." Ponthus was asshamed therwith and turned
the tayle into an othre matie*r*.

15   The kyng made hym to sytt betwen the quene and his
doght*re*, whethre he wold or not. Aftre soppe*r* they went to
dyssporte theym in a garthyn. Ponthus come to the kyng
and sent for the kyng of Scottes, for the kyng of Irlond,
for the kyng of Cornewale, and for mony othre lordes and
20 barounes ; and they sett theym in an herbe*r*. And then
Ponthus sayd, "My Lorde, and all my lordes, and frendes,
I wold make a request of a thyng that I haue doon."[2] And
said, howe the sowdeyn sonnes has wered vpon the Cristen,
and by the g*race* of God two of theym we*r* distroyed ; and
25 howe the thirde revoled hym in his contrey of Spayne—
and by engyne entred into the londe and scaled the citee
of Colloigne ; and tolde theym the myschief that the londe
stode in ;—and howe his fadre was slayne ; and howe that
a goode prest that taghte hym and xiij childre, and[3] hyd
30 theym in a cave moo then[3] two days withouten mete or

---

[1] R, *se doil pou priser.*

[2] R, *une requeste de mon fait,* is mistranslated by D, correctly rendered by
W,—*of a nedefull mater of myne.*

[3] MS. *And moo had then in a cave theym.* R, *Et les cela deux iours.* W, *hydde.*
The emendation will appear violent, but it all follows from the substitution
of *hyd* for *had.* I interchange *theym* and *moo then,* the illogical *and* at the
head of the clause is allowed to stand, for such constructions are not un-
common in the text.

drynke; and as the wolfe goos oute of the wodd for hungre, so the xiij went oute of the cave and weꝛ taken as son as they went oute; and howe the knyght saued theym. And also he told howe the shipp brake ayeinst a rokkete of the 5 see; and how they arrived in Litle Bretan; and all the maner howe they weꝛ saved. And as he told his tale, the teres ran doune frome mony of the lordes eyen, to heꝛ the perell and the sorowe that they had escaped.

And when that he had tolde theym all the matieꝛ, he said 10 that he wold goo into the contrey of Spayne to conqueꝛ his awn ryght, by the grace of God,—"for I thonke hym I haue ben in the fellyschipp of theym that has dystroyed twoo of the sowdeyn sonnes; so theꝛ be noon of lyve bot the thirde, [*Fol. 188ᵇ.] whiche holdes the roialme that shuld be myn. And I vndre- 15 stond that the roialme is wele and wysly gouerned, * and that they haue slayne bot fewe people; for they be made tribu- torye and euery hede pays a besaunt of gold, and for the grete goode that they pay, they soffre euerych of theym to holde and to kepe the lawe that theym best likes." "Ser," 20 said the kyng, "I offre me with all myn hertt to goo with you, althogh I be olde, with my people and my goode." "Ser," said Ponthus, "God yeld it you."

The kyng of Scottes and the othre kynges, erles, and barounes, offred theym to goo with hym. And Ponthus 25 thonked the kynges and the lordes of theiꝛ goode and grete worshipp that they offred hym, and said that he wold haue noon bot men of armes and souldioures, aboute the noumbre of xijᴹᴸ·,—"the whiche I wolle wage, for I thonke God I haue god enughe." And he said sothe, for at the last batell 30 he founde enughe in Corbatan shippes—so myche that itt was grete mervell to see, for he had grete payne to noumbre itt. And wold noo thyng take bot the best knyghtes and men oꝛ armes, aboute the noumbre aboue said. And ordaned ship- pyng and sowded theym, so that they held theym plesyd and 35 they had ioye to goo with hym. Also he desired to haue the Erle of Gloucestre, the Erle of Richemound, the Erle

of Darby, to be captaynes of the Englyschmen—and they
graunted with goode wyll—the Erle of Darsy,[1] the Erle of
Dace,[1] for the Scottes, and he had an erle of euery contrey
forto warne[2] the people of the contrey.

5   And then they toke leve of the kynges and of the lordes
and went to shipp and pulled vp their sales and departed
with grete ioy fro the porte of Hampton. And the kyng
desired that he shuld come agane as sone as he myght. And
he thonked hym of the grete worschip that he had doon hym.
10 The kyng of Scottes, the kyng of Irlond, and the kyng of
Cornewale convehed theym to shipp and toke theyr leue, full
sore wepyng. And the kyng of Irlond said vnto Ponthus,
"Ay fair frende, now see I wele that ye loue me not, sith that
ye haue doon me so myche goode that I ne all my reaume
15 may not deserve itt, and now wolle not let me goo with you
to helpe you." "Ser," said Ponthus, "God thonke you. I
refuse not your helpe, aftre that I haue uede in my iourney,
bot I wolle not haue you with me as nowe, ne noon of myn
othre lordes, vnto the tyme that I knowe the maner of the
20 contrey—and for othre certan causes. Then they kyssed to
gedre and toke leve aythre at othre.

Thus departed Ponthus and his armye fro the costes of
Englond and saled day and nyght vnto the tyme that they
come neghe to Vennys. And then he ordaned his grete navie
25 to abide in the highe see, and said that he wold that ther
were asspyed no moo bot xv[3] shippes, and that they shuld
make theym like marchaundes of salt, to come into the towne.
So he ordaned full wele his dooyng, and toke certayn vesselles
with hym, in the which wer iij C wele fightyng men; and made
30 theym to londe be nyght in a grete wodd betwyn Amroy[4]
and Vennys; and charged theym that they shuld not be farre
of, vnto the tyme that they had tithynges fro hym, and that

---

[1] R, Le conte dars et le sire de Duglas, nothing is said about the Scots.
W mentions only—Of the scottes the Erle of Douglas.

[2] R, gouuerner. W, gouerne.

[3] R, xl. W, a forty.   [4] R, roye. W, Auroy.

they shuld come when they weꝛ sent for. This was the moneday in Whitsontyde, and the tuysday shuld be the weddyng
of Sydone and of the kyng of Burgone.

Ponthus leped to hors and toke bot a yoman with hym.
5 The tuysday erly, as he rode, he founde a pylgreme that had
his govne sved full of patches and a cappe full of broches.
And anoon he lyght donne and said to the pylgreme, "Frende
we wolle chaunge ouꝛ govnes and I wolle haue your cappe
and ye shall haue myn." "Ay Ser," said the pylgreme, "ye
10 scorne me." "In goode faith, that doo I not," said Ponthus.
[*Fol. 189.] And * so they chaunged. And Ponthus did vpon hym the
pylgreme govne, his hatt, and his hosen; and toke the Burdone that he baꝛ in his honde. And his yoman said vnto
hym, "Ser, ye be oute of youꝛ wytt. Why chaunge ye youꝛ
15 riche array with this pouere clothyng?" "Hold thy peace,"
said Ponthus, "and holde thes twoo horses att the tounes
ende, and remeve not vnto the tyme that I come to the."

And then he went furth his way wheꝛ as the kyng of Burgone was; and anoon aftre he sawe his somers and his horses
20 come with his officers; and aftre he sawe the kyng rydyng
on a palfrey all blak. And the kyng and Guenelete rode
talkyng to gedre. As they rode furth, Ponthus said to theym,
"Loo heꝛ be twoo wele noryshed !—for bothe twoo has goode
fatt belles, and wele fed. Ay Sainte Mary !" said he to Guene-
25 lete, "youꝛ bellye has getten mony fatt soppys of courte."[1]
Guenelete waxed rede for shame and was full wroth and
turnyd his hors and said, "Beggaꝛ, what says thou?" and
was aboutward to smyte hym with a tronchon that he baꝛ in
his honde. And Ponthus turned his burdone and said that
30 he shuld make his berd,[2] and he tovched hym. Then the
kyng of Burgone said to Guenelete, "Leve ye this trowane,
for ye can haue no worshipp of hym." And so they passed
furth toward the courte. And Ponthus, that louyd theym not,
playd the foell befor theym and mokked theym as they rode.

[1] W adds with R, *ye are full well shapen to be a veray grete flaterer of the courte.*
[2] R, *dist qui lui fera sa barbe.*

7

And euer Ponthus foloed theym to they come to the courte.
And when he sawe men entre in at the gate, he folocd in
aftre theym. And the porteř wold haue putt hym oute, bot
Ponthus shote hym so fro hym that he made hym fall; and
5 said to hym that he was oon of the xiij pouere men that was
chosen. "Goo! A myschaunce come to the!" said he, "Thou
be a strong beggeř."

At that tyme itt was the custome at the weddyng of grete
astates, theř shuld be xiij pouere men ordanyd, the which
10 shuld sitt at mett befor the bride at a table by theym selfe—
in the worshipp of God and of his xij apostelles.[1] And aftre
the dynneř, she that was maryed shuld yeve drynke to eueryche
of the pouere men, in a copp of golde. And thus went Ponthus and satt doune for oon of the xiij.

15 The fest was grete and of mony dyuers seruices, Ponthus
ete bot litle and beheld ofte tymes his lady Sydone, which
was bot of simple chere, and all be-wepte; for Guenelete told
hiř that Ponthus was deyd in Irlonde—and she trowed itt
bot a litle. When the tables was taken vp, they led Sydone
20 to hiř chaumbre to chaunge hiř arayment and hiř attyre, forto
goo to the scafoldes to see the iustes and the dyssportes. And
in the comyng to hiř chaumbre theř was a gallerye, in the
which weř the xiij pouere men. And ther was ordaned twoo
gentyllwommen—that oon had a potte of syluer full of wyne,
25 that othre hade a cupp of golde—and wated vpon Sydone.
And when she come, she gave drynke to euery pouere man—
and Ponthus was the last. And as he dranke he lete fall the
ryng with the diamaunte, that Sydone yeave hym at theiř
furst aquantance, into the cupp; and when he had dronken,
30 he sayd softly to Sydone, "Madame, I pray you to drynke
this litle for the loue of Ponthus." And when she harde the
name of Ponthus, itt reiosed hiř gretly and she toke the cupp
and dranke; and in hiř drynkyng she sawe the ryng a[nd]

[1] This custom of having poor men at thé feast is dismissed with a word in
W, nor is the reason for the custom given. The description in the text
follows R literally.

knewe itt wele anoon and was ravysshed for ioye, so that she
wyst not wele what she dyd. And then she called hiꝛ damesell
Ellious and said to hiꝛ in counsell, that she shuld lede the
grete pouere man aftre hiꝛ into hiꝛ warderopp; and so she
5 led hym with hiꝛ. And thos othre pouere men demyd that
she wold yeve hym sum maner of gyftes for the loue of God.

And when she was in hiꝛ warderopp, and noo moo with
[*Fol. 189ᵇ.] hiꝛ bot he and Ellyous—and he * was dysgysed, that noo
man myght knaw hym—with grete payne Sydone spake furst
10 and said, "Swete frende, who betoke you thys ryng that I
fonde in the cupp?" "Wote ye not," said he, "to whome
ye gave itt?" "Yis," said she, "ryght wele. Bot is he deid
or on live?—I pray you tell me truly." Said he, "He is on
live, Madame, trowed ye that he was deid?" "Yea, sothely,"
15 said she, "for Guenelete and mony otheꝛ told me so." "And
if ye see hym, what wold ye say?" said he. "I may say,"
said she, "that I had neuer so mych ioy in my hertt, as I
shuld haue then." When he hard that, he said no more, bot
rubbed a litle his vyssage that he had peynted; and anoon
20 she knewe hym, and said, "Ay, ye be Ponthus! and ther is
noo thyng in this world that I loue more, aftre God and my
fadre." Then they had gret ioy and cleped and kyssed to
gedre.

And then he said to assey hir pacience, "Ma dame I be
25 ryght wele pleased that ye be so wele and rychely maryed."
"Ay," said she, "my swete frende, I pray you nomor therof,
for he lives not that I wolle haue, bot you, if itt pleasse you
to haue me,—the whiche I sweꝛ to you and has sworne ofte
tymes, with mouthe and hertt,—for the laste promys avayles
30 not, bot oonly the furste." "Ay Madame," said he, "thinke
ye neuer to take so pouere man, beggyng his bred, and for to
leve a ryche kyng. I shall neuer counsell you, to acquyte my
trouthe, to leve hym." Then said she, "Truly my swete
frende, I wolle neuer haue othre bot you, for I shall neuer be
35 wele att ease,—bot a thowsant tymes mor at ease to soffre in
youꝛ companye the mysease and the povertie that ye soffre,

then to haue all the ryches of the world wit*h* the myghteyst
kyng that is; for that pou*er*tie that God has sent you is bot
to assay you,—that may aftre yelde you rytches[1] and worshipp double folde if ye putt holle you͠r trust to hym.

5   When Ponthus hard the grete trouthe and stedfastnes of
hi͠r, the teres fell doune from his eeyn, and aftre he smyled
a litle, and said, "Madame, by my trouthe the͠r was neu*er*
fonde a bettre, a faire͠r, ne a more stedfaste lady then ye be;
and sith I see you͠r grete trauthe, I wolle hyde no thing
10 frome you no lenge͠r. For I tell you for trouthe, that I haue
more gold and sylu*er* and *precious* stones viij[2] tymes told,
than eu*er* had my fadre; and also I haue xij^Ml men of armes,
sowded and payd for alf a ye͠r, forto goo and conque͠r my
contrey that was my fadres. And dysmay you not for I shall
15 tell you what ye shall doo; ye schall goo to the scafoldes to
see the iustes and ye shall take with you Pollides my cosyn,
and my fellawes, so that the[i] be aboute you; and itt shall
not be long bot I shall see you. I may no lengre tarrye with
you." Then they kyssed[3] and dep*ar*ted.

20   And he went furth haltyng and come to his yoman, that
abode hym, and toke his hors and rode to the wodd whe͠r he
had lefte his people. And when they sawe hym, they knewe
hym not; and they went to haue taken hym for a spye. Bot
he began to laghe and said, "I am Ponthus;" and then they
25 knewe hym. And the Erle of Gloucestre said, "S*er*, ye had
almost doon you a vylleny. How be ye thus dysgised?"
"S*er*," said he, "I haue doon itt for a cause that I wold not
be knawne." And then he sett theym in ordenaunce, aftre
the noumbre of xl knyghtes, all of oon suyte,—of the worthiest
30 of his companye. And he told theym his entent. ⁴And then
they come rydyng by x and by x thorow the stretes, so that
it was grete ioy to see.⁴ And then the Bretanes had grete

---

[1]An unfinished *h* is changed to *c*.   *W, *seuen*. R, *sept*.

[3]R, *Si lacole et encore ne losa baiser ne Requerre*. W, *And toke his leue and
folde her in his armes & halsed her/and yet durste not kysse no desyre for to kysse her*.

⁴This sentence is found neither in W nor in R.

mervell, and the Burgones bothe, what men they weꝛ, that weꝛ so wele armed and so wele besene.

And by that tyme Sydone was comen to the scafold with [*Fol. 190.] mony faiꝛ ladys and gentyllwommen. * And Pollides toke 5 the reyne of hiꝛ bridle and convehed hiꝛ to the scafoldes,[1]— for the whiche Guenelete was inwardly wroth, that Sydon had commaunded hym to doo so. And Sydone told Pollides that he shuld se his cosyn Ponthus. Then Pollides had full grete ioy in his hertt and told all his fellawes, and they had 10 full grete ioy in theyꝛ hertes of the tithynges.

Also it nedes not to aske whethre that Sydone was ryght ioyfull in hiꝛ hert or not. And when sche saw Ponthus so large, so wele armed, and so wele syttyng vpon his hors,— and iusted rowe by rowe, and threwe doune knyghtes and 15 horses, and brake mony sperys, and did mervellously,— Sydone waxed rede a litle for ioye and said, "Se ye hym that is armyd in purpyll and asure, and has a white ladye in his creste holdyng[2] a lyon enchyned—and the lyon has lettres of golde, whiche says 'God helpe'[3]—and has aboute xl fellawes 20 of his suyte, savyng they haue no lettres of gold;—for he with the lettres of gold is Ponthus, and the othre be his fellawes." "Ay Ma dame," said Pollides, "I knowe it wele by his rydyng and by his dedes of armes." Then Pollides schewed hym to his fellawes, the which held theym nyght[4] 25 Sydone, like as she had commaunded theym.

The kyng of Burgone come into the feld vpon a grete stede of Spayne, and he was wysly arrayd and wele armed, and he had aboute xxx[5] knyghtes of his suyte. Euerych theyꝛ speres raysed redye, and began to spuꝛ and to iuste by 30 rowe with the Bretanes that held the fest.

Then Ponthus sawe the kyng of Burgonne and dressed hym toward hym and his fellyschipp. And then they ouer-

---

[1] An erasure, some six letters long, follows *scafoldes* in the MS.

[2] MS. *holdyyng.*

[3] W misrenders,—*God helpe the fourty felawes.* R, *dieu aide.*

[4] See the glossary for the similar forms *neghtboures* and *hight.*

[5] W, *forty.* R, *xx.* O, *xxx.*

threw knyghtes and horses, so that euerych of theym were
abasshed.   The kyng of Bretan, which was on the scalfold
with the ladys and olde knyghtes, asked whoo that thoos
grete knyghtes weŕ, and what he was that had his lady in his
5 sheld, which holdes a lyon enchyned with lettres of gold,—
and has so mony fellowes of oon suyte.   And eueryche said,
they knew hym not,—"bot he doos mervelles, for he ouer-
reches noon bot that he throwes theym doune."   "See ye
not," sayd oon, "how he ouerthrowes knyghtes and horses,
10 and what mervelles he doos?"   "He is an aduersarye," said
the grete ladyes.   "Sothely he is a goode knyght," said the
Lady of Doule, the which was both faiŕ and wyse.   "I sawe
neuer knygth," said she, "doo so wele on hors bak, ne mor
like to Ponthus,—of whoes savle God haue mercy.   Amen."
15 Then said the kyng to Sydone, "Faiŕ doghtre, I wold not
the knyght met with youŕ housbond, lest he threwe hym
doune, or distroyd hym ; for his strokes be mervellous sore
and grete."   "Ser," said she, "and he be wyse, he wolle kepe
hym from hym, for he be a full hardy knyght, and ryght
20 manly."   They made grete languege of Ponthus and of his
knyghthod, bot all weŕ abasshed of hym, what he myght be.
    He tarryed not long ; bot of aventure he encountered the
kyng of Burgon and smote his hors with the spurrys and
smote the kyng myghtely in the sheld,—and the spere was
25 grete and strong, and he handeled itt as he had strenght and
hardenes enughe, and in esspeciall forto doo dedes of armes
befor his lady, which of long tyme had not seen hiŕ;—so this
stroke was so grete that he felled hym doune vppon the
crowpeŕ of his[1] stede and made hym to lose the reynes of his
30 brydle.[2]   And the horse was yong and strong and baŕ hym

---

[1] After his, sadle stands in the MS. cancelled by the rubricator.
[2] From here to the end of the paragraph D follows K literally. W shows
a curious confusion, which makes both Ponthus and the kyng attempt to leap
the pit and, apparently, both fall in,—and that other was yong and strong
and bare hym backwarde & fell into a grete pytt full of stones and Ponthus wende
for to haue lepte ouer/but they fell in so sore the kynge vndernethe all that he was
deed and his hors deed.   W omits also the final clause of the paragraph.

furth and with grete myght leped into a pytt full of stones, wenyng[1] to haue leped ouer, and fell in so mervellously, and the kyng vndre hym, that the hors was deid, and vnnes the kyng myght haue confession.

5 Burgonnes weꝛ wrothe and sorofull for theyꝛ lorde, for euery body cryed—" The Duke[2] of Burgone is deid." Pon-
[*Fol. 190ᵇ.] thus hard itt,. which roght bot * litle. And nomore dide Sydone. Ponthus and his fellawes light doune of theyꝛ horses, and went vp vnto the scafold and did vp his helme, 10 so that euery man knewe hym. And then he come to Sydon and toke hiꝛ by the honde and said, " Ma dame, ye must be my prisonner, bot ye schall haue goode prisonement." She waxed rede for shame and had more ioye then any man couthe thinke, and said, "If I shuld be prisonneꝛ, itt behoves 15 me to enduꝛ."

The kyng was comen doune of the scafold, full sory for the kynges dethe, bot when he wyst that itt was Ponthus that dide all the mervelles and that he had taken his doghtre, he had grete ioy, and said, "God has ordaned that he shall haue 20 my doghtre, and we may not gyf hiꝛ to a bettre knyght. Truly in hym be so mych worschipp that he is able to haue the kynges doghtre of Fraunce. Bot truly I wenyd that he had ben deid, as sume men made me to vndrestond." Then he came toward Ponthus, his armys spredyng, and said that he 25 was right welcome. And Ponthus bowed doune to hym and said, "As Gode live, God yeve to you my souerene lorde, as ye haue of me, grete ioye." Then the barounes and the ladyes both made myche of hym. And his cosyn Pollides and his othre fellowes welcomed hym with grete ioye. And Guene-30 lete made grete ioye in his countenaunce, bot not in his hertt. The people of the contrey thonked God and said, " God has

---

[1] After wenyng a superfluous to haue is cancelled by the rubricator.

[2] Elsewhere always Kyng, but R and H have consistently le Duc. W, ye newe wedded kynge is deed. R, le bruit fu que le marie estoil mort. The lapse shows pretty clearly that the original of D used Duke throughout, and that the change to Kyng in D and W is arbitrary.

sent vs a goode knyght that wolle kepe vs frome ouꝛ enemes."
Grete was the ioye of that aventure.

Ponthus keped with hym all the lordes of Englond, and so
did Sydone, and made theym grete chere—and specially the
5 Erle of Gloucestre, that was a full goode knyght. And asked
hym how his cosyn the kyng fared. The Erle said, "Ryght
wele, blessed be God;" and told the kyng of the mervelles
and of the aventures of the kyng of England;—and how
by Ponthus he toke and ouercome the kyng of Irlond;—and
10 how he toke hym among his men and baꝛ hym away, whethre
he wold or noo;—and how he raunsouned hym not bot made
peace betwen theym;—and howe that by Ponthus was sleyn
the son of the sawdeyn, called Corbatan, and theꝛ was so myche
tresour with hym that itt was mervell to here tell therof, for
15 he had not cessed xij yeꝛ afore to pyll the iles of Cristendome
that he myght ouercome. Also he told hym howe Ponthus
named hym Surdyte de Droyte Voy, and said he was bot a
pouere knyght son. When the kyng herd that he named hym
soo, [he thoght it was]¹ by cause itt was putt vpon hym, that
20 he lovyd in vylanye, and the surenome that he toke was by
cause that he offred hym to fyght with ij or with iij in the
quarell, and myght not be soffred. Also the Erle told hym
howe the kyng of Engloud offred to hym Geneꝛ his eldest
doghtre, and to be kyng (of) Englond aftre his discesse, and
25 duryng his live to be honored of all the reaume;—and how
he disprased hym selfe and wold not thereof;—and howe by
a knyght that was evyll clethed he² was known—and that
was Oliveꝛ the son of Herland;—aud howe the kyng and all
the courte was asshamed that they had doon hym no mor wor-
30 shipp, sith that he was a kynges son.

Itt did the kyng of Bretan myche goode to here hym, and
yitt more goode to his doghtre, and to the barounes that there
were; for it was a noble thyng to here of. And aftre the
Erle had said, the barounes come to the kyng, and said, "Seꝛ,

---

¹ R, *Si pensa que cestoit pour ce quil, etc.*
² R, *qui estoit tout nu.* W, *a naked knyght.*

what thinke ye to doo? Lete hastely speke to Ponthus to
take youꝛ doghtre, and so shall ye and youꝛ contrey be keped
in peace; for we doute vs gretly that he wolle not take hiꝛ,
because of the kynges doghteꝛ of Englond, for itt is myche
5 bettre mariege then this is; also he has so grete tresouꝛ that *
he settes not by noo daungerous lordes." Sayd the kyng, "I
pray you all to thinke theron for ther be noo thyng that I
desire so myche—for theꝛ fell neuer grettre goode to me, ne
worshipp." Then the barounes spake to gedre; and the
10 Vicounte of Leon was charged with the matieꝛ; and he went
to Ponthus and said full wysely, howe he had furst ben savyd
in Bretan, and howe the kyng loued hym wele, and howe by
lies and envye the kyng had ben wroth with hym, and howe
that the kyng is olde and beleved a tale lyghtly—and that
15 theꝛ is noo body bot that he has sume tache,—and that the
kyng with all the wyll of his londe offred hym his doghtre,
and to be kyng aftre hym. Ponthus, the which desyred noon
othre thyng, said, God yelde itt the kyng and all his londe;
and that he is the furst lorde that so myche goode and wor-
20 shipp did hym; and that he myght neuer deserve itt vnto
hym; thogh he weꝛ of havyng and of pusaunce to haue the
myghtiest lady of the worlde, he wold (not) take hiꝛ—to
refuse Sydone; and that he is beholden to the kyng, to the
barounes, and to the contrey, aboue all othre people. The
25 barounes had grete ioye of the answeꝛ and told the kyng
therof, and he was ryght glad.

Then he sent for the byschop and lete hondfest theym.
And the monday aftre was the weddyng. And it nedes not
to aske if Ponthus and Sydone weꝛ glad, and an hundreth
30 tymes more then they made semblaunce. Grete ioye theꝛ was
thorowe oute all Bretane of this assemble.

Ponthus, which was wyse, keped not to be blamed of noo
man. He excused hym to Guy Burgonne, the kynges brothre
of Burgonne, and to the Erle of Mounte Belliard, the which
35 weꝛ comen thedre, and said to theym that he was full sory of
that aventure that befell, of the kynges dethe ;—" for sothly

[*Fol. 191.]

when I iusted with hym I knewe not what he was." And
they beleved hym wele, and that itt was bot aventure of armes,
and that he myght[1] not doo thertoo.[1] And he offred hym
gretly to thcym; and on the morowe he lete ordeyn for
5 hym a full faiȝ seruice and gave iiij[2] penes sterlinges to euery
pouere man that come thedre, and they had neuer afore seen
so faiȝ an almus. So he was gretly prased; and the kynges
frendes thonked hym myche, and said that they wer myche
be-holden to hym. The bodye was embawmed and[3] chisted;
10 and theȝ was ordaued faiȝ horses to carye hym to his contree; and Ponthus convehed the corps iij[4] myles with grete
torches and did hym as myche worshipp as he couthe, notwithstondyng he was bot litle displeased with his deth. So
with grete payne the lordes of Burgonne made hym to
15 retourne, and toke leve eueryche of othre, and they prased
gretly Ponthus and said, that was a verray knyght aboue all
othre; of worthenes, larges, curtesie, and louyng God and the
chirch, noo man myght passe hym as they[m] semed varrely;
and said that God loved hym, when he ordaned hym, so wele
20 manered,[5] so wele gouerned, and vertuously disposed.

[Cap. XXVII. How Ponthus made a maundement of the
  barounes and knyghtes for to goo into Galice to conquer
  his contrey, that the Saresyns helde.]

POnthus retourned to Vennys and come to Sydone and
25   iaped with hiȝ and asked hiȝ if she weȝ oght displeased
with hym, because that he had deliueryd hiȝ of hir housbond.
And she waxed rede and said, "Ser, itt is perilous to doo dedes
of armes with you, but yitt I conne you thonke for that ye

---

[1] This idiom is also in W. It appears to mean " He couldn't have helped
it." The rendering departs from R's, et que nul ne sen deuoit en riens merueiller.
[2] W. iii. d.   R, trois esterlins.
[3] W, and layde in a chayre.   R, et porte en ung chariot.
[4] R, bien trois lieues.   W, well a .vi. myle.
[5] MS. manered hym.   Om. hym.

haue doone." "Ma dame," said Ponthus, "the thynges that
be doone may not be vndoone."

Then he went to the kyng and to the barounes, and·said,
[*Fol. 191ᵇ.] "Seris, ye haue herd say that I haue an * armye to conqueꝛ,
5 with helpe of God, my roialme, whiche the Saresyns holdes
fro me. So I wolle haue, if itt please you, sume people of youꝛ
contrey that wolle take wages, aud I wolle pay theym with
full goode wyll to All Halowe¹ day, before the honde." "Ay,
swete, faiꝛ son, ye shall not aske, bot take my people," said
10 the kyng, "at youꝛ own wyll to conqueꝛ youꝛ contrcy, and
take my tresouꝛ with you, all that I haue; and if itt please
you, I wolle conne you myche thonke to lete me goo in youꝛ
companye, for I be olde and itt shall be noo grete losse of me
—ne in bettre seruice myght I not dye, for my saule is then
15 in Godes seruice." Ponthus thonked hym then//and said,
"Att this tyme ye shall not goo, bot kepe ye this contrey; and
I wolle noon of youꝛ goodes, for God has sent me enugh for
this iourney; bot I wolle haue of youꝛ people, for I trast most
to theym afor all othre." The barounes and the knyghtes
20 had grete ioye of that iourney, and euery man desired to goo
with hym.

And he bad that euery man shuld be redy within **xx**² days
at Vennys; and he ordaned by all contres for shippes and
vitell. And that day euery man arrayd hym wele and gar-
25 nysshed theym of men in the best wise they couthe. Ponthus
said to the Barounes of Aniou and to othre neghtboures, as
to Geffray de Lazynyen and Andrewe de La Touꝛ aboue all
othre, for itt was told hym that they weꝛ comen late oute of
of the contrey wheꝛ they had bene twoo yere in were vpon the
30 Saresyns,—"Ay," said Ponthus, "they be ryght goode knyghtes
and noble men of armes, and he is wele at ease that has theym
in his companye."

Then the lettres come to theym and to mony othre of dyuers
contrees aboute. The messyngers departed. And when they
herd thes tithynges and the cause to goo vpon the Saresyns,

¹ R, a la tous sains. W, for halfe a yere.　² R, xv iours. W, .xv.

that held his roialme, they had grete ioy to goo and euery
man ordaned hym to goo to that iourney.

[Cap. **XXVIII.** Of the grete presente that Ponthus made to
Sydone on the day before the weddyng; and of his vowe
5   that he wold not marye hir vnto he had conquered agane
his reaume of Galice.]

A nd aftre, Ponthus sent for his grete shipp and lete bring
furth therof parte of the riches the day before his
weddyng. And then he sent a presente to Sydone of crounes,
10 cronocles,[1] chappeletes, gyrdles of perles and precius stones,
gybsers of purpyll with perle, furres of sables, armyns, and of
gray, and of othre i[e]welles that itt was mervell to see the
riches that theᷓ weᷓ, for they weᷓ prased to more value then
x[2] thovsand besantes of golde. The kyng said to his doghtre,
15 "Ye be not maried to a prince disherite; bot God has sent
you a goode, a faiᷓ, and a ryght noble lorde. So ye ought
gretly to thonke hym of his grace."// And aftre, he gave to
the kyng mony faiᷓ iewelles, precius stones, cuppys of gold;
and to eueryche of theym that weᷓ barounes and lordes of
20 Bretan, a gyfte of golde, aftre theyᷓ astate. And he was
gretly prased for his grete larges.

The day of his weddyng the lordes of Englond, Scotlond,
and of Irlond weᷓ nobeely arrayd, and of Bretan also, which
did hym worshipp. The feste was grete, and there was grete
25 ioye of herodes and of mynstrelles withoute noumbre, and
Ponthus gave theym grete gyftes. Ther was mony straunge
metes and drynkes. Ponthus made a vowe which was mych
spoken of, for he said thus, "Bycause the people of the courte
shuld not say that the kyng had gyven his doghtre to a man
30 withouten livelode,[3] I make myn avowe to God, that I neuer

---

[1] Coronets. See the Oxford Dict. for *cronicle* and *coronacle*. W, *sercles*.
[2] R, *xx.* W, *thyrty.*
[3] R, *terre.* W, *londe.* R adds,—*Ie voue que iamais ne coucheray en son lit
Iusques a ce que ie soye sires du royaume qui fu mon pere.* W translates literally
adding, *& crowned or elles I shall dye therfore.* To this omission, D sacrifices
the significance of the vow.

kyssed hiƿ requiryng vylleny, when I went oute of this con-
treye, ne I thoght neuer to doo othre wyse to hiƿ, then I myght
to myn awn modre." And he said that, because of the wordes
[*Fol. 192.] that the kyng said to hym when he departed oute of Bretayne.
5 When Sydone herd thes// * wordes, she had grete ioye in hiƿ
hertt and loued hym myche bettre. So that was myche spoken
of, for sume sayd that he was a trewe knyght, and sume said
that he wold not abyde so long vnmaryed, bot that he hoped
to haue sume solace of hiƿ and she in like wyse of hym. Then
10 said the kyng, " In goode faith, I be a verray coward to beleve
so lyghtely a lesyng that I haue herd.

[Cap. XXIX. How Ponthus departed from Bretayn to go
conquer his contrey; and howe he found in a chappell
the Erle of Destrue, that was his vncle, and Ser Patryk
15   that afore tyme saved hym; and how by their counsell
he wanne the grete batell and slewe the kyng Brodas
and took the toune of Colloigne; and how the land of
Galice was clensed of the Saresyns.]

The feste was grete and the kyng wold not that they had
20   noo iustys, for the aventure that the kyng of Burgonne
was deid, lest any myschief myght happen, bot he made theym
to daunce and to syng and mad mony newe dissportes// Att
nyght Ponthus come into the chaumbre of Sydone and said
to hiƿ// "Ay my swete frende, my loue and my ioye, my
25 hertt and all the sustenaunce of my live, I haue ben hasty to
the vòwe that I haue made, bot in goode (faithe),[1] I did itt for
ouƿ worshipp, for the wordes that has ben said afor this tyme.
¶ " Bot in trouthe I soffre more disease then any man on live
doos in like case, for the grete desire that I haue to be betwen
30 youƿ armes. Bot by the grace of God I shall be in shorte tyme,
for itt be oon of the grettest desires that myn hertt (has)."[2]
¶ "My swete lorde and loue, wytt ye wele that all youƿ
desiƿ be myn, ne we ought to desiƿ noo thyng bot that

<hr>

[1] W, fayth. R, en bonne foy.   [2] W, hath. R, ait.

shuld turne to goode fame; so ye haue doone ryght wele—for evyll sayers." Thus spake they enughe to gedre and aftre they clipped and kyssed to gedre and conforted aythre othre. And thus the fest lasted xv days.

5 ¶And when all was doon, he mustred his people. And the Bretanes weꝑ by estimacion iiij^Ml and v C men of armes; and of the Normanes xij C all redy—and weꝑ payd for vj monethes. Itt was a faiꝑ sight to see theym all to gedre, with the men of Englond.

10 Ponthus toke leve of the kyng and of Sydon. And by grete flaterye Guenelete laboured so that he abode with the kyng and with Sydone as gouernouꝑ of theym; and Ponthus betoke hym a grete part of his tresouꝑ to kepe. So ther was wepyng enughe at the departyng of Ponthus and of Sydone 15 and of hiꝑ gentyllwomen. Ponthus kyssed hiꝑ and betoke hiꝑ the moste parte of his tresoure to kepe.

And then he departed and went by londe and passed by Namptes and[1] yelde hym to the havyn of the toure of Dorbendelle,[1] wheꝑ as was a grete navye; for theꝑ arrived Geffray 20 de Lazynyen and Andrewe de La Toure, whiche had a grete fellishipp. And Ponthus receyved theym with grete ioye as for twoo of the best knyghtes, that he loued, and gave theym grete gyftes. And aftre arrived Guyllem de Roches and othre moo of dyuers contrees. Ponthus gave theym mony 25 grete gyftes, so that they mervelled of his grete larges and said, "He is worthie to gouerne and to conqueꝑ all the worlde by his curtesie and faiꝑ gouernaunce." And of his largenes he made to deliuer shippes to the capteyns, aftre theyꝑ people //and itt was not long to all weꝑ shipped. And itt was a faiꝑ 30 syght to see the sales to gedre, for itt semed a forest.

They had wynd att wyll and passed the Ile of Lyon.[2] When they weꝑ iiij[3] myles fro Colleyn, then Ponthus lete

---

[1] W, *& came to sable danlon & to derbendelles.* R, *Et se rendit es salles de la tour dorbendelle.*

[2] W, *yle of doloron.* Not in R. O, *lisle dauleon.*

[3] W, *a .vi.* R, *trois lieues.*

caste ancoᵽ and sayd to the captanes// "Itt behoues vs to
entre into the contrey toward Colloigne I myle or twoo thens
and lete withdrawe the navye, for I wold not they knewe
ouᵽ powaᵽ—for mony causes." So they ordaned that in the
5 begynnyug of the day they departed. And so itt was doon.
And they arrived aganes the farthre side of the toune and
[*Fol. 192ᵇ.] londed * all by nyght and then withdrewe the vesselles agane
faᵽ into the see, that they weᵽ not perceyved. And they that
weᵽ londed putt theym in a valley beside a wode and hid
10 theym in the most prevey wise that they couthe.

And then Ponthus leped on hors bak and come to the wod
·side to se wheᵽ he couth fynde any pouere man to euqueᵽ of
the gouernaunce of the contrey. And att the last he come to
a chapell ryght devoute. And a litle befor day the Erle
15 of Destrue, which was vncle to Ponthus, and Patrices the
knyght, whiche had saved Ponthus and the xiij children and
had ben fauorable to the Cristen people and abode afteᵽ the
grace of God, when he wolde delyuer the contrey,—went on
pylgremege to this chappell, by cause they wold not be aspyed
20 of the Saresyns. Whils they weᵽ theᵽ in theyᵽ prayers, so
come Ponthus rydyng by the chappell, and lyght doune of
his hors and entred into the chappell. And when he saw
twoo men knelyng on theiᵽ knees, he had grete ioy therof
and trowed that they weᵽ cristened. And when they had
25 asspyed Ponthus, they weᵽ a ferde and rose vp sodanly. And
Ponthus asked, "Who be ye? Name youᵽ selfe hardely and
tell me what lawe ye hold." Then they answerd and said,
"With Godes mercy, we wolle not forsake ouᵽ Creator, for
we be cristened." Said his vncle, "And we pray you tell vs
30 your name, for we like youᵽ fellishipp passyngly wele in ouᵽ
hertes." "In feith," said he, "my name be Ponthus, sonne
vnto the kyng of Spayne, on whoes saule God haue mercy."
And when his uncle herd that, he ranne and toke hym in his
armys and said, "Ay Lorde God, I haue nowe my desire.
35 Blessed be ouᵽ Lorde Ihesu Crist, that I thurgh his grete
grace may see you." And when Ponthus knewe that he was

his vncle and sawe the goode chere that he made hym, then
he had grete pitee and said, "By God S*er*, ye reioyse me
gretly in myn hert, and ye say me trouthe." And anoon it
waxed lyght day, that he knewe hym wele; and then they
5 caste wepyng eycn echon on othre.

The Erle said, "Ay swete frende, howe durste ye come thus,
for if ye weŕ asspyed, ye be bot deid." " Fair uncle," said
Ponthus, " I am not allone, bot I haue ryght neghe me xviij[1]
thovsand armed men, as all the floure of Englond, of Scotland,
10 of Irlond, and of Bretan, and of the contree aboute." And
when he herd that, he kneled doune and thonked God, and
said that the (countre) is all holle as itt was wonte to be
before, bot that they be tributories to the kyng Brodas. And
then he shewed hym the knyght Patrices, that had saued hym
15 and his felowes in the shipp, and told hym that he had saued
the contrey. Then Ponthus thonked hym hertely and led
hym furth to see his people. And when he sawe theym, he
had grete ioye.

"Theŕ be nomore to doo," said the knyght, "bot lete
20 ordayne youŕ battelles and putt theym theŕ as I shall tell you
in oon p*a*rtie." So they ordaned the batelles and putt thre[2]
thovsand men aside in a valey; and the remen*a*unt abode
styll, excepte v hunderith which went with Patrices into a
secrete place, into the tyme that the Saresyns weŕ issued oute
25 of the toune;—and shuld Patrices and his people come to the
toune as thogh they weŕ sent fro the kyng to kepe the toune.

And when the Erle of Destrue sawe his sonne Pollides,
which was a faiŕ knyght, he blessed hym and said, " This
assemblye be made by ouŕ Lorde Ihes*u* Criste, which has
30 gyven vs grace to fynde the ryght lorde of this contrey."
[*Fol. 193.] And then he said, " Lordes, ordayne you in array, * for I
wolle goo to the kyng Brodas and tell hym that Cristen people
be entred into the londe to pyll the contre. And then he wolle
haste hym as faste as he canne, with fewe people and withouten

---

[1] R, the same. W, .xxviii.   [2] R, iiij[m]. W, *foure th.*

ordenaunce, wherby he shall be more easly conquered. Ther
for sendes a litle balangeȓ to feche and make redy all the othre
shippes, and wheu they be comen, putt fire in sume olde hous;
and then he wolle trowe that youȓ poweȓ be not so grete as it
5 is, wherfor he wolle dysordeyn hym, withouten any ordenaunce
makyng."

Then the Erle toke his leve and departed and come to the
toune ryght erly. He come to the kyng as man affrayd; the
kyng rose vp, and he saluyd hym by Mahounde; and then he
10 said vnto the kyng, "Seȓ, the Cristen be comen to robbe and
to pyll the contrey, and they be bot a leke frome the toune."
"Be they mony?" said the kyng. "Ser, I wote neuer," said
he, "bot as faȓ as I canne vndrestond, they be into a ӎ¹
shippes." "Fye!" said he. "Be they noo moo? By Ma-
15 hounde, iu evyll tyme be they comen, so I shall tell you; for
I dremed this nyght that I become a grete, blak wolfe, and
that sett vpon me a grete, whyte grehounde and a brachete,
and the grehounde slewe me." "Ay Ser," said the Erle, "ye
shuld not beleve in dremes." "Ye say sothe," said the kyng.
20 "Goo and make to bloo trumpettes and doo crye that euery
man arme hym. So we (shall) take the fals rebawdes and
robbers on the see, whiche I shall make all to be slayne and to
be drawn at² hors tales." "Ye say wele," said the Erle,
whiche thoght that itt shuld not be so.
25 The Erle went furth and armed hym and made to crye that
euery man shuld arme hym. So euery man armed hym and
leped on hors bak. The kyng went oute armed ryght rycheley
and weut oute of the toune withouten makeng of any ordenaunce,—bot who so myght goo, went. So there went furth
30 moo then xij thovsand on hors bak beside fotemen, as archers
and alblasterers.

Ponthus had ordaned his batelles and had sett in a valey
iiij thovsand men of armes for to fall betwene theym and the
toune. And Ser Patryke come with v hunderyth men into a

---

¹ Exactly the *thre score* of W.   ² MS. *and.*

8

secrete place to wynne the toune, and he abode tyll he sawe his tyme to departe.

The kyng smote his hors with the spurres on that partie wher as he sawe the smoke and loked to the see and sawe not
5 past lx schippes, and said, "Nowe on theym! They be all shent. Theyr Ihesu Criste shall neuer helpe theym, bot they shall dye ane[1] evyll dethe." He abode not, to he was past the place where as the iiij thovsand wer. Then he beheld befor hym and sawe the grete batelles in ordenaunce. So he
10 was amervelled of this dede and went to haue withdrawn hym and to haue sett his men in ordenaunce. And yitt he ordaned so that a grete partie was in ordenaunce, for he was a wyse knyght and a hardye in armes; and as he made an ordenaunce, he herd a grete crye betwen hym and the toune
15 and sawe his men flee toward hym. Then he said, "There is noo fleyng. Rynne we vpon [theym] sharpely." So he smote his hors with the spurrys and assemelyd with the batelles. So he iusted with Geffray de Lazynyen, the whiche was not all redye, and they gave grete strokes. Bot the kyng toke
20 Geffray at a trave[r]s and ouerthrewe hym. The kyng lad hond vppon his sworde and said, "Mahounde helpe!" And the furst that he smote he ouerthrewe hym, and did mervellous dedes of armes.

The batell beganc ryght hard and sharpe. Ponthus, that
25 hade grete desire forto doo dedes of armes—in esspeciall on theym that held his roialme, he smote on the ryght syde and
[*Fol. 193b.] * on the lefte syde and bett doune Saresyns and slewe all that euer he smote. The Saresyns held theym aboute their kyng, the which slewe and manhened mony of our men. Andrewe
30 de La Tour sawe Geffray de Lazynyen on fote, that myght not lepe vp agane and was sore bressed and in grete perell; so he smote a Turke and ouerthrewe hym and toke his hors and, in despite of theym all, led hym to Geffray and said vnto hym, "Fair fellowe, lepe vp, for her be perilous abydyng on
35 fote." Geffray lepe vp and thonked hym; and when they

---

[1]An imperfect d is changed to an e.

twoo were to gedre, they made grete slaghtre of Saresyns.
And wele bestirred theym the Bretanes and the Herupoyse.
Ther was grete cry.

The kyng did bloo a trumpett and gederyd his menye and
5 gave stronge batell to our men. Ponthus loked vp and perceyved the kyng, that had slayne his fadre, and howe that by
hym mony men wer slayne, for he did grete dedes of armes
with his bodye, and was ryght richely arrayd and bar a croune
vpon his helme. Ponthus had ryght grete ioye that he had
10 founde hym and went toward hym and gave hym a grete
stroke, and the kyng smote hym agayne. So ther was stronge
batell betwen theym, for the kyng was ryght strong and of
grete hertt; bot Ponthus gave hym so mony strokes that he
mad hym all astoned and to stowpe; and then he cutted the
15 lases of his helmete, and then the kyng had bot litle strenght
to endure. And Ponthus smote hym wele with all his strenght
and smote ay to his neke vndre the helme, so that he fell doune
deid. And when his men sawe itt, they wrong theyr hondes
and wer all dyscomfeted.

20   And on that othre side the iiij thovsand men come behynd
theym and keped theym in, soo that ther escaped noone, bot
all went to the sworde. They wer all putt to dethe withouten
any mercy.

Ser Patryke went oute of his enbushement and come furst
25 with .l. armed men to gete the gate of the toune, and commaunded that the remenaunt shuld folowe aftre. So he come
to the gate, and they knewe hym wele and asked hym, howe
itt went with the kyng and his people. And he said, "Ryght
evyll."[1] Then he entered and wanne the gate and keped itt
30 to the remenaunt come to hym. Then he sett goode kepe at
the gate and bad that noo man shuld entre, vnto Ponthus
come. Then he went into the toune, sekyng houses[2] for
Saresyns, & thoo that he founde he putt theym to dethe. So
Ser Patryke went crying into the toune, "A morte Saresyns!"

---

[1] *evy* is written upon an erasure.
[2] MS. *horses.* R, *hostelz.* W, *houses.*

and, "Live¹ cristened!" The Cristen men that weꝛ in the
toune, which weꝛ in seruage and yelded truage, they made a
crosse with theyꝛ armes, and so they founde noo body that
dide theym harme—no of noo thyng that longed to theym,
5 for Ser Patryke had so ordaned. The toune was wonne, for
all men of defence were goon to the batell² wheꝛ as they weꝛ
slayne, moo then xxvij³ thovsand.

When this discomfatuꝛ was doon, the Cristen people soghte
the feldes, euery man to fynde his frende, his cosyn, and his
10 maistre. So there were not mony sleyn of grete men of name.
Of Bretane, theꝛ was found deid of barounes and of knyghtes;
—Geffray d'Auncenys and Bryan de Pounte, Roland de Cor-
quyan, Henry de Syen, Barnaby de Seynt⁴ Gyles; Herupoys,
—Huberd de Brice, Hamelyn de Mountelyes, and Eustace de
15 Lay Poys; of Petons,—Andrewe de Lay Marche, John de
Lay Garnache, and Huberd d'Argenten, and of knyghtes,—
Amaulry de Lay Forest and Henry de Basoches; and of
Mayn,—Hardenyr de Sylle and Oliveꝛ de Douncelles, and
[*Fol. 194.] of knyghtes,—Graue de Crusses, William du Sages; of Nor-
20 mandes,—* William Tesson, Guy Pamell and Piers de Villers
and othre v knyghtes moo. And of Englond and Scotelond
ther were fewe slayne, for they weꝛ in the rereward; and they
of the base marches bare the bronte, for they weꝛ in the
voward. Ponthus commaunded to take all the deid bodies of
25 the Cristen and maked theym to be buryed in the chirche
of Columpne and did ordeyn for theym all the seruice and
worshipp that myght be doon, in so myche that euery man
prased hym for his goode dedes. The Cristen people were
serched and layd to gedre, the deid on that oon syde, the hurtt
30 on that othre side.

When this was doon, Ponthus and his batelles did ryde
vnto the toune. Theꝛ was delyuered to euery lorde, aftre that
he had of men, stretes and howses, and did fynde so myche

¹ ᴍꜱ. love. R, viuent. W, lyue.   ² b written over a p.
³ R, par extimacion xxviᵐ. W, .xxv.
⁴ ᴍꜱ. Syen. W, Bernarbe de saynt Gyle. R, bernard de saint gille.

riches and vytell that the pou*erest* had enughe. It was cryed
that noo man shuld take noght fro the Cristen people of the
toune, ne doo theym noo wrong—and noo more they dide.

Ponthus rode streght to the grete chirche and offred vpp
5 his hors and his harnes and did (do) syng thre messes and
thonked Gode, weppyng, of his grace that he had sent hym.
Aftre that, the Erle his vncle and S*er* Patryk come to hym and
asked counsell what they shuld doo. And S*er* Patryke said,
"I counsell you befor all thynges, that vnto theym that has
10 any castelles or tounes iu kepyng, or fortresses, be l*ettres* wreten
and sent to theym, as it wer̃ frome theyre kyng, that aftre the
syght of the l*ettres*, they come to this toune, bothe day and
nyght, in all the haste that they myght. And sume shall be
taken here and sume we take by enbushementes that we shall
15 lay in c*er*tayn places. And so we shall haue the moste parte
of they*m*, and so shall we eu*er* haue the lesse to doo." This
goode counsell was holden in suche man*er* that frome the
tounes and castells all they come forward toward the toune
of Columpne; and sume wer̃ take in the toune and putt to
20 dethe and the remena*unt* distressed by enbushements, for they
wer̃ ou*er*thrawn in dyu*er*s places. When the Cristen people
herd of the dyscomfatur̃ of the Saresyns, they rosse by tounes
and by castelles and slewe of theym as mony as they couth
fynde, and so long was the were led that all the londe was
25 clensed of theym and deliueryd ; for sume of theym dide yeld
theym and were conu*er*ted, and Ponthus gave theym goode
enughe to lyve vpon ; and the remena*unte* that myght flee,
fled, wherof sume were slayne by the Spaneyardes and by the
reaume of Castell, and othre were p*er*ysshed in dyu*er*s places
30 myschevously.

¶ Wherfor the Sawdeyn of Babilone was ryght sorofull thus
to haue loste his thre sonnes and his men. He was ryght
angre with Mahounde and said before all men, as a man oute
of his wytt, that the God Crucifyed had ou*er*comen hym and
35 that he was of more vertue than Mahound, when he had not

saved his sonnes and his men. And so there was grete com-
playnte for theym in Babilone and in Damasse.

So I turne agane to Ponthus and so here folowes aftre the
polytyke rewle and demeane of Ponthus and of his gouer-
5 naunce.

[Cap. XXX. How Ponthus was crouned kyng; and how
at the feste he knewe his modre among the xiij pouere
people; and how he made the Erle of Destrue and Ser
Patryk to be kepers of his reaume and to obey vnto the
10   quene, his modre.]

POnthus made leches to be soght forto heall the people
that was wonded and hurte in the batell, and hym self
did visete theym ofte tymes and made to be broght to theym
all thynges that theym (neded). He fested the lordes and all
15 his fellisshipp and gave theym gyftes. And also he founde
in a toure the grete tresoure of the kyng Brodas, the which
[*Fol. 194ᵇ.] was * a grete thyng to tell. And when he had ouerryden the
contrey and clensed itt of the mysbelevers, he founde myche
people and the londe wele belabored, both of vynes and of corne.
20 From all the contrees the people come rynnyng to see theyr
ryghtwyse lorde, and as it had been to myracles. And they
loued hym wele for his grete renoune and worthenes, his
bountee and curtesie; for ther was noon so simple ne so
pouere bot that he wold speke to theym and here theym
25 mekely. He was right petuouse of the pouere people—he
loued God and holy chirche.

And when he had doon this dede, he come to Columpne
and made there a grete feste and was crouned by the hondes
of oon holy bischop. And thedre come to hym the kyng of
30 Aragone, his vncle, that was brothre to his modre, the which
had grete ioye to see hym and of his victorye. And he tolde
hym howe the kyng Brodas had wered vpon hym and howe
ther was taken a trety betwen theym to a certan day—vnto
the tyme that God wold sett a remedye,—"and thurgh his

grace he has ryght wele purveyd of his pitee by you." Thus
complened the kyng to his neviewe and yitt he told hym howe
that he abode the comyng of the kyng of Fraunce and the
kyng of Spayne, that shuld haue comen this somer,—"bot itt
5 is no nede."

The feste was grete of the kynges coronacion and ther wer
made mony straunge thynges. The grete lordes of the contre
come and did theyr homage. And also the fair ladyes had
grete ioye that they were comen oute of hell, and of seruage
10 wher as they had levyd in sorowe and in hevynes; and nowe
the[i] be broghte into ioye and into myrth and into Paradise,
as theym semeth. They liked wele theyr kyng, in so myche
that they hade grete ioye to luke vpon hym. And all maner
of people thonkhed God deuoutely of theyr delyueraunce.
15 Betwen the courses the ladyes did syng,[1] and ther were mony
vowes to the pope,[1] the which were longe to tell. And the
kyng did bryng and presente by xij fair ladies and xij olde
knyghtes grete gyftes and iewelles—sume of fair coursyrs and
sume of fair cuppys of gold and of sylver, of fair clothes of
20 gold and of sylke, and of mony othre grete iewelles,—to the
knyghtes and to the cheftanes, so that all men wer amervelled
of his grete larges. He was a man ryght plesaunt and of
grete curtesie aud of goode condicions.

So ther fell a grete mervell of the custome that was that
25 tyme vsed; for itt was so, that befor the kyng, shuld be
serued xiij pouere men for the loue of God and his apostelles.
So it befell that the Erle of Destrue, the kynges vncle, went
visyttyng the tables, and as God wold he beheld the table of
the pouere people and sawe a womman lukyng vpon the kyng.
30 And as she beheld hym, the teres fell doune from hir eyn.
The Erle luked wisely vpon hir and avised hir so wele, that
by a token that she had in hir chyn he knewe wele that it was
the quene, modre vnto Ponthus. And when he see hir in so
pouere astate that hir gooune was all clovted and to-rent, he

---

[1] Not in R. In W only,—*There was songes and many mynstrelsyes.*

myght not kepe hym fro wepyng. So his hert swemyd[1] for
pitee to see hiꝶ in so pouere degree, and when he myght speke,
he thonked God and went behynde the kyng his neviewe and
said vnto him, "Ser, heꝶ be a grete mervell." "Wherof?"
5 said the kyng. "The best and the holyest ladye that I knowe,
my ladie the quene, youꝶ modre, is her-in." "Wher be she?"
[*Fol. 195.] said he. And he for grete payne myght not * tell hym, for
pitee; and when he myght speke, he told hym in councell and
said, "Ser, see ye hiꝶ sitt yondre with ,the xiij pouereꝶ at the
10 furst ende of the table." And Ponthus beheld hiꝶ and he perceyved hiꝶ chere; and anoon she putt hiꝶ hoode before hiꝶ eyen
and weped; and the kyng had grete pitee in his hertt. Then
said he vnto his vncle, "Make noo semcland, that noon espie itt;
bot when we be vp fro the table, I shall into my warderopp,
15 and bryng ye hyr prively to me." And so itt was doone.
When the tables weꝶ taken vp and grace yolden to God,
the kyng departed priuely and went into his warderopp, and
the Erle his vncle broght thedre his modre priuely. And
when Ponthus sawe hiꝶ, he kneled dounc befor hiꝶ and toke
20 of his croune and sett itt on hiꝶ hede, and sche toke hym vp
all wepyng and kyssed hym and halsed hym, and sore they
weped, she and hiꝶ sonne and the Erle. And when they myght
speke, Ponthus said vnto hiꝶ, "Ay Madame, so myche pouertee
and dyseasc as ye haue soffred and endured!" "Ay my swete
25 knyght and sonne," said she, "I am comen oute of the paynes
of hell, and God has given me grete Paradyse, when itt has
plessyd hym to yeve me so long live that I may see you with
myn eyn[2] and that I see vengeaunce for the dethe of my lorde
youꝶ fadre, which the tyranes putt to dethc, and also that I
30 see the contree voyded oute of the mysbeleve and the holy
lawe of Ihesu Christe to be serued. And I wote wele that
this sorowe and trouble has endured this xiij[3] yeres, as by a

---

[1] W, symmed. R, Le cuer lui emfla de pitie.
[2] R omits everything from here to the end of the paragraph except the
single sentence,—Car les aduersitez qui sont venues en ce royaume est une ven-
gence de dieu. H and O agree with D and W.   [3] H, xiiij.

chastesyng of God (for) the grete delites and lustes that were
vsed in this reaume. So me semes nowe that God has mercy
of his people, that he has keped you and sent you to deliuere
the contrey of the mysbeleve." Ryght wele spake the quene
5 and wisely, as an olde[1] lady as she was.

"Nowe I pray you," said the kyng, "tell me howe ye
escaped and howe ye were saved." " My faiȝ sonne, I shall
tell you. When the crye was in the mornyng in the toune,
and youȝ fadre slayne, I was in my bed; and he armed hym
10 with nomore then with an hawberke and his helme and ran
furth withoute any more abydyng, as the hardest knyght that
was, as men said. When he was departed and when I herde
the crye, I was sore aferd and toke oon of my wommens
gounes aud went my way with my lavendeȝ; and I fonde of
15 aventure the posterne gate open, that sume people had opened,
and so I went oute and went into the wod fast by the laundes,
wheȝ as dwelled an holy hermyte, the (whiche)[2] had a chappell
and a well and a lugge at the wod syde; so I abode ther.
And my chaumberlane,[3] which was wele aged, come euery
20 day to feche almus att the kynges hous, and therby we lived,
the hermyte, she, and I. And so ye may see that God has
saved me." " In goode faith," said the kyng hiȝ son, " ye led
an holye live." And so sche did for she wered the hayre and
went gyrd with a corde, and fasted myche, and was a full
25 holy lady.

The kyng had grete ioy and grete pitee of his modre.
Then he sent for hys tailyouȝ and did shape for hiȝ gyrtelles,
gounes, and mantelles—bot[4] blewe and purpyll—and made
theym to be furred with armyn and sables.[5] And when she
30 was so arrayd, hiȝ semed a full faiȝ lady.[5] And when they
come to sopeȝ, they broght in the quene rychely arrayd.
And when the kyng of Arragonne, hiȝ brother, sawe hiȝ, he
toke hiȝ in his armes and kyssed hiȝ, for he wened she had

---

[1] W, holy. H, saincte.
[2] MS. roche. R, qui.
[3] W, chamberer. R, chamberie.
[4] W, bothe.
[5] Not in W and R.

[*Fol.195ᵇ.] ben deid. The lordes and the ladys of Galice had grete *
ioye of the quene and did hiꝰ myche worshipp, for they held
hiꝰ for a goode and an olde¹ ladye and were all amervelled
fro whens she come, for they went all that she had been dede.
5 Hir brothre the kyng of Aragon was sett at soperꝰ at the table
ende, and aftre the quene, and then hiꝰ sonne Ponthus, for
the day of his coronacion he must kepe his astate. The quene
was of goodly porte and semed wele to be a grete ladye. She
was ryght humble and had ryght grete ioye of the worshipp
10 and goodnes that she sawe in hiꝰ son. Then she said to hiꝰ
son, "Fair son, I haue grete desire to see ouꝰ doghtre youꝰ
wyf, for the grete goodenes that I haue herd of hir." " Ma
dame," said he, " ye shall see hiꝰ hastely, if it be pleasyng to
God." That day passed with grete ioye and dissportes of
15 ladis and daunsyng and synghyng, and of othre maner
of plays.
    That nyght Ponthus dremed that a bere had dovoured his
lady Sydone, and that she cryed and said, "Ay Ponthus my
swete lorde, for the loue of God, soffre me not thus to dye."
20 Thus a vision² fell to hym twys or thryse; and so he was
sore affrayd therwith and had grete mervell in his hertt what
itt betokened. Att morowe in the sprynhyng of the day he
called vp his men and sent for his vncle and for Ser Patryk.
So they come to hym and he told theym his avysions and
25 said, " Myn hert telles me that my wyfe has sume sekenes, or
is in grete trowble. She be so, that I wolle no lengre abyde
here; bot I wolle go to see as faste as I canne for to see hiꝰ."
When they sawe his wyll, they ne durst ganesay hym.
    Then said the kyng, " Faiꝰ Lordes, I thonke God and you,
30 this contrey be clensed of the mysbelevers and I thynke that
by you twoo the contrey has ben saved and the people keped
fro the dethe,—by youꝰ goode revoles. It was Godes wyll.
So I bethinke me of Moyses and Aaron that God sett to save
the people of Israel. So ye shall haue grete merite and the

¹ W, holy. And did . . . ladye is lacking in R.
² W, This auysyon. R, ceste aduision, is probably the original reading.

guerdone of God ; and as for me, I be ryght myche beholden
to you. Wherfor, faiꝛ vncle, I make you my lyeu-tenaunt,
and Ser Patryk shall be senysshall and constable of this
reaume; for it be goode reason that ye, that has doone so
5 myche goode and saved the contre, haue the revoll and the
gouernaunce therof. And ye, Ser Patryke my dere frend, ye
saued me; so I shall yeve you londe and goode, so largely
that ye shall not lese youꝛ true seruice." Seꝛ Patryk kneled
doune and thonked hym.¹ Then he comaunded theym that
10 the state of his modre weꝛ keped, and that she shuld haue
hiꝛ awn commandemente, as it weꝛ to his awn propre persone;
and also that they shuld sustene as wele the pouere as the
ryche and that the ryche shuld not ouerlede² the pouere.
And then he comaunded theym to repare the chirches of
15 glasen wyndowes and of all othre thynges,—wheꝛ as they
were broken, to make theym vp agane,—"and I shall take
you x³ thovsand besauntes of golde therto. He ordaned ryght
wele for his reaume all that neded.

And then he went and herd thre messes and sent his dynneꝛ
20 to shipp, and toke his leve of his modre the quene and said
vnto hiꝛ, heryng all men, " Madame I leve you the reaume
and the tresouꝛ that I haue, all in youꝛ demeyn and gouernaunce. I haue commaunded and commaundes all men to
obeye you as they wold doo to myn awn persone; and, for
25 the better, I leve you myn vncle and Ser Patryk my goode
knyght, the which I haue made constable and senysshall
of my reaume, and myn vncle my lyeu-tenaunt." So he
toke leve wepyng. And she prayd hym to come agane in
[*Fol. 196.] shorte tyme, for she wold fayne se his wyfe. And he toke
30 his leue of the lordes and * ladys of the contrey and went
to the schippes.

Euery man arrayd hym and dressed hym to the see. The
kyng Ponthus come to the barounes and told what avision⁴
was there befallen to hym; wherfor he myght neuer be at

---

¹ thonked hym is repeated in the MS.   ³ R, xx.
² W, ouerlay.   ⁴ MS. a vision.

hertes ease, to he had sen the quene his wyfe. So he toke the
see and saled so long to he see the costes of Bretan.

And here I leve of the kyng Ponthus and retournes agane
to the kyng of Bretan and to his doghtre Sydone—howe itt
5 befell theym of the tresone that Guenelete wroght when Ponthus was in Galyce.

[Cap. XXXI. How Guenelete by fals lettres, that hir lorde
        was deid, wold make Sydone to marye hym, and she fled
        to a toure for to defende hir; how Guenelete famysshed
10   hir and the kyng of Bretayn in the toure vnto she must
        nedes yeld hir.]

G venelete was made keper of the kyng of Bretane and of
    his doghtre Sydone, for Ponthus had yeven hym all
the gouernaunce as ye haue herd before, wherfor he had grete
15 ioye. Neuerthe les he myght not kepe ne chastie hym selfe
from tresone. So he bethoghte hym that he wold haue Sydone
to his wyfe by sume maner of way, and that he wold be lorde
and kyng of that contrey avthre by fair maner or by fowle,
and that he wold put hym in aventure. So the devyll temped
20 hym so myche that he did stuff the citees and the castelles, and
sent for souldeours and yeve theym syluer in honde forto haue
the loue of men of armys. [1]So thurgh his syluer of evyll
vertue[1] the goode men putt theym self in perell of dethe. And
when he had stuffed all the fortresses (he)[2] did make a fals
25 seale of Ponthus armys and made twoo fals lettres, oon to the
kyng and an othre to his doghtre Sydone, the which specified
that Ponthus recomaunded hym to the kyng, and that all his
men wer dyscomfeted and sleyn and hym selfe hurt to the
dethe, withouten any remedye. So he prayd hym that for his
30 welfare and for the welfare of his, that he wold yeve his doghtre
to Guenelete, and that bettre he myght not besett hir. And

----

[1] W, *So is syluer of an euyll vertue for.* R makes it still more general:—
Si est largent de male vertue. Car pour lauoir len si met a lauenture de mort.
[2] MS. *and.*

forto make the mariege he yeave hym all his tresoure that he
broght oute of Englond. Thes *lett*res wer̃ ryght wele devysed.
And in the *lett*re of Sydone was, how he prayd hir̃ and required
hir̃, for all the loue that eu*er* was betwen theym, to take his
5 cosyn Guenelete.

And when the kyng and his doghtre sawe thes *lett*res, it is
not to aske of the grete sorowe and hevynes that they made.
Sydone swoned often tymes and weped and whisshed aftre
hym, the whiche myght not be oute of hir̃ mynde. She drewe
10 and rent hir̃ [1] fare [2] here and made so grete sorowe that itt was
grete petee to see. So the ladys and the courte wer̃ in grete
hevynes for hym and said, "Allas! What damege! What
pitee! The flour̃ of knyghthode, the flour̃ of all gentyllnes,
the myrro*ur* of all goode man*er*s be dystroyd." The toune,
15 the burgeses, and all the comon people weped and soroed for
they̅r̃ frendes and they̅r̃ kynesmen, for they trowed that they
had ben all deyd.

Ther̃ myght noo man comforth Sydone. "Allas!" sayd
she. "He was that man in whome all bountee and trewth
20 dwelled, and by (whome) I [3] thoght to haue had all my ioye,
and the which was so free and so trewe and loued me so wele
and was so likly to haue holden the people in reste and peace.
How has God soffred suche aventure agane hym and agane
me? Allas sorofull wreche! What shall I doo?" So ther̃
25 was noon so hard a hert bot that it wold haue had pitee of
hir̃; and this sorowe endured more then viij days withoute
cessyng.

And Guenelete come and said to the kyng, howe Ponthus
required hym to gyve hym his dogh*tre*. So he flatered hym
30 full fair̃ and said that he shuld s*er*ue hym and hir̃ and worshipp theym and kepe the reaume, and that Ponthus had
gyven hym golde and sylu*er* more then the reaume was worth.
[*Fol. 196b.] So he offred [4] to hym and * said, "S*er*, I pray you goo and

---

[1] MS. *his*.   [2] *r* apparently altered from a *c*.
[3] After *I, trowed* cancelled by the rubricator. W, *thought*.
[4] *Si lui offre et dit*, the exact original of D's reading. W, *offred it*.

speke with your doght*re*, that she wold consente therto."
The kyng was aged, so he wyst not what to say. And Guenelete did so myche by his subtile wytt that he made the kyng
to consente. The kyng was aged and come to his doghtre and
5 comforthed [hiꝑ] the fairest wyse that he myght, and said to
hiꝑ that dyscomforthe did bot greve to hiꝑ withoute any helpe
to hym, or to his reaume, and sith that Ponthus required it,
that she shuld haue Guenelete, for the loue of hym and for
the grete tresouꝑ that he had gyven hym ; and also that he
10 shuld obey vnto hym and kepe his reaume for to revle it,—
" for if (I) gyve you to any kyng, he wolle lede you in-to his
awn contrey, and so shall we then abyde withouten gouernaunce or gouernouꝑ." When Sydone herd hiꝑ fadre thus
speke, she had grete m*e*rvell and said, that, God be pleassed,
15 he shal not be hiꝑ husbonde and that (she) shuld rathre be
barren.[1] And the kyng, that loued hiꝑ so myche (sayd), sith
it liked hiꝑ not, she shuld not haue hym ; bot bad hiꝑ be of
goode comforth.

So he come to Guenelete and said vnto hym, that his
20 doght*re* wold haue noo husbond at this tyme. " Howe !"
said Guenelete, " Refuses she me ? It shall not be all at hiꝑ
wyll." So he come to hiꝑ and made myche of hiꝑ and gave
hiꝑ faiꝑ languege,—howe t[hat][2] he[2] thynkes to s*e*rve hiꝑ and
to obey hiꝑ, and she to be lady of all, and that noght shuld be
25 doon in the reaume bot by hiꝑ commaundement; and howe
he has the grete tresoure of hir said lorde, that was wonne
vpon the Saresyns, the whiche was yeven hym by hys l*ett*res.
Myche he made of hiꝑ and flatered hiꝑ, bot all avayled hym
not ; for she sware to hym that she shuld not be wedded of
30 all that yere, for noon that spake with tunge. " Howe !" said
he, " If youꝑ fadre *comm*aunde you, wolle ye disobcy hym ?"
" My lorde my fadre may *comm*aunde me, what so eu*e*r that
it pleasse hym," said she, " bot forto dye, I shall abyde all

---

[1] W, *rather dye.* R, *dist* . . . *quelle seroit auant beguyne.* D appears to have
mis-read, *baraigne.*
[2] MS. *the.* W, *that he.*

this yeꝛ. Aftre, say I not bot I wolle obey hym." "Yea?"
sayd Guenelete, "Make ye refuse of me? And ye wolle not
obey to the *lettres* of youꝛ forsaid lorde—the whiche ye desired
and loued so myche, and that theꝛ was no thyng bot that ye
5 wold doo itt for hym—and sith ye lyst not (to) obey to his
prayeꝛ and his *lettre*, and also ye list not to obey to the *commaundement* of youꝛ fadeꝛ,—by the faythe that I owe vnto
hym, bot if ye take othre counsell, I doute ye wolle be
angreed." So he threte hiꝛ, when by fairnes he se that
10 he myght not haue hiꝛ. And then he says, sith that he has
the *lettre* of hiꝛ forsayd lorde and the concentyng of hiꝛ fadre,
that he wold haue hiꝛ, whethre she wold or noo. "Yea," said
she, "be I in that *partie*?" "Yea," sayd he, "by my faithe,
ye shall see what may befall." "Rathre," said she, "I shall
15 haue eue*ry* lyme of me hewen frome othre." "Yea," said he,
"it shall be seen all in tyme." So he dep*ar*ted as a wodeman,
for he wened not to fale of hiꝛ.

Sydone was all abasshed, and thoght in hiꝛ hert that it was
not the furst treson and falsnes that he had doone. So she
20 thoght wele that the *lettres* were fals, for othre tymes had he
doon¹ to vndrestond that Ponthus was deid. So she called
thre² squyers and twoo³ yomen into hiꝛ chaumbre, that she
had, and called Ellyous and othre twoo gentylwomen, and
said vnto theym, that she dovted hiꝛ of Guenelete and shewed
25 theym how he was hote of loue, wenyng to haue hiꝛ by faiꝛ
[*Fol. 197.] man*er* * or by fowle mane*r*,—"for he be malicius and *per*-
aventure wold wyrke by strenght. So I haue purposed that
we shall goo into yonde toure, and doo beꝛ thedre vitell, and
theꝛ shall we abyde, vnto the tyme that we haue sume rescouse
30 of ouꝛ frendes, or of sume of the barounes, or elles haue herd
the trouthe of my lorde Ponthus." They said that she had
wele said. And so it was doon. They dide bere brede and
wyne in botelles, in barelles, and in pottes, flesche and cheses,
and all thyng that theym neded, as long as they had laseꝛ;

¹After *doon, that* cancelled by the rubricator.
² W, *two.* R, *deux.*   ³ W, .*iii.* R, *deux chamberlans.*

and then they schitt the dore, and with barres of yrne, and
bare vp rokkes and stones for to defende it, for Guenelete
had thoght to haue taken hiꝛ agane hiꝛ wyll and to haue
doon hiꝛ outerage, if she wold not haue concented.

5   So he come into hiꝛ chaumbre and when he fonde hiꝛ not,
he serched the warderoppes, wheꝛ as he did fynd a gentyll-
woman, the whiche tolde hym that she was withdrawn into
the toure, and how she had vitelled it and stuffed it ; and
when he herd that, he luked as a wodeman and come before
10 the toure and prayd hiꝛ full fayre to open hym the dore, and
swore by his feith that he wold not mysdoo hiꝛ. But Sydone,
whiche knewe wele his vntrouthe, said he shuld not come in
by that meane. He thret hiꝛ sore and swore that he shuld
take hiꝛ by force & make hiꝛ his wench, if she wold not take
15 with to be his wyfe, and bad hiꝛ chese whethre she wold doo.
"Ay," said she, whiche was ryght angre to here the vngudely
wordes, " Traitouꝛ thou shal not come therto, and God wolle,
for thowe shall dye an evyll dethe for this fals entreprise."
Then he waxed angree and sayd, sith that he had doone so
20 myche, he wold fenyshe itt, what so euer befell.

So he toke the kyng and put hym in prisone, for fere
that he shuld gedre men of armes aganes hym ; and then he
come to the burges and said vnto theym, howe Sydone was
yeven hym of hiꝛ husbonde by goode lettres, and also the
25 kyng hiꝛ fadre was accorded therto by cause that she wold
haue ben weddyd to a man of noght, which wolde haue hated
and dystroyed the contree ; " bot," said he, " if that I haue
hiꝛ, I shal kepe youꝛ fraunches and youꝛ libertees and I shall
kepe you as the gold doos the stone. So I haue sett the kyng
30 in a chaumbre, for he be all doyted and has noo wytt, and he
wold lyghtly concente to the lewde counsell[1] of his doghtre ;
wherby the contree myght be loste, if it befall as they thynke.
Bot I shall (kepe) theym wele therfro, with Goddes helpe and
youres, and to saue the wele-faiꝛ of Bretane." So he gave

---

[1] W, *courage.* R, *fol couraige.*

largely to theym, and putted to theym mony doutes, that myght noye hym,[1] aud he did itt in suche wyse, wenyng to theym that he had sayd trouthe, wherfore they durst not ryse ne meve. And also he had mony straunge souldeoures.

5   When he had spoken to the burges and to the people, he come to the toure and assaled itt. So ther̄ was within bot v men a[nd] four̄ wommen, that threwe doune grete stoues and defended wele the toure. And also there was the most partie of theym that did bot feyne, for the[i] wold not that she were

10 taken. The sawte lasted a grete while and Guenelete had fayled of his entente; so he was ryght sorofull and angree and thoght at the lest he wold famyshe theym. " In goode faith," said Sydone, " we haue vytell enughe for a monethe day, and in the meane tyme God may helpe vs and sende vs

15 rescouse." When Guenelete vndrestode hir̄, he went to haue

[*Fol. 197ᵇ.] ronne wode for angre; for he was half dystrakked * by cause he had fayled of his purpose, and wold and wysshed that he had not begonne; bot sith he had vndretaken itt, he thoght that he wold fynysshe it, or elles dye therfore. So he sett

20 goode warde and watche aboute the toure, that ther̄ shuld come no vytell to theym.

And then he bethoght hym of a grete malice, for he come to the kyng and prayd hym to goo to his doghtre, for he knewe wele that he myght turne hir̄ of hir̄ folye that she has

25 taken on honde; and tolde hym that he wold not famyshe hir̄, bot fall into a tretee. The kyng, that was goode and true and thoght noon harme, went vp to his doghtre and told hir̄ howe she was in a way to be deid and shewed hir̄ mony ensaumples.

30 And she answeryd hym to the contrarye, and howe she thoght wele the lettres was (false);—"and ye wote wele," said she, "that othre tymes he has sayd that he was deid. So I shal rathre dye, bot if I knowe the verray treuthe." " In goode faith," said the kyng, " it may wele be as ye say; for I knowe

_____

[1] ms. theym. W, that he supposed myght noye hym/translating R, qui lui pouuaient nuyre. I. e., "might hinder him" (Guen.).

noo man of knowlege that has ben ther, and harde is the werre,
wher as noon escapes." So they be sumwhat comforthed, for
the grete vntreuthe that they knewe on hym.

Guenelete asked the kyng, that he sawe aboue at the wyn-
5 dowe, " Ser, what wolle she doo? " " So helpe me God," said
the kyng, " I may not spede, for she be yitt all sorowfull and
angree for hir lorde, wherfor I may haue no goode answer."
" No ! " said Guenelete, " by the faith that I owe to God, ye
shall abyde with hir and ber her fellishipp, forto ete pesen
10 and ploumes; for ye shall bot[1] twoo dye for hungre, bot
if I may haue hir fellysshipp." So the kyng abode with his
doghtre, wherfor she had the titter pitee for the hungre and
the dysease of hir fadre. They had mete enughe iiij days or v.
bot the vj[t] day theyr vitelles fayled so that they had navthre
15 bred nor flesch. So the[i] wer twoo days that they navthre ete
ne dranke save a litle chese, and iche of theym a draghte of
wyn. The kyng began forto feble, for Sydone had noo more
mete bot vj apyls, of the whiche she gave euery day twoo to
hir fadre. She weped and sorowed for the grete disease that
20 hir fadre was in, and that did hir more sorowe than hir awn
peyn did. She loked often tymes oute at a wyndowe toward
the citee and the see, if she myght se any thyng. So she
wyshed ofte tymes aftre Ponthus and then she weped and
made myche sorowe, desyryng hir awn dethe, and said to the
25 kyng, "Ay my lorde, it had ben bettre for you that I had ben
deid long agoo, then ye to soffre suche payne and so myche
hungre for me." The kyng weped and sayd, " I had leuer
dye for hungre then to se yonde traitour gete you by this
meane." Sydone called hym,—" Fals traitour and vntrewe,
30 howe may thou soffre the kyng to dye, that is so trewe[2] a
man? Allas ! " said she, " Be thys the nurture that he has
made of the, when thou has beseged hym and makes hym to
dye for hungre and thurst, that oftentymes has gyven the
goode mete and drynke? Be this the guerdon that thou
35 yeldes hym ? " She said hym myche shame, bot all avaled

[1] W, bothe. R, tous deux.   [2] W, good. R, bon.

not; for he made his othe that he shuld make hym to dye
for verray hungre, if she wold not concent to be his wyfe.

The kyng was almost deid for hungre and lay in his bed
and myght not styrre. And when Sydon behelde hym she
5 said that she weᵽ leuer to dye, or to sorowe all hiᵽ live then
to see hiᵽ fadre dye for hiᵽ. Then she said to hym wepyng,
"My ryght swete lorde and fadre, I may noo lengre soffre
youᵽ sorowe ne the hungre that ye abyde. Me is leuer to
[*Fol. 193.] dye, or to be in sorowe all my live days, then to se * you in
10 this case." The kyng weped and wyst not what to say; forto
see that he shuld haue hys doghtre by this way, it greved
hym sore, and on that othre side, to see hym selfe and hiᵽ to
dye to gedre, itt did hym grete harme, for she shuld be cause
of hiᵽ awn dethe. So he sorowed sore and said that he had
15 to long lived. So he couthe not councell hym self and said
vnto hiᵽ, "Faiᵽ doghtre, I wote not how we may doo. I
ne wote what counsell I may yeve you—so myche sorowe I
haue, bot to see you dye, I may not see it; and I wold that
the dethe toke me, so that Ponthus weᵽ in this toune on live
20 on the strong parte, for he wold venge hym wele on the trai-
touᵽ that wold have you agane youᵽ wyll." And the squyers
and the gentyllwomen, the whiche were at the dethe and wode
for hungre,—it was noo mervell, for it was iiij days past or
more sith they ete any maner of mete, and they said, "Ma
25 dame, ye shal be cause of youᵽ awn dethe and of the kynges
youᵽ fadre and of vs. It wer bettre to take the vnhappy ure[1]
then to doo worse."

When she sawe that she must nedes doo it, for to save hiᵽ
fadre more then for hiᵽ awn deth, which she sett bot easy by,
30 then she rose vp and went to the wyndowe and did call
Guenelete; and then she come agane and sent hiᵽ fadre and
badd hym speke to Guenelete, and if he myght fynde noo
tretee that he shuld accorde with hym, so that he myght haue
viij days or more respite to recouer vs of the hungre that (he)
35 has sett vs in. The kyng rose vpp and said to Guenelete that

---

[1] MS. *Vrethen.* W, *vnhappy man.* R, *cellui homme.*

by strenght he shuld neuer haue the loue of hiꝛ; and if he wold leve his entreprise, he shuld yeve hym tounes, or castelles, or what thyng he wold haue. And he answerd agane and said, that he wold not take all the reaume, bot that 5 he wold haue hiꝛ, sith that hiꝛ (lorde) had yeven hiꝛ to hym. Then said the kyng, " Heꝛ be bot litle reason. I dovte that ye shall not reiose hiꝛ long." All avaled not that the kyng said, for he was more in his cursydnes then he was afore, and said, (not) for to dye, he wold leve his entreprise, what so 10 euer befell. The kyng asked hym a monethe respete, and at the monethe ende he shuld yeve hym an answeꝛ. And Guene- lete wold ryght not doo; bot the kyng did so myche that he had iiij days resspete, and aftre the iiij days he shuld wedde hiꝛ; and that (she) concented therto.

15   This[1] was the matieꝛ sworne and agreed. And yit said Guenelete, that she shuld not departe oute of the touꝛ vnto the day come of hys weddyng. He had grete ioye and did bere hiꝛ euery day of the best metes that he couth fynd. And then he helde the kyng wele avysed.[2] Aftre the iiijᵗᵉ 20 day the feste and the array was grete, and Guenelete floo for ioye to haue so faiꝛ a ladye, that he loued so wele. The kyng went and broght hiꝛ doune, and she come all for-weped[3] and was so heuy that she had leveꝛ haue died then lived, and wyssed in hiꝛ hert aftre Ponthus and said, allas in evyll tyme 25 was she borne,—"for a simple chaunge nowe haue I made." So she was led to the chirche, and the byschop did wed theym. The teres fell often tymes and thyk frome hiꝛ eyn.

The mete was ordaned and theꝛ was dyuers mynstrelleses, of trumpes, taboretes, and fydelles. Ryght mery was Guene- 30 lete, bot I dovbte it was aganes his mysaventure, as it pleased God,—for euery man shal be rewarded aftre his seruice. That day was the fest ryght grete.

---

[1] W, *And thus.*
[2] W, *auysed.* The reading appears to be a misunderstanding of R's *bien aise.*
[3] W, *bewepte.*

So leve we here of theym and turne agane to Ponthus, howe he come on fro Galice to the mariege of Guenelete and of Sydone.

[Cap. XXXII. How Ponthus arrived in Bretan the same
5   day that Guenelete and Sydone was maried; and how
he and his fellawes went to the feste as dauncers, and he
slewe Guenelete in playne soppeȝ.]

198ᵇ.] *POnthus was in the shipp and had taken the see and had
taken his leve at his modre and at his vncle and of
10 all the barounes of his contrey, and had all ordaned as ye
haue herd afore. He did drawe vp the sales and had wynd
at wyll and sailed so long that they arrived in the Ile of Ree
fast by the Rochell. Theȝ they toke leve of hym, the Pety-
vynes, the Aungevynes, the Manseoues, the Toryngeaus. So
15 Ponthus toke his leve of theym and thonked theym myche
and gave thcym grete gyftes; and then he toke the see agane,
he and the othre navye of Englond and of Bretan; and the
wynde fell all calme and Ponthus toke twoo litle ballcugers
and thre scoore fellowes with hym, and began to rowe.
20   Sydone had dremed that hiȝ lorde come; wherfore she had
sent oute oon of hiȝ squyers to the see syde, to see if any
thyng come,—which lepe vpon a coursoure. So he beheld
twoo ballengers and sawe in theym a standard. So he supposed that it was of the armys of Galice; wherfor he toke
25 his hoode and made a signe of callyng. Ponthus beheld and
said, "See yondre a rydaȝ, that makes vs a signe of callyng.
Itt semes vs that he has grete haste, or elles he mokkes vs.
Haste you that we weȝ with hym." And when the squyeȝ
knewe Ponthus, he cryed to hym aud said, "Ser, haste you,
30 for Godes loue." "What?" said Ponthus, "Be theȝ any
thyng amys?" Then the squyeȝ told hym howe Guenelete
had serued hym fro poynte to poynte. And then Ponthus
blissed hym aud was all amervelled, that euer he thoght to
doo suche treasone.

"Nowe," said the squyeꝛ, "they wolle anoon be at the soppeꝛ, so it shal be harde to come in." "I shall telle you," sayd Ponthus, "howe we shall doo: we shall dysgyse vs at yonde vyllege and we shall goo in daunsyng with tyboures 5 and with pypers,[1] and we shall beꝛ presentes, sayng that we be fellowes that has grete ioye of the mariage; and by that meane we shall come in with the daunses." "In goode faith," said the squyeꝛ, "it be wele sayd." And so itt was doon.

And Ponthus dysgysed hym[2] in the gounes of the goode 10 men of the subarbes; and then they went daunsyng to the courte. So it was neghe the sonne gooyng doune, and men lete theym entre into the hall, wele dysgysed. Sume had stree hattes and sume of grene bowes and sume had hoodes stuffed with hay, sume were haltyng and sume were croke bakked,— 15 euery man made aftre his awne gyse. Guenelete made ioye and sayd, "Ye may wele see howe the comon people has grete ioye of our weddyng; theꝛ be faiꝛ dysportes that they make vs." Bot he knewe not of the bushement, wherby he was sone angred.

20   When Ponthus and his felleshipp had daunsed twys or thrys aboute the hall and had beholden the hyghe dese, and sawe Guenelete that made grete ioye and grete feste of the daunses and getted[3] at the table, Ponthus come thedreward and kast away his disgysyng, so that euery man knewe hym; and then 25 he said to Guenelete, "Ay thou fals tratouꝛ and vntrewe, howe durst thou thynke so grete a treson aganes me and the kyng and his doghtre, the whiche has norysshed the and doone the so myche goode? A simple guerdone has thou yelded theym agane therfore. Bot nowe thou sall haue thy payment." 30 Guenelete behelde hym, the whiche was full ferd and wyst neuer what to answeꝛ, for he knewe wele that he was bot a deid man. And then Ponthus drewe a litle swerd, ryght [*Fol. 199.] scharpe, and smote hym, so that he clave the hede * and

[1] W, *with pypes and tabours.*
[2] W, *Kynge Ponthus and his felowes dysguysed theym.*
[3] W, *wayted.* R, *deuisoit.*

the body to the navyll, and aftre he cutted of his hede, the which was in peces in signe of a tratoure, and made hym to be draun oute and commaunded that he shuld be borne to the gallowes.

5 When the kyng and his doghtre sawe Ponthus, the[i] lepte from the table and come rynnyng, theyꝛ armys open, and halsed hym and kyssed hym. Sydone weped for ioye and kyssed his mouthe and his eyn and she myght not dysseuer from hym. Bot Ponthus had so grete pitee for the dyscase
10 that they had soffred, that the teres fell frome his eyn, so sore his hert was. And when theyꝛ herttes weꝛ sumwhat lyghtened, the kyng said, " Faiꝛ son, it has bot litle failed that ye shuld haue lost the syght of youꝛ wyfe and of me." Then he told hym of the grete treson, of the fals le*tt*res, and of the
15 hungre he made theym to soffre. Ponthus blessed hym and was all abasshed and sayd¹ that ne*uer* sith Crist [was] borne,¹ was suche a trato*ur* livyng, that thoght so fals a tresoune. " I bethynke me," said he, " of Ih*esu* Crist that had xij apostelles, of the which oon sold hym. And so we come hidre xiiij²
20 fellowes, as it plessyd to God, wherof oon was wors then Iudas; bot thonked be God, he be wele payd for his reward." "Ay," said the kyng, " and ye had bene lengre absente, ye had bene more mokked." " God wold it not," said Ponthus.

" Nowe leve we this talkyng," said the kyng, " for the
25 matieꝛ be wele fynysshed to my plesuꝛ; so lete vs leve of ouꝛ disporte³ and tell ye vs of youꝛ dedes,—howe ye haue sped." " Ryght wele, I thonke God," said Ponthus. Then he told theym of the batell and of the dyscomfetoure of the Saresyns, and howe the contrey was clensed and wele laboured. And
30 then theꝛ weꝛ sum that told all the man*ere* and the revle, howe he was coroned. They had all grete ioye to heꝛ of the faiꝛ aventures that God sent hym. Then they did bryng hym

¹ W, *sayd that neuer erst was borne suche.* R, *car oneques mais ne nasqui si faulz homme.*
² R, *ziiij.* W, *.ziii.*
³ After *disporte*, a superfluous *and tell ve* is cancelled by the rubricator.

doune to soper and aftre songen and daunced and had ioye in
theyr herte. Sydone was merye and glade, and it nedes not
to aske, howe that she in hir herte thonked God mekely to be
escaped frome so grete a perell. That nyght they wer wele
5 eased, for both their hertes wer[1] in dystresse. They talked
of mony thynges and they had enughe of ioy and of dissportes
to gedre, for they loved wele to gedre. They loved God and
holy chirche and they wer ryght charitable and piteous of the
pouere people.
10   That nyght the sowdeoures of Guenelete fled a way,—
whoso myght goo, went. All othre people thonked God of
the commyng of Ponthus, and they went (on) pylgremege and
with processyon, yeldyng graces to God, for euery man wenyd
that he had ben deid. On the morowe aftre arryved the
15 navye of Englond, of Bretan, and of Normandye. And when
they herd the tresoune of Guenelete, they had grete mervell,
howe that euer he durste thynke suche falshode.
      The kyng of Bretan receyved theym with grete ioye; and
the kyng Ponthus withheld with hym the Erle of Gloucestre,
20 and wele a twenty knyghtes, and said that within xv days he
wold goo into Englond to see the kyng and the quene and
theyr[2] doghtre Gener; and said to the Erle of Richemound,
"Recommaunde[3] me to theym, I pray you; and if my lady
Gener be not wedded, I shall bryng hir an husbond, if it
25 pleasse the kyng and hir." So he tolde hym in his ere that it
was his cosyn german Pollides, the which be right a goodely
knyght and of goode condiciones and likly to come to[4] grete
worshipp. "In goode faithe," said the Erle, "ye say trouthe;
[*Fol.199ᵇ.] and the kyng wolle be full glade of hym, as I suppose, and
30 haue hym in * grete chertey, for the love that (he) has to you.
So he convehed hym as far as he myght and aftre toke his
leve of theym. And so they departed and come into theyr
awn contrey with grete ioye.

---

¹ W, had ben.   ³ ᴍs. ther'. W, her. R, leur.
³ ᴍs. recommaumde.
⁴ In the ᴍs. to follows worshipp. I follow the order of W.

The Erle of Richemound come into the courte and founde
the quene and the kyng of Scotes, that was comen to see
theyme. The kyng asked hym of the tithynges. And he
told hym, fro the begynnyng to the endyng, of all the aven-
5 tures: and howe the contrey was deliuered of the Saresyns,
and howe the contree and the people had ben saved by the
Erle of Desture and Ser Patryk, in suche wyse that it was
wele laboured and peopled of men by the truage that they
yelded, wherby they lived in peace. And then he told hym of
10 the treson of Guenelete, and aftre he told theym of the grete
yeftes, of the grete gentylnes, and the goode chere that kyng
Ponthus made theym, and howe gretly he was beloued of all
men. And when he hade all tolde, he toke in councell the
kyng, the quene, and theyr doghtre Gener, and the kyng of
15 Scotes, and tolde theym howe Ponthus woll come thedre
within xv days, and withheld with hym the Erle of Gloucestre, and howe he had spoken to hym of a mariege of his
cosyn german and of Geneuer. The kyng asked what maner
knyght he was; and he answerd that he was the goodliest
20 knyght that he knewe, save Ponthus,—"and I tell you,"
said he, "that he resembled[1] myche to Ponthus, of persone
and of condiciouns, save he be sumwhat lesse." "Be my
feith," sayd the kyng, "I accorde me therto, so that it please
my doghtre." And she kneled doune and said, what it
25 pleased hym to commaunde hir, she shuld doo it. The quene
and the kyng of Scottes agreed theym to the mariege, and
the kyng of Scottes said, "Ser, it nedes not to marye your
doghtre to a kyng, or to a lorde, that wold not dwell in the
reaume; for a kyng, or a grete lorde, peraventure, wold not
30 dwell in this contree, and that wer not goode for the people
ne for the contrey; and witt ye wele, that als longe as the
kyng Ponthus levys ther shall noo man be so hardy, to assayl,
or to greve, this lond." Then said the kyng that he said
sothe. Geneuer, that so myche loved Ponthus, said in hir
35 hert, that the knyght pleased hir more then any othre, and she

---

[1] W, resembleth. R, ressemble.

enquered of hym full farre[1] of the Erle and of the knyghtes,
that had ben at the werre and had seen hym ; and the more
that she enquires, the bettre she fyndes and the more she
loves hym.　Now has she noo desire so grete as to see hym
5 and she prayd to God that he myght come soon.　So leve we
to speke of theym and turne agane to the kyng Ponthus.

[Cap. **XXXIII.** How kyng Ponthus made a grete feste at
　　Vennys for to feste the straungers, wher as he wonne
　　the prys aboue all othre.]

10 POnthus turned agane to Vennys,[2] when he had convehed
　　　the lordes of Englond and of the contrees beyonde.　So
they went to here messe and aftre went to theyr mete ; and
then said kyng Ponthus to the barounes of Bretan, " Faiȝ
Lordes, if it pleasse you, me must see the ladies of this con-
15 trey, for I wolle feste theym for the love of the Duke of
Gloucestre and thes knyghtes of Englond, the whiche muste
be fested, and to dyssporte theym with sume dedes of armes ;
for within xv days we must goo into Englond to see the
kyng, for' certan matiers that I have to speke with hym."
20 They answerd that it shuld be doon.　" Nowe," said he, " I
charge ichon of you, that ye bryng the fairest ladyes and
gentyllwommen of youȝ contrees, and iche of you shall bryng
his wyfe, and ye shall be here all by this day sevennyght."
　　So this was graunted, and euery man went home to his wif
25 and to theyr frendes and eueryche of theym soghte for the
[*Fol. 200.] fairest ladys and * gentylwommen, and the beste synghyng
and daunsyng, that they couthe fynde, and come to Vennys.
And 'the kyng Ponthus went aganes theym and resceyved
theym with grete ioye of mynstrellcie and of othre disportes.
30 　On the morowe aftre weȝ the iustes grete.　Sydone was in
a scafold, and the kyng hiȝ fadre, and the grete ladies of
Bretan and the aged knyghtes.　Ponthus was of the inner

---

[1] W, *frome ferre.*　　　　　　　　[2] MS. *Vennys and.*

partie, and the Duke of Gloucestre, Barnard de La Roche,
Gerrard de Vettrey, Pers de Vettry, Rogeȝ de Loges, the
Vicounte de Dounges, and Endrus de Doule,—for to iuste
aganes all comoners.[1] So the iustes began grete and harde.
5 Ponthus bett doune knyghtes and horsses, so that euery man
dovbted to mete with hym. The ladies prased hym myche
and so did all othre men. Grete was the feste, the iustes, and
the dissportes, and lasted to the sonne goyng doune. Theȝ
weȝ mony faiȝ iustes and harde strokes, that longe weȝ to tell.
10   At evyn they went to theyȝ soupeȝ. and weȝ serued with
mony dyuers seruices; and mynstrelles and herowdes made
grete myrth and grete noyse. The prys of the uttre syde was
yeven to the Lorde Mounteford, for ryght wele and sore he
had iusted. So he had the cupp of gold. And Ponthus had
15 the prys within and he had a chapelete, that the ladys sent
hym.
    And then with (that) come Geffray de Lazygne, Andrewe
de La Toure, Guyllyam de Roches, and Leonell de Mauleon,
the which Ponthus had sent for, to goo with hym into Eng-
20 lond, for ouer all knyghtes he loued theym beste for theiȝ grete
worthenes. And the kyng Ponthus rosse a gane theym and
toke theym in his armes and made theym grete chere. And
they said vnto hym that he dide wrong to rysse aganes theym
and that he was to curtese and to gentyll. Aftre souper the
25 Lorde de Lazigne said, "Ye haue this day iusted withoute
vs, and if it please you," said he to Ponthus, "we iiij that be
last comen shall iuste to morowe." Then said Ponthus, "Ye
shall haue with you my cosyn Pollides and the Vicounte de
Lyon, for to be vj; for I vndrestond this day by the Vicounte
30 wordes, that he was wrothe by cause that he was not of the
inner partie,—for we shall nowe at this tyme ease his hert."
Then he was called, and Pollides told theym that to morowe
they vj shuld iust aganes all comoners.
    So the cry was made that the white fellowes shuld delyuer
35 all maner of knyghtes; and he that withoute shuld haue the

[1] W, comers. R, venans.

pris, he shall haue a gyrdle and a gybser of the fairest lady
of the feste; and he that within shuld haue the prys, shuld
kysse the fairest ladye and of hiꝑ shuld haue a rynge of gold.
So theꝑ weꝑ grete iustes and mony grete strokes gyven; bot
5 who so euer iusted wele, or noo, I lete it passe forto abryge
thys storye. And neuer the lesse, the pris withoute was yeven
to Geffray de Chateawbreaunce, and the price within, to Pollides; bot sum said that Geffray de Lazygne had wonne it,
so theꝑ was therfore a grete debate.

10 [Cap. XXXIV.]¹ Her followes of the mariege of Pollides
     and of [the] kynges doghtre of Englond.¹

On the morowe aftre Ponthus toke his leve of the kyng
     and of Sydone and of the ladys of Bretan, and toke
the see and led with hym xij of the barounes of Bretan and the
15 iiij knyghtes before said. So they passed ouer; for the Erle
of Gloucestre parted before theym a day iourney, for to tell
the kyng of Englond that the kyng Ponthus come for to
see hym.

The kyng vndrestode wele by the Erle of Rychemond that
20 he come; so he was garnysshed and stuffed of all thynges
[*Fol. 200ᵇ.] that hym neded forto receyve hym * worshipfully. With hym
was the kyng of Scottes, his brothre, and the kyng of Ire-
londe and the kyng of Cornewayle, his neviewe, and the erles
and the barounes of his reaume. So they had grete ioye of
25 his comyng. The kyng prayd theym all to doo hym all the
worschypp and chere that myght be doon,—"for," said he,
"ye wote wele howe by hym this reaume was releved both of
negheboures and Saresyns." They said all that they shuld
doo theyꝑ poweꝑ. The kynge lepte on hors bak and thos
30 othre knyghtes and rode agane kyng Ponthus wele a myle,
with all maner of mynstrellcy. They receyved hym with

¹ Since this sentence of the text is quite in the form of a chapter heading,
I have used it as such.

grete ioye and worshipp. The cheꝛ that they made hym be
not to tell of, for itt was ryght grete.

The kyng Ponthus was right rychely arrayd with perles
and precius stones, and he had vpon his hede a cercle of
5 stones and of perles. They weꝛ twenty knyghtes with Pollides, and the vj[1] that I spake of afore and iiij hundreth of
Galyce. Thes twenty knyghte[s] weꝛ cled in singulatones
furred with[2] wyld ware all in oon suyte. They weꝛ wele and
richely arrayd of gyrdells of gold and of gyspers, faiꝛ and
10 ryche, the which apered vndre theiꝛ ryche mantylls. They
weꝛ myche luked vpon, and theiꝛ ordenaunce was holden
riche, both faiꝛ and goode. With grete ioye intred the kyng
Ponthus into London and theꝛ he founde the quene and hiꝛ
doghtre and hiꝛ ladyes in the courte abydyng hym.
15 So when he sawe the quene, he lyght a farrom and went
rynnyng toward hiꝛ, and she kyssed hym and halsed hym,
and he was receyved with grete ioye and worship. The quene
asked hym howe he had doon sith he departed from thens;
and he said, "Ryght wele." Geneuer the kynges doghtre had
20 alwey hiꝛ eye to see Pollides, the which she had grete desire
for to see. So she knewe hym by the tokens and the liknes
of his cosyn Ponthus, and she se hym so gracius and so
plesaunt that she liked hym aboue all othre. And yit, to be
in more certan, she asked the Erle of Gloucestre of hym; and
25 he shewed by a signe whiche was he. Then she said in hiꝛ
hert, that she had not faled to chese hym and that hiꝛ hertt
told hiꝛ wele that it was he. They went to mete, and theꝛ
weꝛ mony straunge seruices and notablely serued; for the
barounes serued by the kynges commaundement. Aftre mete
30 they ete and dranke and toke spices. And Geneuer had grete
desire that they shuld speke of hiꝛ matieꝛ; so she said to hiꝛ
vncle the kyng of Scottes, laghyng, "I wote not what shall
be of the speche that the Erle of Richemound broght." And
the kyng smyled and said, "Ye haue seen hym. What say

---

[1] W and R have the correct reading, .xvi.
[2] W, with veer, following R.

ye by hym? Plesys itt you of hym?" She waxe rede. "I
shall doo as my Lorde my fadre and ye wolle." So he sawe
wele that she liked hym and come to the kyng and said vnto
hym, it was goode to wytt of the matieꝛ of his nece.

5 Then said the kyng of Englond, "Ye say trouthe. Withdrawe you into yonde chaumbre." And the kyng withdrewe
hym, and sent for the kyng of Irlond and for the kyng of
Cornewale and for the lordes and barounes of his reaume.
And when they weꝛ comen, he tolde theym howe the Erle of
10 Rychmond had spoken vnto hym fro the kyng Ponthus of the
mariege of his doghtre and of Pollides; and he said vnto
theym, "Faiꝛ Lordes, ye knowe wele that I be aged, so it
behoues that ouꝛ doghtre be maried to a man that weꝛ likly
to kepe you in reste and in peace. If ye take a grete lorde, a
15 kyng, or a prince, peraventuꝛ he wolle make his dwellyng in
his awn contrey, and so * shuld ye be withouten gouernouꝛ;
and if any wrong be doon to any of you, or to this reame,
or to any of ouꝛ pouere[1] comones, they shuld be fane to goo
oute of the contrey to seke ryght of his request. Therfore,
20 as me semes, it weꝛ bettre to haue a yonge knyght of high
kynrede, that wolle abide and dwell with you, and that wold
thynk hymself to (be) beholden to haue worsshipp by hys
wyfe; and in so myche he shuld be the more enclined to obey
you and the reaume. So I wolle tell you all the matieꝛ that
25 has ben spoken vnto me." Then he declared theym howe
the kyng Ponthus had spoken to the Erle of Richemound of
his doghtre and of Pollides, the whiche men holden for a goode
knyght and wele condicioned. So theꝛ was myche talkyng
both of oon and of othre, that longe were to tell; bot the ende
30 was that all was accorded, and said, that they myght noo
bettre doo for the welfare of the reaume and forto be obeyd
and oute of trouble, and that as long as his cosyn Ponthus
levys, theꝛ shuld noo man be soo hardy to meve any werre
aganes theym.

[*Fol. 201.]

[1] After *pouere, me* cancelled.

And when the kyng sawe that they concented, he said to
the kyng of Scottes and to the Erle of Richmound, the which
were worshipfull knyghtes, "Goo ye," said he, "to the kyng
Ponthus and doo hym to wytt of all thes maters and say
5 hym that for his love we wolle haue his cosyn." Thes twoo
departed and called the kyng Ponthus aside and tolde hym
ryght graciusly howe the kyng and his lordes weř concented
for the love[1] and worshipp of hym vnto the mariege that he
had spoken of to the Erle of Richemound. Ponthus thouked
10 the kyng and the barounes full mekely and said that they did
hym myche worship, for the which God graunte hym grace
forto deserve it. And so long went and come the kyng of
Scottes to he assembled theym in the kynges[2] chaumbre and
theř come the Archbysshop of Caunterbury, the whych fyanced
15 theym.

It be not to aske if Geneuer had ryght grete ioye in hiř
hert, all thoghe she made theř bot simple chere outeward.
Sche loued hym and praysed hym myche the more for his
gudelenes and the gude name that men gave hym and also
20 for the love of his cosyn Ponthus, the which she loued myche
afor tyme. And also Pollides thonked God devoutly in his
hert for the grete worship that he had sent hym in this world,
and to haue so faiř a lady and of so goodely behavyng. So
the day of the weddyng was sett the viij[t] day aftre. Grete
25 was the feste and grete weř the iustes, the which begane the
morowe aftre the day of the mariege; for the kyng Ponthus
said that he wold not accorde that theř shuld be any dedes of
armes doon the day of the mariege, and that he said was by
cause the kyng of Burgon deid the day of his mariege. Forto
30 say of all the goode iustes[3] it weř to long to tell, bot ouer all
Ponthus iusted wele, for he was withoute[4] any pitee or[4] pere.
Right wele iusted Pollides and the kyng of Irlond, the Lorde
de Lasigne, the Lorde de La Toure, the Lorde Maunford of

---

[1] After *love*, a superfluous *and worship* stands cancelled.
[2] R, *c. du roy.* W, *quenes.*
[3] W, *well Iusters.*   [4] W omits.

Bretan—thes had all the voice of the wele iusters. It were
long to tell all, so I lete it passe lyghtly; for it were a grete
thyng to tell of the grete feste, of the ordenaunce, and of the
seruices, and of the price that was yeven, and of all the dys-
5 sportes. The feste endured fro the monday vnto the fryday.

Aftre mete the kyng Ponthus toke his leve of the kyng
and of the quene, bot with grete payne they gave hym leve.
Geneuer convehed hym wele two myle, and they had myche
[*Fol. 201ᵇ.] goode talkyng to gedre, and she said vnto hym howe * she
10 loved hiȓ lorde Pollides myche the more, by cause that she
had loved hym covertly before, and that she prased hym the
more, by cause that he had keped truly his furst love. Ponthus smyled and said that theȓ was noo wyle bot that wommen
knewe and thoght. So they spake enughe of dyuers thynges;
15 and then he made hiȓ to turne agane, with grete payne, and
said vnto hiȓ, " My lady and my love, I be youȓ knyght
and shall be as long as I live ; so ye commaunde me what it
pleasse you, and I shall fulfyll it at my poweȓ." And then
he said befor Pollides, " My faiȓ lady and my love, I wolle
20 that my cosyn here love you and obey you, and that he haue
noo plesaunce[1] to noon so myche as to you. And if theȓ be
any favte, doo me to wytt and I shall correcte hym." " Ser "
said she, " he shall doo as a goode man owe to doo." " God
graunt it," said he. So he toke his leve and departed.
25 Then the kyng of Scottes, the kyng of Irlond, and the kyng
of Cornewale wold haue convehed theym,—that is to say,
Ponthus and his felisship, vnto the porte, bot Ponthus wold
not soffre theym. Bot theȓ was hevynes and curtesie at theyȓ
departyng. And aftre they toke theyȓ leve at hym and turned
30 agane to the kynges hovs. And the kyng Ponthus come to
the porte and called to hym his cosyn Pollydes aside and said
vnto hym, " Thonked be God, ye owe grete guerdon vnto
God, for ye be in the way to by ryght a grete kyng and
myghty of armys and of haviȓ and of notablenes, and grete
35 lordes youȓ subiectes ; so ye owe to thonke God highly, and

---

[1] ᴍs. plesaunt. W, *pleasaunce.*

therfor it behoves you to have foure[1] thynges, if ye wolle
reiose all in peace and to live peacyble :—

"The furst, it behoves that ye be a verray true man,—that
is to wyte, love God ouer all thyng, with all youꝛ hert, and
5 drede to disobey hym ; if ye love hym, ye shall faire the bettre
and he shall helpe you and sustene you in all youꝛ nedes.
Love and worship holy chirche and all the commaundementes
therof truly kepe.   This be the furst seruice that men shuld
yeld to Allmyghty God.

10   "The secunde be, that ye shuld bere worshipp and seruice
to theym that ye be comen of, and to theym of whome ye haue
and may haue worship and riches,—that is to say, love to
serue youꝛ fadre and youꝛ wyfe, wherof myche worship shall
befall you.   Be to hym a verray ryght sonne; kepe you that
15 ye angre theym not; soffre and endure what langu ege and
wordes that shal be said vnto you, or of whate tales shall be
reported vnto you,—sum to please you and some to flater you,
or elles for malice coverte of suche men as wold not the peace
betwen you and theym ; for faiꝛ cosyn, he that wolle soffre
20 of his bettre and of his grettre, he ouercomes hym.   It is
a grete grace of God and of the worlde, a man[2] toward hym
self[2] to haue sofferaunce, for dyuers resones, the which shuld
be long to tell.

"The third resone is forto be meke and amyable, large
25 and free, aftre youꝛ poweꝛ, to youre[3] barounes and to youꝛ
knyghtes and squyers, of whome ye shall haue nede ; and if
ye may not shewe theym largesse and fredome of youꝛ goodes,
at the lest, be to theym curtes and debonere, both to the grete
and to the litle.   The grete shall love, the litle shall prase
30 you ouer all of youꝛ goode cheꝛ; and so[4] it shal gretly avale

---

[1] W's reading. MS. *thre.* Ponthus' homily is actually divided under four
heads.

[2] W omits *a man* and has *towarde hymselfe* immediately following *worlde*
and modifying *grace*—probably the true reading.

[3] The *e* of *youre* shows a tag apparently for a second, unfinished *e.*

[4] W, *so he shall auayll you a ryght heralde.* R, *Et vous vauldra ung droit
herault.*

you,—so myche ye shall be prased ou*er* all. And also it is
to vndrestonde that ye shuld be curtes and gentle vnto you̅
wyf afor any othre, for dyu*er*s resons; for by worshipp and
by curtesie[1] beryng vnto hi̅, ye shall hold the love of hi̅
5 bonde vnto you; and forto be dyu*er*s and roode vnto hi̅, she
[*Fol. 202.] myght happenly chaunge, and the love * of hi̅, so shuld ye
wors reioys; and p*er*aventur*e* she then myght gyve it to an
othre, whe̅ as she myght take suche plesaunce,[2] wherof ye
myght be right sorye,—and that ye shuld not withdrawe it
10 when ye wold. And so the̅ be grete p*er*ell and grete maistre[3]
to kepe the love of mariege. And also be wa̅ that ye kepe
selvyn true vnto hi̅, for it be said in Gospell that ye shuld
chaunge hi̅ for noon othre. And if ye doo thus as I say, God
shall encrese you in all goode welthe and worship. If ye see
15 hi̅ angree, apese hi̅ by fairnes, and when she comes agane
to hi̅ selfe, she shall loue you myche the more; for the̅ be
noo curtesie doon to a good hert bot that it is yolden agane;
and when an hert be fell and angre and men wrath it more, it
imagyns thynges wherof mony harmes may fall.
20 "The fourte reson be, that ye shuld be petuous of the
pou*er*e, the which that shall require right of the ryche, or
of the myghty, that wold greve theym; for therto be ye sett
and ordaned—and all othre that has grete lordeshipes,—for
ye come into the worlde as pou*er*e as they dide, and as pou*er*e
25 shall ye be at the day of you̅ dethe; and ye shall haue noo
more of the erthe, save oonly you̅ lenghte, as the pou*er*e shall
have, and ye shall be lefte in the erthe allone, as the pou*er*e
shall be. And the̅ (fore) shall ye haue noo lordeship, bot forto
holde ryghtwysnes, withoute blemyssyng, or doute of any grete
30 maistre,[4] or repreve, nethi̅ letyng for the love ne for the hate,
for thus commaundes God. Eu*er*y friday in esspeciall he̅ the
clamou̅ of the poue̅ people, of wommen and of wydoys. Putt
not thei̅ right in resspete ne in dilacion, ne beleve not allway

---

[1] W, *courteys.*
[2] MS. plesaunt.
[3] W, *maystry.*
[4] MS. *maistrie.* W, *mayster.*

youꝛ officers of euery thyng that they shall tell you; enqueꝛ
befor the truthe, for sum of theym wolle doo it to purchese
damege to the pouere, for hate, and sume for covetyse, to
haue theiꝛ goodes, when they see that they may not doo so
5 with theym as they wold. So, if they come with fals reporte,
it is a perilous thyng for a grete lorde to be lyght of beleve."

He taght and[1] shewed mony goode ensaumples. And Pollides thonked hym and said vnto hym, "Ser, I knowe wele
ye loue, and of youꝛ goodnes ye haue purchesed, me the wor-
10 ship and the welfare that I haue; therfor I pray you, by the
way of charitee, that we may euery yere mete and comon[2] to
gedre; for that shall be my comforth, all my sustenaunce and
ioye." "I graunte therto," said Ponthus. And aftre, when
they had spoken and talked of mony thynges, they toke theyꝛ
15 leve echon of othre and halsed and kyssed to gedre; and
navthre of theym had powaꝛ to speke oon worde, for mervellously they loved to gedre.

When the kyng Ponthus had his hert sumwhat clered,[3]
that he myght speke, he toke his leve of the lordes of Eng-
20 lond and offred hym self myche vnto theym. And Pollides
turned agane vnto the kynges hous, wheꝛ as men made hym
right grete ioye.

Pollides helde wele the goode doctrine of his cosyn Ponthus,
for he serued and obeyd the kyng and the quene, and made
25 hym selfe to be loved both of the ryche and of the pouere by
his larges and curtesie. Ryght wele he loued God and holy
chirche and was pituous and charitable vnto the pouere people.
The kyng and the quene loued hym as theiꝛ awn childe, and
aboute vij yeres aftre, the kyng died; and then was Pollides
30 crowned kyng peascablely, and ryght goode (loue) was betwen
hym and his wyf and the olde quene, and so he reigned in
peace and in goode ryste.

So leve we heꝛ of hym and turne agane to Ponthus.

---

[1] After *and, swe* cancelled. [3] R, *le cuer luy esclaircist.*
[2] W, *se vs.*

[Cap. XXXV. How kyng Ponthus returned to Bretan and
gouerned the realme wysely vnto his dethe.]

[*Fol. 202ᵇ.] *K̄ ¹yng Ponthus saled so long on the see, he and his
barounes, that they come and londed in Bretan and
5 then they went to the kynges hous, wheꝛ as they weꝛ receyved
with grete ioye of all maner of people. And when they had
sodiourned wele vij days, Geffray de Lasigne and Andrewe
de La Toure and the straungers toke their leve and departed.
Ponthus gave theym mony grete gyftes and riche presentes
10 and thonked theym and witheld theym as his fellowes and
his frendes, and then he convehed theym a liege,² whethre
they wold or not. Then they toke leve echon of othre.
The kyng of Bretan lived aboute space of thre yeres aftre,
for he was ryght wele aged; and so was Ponthus kyng and
15 was ryght wele beloued of the astates and of all maner of
people. He was right goode and rightwys of iustice, charitable and petuouse of the pouere. Ryght wele they loued to
gedre, he and the quene his wyfe, and led a ryght goode, holy
live and did mony almus dedys. And when the houshold
20 shuld remeve from oon place to an othre he did crye that all
they that he owed any goode vnto, weꝛ itt for his houshold,
or for any othre thyng that weꝛ taken for hym, that they
shuld come to hym or to his officers, and all he did pay for,
that was taken of any man;³ for he said that all that witheld
25 any goodes or det frome the pouere shuld haue litle merite
therof. He vsed and led right a goode, holy live.
And so then the[i] went and wonned a yeꝛ in Galice, wheꝛ
as they weꝛ right wele beloued, dred, dovbted, and worshipped.
The Erle of Destrue thonked myche the kyng his neviewe of
30 the worshipp that he had doon his sonne. The kyng Ponthus
gave grete heritage and londes to Ser Patryke, which had
saved hym in the shipp and had doon so myche goode to the

---

¹ This K extends through four ll. of the MS.   ² *a two myle.*
³ W inserts, *for he sayd that they were foles that abyde to theyr heyres or to
theyr executors/for fewe were contented*—following R literally.

contrey. Right grete reuerence bare the quene Sydone vnto
the olde quene hiꝛ lordes modre. The kyng sent for his vncle
the kyng of Aragon and for the lordes and barounes of the
contrey aboute, and made grete iustes that dured wele x days.
5 And aftre the quene and the houshold went on pilgremege to
Sainte Iames in Galice.

And aftre his turnyng agane, he dwelled not long bot that
he went to the weres in Spayne aganes the Saresyns. And
he led with hym the barounes of Bretan, of Anyoye, of Mayne,
10 of Petowe, of Tourreyn, of Normandie. Of the Normandes,
he led the Erle of Morteyn, the Vicounte of Avrences, Tesson,
Panell, and mony othre knyghtes; of Mayne, Huugres de
Beamounde and Guy de Laball[1] and dyuers othre; of Anyoye,
Piers de Doune, Andrewe de La Toure, Guyllen de Roches,
15 the Lorde of Marmonte,[2] John de Petowe, the Lorde de Lasigne, Guy de Towars, Leonell de Malleon, Hungres de Par-
teney; of Turreyn, Hubberd de Malle, Hondes de Bausy,
Patryk d'Amvoys;[3] and mony of theym of Bretan and of
Gascoigne. They weꝛ wele xv^{MI}, and discomfeted the hethen
20 people, and ther they did mony grete dedes of armes and toke
mony grete tounes and castelles; and then vpon the wynteꝛ
euery man turned home agane into his awn contrey. And all
gave grete love and prasyng[4] to Ponthus, for he payd theym
wele the[i]ꝛ wages and gave theym grete gyftes,—in so myche
25 that they said, theꝛ was no right cheften bot he, and that he
[*Fol. 203.] was likly to conqueꝛ all maneꝛ of contrees * be his knyghthode,
larges, and curtesie,—" for all goode condiciones be in his persone, aftre the revle of God and of the world, and in hym be
all goodelynes, so that it be mervell of hym before all othre,—
30 he owe grete guerdon vnto God."

He dwelled a while in Galice, and aftre he come agane to
Bretan, and then he went and sawe his cosyn Pollides, the
which was croned kyng of Englond, wheꝛ he was receyved

---

[1] W, *la vale.* R, *laual.*
[2] W, *Nermount.*
[3] MS. *Damvoys.* W, *damboise.*
[4] W, *loos and pryce.*

with grete ioye. It be not to aske if the quene Geneu*er* sett a grete payne forto feste hym and make hym grete chere.

And aftre that went the kyng of Englond into Gascoigne and into Galice to see his fadre and his kynesmen and he gave 5 theym grete gyftes. And then he turned agane into Bretan, whe͞r as he was myche made of and had grete chere. And aftre he went home agane into his awn reame.

The kyng Ponthus and the quene leved long enughe and reigned to the plese͞r of God and then they discesed and 10 finisshed to the grete sorowe and hevynes to they͞r people.

Bot thus it is of this worldly live; for the͞r be noon so fai͞r, ne so ryche, so strong, ne so goode, bot at the last he must nedes leve this worlde. *Explicit.*[1]

---

[1]After the last l. of the romance are four ll. blank. The rest of f. 203 has been cut out.

ß.